THE LAWYER'S LAWYER

THE LAWYER'S LAWYER

JAMES SHEEHAN

CENTER
STREET

New York Boston Nashville

Copyright © 2013 by James Sheehan

Center Street
Hachette Book Group
237 Park Avenue
New York, NY 10017

www.CenterStreet.com

Printed in the United States of America

RRD-C

First edition: January 2013

10 9 8 7 6 5 4 3 2 1

Center Street is a division of Hachette Book Group, Inc.

The Center Street name and logo are trademarks of Hachette Book Group, Inc.

The Hachette Speakers Bureau provides a wide range of authors for speaking events. To find out more, go to www.HachetteSpeakersBureau.com or call (866) 376-6591.

The publisher is not responsible for websites (or their content) that are not owned by the publisher.

Library of Congress Cataloging-in-Publication Data
Sheehan, James, 1949-
 The lawyer's lawyer / James Sheehan. -- 1st ed.
    p. cm.
 ISBN 978-1-4555-0866-2
 1. Lawyers--Florida--Fiction. I. Title.
 PS3619.H438L45 2013
 813'.6--dc23
                          2012016136]

*To my Aunt Ann: my mother's twin sister, my second mother,
and my biggest fan; and to my lifelong great friend,
Christopher Anthony Dennehy, who we lost recently and
who was an inspiration for so many of my literary characters*

THE LAWYER'S LAWYER

PROLOGUE

Oakville, Florida, December 30, 1991

C an I have a Budweiser?" the young man shouted at the bartender. He had to shout because the place was packed and everybody was crowded around the bar jostling and yelling above the din for beer, the only commodity being sold, the wine having run out hours ago.

"No Budweiser," the bartender said. "All we've got is Lone Star and it's not that cold. We're selling it too fast."

"Shit, man. What's that about?"

"It's *about* three bucks and you've got three seconds to make a decision. Otherwise, this beer is going to the guy behind you. One, two—"

"All right, all right. Here's the money."

The bartender took the bills, placed them in the cash drawer, opened another beer, and found another customer. There were three men behind the bar, the oldest guys in the place, all performing the same function. They had experience tending bar, but it was rusty experience. Two of the men at least owned bars. The third, Jack Tobin, was a very successful lawyer from Miami.

The havoc continued until seven thirty when it died abruptly. A couple of young women lingered at the bar flirting with the older men, who still looked good despite their age. Basketball was their sport and they played regularly to stay fit, although Jack did triathlons as well.

At about eleven thirty, the revelry ignited again. College kids descended on the place like locusts. At least the Lone Star was cold this time around.

The Gator Bowl was in Oakville that year because a new stadium was being built in Jacksonville. Jack Tobin's close friend Ron had chosen to open his new bar, The Swamp, on that day. Ron called on Jack and another friend, Pete, who owned a college bar in Blacksburg, Virginia, to help him. The three men had been friends for over twenty years.

By 2 a.m., when they finally closed the doors, they were beyond exhaustion. Sitting at a large round table, each one pulled up an extra chair to rest his legs on while drinking the beer they had been serving all night, Lone Star.

"This stuff isn't bad," Jack said, taking a sip. "I never had it before. Never even knew it existed."

"Me neither," Ron said. "Until the local distributor showed me the sheet with all the beers he was carrying and the prices. This stuff is cheap—a good bang for your buck. I needed a lot of beer tonight so I needed cheap."

"So what do you think of our boy's bartending debut tonight?" Pete asked, pointing at Jack.

"Him?" Ron said. "He doesn't have a prayer. He's too polite. The house is caving in and he's having conversations with people. Me— if I don't see three dollars in your hand, you're not getting a beer. Nothing to discuss. Case closed."

Pete laughed. "Looks like you're going to have to go back to making millions as a big-time Miami lawyer, Jack." Jack had started his own firm in Miami twenty years earlier. It now had a hundred lawyers.

"Not for long," Jack replied. "I'm going fishing soon. Five years, max."

"Retiring?" Pete asked. "At your age?"

"Yeah," Ron cut in. "Jack's planning on moving to some rinky-dink, hole-in-the-wall town called Bass Creek, down by the Okalatchee near the big lake. He fancies himself a fisherman. You'll be bored stiff in a year, Jack. Are you going to find yourself a toothless old woman to hang out with?"

They were all laughing now, letting go of the exhaustion from the evening's work. Jack was the foil for the moment and he relished the role. Nothing like old friends to keep you grounded.

"Maybe I'll get along without a woman," Jack said. His third wife, Renee, had divorced him less than three months before. "Maybe I'll find peace in solitude."

"Shoot him now, Ronnie. He's finished," Pete said. When they were younger, Pete had been the ladies' man of the group. He was of eastern European descent with a handsome face, piercing brown eyes, and thick dark hair.

"No, he's not," Ronnie objected. "He's just taking a break from women. You would too if you'd been married to the princesses he's been with. Sorry, Jack, but you haven't chosen well, at least not up to this point."

"I'm sorry I haven't lived up to the expectations of such an esteemed pair as you two. If I meet another woman, I'll be sure to run her by you guys."

"That's a good idea," Ron continued. "But I've got a better one, Jackie boy. Move up here. I'll introduce you to some beautiful women."

"Thanks, Ronnie, but I've got my heart set on being a small-town country lawyer and fishing a little every day."

"This is the place for you, Jack. We've got running trails, hiking trails, natural springs, and the most beautiful rivers in all of Florida."

"Sorry, Ronnie. I'm hooked on Bass Creek. It's a sleepy little backwoods town that sits next to a pretty big fishing pond. A man can lose track of time in a place like that." The "pond" Jack was referring to was the great Lake Okeechobee.

"That'll change. As a matter of fact, I predict someday you'll come here to Oakville, Jack, maybe for a case or something, and you'll decide to stay."

"Wow, this is getting heavy," Pete said. "Predictions of the future."

"Mark my words," Ronnie continued. "Jack will be here. It'll be for either a big case or a woman or both."

"Look at him," Jack countered. "He has one good night and all of a sudden he thinks he's Carnac the Magnificent."

"It *was* a good night," Pete said.

"Yeah," Ron replied. "Now if I can just find a way to have a championship football game played at the stadium every night of the week, I may survive in this business."

PART ONE
October 1993

Oakville, Florida

CHAPTER ONE

Stacey Kincaid had been at the University of North Central Florida at Oakville all of two months, but she already knew her way around. A pretty brunette with large greenish-hazel eyes, she stood out among the sea of blue-eyed blondes on campus.

It was a gloomy Monday afternoon. The rain had just stopped as she descended the steps of Fogarty Hall reading from her psychology textbook, a dangerous practice even on dry, sunny days. She looked up for a moment and spotted him walking in the grass about a hundred feet in front of her, stooped over, limping along, his right leg in a cast below the knee.

Carrying too many books in his outstretched arms, he appeared to slip on the wet surface. Both he and the books flew into the air as he performed an awkward and involuntary swan dive, hitting the ground headfirst.

Instinctively, Stacey rushed to the rescue.

"Are you okay?" she asked as she helped him to his feet.

"Yes," he said in a soft, almost helpless voice. "Thank you so much."

The books were scattered everywhere and he began to pick them up, his mannerisms deliberate, like those of an older man, although he looked to be in his midtwenties—thirty at the most. Thin, with shoulder-length blond hair and a scraggly beard, he was dressed like a sixties hippy in jeans, a tie-dyed tee shirt, and one dirty white Converse All-Star. The cast leg was shoeless. The front part of his body was soaking wet.

"Let me help you," she said as she started to pick up some of the books.

"Thanks. I don't know if I can make it to my car. It's just a block off campus," he said when the books were all gathered and she was still holding a few in her hands along with her own psychology textbook and a notebook.

"I'll come with you."

She walked beside him until they reached the car, an old beat-up, two-door orange Volkswagen Bug. The man struggled to find his keys with the books in his hands, then fidgeted with the lock. Finally, he succeeded in opening the car door. Stacey smiled patiently as she watched him.

What a klutz, she thought. *No wonder he's in a cast.*

The man pulled the passenger seat down and deposited his books in the back. Stacey didn't notice him linger for a moment before he withdrew himself from the rear of the car.

"You can put those books on the floor in front," he told her, pointing to the empty floor on the passenger side.

Stacey leaned down and set the books on the floor of the front seat. For some reason, she stole a glance back at him as she set the books in place. She didn't know why she did it—perhaps it was simply intuition, perhaps it stemmed from her training in tae kwon do. Whatever the reason, that quick glance saved her life.

She saw the man raising his right arm to strike her with a small club that had appeared in his hand. She pivoted quickly, placing her left forearm high enough to blunt the force of the blow before the man's arm had gained enough speed on its downward trajectory. Without thinking, she latched her left hand onto his right shoulder as she used him to pull herself up and toward him. When she was almost standing, her right leg came forward and she kneed him hard in the groin and whirled him around using both hands.

He first doubled in pain from the blow, then lost his balance and found himself on the ground on his back. She had deftly twisted him off his feet.

He instantly regained his balance, however, reaching for something lodged under his left pant leg and turned back toward her catlike, swinging his right arm as he did so. The awkward, bumbling fool of minutes ago had disappeared. The cast, obviously fake judging from the maneuvers he was now making, had fallen off. Stacey saw a new object in his right hand: a large bowie knife. *No time to run.* When he shifted his weight forward, she took a step back with her left leg and swung her right one as a soccer player might, snapping it quickly as it connected with the man's wrist. The wrist hit the top part of the doorframe. The man screamed in pain as the knife went flying into the air. Stacey kicked him twice more, once in the throat and once in the jaw. He fell back into the front passenger seat as the knife landed harmlessly in front of her.

She stared at it for a moment. It had an unusual handle. She'd seen the design before in one of her classes—a grotesquely carved figure popular in the Middle Ages called a gargoyle.

The fight was not over, however. The man reached for something again, this time under the passenger seat.

It's a gun! Stacey thought. There was no time to stop him. She could take a chance and try to knock the gun out of his hands, but the element of surprise was gone. The better decision was to run, and she started at full speed toward College Avenue, a block and a half away. There would be plenty of people on the avenue. She ran with total abandon as if the bullet were already in the air and she needed to distance herself from it. But the bullet never came. And when she finally took a look back, her attacker was nowhere in sight. Still, she kept on until she reached The Swamp, a popular bar and restaurant in town.

"Please call the police!" she said to the bartender, a woman not much older than herself. "A man just tried to kill me. I think he's still after me."

CHAPTER TWO

I want you to do me a favor," Detective Danielle Jansen said to Stacey. They were sitting in one of those sterile interrogation rooms in the Oakville Police Department: white walls, metal desk, four metal chairs. Stacey felt a little like a suspect who was being interrogated although Detective Jansen was very nice.

"What?" Stacey asked.

"This will be a little hard because of what you've just been through, but I want you to close your eyes and bring up the image of the man who attacked you. Can you do that?"

There was another person in the room with them, a sketch artist the department had borrowed from Dade County for a few weeks. He was sitting off in the corner with a sketchpad on his lap. And behind the window that looked into the room were seven men: another detective from the Oakville Police Department, two detectives from the Apache County Sheriff's Department, and four FBI agents.

"I'll try," Stacey replied. It had been a long day already and she was tired. When the attack came, she had acted forcefully without thinking. Now, after learning *who* her attacker might have been, she was a bundle of nerves. It was going to be difficult to bring that man back to life in her mind. She closed her eyes.

"Can you see him?" Detective Jansen asked.

"Yes, ma'am."

"Can you see his eyes?"

"Yes."

"What color are they?"

"Blue, I think."

"Are they large or small?"

"I'd say large."

"What about his eyebrows—can you see them?"

"Not really. I mean, he's got eyebrows but they don't stand out."

"What about his nose?"

"It's straight, almost pointy. Not big."

"That's good, very good. What about the lips?"

"Thin."

"Chin?"

"It doesn't stick out or anything."

"Ears?"

"Can't see them. His hair is covering them."

"You said he had long blond hair—is it straight or curly?"

"Curly."

"And his beard—is it full?"

"No, it's kind of stubbly, not very long."

"How about his teeth?"

"Can't see them."

"Anything else? A mole maybe, or a scar—something that will help us identify him?"

"No, ma'am."

"Okay, Stacey, you can open your eyes."

Stacey took a deep breath. It hadn't been so bad. The sketch artist came over and showed them the face he had drawn based on Stacey's observations.

"Does that look like him?" Detective Jansen asked her.

"Kinda."

"Is there anything you would change?"

"I think his face is thinner, that's all."

The man went back to his desk and started working on a revision. Within minutes he had a new sketch, which Detective Jansen again showed to Stacey.

"That's good," Stacey said.

"You're sure?"

"Yes, ma'am."

"Okay. Come on over and sit with me at my desk." Detective Jansen put her arm on Stacey's shoulder like a mother comforting a troubled child and walked with her out of the room and over to her desk.

Stacey liked Detective Jansen. There was something about her that made Stacey calm down even though she felt like a Mexican jumping bean inside. "Can I ask you a question, Detective Jansen?"

"Sure, and call me Danni. That's what everybody around here calls me."

"Isn't this a hard job to do, I mean, for a woman?"

Danni smiled, looking around the room and seeing what Stacey was observing for the first time. "At times it's a challenge, but I love what I do."

Detective Jansen's desk was located in a large room with other desks. Men were everywhere, bustling about, hairy arms protruding from long-sleeved shirts that were folded just below the elbows as if they were all in uniform even though they were detectives. Stacey noticed that Danni was dressed somewhat like the men: She wore pants and a long-sleeved shirt with the sleeves folded to just below the elbow. She even had a man's nickname. Her shirt was pink, however, her arms smooth and tanned, her short hair fashionably styled, and she wore makeup. There was no mistaking her radiant face amid that sea of stubble. She was fitting in with the boys but only so far.

"Have you called your parents and told them what happened?" Danni asked.

"Yeah," Stacey replied. "Right after I called you guys. They're coming up."

"From where?"

"St. Petersburg. I think they might take me out of school. I don't want that to happen."

She was sitting in a chair next to Danni's desk now. It was Danni's turn to take a good hard look at this young girl who had so recently fought off a serial killer. She was about five foot six, a couple of inches shorter than Danni herself but taller than the five other victims. And she had the look of an athlete, her body firm and toned. None of that would have helped if it weren't for the martial arts training. That training had made her the only coed so far to survive the attack of a serial killer. By doing so, Stacey had given the police their first real evidence to work with.

Danni put her hands on Stacey's shoulders and looked into her eyes.

"Listen to me. I don't know if you appreciate fully what happened today. You saved your own life because of what you did. You were unbelievably brave but you were still lucky. We'll keep your name out of the papers and we can keep tabs on you for a few days, but eventually you're going to be on your own again. We haven't established a pattern for this killer yet. Once he knows that we have an accurate description, he will realize that you are the only person who can identify him. It may be wise to take the semester off while we catch this guy."

"But I don't want to."

Danni understood the sentiment. She'd been eighteen once. All eighteen-year-olds were immortal in their own minds no matter what the potential danger. However, she understood Stacey's parents' concern as well. She had a daughter of her own, Hannah, and she was a single parent. The fact that her daughter was only ten years old did not allay her fears.

"I've got to talk to some people for a few minutes. Stay here at my desk and I'll let you know when your parents arrive."

"Are you going to encourage them to take me home?"

"No. I'm going to provide them with the information they will need to make a decision."

"That's what I'm afraid of."

Danni smiled again. She liked this young girl. Stacey had a lot of spunk and tremendous instincts. Danni was certain, however, that Stacey's parents would take her home. Every parent of a female student at the university was considering taking his or her daughter out of school. After what had happened to this young woman, it was a no-brainer.

They would never be able to live with themselves if they didn't do it.

CHAPTER THREE

You handled her very well," FBI Agent Allan Peterson said to Danni when she entered the observation room where some of the agents and detectives were still huddled. Peterson was Danni's partner on the task force formed to find and capture the killer.

"I wasn't *handling* anybody," Danni snapped. The words were out before she could catch them.

"Whoa! Excuse me," Peterson replied. Danni realized immediately that her response was uncalled for. Peterson was trying to give her a compliment. The stress was getting to her.

"Sorry. Can we get down to business now?"

"We already have," Peterson said. "We're running down the Volkswagen and trying to decide what we're going to do with the sketch besides giving it to every police officer within a hundred-mile radius."

"Is somebody actually thinking of sitting on it?"

"Maybe. If he knows we have a good description of him, he might run."

"And young college students may no longer be killed."

"Be killed *here*, you mean. If he's got the urge to kill, he's going to continue no matter where he is."

"That's not necessarily true. Some serial killers have been known to stop for no apparent reason. If we can interrupt his pattern, he may stop."

"Danni, we're not in the hoping business. We're in the catching business. And if we decide that distributing this sketch is going to cause our killer to run, we're going to keep it on the down low."

Danni knew he was right although she hated to admit it.

"And who's making that decision?"

"The higher-ups," Peterson replied. "They're meeting as we speak. Where's the girl?"

"Sitting at my desk waiting for her parents to arrive. I think they're going to take her home."

"Good decision. This guy knows she's out there. He's got to take another pass at her if she stays in school. She's the only one who can identify him."

CHAPTER FOUR

O kay, let's take this new information and try to develop some leads from it. We'll meet back here at eight tomorrow morning," Captain Jeffries said as he dismissed the task force on Tuesday morning. Jeffries was the head of the homicide division at the Apache County Sheriff's Office, and Danni had known him for over ten years. His appointment as head of the task force was a little controversial since the FBI normally liked to run its own show.

The sketch had been distributed to every police officer in the Oakville Police Department, the Apache County Sheriff's Office, all FBI agents on the case, and all other law enforcement agencies within a 150-mile radius. That geographical limitation would expand, as would the number and type of people who would receive the information. The decision had been made not to release it to the general public at this time.

The task force had set up a hotline after the third murder and encouraged people to call into it with any information they thought might help. There were two operators assigned and trained to take the calls, which were recorded. They had a series of questions to ask. Two secretaries typed up the recorded questions and answers, which were then divvied up among the task force teams. Every morning after the briefing, Danni and Peterson would go through their allotted interviews and make callbacks if they felt the need to follow up. It was tedious work and, so far, fruitless.

The murders had taken place throughout Oakville over a four-month period of time, and there was no discernible geographical pattern—or any other pattern, for that matter. Some had occurred during the day, some at night. Victims one and four had been killed at separate student-housing facilities on Arthur Road south of the campus. Victim one had been strangled while victim four had been stabbed repeatedly in the chest and abdomen. Victim two was living in a similar complex off Thirty-ninth Street, northwest of the campus. She had been stabbed and eventually choked to death with her own pantyhose. Victims three and five lived in houses with other students: three, a few miles east of town, and five, northeast of the campus. They had both had their throats cut, victim three almost to the point of being beheaded. Two of the victims were blondes; three were brunettes.

Stacey Kincaid was the first coed the killer had attempted to make contact with on campus. He was getting bolder.

Murder number three was the one that hit Danni the hardest because of the sheer brutality. The task force was formed after that murder. Three was the magic number for the FBI to label someone a serial killer. Before that it was just murder and that was a local issue. Although Allan Peterson was on the task force, he had not been assigned as Danni's partner until recently. He was a tall, handsome blond, not bad to look at, but they were still feeling each other out as partners.

"Anything on the Volkswagen?" she asked.

"Yeah, it's registered to a female student," Peterson replied. "She parked it at the spot where the victim was attacked but didn't lock the doors. Said she had no reason to. Nobody would steal a broken-down old Bug. And get this: It had been there for three or four days—she couldn't remember exactly."

"What are these kids thinking?" Danni said. "Leave your car in the same spot unlocked for days and expect nothing to happen. I don't get it."

"She probably figured nobody would want it—at least, not to stage a murder in. I'll bet if he knocked her out he was going to hot-wire it and take her somewhere to do the killing. Those old Bugs are easy to steal."

"You're probably right," Danni replied. "So he had to set that whole scenario up. He knew where the car was. He knew the door was open. He put his weapons in there. Then he got some books, put on a fake cast, and waited for Stacey to walk out the front door of Fogarty Hall. He even pretended to open the car door as she watched. Now that's what I call calculating."

"Like he was writer, director, and star of his own play," Peterson observed. "He's an organized killer all right. No doubt about it."

Danni knew exactly what Allan was talking about. There were three types of serial killers: organized, disorganized, and mixed. Organized killers were usually very bright and plotted their murders, sometimes very intricately. They were usually male and, in this case, considering the victims, the killer was almost definitely a man. Murders like this didn't happen in small-town America every day, but they did happen on college campuses from time to time.

"Did you read that information we received last Friday on serial murders that have occurred in the last ten years?" she asked.

"I've seen it before."

"So you know there was someone killing coeds on the campus of the University of Utah two years ago?"

"And two years before that at Florida State, and before that the University of Texas," Allan replied.

"Any discernible patterns?" she asked.

"They were all organized killers. The killings in Utah and at Florida State, like here, had no pattern or ritual to the murders themselves. And the killer was never caught. He apparently just moved on."

"Any people we know of who were in Utah and are now here?"

"There was a first-year law student who did undergraduate work at Utah. Somebody already talked to him though."

"Law student? That doesn't necessarily mean he's intelligent, but it could."

Peterson had a law degree and Danni knew it.

"Simply because somebody is a law student and goes to a different graduate school for their studies is not grounds to put them under suspicion," he said.

Danni had made the remark as a joke, but they obviously did not have the same sense of humor. She let it go.

"Maybe not, but he's here, so let's go talk to him again and see for ourselves if he fits our profile in any way."

"It can't hurt," Peterson replied.

CHAPTER FIVE

The young man's name was Thomas Felton and he lived in an apartment on Arthur Road. Luckily, he happened to be home when they came to visit.

"I talked to a police officer the other day," he told them after inviting them in. "What's this about?"

Although he was pushing back a little, he didn't appear angry or defensive. *Anybody would ask that question*, Danni told herself as she studied the details of his face and compared them to the sketch that Stacey had helped them come up with. He was slim, his nose was straight, and his lips were thin, but that's where the resemblance ended. His eyes were green, his brown hair was short and straight, and he was clean-shaven. *It could have been a disguise*, Danni surmised, not ready to let him go on appearances alone. *After all, the perp was wearing a fake cast.*

"What do *you* think it's about?" Peterson asked.

"I don't know. The other two guys who were here asked me questions about Utah, so I assume it has something to do with Utah and here."

"Anything else?" Danni persisted.

"Well, the only thing I can think of was that there were some female students murdered in Utah when I was there, and the same thing is now happening here."

He said it nonchalantly, not a bit ill at ease. A guilty person would probably not make such an honest and open analysis to the police, she thought, although it would have had to be a calculation in anybody's mind. *Maybe he's smart enough to know that. Maybe he's a little too relaxed.*

"Well?" Peterson asked.

"Well what? It's true I was in both places. But I went to undergraduate school in Utah and law school here. That's not unusual, is it?"

"I don't know," Peterson replied. "Why did you go all the way across the country?"

"Money, mostly. I came here a year ago and established residency. In-state tuition is a lot cheaper here. Besides, the law school is good and I like the climate."

"Ever been arrested?" Allan asked. It was a good question to just throw out there to test Felton's reaction. He didn't react at all.

"I was arrested once when I was fifteen. They took me down to the station, booked me and everything, and then they found out it was a mistake and let me go."

"Where was this?"

"Idaho, where I grew up."

"That it?"

"That's it."

Danni made a mental note to check on the arrest record and to compare the in-state tuition rates as she scanned the apartment. It was very clean and orderly and tastefully furnished in autumn tones—browns, oranges, reds—that gave the place a warm feeling. Several framed Monet prints hung on the wall—not a typical student's apartment or even a typical Florida home.

"You live here alone?" she asked, her eyes noting that there appeared to be two bedrooms. One door was open, the other shut.

"Yeah," he said, offering no explanation for the second bedroom.

"You wear contacts?" Peterson asked. Danni cringed at the question. *Why did he ask that?* She forgot about it, however, when her eyes spied a knife on display on a bookshelf in the living room. It was ornate with a curved black pearl handle and a long thin blade, perhaps from the Middle East. Danni picked it up and studied it.

"It's a nice piece, isn't it?" Felton asked as he walked toward her.

"It's unique. Are you a collector?"

"No. That was my father's. He died when I was young. It's one of the few things of his that I have."

As he started to walk away, Danni reached into the small purse she carried with her. A cigarette case fell from the purse right at Felton's feet. He politely picked it up and handed it to her.

"Thank you," she said.

"You're welcome."

They left minutes later. Danni had wanted to look around the entire apartment but Felton denied the request. He did it pleasantly and politely just as the two detectives probably would have done themselves if it had been their home. As a law student, he probably knew they had no basis for a search warrant.

"I didn't know you carried a purse," Peterson said as they walked toward the car.

"I don't," she replied.

Peterson was confused. "And I didn't know you smoked either."

"I don't."

Peterson was so confused now, his face was visibly contorted. Danni relieved his stress by reaching into the purse and pulling out a plastic baggie. The cigarette case was inside the baggie.

"Now we have a fresh set of prints in case we ever need them," she said.

Peterson gave her an understanding smile even though he didn't approve of her tactics.

"What was the contacts question about?" she asked when they were in the car and driving away.

"Well, the girl said the killer had blue eyes. His were green. The only possible explanation for the change in color would be contacts. Why?"

"Just what you said," Danni replied. "The only possible explanation for a change in eye color would be contacts. You may have tipped him to the fact that we have a description."

"Come on, will you, Danni? Give me a break. Whoever our killer is knows that his most recent victim got away. Therefore, he knows, or at least he has to assume, that we have some type of a description. Asking Mr. Felton, who, by the way, I believe had nothing to do with these murders, if he wore contacts does not give away anything."

"You're probably right about that, but I'm not ready to abandon this guy as a suspect. Did you see that knife?"

"Yeah. It's nothing like the knife we're looking for."

"Maybe he's a knife collector. Maybe he's got other knives in that second bedroom."

"That's a long shot."

"I know, but if we're ever going to catch this guy, we're going to have to start making some educated guesses and going with hunches because he's not leaving any evidence behind."

"Hunches get you nowhere," Peterson said. "Somewhere along the way he'll make a mistake. You watch."

"I hope you're right."

CHAPTER SIX

Stacey wasn't happy with her parents' decision to take her out of school and back to St. Petersburg with them, but she understood. Before she left, she'd had a long conversation with Detective Jansen.

"Your parents are making the right decision," Danni had told her. "I have a daughter who is only ten years old, but I don't want her living here. If I could send her away, I would. Your parents have no choice after what happened to you.

"I know it seems like the end of the world, but we'll catch this guy soon and you'll be back here before you know it."

Stacey had just nodded, but as the days went by, she'd thought about what Danni had said. It made sense so she decided to accept her parents' decision and not be angry with them. Besides, she still had a lot of friends back home who were going to the junior college, and there were plenty of opportunities for fun.

Saturday night always brought a party and tonight's party was on Snell Isle at one of the estates on the water. Stacey was standing on the seawall talking to Jason, whose last name she couldn't remember. Jason had been a few years ahead of her in high school, and she'd had a crush on him for the longest time. Now he was finally paying attention to her, and she wasn't all that interested.

She had walked out to the seawall to be alone for a few minutes.

The grounds were so large she could hardly hear the revelers inside. Jason had followed her a short time later. It was a little awkward since they really didn't know each other that well. Jason thought the conversation might go a little more smoothly if alcohol was involved.

"Can I get you a beer?" he asked.

"Sure. Make it a light beer."

He'd been gone only a few seconds when someone else showed up—a tall thin guy with short black hair. Stacey didn't recognize him from school or the neighborhood.

"Beautiful night, isn't it?" the new guy said.

"Yeah," Stacey replied. "This is perfect Florida weather."

"Especially out here away from the crowd and the lights. You can really see the stars out here."

"Too bad there's no moon," Stacey added.

"Having no moon makes it perfect," he said as he inched closer to her. "I just wish I had the luxury of taking my time with you."

Stacey was puzzled by the remark. As she turned toward him, she started to understand too late. He was next to her now, plunging the knife deep into her belly while capping her mouth with his left hand. The second stab penetrated her chest right into her heart.

"Not so tough tonight, are you, honey?" he said as her body sagged to the ground.

As he walked toward the seawall with two bottles of beer in his hand, Jason wondered where the hell Stacey had gone. Had she ditched him already? He didn't identify the large dark object lying in the grass until he was upon it. He saw the bulging eyes first, then the mouth agape, and the blood... He dropped the beers and opened his own mouth to scream, but no sound came out. His mind told him to turn and run, but his legs wouldn't move.

CHAPTER SEVEN

Danni was up early on Sunday morning making sandwiches and packing the cooler. She and Hannah were going to Whiskey River Springs for the day. They both needed it. Danni hadn't taken any time off in a month, and some days she worked round the clock. Thank God her sister Mary was a stay-at-home mom and was willing to watch Hannah. Otherwise, Danni would have had to quit her job.

Hannah was a little lost without her mother around constantly correcting her, keeping her in line, and loving her to death. Dad lived in town but he was usually "tied up" with work or, worse yet, a new woman. Whiskey River Springs was Hannah and her mom's special place. They'd swim and hike and just hang out together. They almost weren't mom and daughter at the Springs. They were girlfriends.

The doorbell rang as Danni was filling the cooler with ice. She first checked to make sure she had her gun.

"Who is it?" she called out from a distance. Hannah was still asleep, but it didn't matter. Even if she were awake, the rule these days was that Mommy always answered the door. Hannah was never alone in the house.

"It's me—Allan."

Even though she recognized the voice, Danni looked through the peephole to be sure. Maybe she was overly cautious, but whoever the murderer was, he knew she was on the case. And if he took her out, her daughter was defenseless. She finally opened the door.

"I don't care what you've got, I'm not going with you. Hannah and I need this day."

"I'm not going to take you away from your day. I just have some bad news," Allan said.

"What is it?" she asked impatiently. She had no idea what was coming.

"Stacey Kincaid is dead. The St. Petersburg police contacted us early this morning. She was at a party and apparently went for a walk on the seawall. Some boy found her. She was stabbed twice: once in the abdomen, once in the chest."

Danni felt like she had been stabbed in the chest herself. It was a totally different experience to find out about the murder of someone you knew. Danni had taken Stacey under her wing and given her motherly advice. They hadn't known each other that long or that well, but they had touched. She didn't want to show her emotion though, at least not to Allan, although she could tell he understood that this was different.

"Anything we can use?" she asked.

"Nothing. Nobody saw anything and there was nothing at the scene but the body."

"It's him though. Had to be. She was his loose end."

"No doubt about it," Allan replied.

Danni's mood had dissipated somewhat by the time she and Hannah reached Whiskey River Springs. It was partially her own attitude adjustment and partially the springs themselves.

As for her attitude adjustment, Danni only needed to remind herself that every one of those victims had a mother and father, relatives, friends, and acquaintances who loved and cared for them dearly. The difference between Stacey and the others was that she, Danni, had been one of Stacey's acquaintances and not just the investigating officer. Danni had to put her personal feelings aside and do for Stacey exactly what she had to do for those other girls and for future victims: Find the murdering bastard who killed them and who would kill again.

The other part of her mood change was Whiskey River Springs. Set outside the town of White Springs in northern Apache County, the underground springs were one of the many natural wonders of Florida that tourists who stayed on the main drag would never see. This was farm and ranch country, where the cypress, pine, and great oak, their branches littered with Spanish moss, sheltered and protected their hidden jewels, the spring-fed Suwannee, Ichetucknee, Crystal, and Santa Fe Rivers that meandered across the interior landscape of north central Florida like the fingers of a giant celestial hand.

Whiskey River Springs was actually a series of underground springs that fed the Santa Fe. You could rent a tube and float down the river from one spring to another, which Danni and Hannah often did, or you could just lounge at one spring as they were doing on this particular day.

Hannah at ten was like a fish in the water. Danni and Mike, Hannah's father, had put her in lessons before she was a year old and it had paid off. She loved the water, especially the springs.

"How did they get here?" she had asked Danni not so long ago.

It was a teachable moment that Danni luckily was prepared for. "The springs have been here for thousands of years, honey." She told her daughter how ordinary rainwater over thousands of years had carved out underground caverns and caves in the limestone. "As the water travels in these caves and caverns, it has to come out somewhere. The springs are where it comes out."

They always carried goggles, and Danni had shown Hannah

where the caverns were in each one of the springs. "Promise me you'll never swim in there."

"I promise, Mommy."

Danni had firsthand knowledge of both the danger and the spectacular nature of the caves and caverns of these particular springs. She was a certified scuba diver, and she and Mike had explored these caverns years ago before Hannah was born and before she discovered that Mike was one of those assholes who needed more than one woman to satisfy his needs. She kept forgiving him and letting him come back home until finally he'd left her for a woman ten years her junior. There was no coming back after that, and the experience had soured her on men in general.

Hannah's promise not to explore the caverns was enough for Danni. On this day, after about an hour of swimming in the crystal clear water, which was a constant seventy-two degrees year round, Danni retired to her beach chair to read while Hannah continued to play.

The springs were literally holes in the ground that you had to walk down into, and stairs had been constructed for that purpose. The cedar, the oak, and the pine formed a canopy above so that very little direct sunlight filtered in. Again, it was a Florida the ordinary tourist would never see.

Danni left her book every once in a while and walked over to the springs and looked down on her daughter who was having a ball. She had found a girl her age to play with.

While Danni was sitting in her beach chair reading and relaxing for the first time in months, her cell phone rang.

"Hello."

"You lost your only witness, didn't you?" the voice on the other end said.

"Who is this?"

"You know who it is."

Danni could feel her blood pressure rising. He was getting pretty brave now. "You piece of shit. I'm gonna nail your ass."

"You shouldn't leave your daughter in a watering hole where you can't see her."

The words took a moment to register. Danni threw the cell phone down and raced for the water, not knowing what to expect. Was that son of a bitch down there? Had he grabbed Hannah?

Hannah was fine. She was still playing with her newfound friend. Danni took a long deep breath and exhaled. For just a split second her life had hung in the balance. Then the cop in her took over. She looked around. There weren't too many people at the springs that day and most of them were women with their children. She couldn't see him, but he had to be there somewhere. She ran back to the blanket and chair, retrieved her cell phone and called the desk sergeant at the Apache County Sheriff's Office. She recognized Bill Rose's voice right away.

"Bill, this is Danni Jansen. I'm out at Whiskey River Springs and I just got a call from our killer. He's out here somewhere."

"I'll get some cars out there right away, Danni."

"There's only one road in and out of here, Bill."

"We'll set up roadblocks at each end. If he's still in there, he won't get out."

Danni next called Captain Jeffries directly and gave him the news so he wouldn't get his information secondhand over the radio.

"I'll send a task force unit out there as well, Danni. Why don't you take your daughter home. This could get a little hairy."

Danni wanted to be there, but she knew that his advice was sound. "I will, Captain. Thanks."

Getting Hannah out of the water was no easy task.

"Come on, Hannah, we have to go."

"We just got here, Mommy."

"I know, honey, but we've got to go now."

The sheriff's deputies arrived on the scene just as Danni and Hannah finished packing up. Everybody was ordered out of the Springs and checked out individually before being allowed to get in their cars and leave. Each car got a pass placed on the inside dashboard by an officer just before leaving, and the people inside received some verbal instructions: "Lock your door and don't stop for anyone for any reason until you get beyond the police blockade. When they see your pass at the blockade, they'll let you go."

The cars left single file so there would be no way for the killer to stop one of them without somebody else observing. Danni and Hannah were in the last car.

The next morning, Danni called the office to say that she wouldn't be in. She talked directly with Captain Jeffries.

"We didn't get him," Jeffries told her.

Danni wasn't surprised. "Did you check out that phone number he called from?"

"Yes. It belonged to a woman who lives in White Springs. She was at Whiskey River Springs yesterday and she said she'd lost her phone. We're checking her out, but she sounds legit."

"He was probably at the Springs, stole the phone, and called me from the road as he was leaving."

"That would be my guess," Jeffries replied.

"Listen, he made a veiled threat against my daughter yesterday, and I've got to take care of that. It's going to take me a couple of days."

"Understood. Need any help?"

"Nope. The fewer people who know about this, the better."

"I hear you. Let me know when you get back to the office."

Danni accompanied Hannah to school that morning. They went right to the principal's office where they waited an hour to see the principal, an elderly black woman named Mrs. Demps. Danni went into the office alone but not until she had one of the office ladies swear she would not let Hannah out of her sight for any reason.

"Not even to go to the bathroom."

"Not even to go to the bathroom," the woman repeated.

Inside the principal's office, Danni revealed her plan.

"I don't know if you know this or not," Danni began, "but I'm a homicide detective with the Oakville Police Department. Yesterday the man who is killing these young coeds threatened my daughter directly. I have to take her out of school, and I have to take her out of this area and reenroll her somewhere else under a different name. I will need to take all her records with me."

"That may take a few hours."

"We have some packing to do, and I have some calls to make. I can come back in three hours."

"Make it two," Mrs. Demps said. "We'll have the records ready for you."

Danni had already called Mike's cousin, Eleanor, who lived in a suburb of Denver. The two women had become friends during the marriage and had maintained that friendship after the divorce. Eleanor had two kids of her own. Her son, Tim, was fourteen and her daughter, Patricia, was twelve.

"Eleanor, I have a big favor to ask of you," Danni began. "You are kind of off the radar in the sense that few people knew that we were friends and nobody knows that we are still, including Mike." Danni then told her what had happened recently.

After picking up the records at school, Danni and Hannah took a very circuitous route to Tampa, making sure they were not followed. Late that afternoon they boarded a plane for Denver. During the drive to Tampa and the flight to Colorado, Danni drilled Hannah on the details of her new life.

"You can't get close to anybody, honey, except Aunt Eleanor and Uncle Charley and Tim and Patricia. You are still going to be Hannah, but your last name is going to be Olson like Tim and Patricia. Do you understand?"

"Why, Mommy? And when am I going to see you?"

It was a process but Hannah was starting to get it by the time they landed. Eleanor was waiting at the airport. Danni spent the next morning making copies of Hannah's school records, then altering the copies, then copying the altered documents until they looked as good as the originals. Early that afternoon she and Eleanor met with the principal of Parker Elementary School. Danni told the woman the whole story.

"Hannah can't live with me while this maniac is free and she needs to go to school. I have her records here which show her name as Olson and show that she is a fourth-grade student."

"I need to check with the school board before I can approve this," the principal said.

"You can't," Danni replied. "I don't want *you* to know. I don't want anybody to know. If you can't take my daughter under these conditions, then she's not going to go to school while this madman is loose. I'll sign whatever waiver you need just as long as you don't show it to anybody until this is over." She didn't say what "over" meant, but they all knew there were several possibilities.

The principal, Mrs. Hoffman, thought about it for a long time.

"The child needs to go to school," she said finally. "And nobody can fault us for doing what we're doing under the circumstances."

Danni was on a plane home that night. Every nerve in her body was on edge. Every fiber within her wanted to be with her daughter in Denver. Finally, she started to feel just a speck of what Stacey Kincaid's parents and all those other victims' parents had felt when they heard the news that their daughters were gone. *My little girl is still alive*, Danni thought.

We've got to find this bastard.

CHAPTER EIGHT

Danni didn't get good news when she walked into the morning meeting on Wednesday.

"We've got another body," Captain Jeffries told the group although most of them knew already. "A junior at the university; they found her on the north side of town. She'd been lying dead in her apartment for three days. Throat was cut. Can you imagine that? She was living in an apartment complex and nobody even noticed the smell. It's like people these days live in cocoons or something."

Danni was already making the connection. Three days ago was Sunday, the day she was at Whiskey River Springs. She didn't say anything to the captain until the meeting was over.

His door was open when she walked in the office, but she knocked anyway. Captain Sam Jeffries looked up from the paperwork on his desk and smiled. He was a big man with broad shoulders and a gut to match, but he was a good leader and everybody on the task force respected him, including the FBI guys who had a tendency to respect nobody but their own.

"Good to have you back, Danni. Did you get everything taken care of?"

"Yeah, thanks. I appreciate your giving me the time off."

"No problem. Family comes first. I know you've probably lost some sleep worrying about your daughter and all. What's up?"

Danni and Sam Jeffries had worked on many cases together over the years and she considered him a friend. Danni had an idea and she needed his help. She hoped those years of friendship would come into play in their ensuing conversation.

"It's about that murder, Captain. When did it happen exactly?"

"Sunday, late in the afternoon, about the time we were chasing around Whiskey Springs looking for our killer."

"So he set us up."

"Looks like it."

"Why didn't you tell everybody at the morning meeting? You weren't trying to protect me, were you? I mean, I was the one who got everybody out there."

"No, you weren't, Danni; he was. He got us out there. And he could have used anybody to do it. It must have just slipped my mind at the meeting. The forensics from this recent murder don't add anything to what we already know anyway."

"She was a college student at the University of North Central Florida, wasn't she?"

"Yeah. Just like all the rest."

"Don't you find it intriguing, Captain, that the murders are happening all over the city, including areas not necessarily associated with the college, yet only women who are students at the University of North Central Florida are the victims?"

"That's pretty obvious. What's the point?"

"These aren't just random campus killings. The killer is setting out to kill just students from this university."

"Okay?"

"Maybe there's a further connection, a common class, a major, or a minor or something like that."

"The FBI has looked into that. No pattern has emerged yet." At least she was thinking outside the box. Besides, even though he was ten years her senior, Jeffries still enjoyed watching Danni pace back and forth in his office, her hands on her hips, her body bouncing with every step. It was more fun by a long shot than looking at the paperwork on his desk.

"Maybe it's about him. Maybe he was a student, maybe he *is* a student, and some coed rejected him."

Jeffries stood up at that point.

"The FBI has profilers looking into that type of stuff, Danni. We have to concentrate on good old-fashioned police work and find some hard evidence. Let them work on the theories."

"We need a search warrant to get the proof."

"What are you talking about? A search warrant for what?"

"Thomas Felton's apartment," Danni replied.

"Thomas Felton? Refresh my recollection. Do we have a file on him?"

"I do."

"Get it."

The file was on top of her desk. Danni had figured he might want to see it when she brought up the issue. She returned moments later and handed it to him.

"He's the law student who was in Utah during the serial killings there, and he's now here."

"Didn't we already check him out?" Jeffries asked.

"We spoke to him a couple of times but that was it."

"Well, it says here that he went to undergraduate school in Utah and came here to go to law school. He came a year ago to establish residency because the tuition is cheaper here for in-state students than it is in Utah. Danni, you verified that his story was true. Isn't that right?"

"Yeah."

"So what would be our basis for a search warrant?"

"He fits a portion of the eyewitness description, at least that portion that could not be disguised."

"And that is?"

"He's tall, thin, and he's got fine features—a straight nose, thin lips."

"That's it? How do we know the killer was in disguise when he tried to kill that young girl? What was her name?"

"Stacey Kincaid. We don't know for sure, but we have enough evidence to make the assumption."

"What's that?"

"He eventually killed Stacey in St. Petersburg at a party. If you recall, he stabbed her twice at close range."

"Okay," Jeffries said.

"He had to be confident that he could get that close to her at a party without her recognizing him."

Captain Jeffries folded his arms and scratched his chin with his right hand. It was an obvious conclusion, but nobody had even brought it up before Danni mentioned it. So much for all the sophisticated equipment; it never replaced good police work.

"Okay, let's assume he was disguised. What else do you have?"

"I found a very rare knife in his apartment. It was long and thin with a black pearl handle. I'd never seen a knife like that before."

"I'm not following you, Danni. Was that knife or one like it used in any of the murders that we know of?"

"Stacey Kincaid said the murderer tried to kill her with a very unique knife. The description was something like a bowie knife with a gargoyle carved on the handle."

"A bowie knife isn't thin—it's broad. Makes a wide cut. Where's the connection?"

"Maybe he's a knife collector. Maybe he's got a collection of knives in that second bedroom we didn't see and he wouldn't let us into."

She lost him there. She could see it in his face.

Jeffries didn't comment on that theory directly. He knew Danni had been through a lot in the last forty-eight hours, and it was understandable that she wanted to get this guy as soon as possible. He didn't want to tell her she was grasping at straws so he waited a few moments.

"We won't get a search warrant with that evidence, Danni. It's not probable cause."

"Probable cause is what the judge says it is. Who knows? We might get Judge Reed. He pretty much signs anything that comes across his desk."

"I don't think so. Not even Judge Reed would sign this one once he knows all the facts. Look, I know this is personal now and you want to get this guy, but you're targeting someone without evidence. It's what we tend to do when we get antsy."

"I'm not antsy, Sam. I think we need to try for this search warrant. If we're wrong, we're disrupting this guy's day for a few hours. If we're right, we might save somebody's life. We need to do something."

"All right, Danni, you prepare an affidavit and copy this file and I'll ship it over to the state attorney's office. If they think it's worth it, they'll go to the judge for a warrant."

"That's not good enough, Sam. Jane Pelicano is the assistant state attorney assigned to work with us on this case. You need to talk to her and convince her to go get that warrant for us."

"Look, Danni, I'm the head of this task force. I don't mind going out on a limb and trying new ideas, but I can't start lobbying on your behalf for something I don't believe is going to work.

"Having said that, you write a memo along with your affidavit stating every reason you can think of to justify getting a warrant and

I'll send it along. If you want to talk to Jane yourself after that, I have no problem with it."

Danni knew that was the best deal she was going to get.

"Thanks, Captain."

"No problem. Keep thinking, keep pushing. We'll nail this guy."

CHAPTER NINE

A few days after her memo and affidavit had been sent, Danni went to see Jane Pelicano. She'd called first and made an appointment so Jane was ready for her.

Jane Pelicano was the top assistant state attorney in Lou Daniel's office. She tried many of the high-profile capital felonies, so it was no surprise that she'd been assigned to this case. Danni had her work cut out for her but she was ready. She wasn't sure why, but the desire to get a warrant and search Thomas Felton's apartment was starting to consume her.

Jane Pelicano was standing up when Danni walked into her office. She came around her desk to greet Danni. The two women knew each other professionally because they'd worked on a lot of cases together.

"I read your memo and your affidavit, Danni. Sam sent me a memo, too, along with the file. I'm with him on this: Suspicion isn't probable cause. We've got nothing to connect this guy. The fact that he was in Utah and is now here is totally explainable and his story checks out. After that what do we have? He fits part of the description, and the killer probably used a disguise, but that's not going to cut it and you know it."

Jane Pelicano was a tall woman with short, drab, brownish hair. Nobody would ever call her pretty nor would they call her ugly.

Her features were ordinary and she did nothing to enhance them by wearing little makeup and conservative pantsuits every day. Her success was intrinsically tied to the fact that nothing was about her. She approached the job in a businesslike manner; she got the jury to focus on the evidence, and she had the ability and the confidence to out-lawyer even the best criminal defense lawyers and ram home the conviction. Under normal circumstances, Danni was no match for Jane Pelicano.

"What's the harm, Jane, in putting it before the court?"

"The judges rely on us to screen these affidavits so they're not dealing with frivolous motions all the time."

"So this is about your reputation? Seven women have been murdered already. We need to have a sense of urgency here."

Jane walked over to where Danni was standing. She didn't get in her space but Danni could feel her.

"How long have you known me, Danni? Do you ever think I would put my own interests over getting the evidence against a serial killer?"

"No, I don't. But explain to me again why you won't even try. And leave out the part about the judge relying on you—because that seems to be about your reputation."

Jane walked away from her at that point and stood behind her desk with her arms folded across her chest.

"Do you know how many reporters are here in town writing about these murders?"

"A lot."

"More than a lot, Danni; there are reporters here from all over the globe. Let's say we get the search warrant with this flimsy evidence, which is no evidence really, and search Mr. Felton's apartment. And let's say we find nothing. That day, not the next day but that very day, Mr. Felton will be known worldwide as a suspected serial killer. His reputation will be ruined forever. No matter what happens in this case, he has been labeled and he will be hounded by the press and other assorted sickos. People who have been labeled like that in the past for the most part never recovered. They got sick, they committed suicide, whatever.

"Sam told me that you said something about Mr. Felton being inconvenienced for a couple of hours—that is so far from the truth. The judge's reputation would suffer as well. The Fourth Amendment protects the innocent from unreasonable searches and seizures. That's also part of my obligation as a prosecutor."

Jane had certainly given Danni a lot to think about, and she did it in that way of hers, with that air of certainty that she used in her closing arguments to convince the jury there was no other conclusion to reach. Danni didn't come back at her right away. She paused for a few moments to give Jane and her speech the proper amount of respect.

"I hear you, Jane, and everything you said is true. You're right. I haven't considered all the ramifications for Mr. Felton nor do I want to. I want to keep my focus on those seven girls and the next victim, whoever she may be. If I can save her life and her family and her friends the heartache, I'll move mountains to do it. This killer has talked to me. He's intimated to me that he could kill my own daughter. He's got to be stopped. As a matter of fact, now that I mention it, I talked to both Mr. Felton and the killer and their voices sounded familiar. I can add that to my affidavit."

"I'm going to pretend I didn't hear that, Danni. A professional like you meeting with her superior and then with the state attorney, preparing a memo and an affidavit, and then suddenly recalling that the voices of the killer and *her* suspect were familiar—that is so outrageous it could get you fired.

"Look, I know this is personal for you. Sam told me all about your daughter's situation, but that doesn't justify bending the law. We have to follow the law. Having said that, I'll tell you

THE LAWYER'S LAWYER 45

what I'm going to do. I'll ask for the search warrant. I'll sit down with the judge and I'll lay it all out for him or her, whoever we get, the pros and the cons, and we'll let the chips fall where they may."

Danni couldn't believe her ears. Had she actually gotten through to Jane?

"Fair enough," she said.

On the way out of Jane's office, Danni realized she'd been had.

Danni had another meeting that day, with her ex-husband Mike, that she had put off for as long as she could. They met at The Swamp.

Danni was already sitting at a table when he arrived. She had gotten there early so she could pick out a spot where she felt comfortable, a table by the window, away from the bar and the crowd, looking out on the patio with College Avenue in the background. They could talk privately here.

Mike, a very successful pharmaceutical salesman, was dressed in a tailored blue suit with a pink shirt and lavender tie. *He was always a bit of a dandy*, Danni thought as she watched him walk to the table. He had a smile on his face and a look of confidence as if seeing him made it her lucky day. An objective observer would say he was a handsome man with thick black hair and a muscular physique, but Danni no longer saw him that way. He leaned over the table and kissed her on the cheek.

Danni cringed at his touch.

"So what is it that you needed to see me about?" Mike asked. "And how is our lovely daughter? I'm looking forward to my time with her this weekend."

"That's what I wanted to talk to you about, Mike."

"What? Is something wrong with Hannah?"

"No. She's fine. She's just not here."

"I know she's not here. She's at school, right?"

"No. She's not here in the state of Florida."

Danni told him what happened at Whiskey River Springs and how she had had to take Hannah out of school. She even told him where his daughter was. She had debated about that in her own mind for some time but decided that he had a right to know. He was her father, after all. Not a very good one but still her father. Danni made sure she kept her voice low so nobody could possibly hear that particular part of the conversation.

"You can't say anything to anybody about where she is. Secrecy is her only protection."

"I can protect my own daughter," he said haughtily.

Danni didn't reply.

Mike's smile was now gone, replaced by a sneer. "You had to be a cop, didn't you? You had to go out there in a man's world and prove yourself no matter what."

Danni had figured it was going to get ugly although she didn't know what Mike's weapon of choice for today's battle would be until that moment.

"This isn't about me, Mike."

"Oh, yes it is, Danni. How many other cops are there on your task force? How many of them are women? Who else's children have been threatened? It's definitely about you, Danni. It's always been about you."

There was some truth to the statement but so what? This conversation was about Hannah and her safety. She wasn't going to let it deteriorate into another discussion about why their marriage had failed.

You slept with other women, you asshole! Remember?

"Look, Mike, I don't want to argue with you. I just want you to know what happened and where Hannah Jane is. You can call her anytime you like."

"I know that," Mike snapped. "And when this is over, we're going to revisit the issue of custody. Your house is a dangerous environment."

"Fine," Danni said and stood up to leave. "Thanks for your concern."

She smiled to herself as she walked out of the restaurant. *He wouldn't dare ask for custody. It would interfere too much with his social life.*

CHAPTER TEN

Alice Jeffries was a lonely woman these days. Her husband, Sam, was spending fourteen- to sixteen-hour days at the office with the occasional middle-of-the-night rendezvous at murder sites around the city of Oakville. It had started the night of the first murder four months ago. Sam ran the homicide division at the Sheriff's Department. *If all the murders are in Oakville, why is my husband, a captain in the Apache County Sheriff's Department, responsible for solving them when Oakville has its own police department?* Alice asked herself, usually in the middle of the night when he had gone out to a scene and she was left alone in their bed. She knew the answer, but she asked the question anyway because she was angry and exasperated.

Oakville was *in* Apache County so it was part of the sheriff's jurisdiction. Besides, this case was a different animal. Hell, the FBI was here. And Sam was now the head of the whole investigation. That acknowledgment didn't make her feel one bit better. Oh, she was proud of Sam, but this murderer was killing their marriage along with those coeds. *I guess I'm being a little selfish*, she told herself from time to time.

Alice was the second-grade teacher at White Springs Elementary School, a five-minute drive from her house. She went to work at seven every weekday morning during the school year and was home at four most days. Before the murders had begun, she would often meet Sam as he was pulling into the driveway, his job hours being as predictable as hers. They'd married when they were both twenty. It was a shotgun wedding with little Johnny arriving six months later. Kathleen was born two years after that. The kids had gone off to college now and were pursuing their own careers, Johnny in D.C., and Kathleen in Miami. At the ripe old age of forty-five, Alice was living in the proverbial empty nest.

It was fine when she and Sam were on the same schedule. They'd go out for a bite to eat, maybe a movie if they felt up to it. Or they'd prepare a meal together at home. Cooking was a hobby they both enjoyed. After the first murder, Sam started working ungodly hours. Alice just went home and amused herself with a good book or the television. A couple of months later, however, she'd taken to going out a night or two during the weekend with some of her girlfriends from work. Nothing fancy, just a few drinks at the local tavern. She overdid it a few times, but not very often. It was awkward at first since most people knew she was the wife of a captain in the Sheriff's Department. But after a while she fit right in. She'd always get home early, well before Sam arrived.

Alice was a petite, pretty woman, with short brown hair and green eyes, and she maintained her figure with a strict diet and regular exercise on her home treadmill. She and Sam made an odd couple because he was so massive. Many times when they were out to eat she'd catch people looking at the two of them. She knew what they were wondering. *Yeah, I get on top*, she'd wanted to say, *and it's great.*

This Saturday night, she'd had a little too much at the bar because a man she'd never met before—actually, she didn't even meet him that night—kept sending over drinks for her and her girlfriends. She'd swerved a little bit on the five-block drive back to the house. *Keep it steady*, she told herself. *Sam would not be too happy if you got a*

DUI. Fuck you, Sam. No fuck me, Sam. Please. Just so I can remember what it feels like once again before I die.

It was a tad overdramatic, she knew. After all it had only been four months and there was a reason for it. Poor Sam was working his ass off, night and day. Some couples their age never had sex. She stumbled out of the car and up to the doorway. It took her almost two minutes to get the key into the door. She chuckled to herself as she kept missing the keyhole. Finally she was in. She slammed the door behind her and headed upstairs to the bedroom. When Sam got home, she wanted to be asleep. *You can't question a sleeping beauty,* she reasoned.

Standing in the bathroom in her bra and panties brushing her teeth with her eyes closed, Alice started dreaming about this guy she'd met at the bar a couple of weeks back. He'd asked her to dance. She'd refused, of course, but she'd wanted to and now she pictured herself on the dance floor twirling around, carefree. *You're not an old maid,* she told herself as she swayed to the imaginary music. *You've got your whole life ahead of you.*

She didn't see the lights go out because her eyes were closed and she was more than a little drunk. In her dreamlike state, she didn't even hear the click of the switch. The first sign of trouble for Alice was when she felt a sharp pain at her throat. Suddenly she was yanked off the ground by something around her neck. She opened her eyes then but couldn't see anything. She felt him behind her and tried to turn and grab him, but she had no leverage. The pain was unbearable now. She was gasping for breath and flailing her arms. Whatever it was around her neck was cutting her badly. She tried to grab hold of it and release the pressure but she couldn't. It was a wire! She made a last-ditch effort to scratch his face but it was too late. She felt herself slipping into unconsciousness.

Sam came home a half hour later. He headed for the kitchen and made himself a ham sandwich. Then he turned on the TV in the living room and watched it for an hour or so before heading up to bed. As he flipped on the light switch in the bathroom to take his last piss of the evening, he almost fell over Alice's corpse.

"Jesus!" he exclaimed, recoiling from the body on the floor. He could feel himself starting to hyperventilate as Alice's cold dead eyes seemed to stare right at him. Then the cop took over. He knelt down and checked her pulse. There was no doubt she was dead. He called 911 and made his report. After that, he checked the entire house for clues.

When he was finished, the twenty-year veteran who had recently presided over so many ghastly crime scenes of young women went back up to the bathroom, sat down next to his wife, held her cold, rigid hand in his, and wept.

CHAPTER ELEVEN

After she checked out the crime scene with the other members of the task force, Danni went looking for Sam. She found him downstairs in his den with the door closed, sitting at his desk smoking a cigarette. Sam was not a smoker.

When she walked in, Sam stood up and gave her a hug and started weeping again with his head on her shoulder.

"I don't want anybody to see me like this."

"They're your friends, Sam. They understand."

Sam let her go at that point and sat back down in his chair. "It's funny—up until a few minutes ago I believed wholeheartedly what you just said. We're in the business of murder. We understand. The reality is I never understood all those people who were crying over *their* loved ones. I never got it until now. Now it's my Alice." He fought back the tears again. "Twenty-five years we were together. Twenty-five years. What am I going to tell my kids?"

Danni didn't know what to say so she said nothing, just stood next to him with her hand on his shoulder. They stayed there like that for several minutes.

"We've gotta get that bastard," Sam finally said.

"We will, Sam. We will."

"If he finds out where your daughter is, he's going to kill her. You know that, don't you?"

It was the first thing Danni had thought about when she heard about Alice. "Yes, I know."

"I should have gotten that search warrant for you. I don't know if that kid is innocent or guilty, but we can't leave any stone unturned. I know how you feel now."

"It's too late for that, Sam, but we'll catch this guy."

Sam wasn't listening though. He was in his own nightmare.

"I put you off," he said, standing up and walking around the room. He was such a big man that he immediately made the room look smaller. "I sent you to Jane and then I sent her a memo basically telling her to give you lip service. She told you she was going to go to the judge but she did the same thing with him that I did with her. People are dying out there and she's sitting with the judge telling him about a hysterical police officer. What the hell were we thinking?"

Danni had already figured out how the search warrant deal had gone down so she was not all that upset by Sam's confession. She was worried about him though. He was losing it. She stopped him and put her hands on his shoulders as she looked him in the eye.

"Look, you were right about the search warrant. Besides, it's not important now. You've got to pull yourself together, Sam. Your kids are going to need your strength. They're going to look for it."

Sam loved his kids. Danni expected him to straighten up when she mentioned them but he didn't. The head lowered again.

"I don't know what to say to them."

"You'll find the words."

"I can't."

"I'll help you. Now, I know this is not going to sound that reassuring, but I want you to give me your gun."

Sam lifted his head and gave her a quizzical look. "My gun? What do you think I'm going to do?"

"Nothing, but I don't know for sure. Neither do you. Nobody

knows how they will handle a situation like this. Give it to me. I'll hold it for seventy-two hours, then I'll give it back to you. I'll tell the sheriff informally what I've done so they don't try to do anything formally."

Sam knew the protocol. He knew they could put him on leave and ask him for his gun. Danni was trying to save him from all of that.

"I don't want to miss a day looking for this guy."

"Come on, Sam. You've got to bury your wife. You have to tend to your children. You need at least a couple of weeks."

"I'm not taking that long." He almost shouted the words. "I'm gonna get this piece of shit."

"We'll see. For now, give me your gun for seventy-two hours."

Sam took his Glock out of his holster and reluctantly handed it to her.

"I'm sure this isn't the only gun you have," she said as she took the Glock.

Sam looked at her again. "Do you want to leave me defenseless?"

"He's not coming after you, Sam. You're the wrong sex. Now where's your other gun?"

Sam reached into the top drawer of his desk and pulled out a key. "I've got a few," he said and opened the door to what appeared to be a closet. Danni watched, expecting him to pull a gun out of his shoebox or something. Instead, he walked into the closet, which was free of clothing, reached down to an almost invisible latch on the right-hand side of the back wall, inserted the key, turned it, and the wall became a sliding door revealing a small room on the other side that contained a mini arsenal. Sam entered the room with Danni right behind him. There was a rifle with a scope (Danni couldn't make out the model) mounted on the wall with several shotguns, and an AK-47. Sam had built a long thin table underneath the mounted guns. In the middle of the table were some tools, cleaning materials, two high-intensity lamps, and a chair for Sam to sit in while he was doing his work. On each side of the chair, laid out in a row, were five semiautomatic guns: two to the left, three to the right.

"I built this den with my own hands," Sam said. "And I put this little room in for myself. Nobody knew about it but Alice, and now you."

"What the hell are you getting ready for, World War III?" Danni asked.

"I'm a collector. It's my hobby. Rifles, shotguns, semiautomatic weapons."

"No revolvers?" Danni asked for no particular reason.

"I don't like revolvers," Sam replied.

Danni thought for a brief moment about how Sam had dismissed her argument that Thomas Felton might have been a collector of exotic knives, but she let it pass. This was not the time. She put the Glock on the left side of the table to make the distribution even.

"Is that the only key to this room?" she asked.

"It sure as hell is."

"Why don't you lock up and give me the key."

To Danni's surprise, Sam did exactly as she requested, which made her believe he had another gun hidden somewhere else.

"I'll give this back to you in a few days, I promise."

"I wouldn't have given it to you if I didn't trust you, Danni."

CHAPTER TWELVE

Vanessa Brock and Pedro "Pete" Diaz had their own plan to deal with the danger and peril associated with a serial killer loose in the city of Oakville. Vanessa told the plan to her parents, who were insisting that she come home to Missouri. Both she and Pete were seniors and very anxious to graduate and get on with their lives—she as a teacher and Pete to go to graduate school for his MBA.

"We'll be fine," Vanessa said. "Pete is going to stay at my apartment and sleep on the couch. He's got a license to carry a gun and he knows how to use it. He goes to the firing range every week and he says he won't let me out of his sight."

Vanessa's parents knew the sleeping on the couch part was a lie, but they weren't going to call their daughter out on that one. The rest sounded mildly reassuring. Vanessa had always been headstrong and they weren't going to talk her out of anything she wanted to do anyway. And Pete was a barrel-chested powerful young man. They had met him several times on their visits to Oakville. So they accepted her assurances.

Except for the couch part, the rest of the story was substantially true. Pete didn't have a gun permit but he did have a gun that he kept under their bed at the apartment. He did go to the range regularly to shoot and he was not going to let Vanessa out of his sight. That part wasn't hard for Pete. He worshipped the ground she walked on. Nobody was going to get near Vanessa while he was still alive.

On Saturday night, Vanessa and Pete returned home after watching the football game at The Swamp. There hadn't been a murder in a couple of weeks and there was a fairly decent crowd at the bar. It was almost as if everybody had learned collectively to deal with the fact that they lived in a city under siege, so they continued to go about their daily lives—working, going to school, drinking, watching football. Somewhere in the recesses of their brains, however, they knew that murder and mayhem could, and probably would, rear its ugly head again, but that did not deter them. They still had to live and breathe and play.

Pete had had a little too much to drink. He was okay when he stuck to beer but the lemon drop shooters always did him in. Vanessa drove home although she was a little tipsy herself. It was only nine o'clock but they stripped their clothes off in a matter of seconds and practically passed out in bed. Neither one of them heard the telephone ring at ten, or ten thirty, or eleven.

Somewhere around midnight, Pete woke up to take a leak. His head was pounding as he fumbled in the dark to find the bathroom. Vanessa did not stir although he was making a racket on his journey.

Ten minutes later he was back in bed sidling up next to her naked body. She moaned when she felt him put his arm around her and pull her close. She was half asleep as she felt him working his way inside her. It was almost like a dream when they started moving in rhythm although it felt somehow different this time. *Pete* felt different. Not bad, just different. Then she felt a sharp pain in her stomach and another one. *What is going on? Oh my God, what's happening?*

It was already too late. His hand went to her mouth to stifle any scream she might attempt as he stuck the long thin blade one last time through an opening in her rib cage into her heart.

*   *   *

Danni got the call at five that morning. It came from Allan.

"We've got a double homicide," he said.

"Is it our guy?" Danni asked. This was the first double homicide.

"Can't say for sure, but I think so. She was a student at the university and they were both stabbed."

"That's close enough," Danni replied. "I'll be there as soon as I can."

When she arrived forty minutes later, there were cops everywhere—and reporters and crowds behind the barricades that the police now knew to set up at each murder site.

"Where've you been?" Allan asked. "I expected you a half hour ago."

"I made the mistake of lying back down in bed," Danni told him. "Did I miss anything?"

"Absolutely nothing. The mother called the station when she couldn't get her daughter on the phone. She was frantic, so two uniforms came over to check. They found the bodies just like they are now, the boyfriend in the bathroom and the girl in the bed. He had one stab wound in the back that went right into his heart. He must have died instantly. She had several stab wounds in the stomach and chest. There were no signs of a struggle. Jeffries postulates that the killer was in the apartment waiting for them when they got home. The boyfriend probably got up in the middle of the night to take a whizz—there's urine in the toilet, probably his. The killer took care of him and then got in bed with her, maybe even had sex with her before he killed her."

"What a sicko."

"Goes without saying," Allan replied.

"So Jeffries is here?"

"Yeah. He must have been listening on the radio. He got here right after the uniforms. He's outside searching the perimeter right now."

It had been two weeks since Alice Jeffries died. Since that day Sam Jeffries had taken time off to be with his kids. He'd only appeared in the office once. Danni had seen him leaving in the middle of the afternoon. She had no idea why he had been there.

She also saw him at Alice's funeral.

"I'm taking your advice," he told her. "The kids are going to be home for at least a week. I'm not going near the office while they're here."

Danni gave him his key back the day of the funeral and had not seen him since. Apparently the kids had gone back to their own lives.

"Anything we can use?" Danni asked Allan.

"Nope. The coroner may come up with something if they had sex but the place is clean as usual.

Just then there was a commotion outside.

"Somebody found something!" Danni heard an officer say. It was a little after six and the sun was just rising. She followed the crowd out of the apartment and into the backyard toward a thicket of woods. The group were all professionals so they moved slowly, not wanting their peers to think they were excited or anything. A few feet into the thicket she saw Sam Jeffries standing over something and directing traffic. As she drew closer, she heard his voice.

"Be careful getting it out of there. If there are prints, we don't want to smudge them."

Two men were on their knees on the ground, carefully moving the dirt away from the object. Allan pressed forward to see what it was. Danni followed.

There on the ground, obscured slightly by some plants, was a large bowie knife: The handle was carved in the shape of a gargoyle!

CHAPTER THIRTEEN

B ack at the station, forensics did the fingerprint analysis on the bowie knife and found a match from the NCIC computer. Five members of the SWAT team accompanied six members of the task force, including Danni, Allan, and Sam Jeffries, to Thomas Felton's apartment to pick him up at eleven o'clock that morning.

When they were sure all the exits from the building were covered, Sam rang the doorbell to Felton's apartment. After that, he moved back as the SWAT team positioned itself in place to break the door down after allowing a reasonable period of time—not more than five minutes—to pass. Danni sidled next to Sam just in case. She knew where his gun was holstered. If Felton opened that door in the next minute or so, Sam might decide to just blow his head off.

Felton did just that: Without even asking who it was, he opened the front door dressed in his skivvies. Two of the SWAT team members grabbed him immediately and forced him to the floor on his knees with his head smelling whatever sweet aroma the carpeting was emitting at that moment. Sam had the honor of reading Felton his rights. It was good to keep him occupied.

"Thomas Felton, you are under arrest for the murders of Vanessa Brock and Pedro Diaz. You have the right to remain silent. Anything you say can and will be used against you in a court of law. You have the right to speak to an attorney. If you cannot afford one, an attorney will be provided for you at no cost to you. Do you understand these rights as they have been read to you?"

One of the uniformed police officers had a small handheld camera focused on both Sam and Felton, memorializing the event. No need to fuck up a good arrest with a procedural violation. Felton nodded his head.

"You need to respond verbally," Sam told him. For a moment, Danni thought Sam might just kick Felton in the head. He was positioned perfectly and Felton's head just hung out there like a soccer ball.

Come on, answer! Danni said to herself. *Just answer the damn question before he loses it and kills you right here and now!*

"I understand what you said to me but I'm innocent," Felton replied. "I didn't kill anybody. You've got the wrong man."

"We'll see about that, dickhead," Sam answered. "You're going down. And don't be fooled: that cocktail they give you up in Raiford—it may be quick but it's awful painful. They just paralyze you so nobody can tell."

Danni looked at the officer holding the camera. Unfortunately, he'd caught it all on tape, including Sam's diatribe. They'd have to explain that away down the road. She slipped her arm around Sam's as the SWAT guys started to move Felton to a police vehicle.

"Come on, Sam. It's all over," she said.

"It won't be over until that son of a bitch is dead. And it won't even be over then," Sam said. "It won't be over till I'm dead and my kids are dead and all those other kids' families are dead. Then it will be over."

PART TWO
Eight Years Later
October 2001

Bass Creek, Florida

CHAPTER FOURTEEN

J ack, will you get me a beer while you're down there?" Henry Wilson asked his friend Jack Tobin as he sat in one of the captain's chairs at the stern of the thirty-two-foot Sea Ray with a fishing pole in his hand. It was a calm, sunny day on Lake Okeechobee. The fish were jumping but they weren't biting.

Jack was in the galley frying hamburgers for lunch. It was just the two of them, as usual on a Saturday afternoon.

"Sure, Henry. Can I get you anything else, like an extra cushion for your chair or a frosty mug for your beer?"

"Just the bottle will do, Jack, but hurry up, will you?"

"You'd better be careful. You don't want to mess with the cook," Jack said as he handed Henry his beer.

"I forgot about that rule. Don't spit on my burger. By the way, Bobby Flay, when are we eating?"

"Why? Do you have something important to do out here on the lake that I don't know about?"

The lake was empty. There wasn't a boat in sight.

Henry took a sip of his beer.

"You never know. It's kinda like these fish. One of them is going to show up in this boat sooner or later."

The banter went on like that all day. They were an odd couple, to say the least, and the origin of their friendship was even more unusual. Henry had been a prisoner on death row with eight weeks to live when Jack became his lawyer. Eight weeks later he was a free man. Jack's wife, Pat, was sick at the time, and she eventually died. Henry had helped Jack through those bad times, and they'd been close friends ever since.

Henry lived in Miami and Jack in a small town called Bass Creek that bordered the lake. Henry came up most weekends and they usually went fishing. It was a good-sized boat, but there was barely room for both of them. Henry was a six-foot-five bear of a man and Jack was six-foot-two although he was much thinner.

"You need to put some meat on those bones," Henry told him when the burgers were cooked and Jack was sitting next to him. "Maybe you need to add fries and onion rings and some ribs to these meals."

Jack laughed. He had a good appetite but he worked out almost every day and stayed slim. Besides, nobody could eat like Henry.

"The women like me just the way I am, Henry."

"What women? I haven't seen you with a woman in ages. Probably 'cause they think you're too skinny. I don't know about your white women, but black women don't like skinny men. Won't even look at you twice."

Henry had unknowingly hit on a sore spot. Jack had been feeling a bit lonely lately and thinking that perhaps it was time for him to find a companion to share his life. There would never be anyone to replace his late wife, Pat, but he knew Pat didn't want him moping around the house either. She wanted him to be happy. He couldn't see her but he knew that she was the one pushing him out the door.

"I've been thinking about moving, Henry."

"Where the hell did that come from?"

"I don't know. Don't get me wrong. I love Bass Creek but it's dead. And there's only so much fishing a man can do."

"I hear you, brother. You're still a young man and, frankly, there are too many memories here that might keep you from starting fresh. Where were you thinking of going?"

"I don't know. I've just thrown it out there to the universe and I'm going to wait to see what comes at me in the near future."

"You know I love you, Jack, but you're weird. What the hell is that—you're going to wait for the universe to throw something at you? Is that some kind of religion you and Pat cooked up in that little cove of yours?"

Henry had heard many stories about Jack and Pat's special place, a little cove hidden off the Okalatchee River near where the river intersected with the lake. They claimed that they communed with nature and the spirits there. Henry had never visited it because it had been so special to them.

"You might call it that, Henry. Just look around. Out here where man has not been, it's perfect. Didn't the Indians look to nature as their god?"

"You're a good lawyer, Jack, but that's a bad argument. Look what happened to the Indians. They suffered more degradation at the hands of the white man than my people did. And that reminds me, what am I hanging around with you for?"

They both laughed and took a sip of their beer.

"The Indians did real well when it was just them and nature."

"Okay, Jack. You're entitled to think whatever you want. I just hope you don't wait too long for some bird to come whispering in your ear."

CHAPTER FIFTEEN

The universe called the next day in the form of Wanda Reardon, an old friend and client of Jack's. Wanda was a single mother with five children, ranging in age from twenty-one to twelve. An attractive African-American woman in her midforties who worked night and day, Wanda had come to Jack a year and a half ago because she had been involved in a car accident.

Jack had made his living and amassed a small fortune defending insurance companies in personal injury actions before he retired to Bass Creek. He hadn't defended a case as small as the one Wanda brought to him in twenty years, and he had represented very few plaintiffs in his career. Besides that, he had embarked on a new vocation representing death row inmates. It didn't pay at all, but Jack was not looking for money at this stage of his life.

Wanda had made an impression on him that first day. She was a determined woman who refused to let life defeat her. Her accident had caused her to be out of work for six weeks and, since she lived on the margin, that brief period of time had almost crippled the family. Wanda had lost her job as a practical nurse and was unable to find another.

It had taken two letters and a phone call for Jack to settle Wanda's case for twice as much as it was worth. The insurance adjuster handling the matter took one look at the name of the attorney representing Wanda and coughed up the money. Jack had left the practice of civil law but his reputation remained. He had also made some inquiries at the hospital about why his client had lost her job after she was in an automobile accident. It didn't take the hospital long to get the message. Wanda was offered her old job back.

It was nine o'clock on Sunday morning when Wanda knocked on Jack's door. Both Jack and Henry were up and about, getting ready for another day of fishing. Jack answered the door.

"Wanda, how are you? Boy, it's been a while."

"Yes, it has, Jack. Yes, it has." Wanda gave him a big hug. "You need to come over to the house for some good home cooking." As she said the words, she gave him the look that Henry had given him the day before. The one that said "you need to put some meat on those bones."

"I will for sure, Wanda, but you didn't come all the way over here to invite me for dinner. Come on in and tell me how you're doing."

He led her to the living room and offered her a comfortable spot on the couch. Henry was in the kitchen making coffee.

"You remember Henry, don't you?"

Wanda smiled. "I sure do."

Henry smiled back from the kitchen. Jack sensed there might be something more between the two of them than just knowing each other's names.

"Can I get you some coffee?"

"No, I don't want to bother you on the Lord's Day. And I'm too troubled to eat or drink." She did appear upset although not too upset to smile at Henry.

"What's the problem, Wanda? How can I help?" Jack sat down on the couch next to her.

"It's my son Julian. You remember him, Jack. You went to one of his football games with me up in Oakville."

"I do. What a great athlete."

A smile again came to Wanda's face, but for only an instant. "Yes, he is, but he's in trouble. He's about to lose everything. Everything he and I have worked so hard for."

"What kind of trouble?"

"Some girl up there at the university claimed he tried to rape her. Now, Julian is no angel, but I talked to him and he told me he's innocent. He says the girl is just making it up. The press is all over him because the football team is having a lot of these kinds of problems. He needs a lawyer bad, Jack."

It was not a case that Jack would normally take. There were plenty of good criminal lawyers who could handle a case like this, but Wanda was a friend and she had no money. That was the unspoken conversation between them. Jack knew Julian and he liked him but he didn't know if he was innocent or not. If he had tried to rape the girl, Jack was not going to help him.

It occurred to him as he sat next to Wanda that maybe something else was going on here. Maybe he was supposed to go to Oakville. He'd been there many times and his good friend Ron owned The Swamp, the most popular bar and restaurant in town. Oakville had a vibrant community of intellectuals, a great arts community, a world-class medical facility, rivers and natural springs, and so much to offer.

He'd long ago forgotten about Ron's prediction that he would come to Oakville someday to live.

"I'll tell you what, Wanda. Henry will be disappointed, but I'm going to forego fishing today and take a drive up to Oakville to see Julian."

"Oh, thank you, Jack. Thank you."

"Don't thank me yet. I'll talk to Julian but I won't help him if I don't think he's innocent."

"That's fine. That's fine. He's innocent. You'll see it right away, Jack. You'll look into his eyes and you'll know."

"Henry is going to be awful disappointed he won't get to spend the rest of the day with me." Jack turned and looked at Henry, who was walking out of the kitchen toward the dining room table with his coffee and a bagel in hand.

"Oh, don't you worry about Henry," Wanda said. "I'll take him over to my house and feed him a good meal." She looked over at Henry and smiled. Henry smiled back.

Maybe the universe is working for both of us, Jack thought.

CHAPTER SIXTEEN

Wat was all that between you and Wanda?" Jack asked Henry after Wanda left.

"Well, back when you were her lawyer and I was your investigator we became kinda friendly toward each other."

"And?"

"And nothing. All those kids scared me away."

"What's changed?"

"I don't know. Maybe I've changed. It's not like I've decided to marry the woman. She walked in the door and she smiled at me and I smiled back and I'm probably going to stop over for some dinner."

"Yeah, right, Henry—some dinner. That's what I got out of it."

Henry smiled. "I know you just as well, Jack. Like I know exactly what you were thinking when Wanda mentioned her son up in Oakville."

"And what's that?"

"You were thinking Wanda was the universe talking to you and you're supposed to go to Oakville." Jack tried to hide his smile, but Henry caught it. "I'm right, aren't I?"

"I don't know. The thought did cross my mind. You still think I'm crazy?"

"Hell, Jack, you're one of the sanest men I've ever known. If you believe in the universe, I believe in it too. Let's see if it'll work for both of us."

"Amen, brother. So I'm probably going to stay in Oakville for a little while even after I get Julian's case disposed of."

"Are you going to take the case?"

"Don't know. Julian is a good kid but things can happen when you're away from home. I'll know once I talk to him."

"Think you're going to need me?"

"Probably. For now, why don't you stay here and keep Wanda happy and look after the house."

"And the boat," Henry replied.

"Especially the boat."

Henry lived in Miami, but he didn't have an everyday job. Jack had convinced the Florida legislature to award him three million dollars for wrongfully imprisoning him for seventeen years, so he basically lived off his investment income. Like Jack, he worked for Exoneration, the nonprofit foundation that investigated cases of individuals who had been wrongfully convicted, especially those like Henry who were on death row.

"Consider it done," Henry said. "Go to Oakville and stay as long as you like."

"I don't want to put you out."

"Trust me, Jack. I'll be just fine."

Jack met Julian Reardon at his apartment on Arthur Road in Oakville. Julian was expecting him as Wanda had called to tell him Jack was coming. Julian was a remarkable physical specimen. Six feet tall, he was all muscle, athleticism, and speed. Jack remembered watching a couple of his games last year when Julian was a sophomore running back, and from what Jack had observed, he was eventually going to be playing professionally. The University of North Central Florida was an elite football school and played in the Southcentral Conference, arguably the toughest football conference in the country, but at times it appeared that

Julian was playing at a different level than the other kids on the field. Every major college had recruited him back in high school: Alabama, Ohio State, Virginia Tech, and Oklahoma, to name a few. Julian had chosen the Fighting Ospreys of North Central Florida because his mom loved the Ospreys, and Oakville was close enough that he could sneak home for a weekend now and then in the off-season.

"Hi, Julian," Jack said when Julian answered the door.

"Hi, Mr. Tobin. Come on in."

Jack walked in and sat at the kitchen table. The apartment was cleaner than any apartment Jack had lived in during his college days. While the two knew each other, it was only because of Wanda. The first few minutes were awkward.

"Do you live here by yourself?" Jack asked.

"No, I've got a roommate. He'll be gone for a couple of hours."

"So we can talk. Tell me what happened, Julian."

"It happened last Saturday. We'd just won a big game against South Carolina and we were out celebrating. I know I had too much to drink but not too much that I didn't know what I was doing. I met this girl, Sandra was her name, and we started talking and stuff and she was kinda hugging on me and we went outside into the parking lot in the back where it was dark.

"I want you to know something, Mr. Tobin. I've got a girlfriend, Robin. I know we're young and everything but we love each other. We talk all the time about getting married when I get drafted into the pros. Anyway, this Sandra was getting very hot with me when we were in the parking lot, you know what I mean?"

Jack just nodded.

"Then all of a sudden I didn't want to be there no more. I stopped her and told her I couldn't do this. I apologized and everything. While I was walking inside, she yelled at me 'You're gonna pay for this.' That was it. I left the bar. I never saw her again until I was called in the other day by my coach who told me this girl claimed I tried to rape her. I never did."

Julian was looking at Jack the whole time he was talking. Jack could tell he was ashamed of his actions. He also could tell that Julian was being truthful. It was the little things. He didn't look away. He didn't rub his hands or blink. He just told it like it was.

Jack had him call his coach, Clint Maddox, and arrange a meeting. Maddox must have been anxious to see him because Jack was in the coach's office within an hour.

"Nice to meet you, Mr. Tobin," Coach Maddox said after Jack introduced himself. He had the handshake thing down. Looking directly at Jack, a perfect smile pasted on his face, he gave Jack's hand just the right squeeze. *Probably part of the training*, Jack thought. *This guy has shaken more hands than a career politician.*

"I know who you are," Coach Maddox said to him. "I've read about you here and there. I'm surprised you're representing Julian."

"I know the family. His mother is a friend of mine."

"She's a very nice woman. How can I help you?"

"I'm not the one who needs help, Julian is."

"I know but I can't help him. This case has already been reported to the NCAA, and there is an active criminal investigation. My hands are tied. All I could do was suspend Julian from the team. He's on his own."

Jack smiled at the coach's words as he sat down in a chair the coach offered him. Maddox didn't seem to like the expression on Jack's face. Jack had read somewhere that the coach had a short fuse. He was a big man, tall and thick, with arms like tree trunks. *Probably somewhere in his fifties*, Jack surmised. *From his size I'd say he must have been a lineman in his playing days.*

"Something funny?" Maddox asked.

"Not at all."

"Then why the smirk?"

"It was more of an ironic smile."

"I'm not sure I understand the irony."

"Well, I was thinking about how you promise these boys everything to get them to come here and all your alumni go crazy giving the school money so these kids will go out there and win one for the Old Ospreys, then one of them gets in trouble and you drop him like a hot potato."

"So what's your point?"

"Isn't there some sort of obligation to this kid, at least morally, to help him through this until somebody determines he's actually done something wrong?"

"The school gives him the opportunity to get a free college education if he plays football and keeps his nose clean. If he doesn't keep his nose clean, I can't help him. You go to bars, you're gonna get in trouble. I'm no different than Julian. I have the opportunity to stay employed if I coach football, keep my nose clean, and win. If I don't, I'm out. People get fired from jobs every day for a good reason, a bad reason, or no reason at all. That's life.

"I'd like to help Julian. The school would like to help him, too. But we can't. The NCAA is all over this and so is the press. Our hands are tied. I think Julian is a good kid and I'm glad he's got you."

That was a sobering assessment, Jack thought as he left Coach Maddox's office and headed for The Swamp.

CHAPTER SEVENTEEN

Jack found a table in the back corner of The Swamp and waited for his friend Ron to make his way over. It was a little after five and Ron was shaking hands and slapping backs as he worked the room. As owner of the legendary restaurant and bar, Ron was one of the best-known people in town after Coach Maddox and the basketball coach, whose name Jack couldn't remember.

Ron made a point of looking at his watch as he approached Jack.

"You've been here for over an hour and you haven't gotten that kid off yet," he said as he gave his good friend a hug. "You're slipping, man. You're not at the top of your game anymore. I told you when you stopped doing it for money you were going to fall apart."

Jack laughed. Ron was always in character as the slick-talking New Yorker who didn't know much except a few common-sense rules such as how to remove the twenties from the cash register every thirty minutes.

"Keep it there any longer, employees get sticky fingers," he'd told Jack on more than one occasion. "It's an occupational disease and prevention is the only treatment. If I wasn't here every day watching them like a hawk, there'd be nothing but nickels and dimes in the register."

Nothing could have been further from the truth. Ron was an astute businessman who put a great deal of faith and trust in his employees and ran a first-class operation with good food as well as drinks, although he would deny those facts until the cows came home.

"I run a gin mill," was his favorite line.

Jack and Ron had been friends since high school back in New York City. They were both poor kids, sons of immigrants. Jack's people were Irish and Ron's were Italian, a distinction that didn't resonate with either of them. After college, Jack went on to law school. Ron started a business and then another one and another one until he learned the right way to do things.

"I'm an overnight success," he would tell people. "It was just a long night."

"So did you meet with the kid?" Ron asked after he sat down.

"Yeah. I met with Coach Maddox too."

"And what did the great man have to say? No wait, let me guess. 'My hands are tied' or some shit like that."

Jack laughed again. Ron brought out the best in him. "That's exactly what he said."

"It figures. They bring these kids up here, make celebrities out of them, expose them to every temptation known to man, and expect them to handle it like they've been doing it all their lives. I'm a big believer in personal responsibility, but this is too much."

"That's a problem I can't solve. I need to find out if Julian is innocent or guilty. If he's guilty, then he deserves to be punished. My sense after talking to him is that he's innocent."

"How can I help, Jack?"

"I thought you might know a little bit about the criminal investigation—who I can talk to and such."

"The person running the investigation is a detective named Danni Jansen. She's an old friend of mine. I've known her since she came on the force twenty years ago. Good person. She used to be one of our best homicide detectives but now she's on her way out. I think she's got less than a year to go before she retires so they've got her doing all kinds of stuff."

"I need to talk to her."

"I'll call her right now and ask her to come by. She lives five minutes away."

"I don't need to meet her here," Jack said.

"Why not? Aren't most problems solved over a drink or two? Don't answer that. It's my mantra and I'm sticking with it. I have to. I own a gin mill, for Christ's sake. Besides, she's a very good-looking woman and she's single. She'd be perfect for you. You can kill two birds with one stone."

Jack just smiled. When Ronnie was on a roll, there was no sense arguing with him. It didn't get you anywhere.

He was back five minutes later with a dejected look on his face.

"She said she'd meet you at the office tomorrow morning at nine."

Jack laughed.

"What's so funny?" Ron asked.

"You are—always playing the matchmaker."

"I was just trying to sell a few drinks. I've gotta pay for these lights to be on, you know."

Jack was at the police station promptly at nine o'clock the next morning but he didn't get to see detective Danni Jansen until nine thirty. It was part of the game to make him wait and he wasn't upset by the maneuver.

"Danni Jansen," she said when she finally emerged from behind a sterile wooden door with a sign on it that read "Authorized Personnel Only." "Sorry to keep you waiting."

Sure you are, Jack wanted to reply. She was a tall woman, maybe five eight or nine, with fair skin, large green eyes, and light brown hair that settled just above her shoulders. She was pretty in a natural way, wearing very little makeup from what he could tell, a pair of navy slacks, a light blue button-down shirt, and no jewelry except a silver watch on her left wrist.

"Jack Tobin," Jack said, extending his hand to meet hers. "No problem. I had some work to keep me busy anyway."

She motioned for him to follow her through the forbidden door and down a long hallway to a small room that had a table and two chairs.

"Can I get you something to drink?"

"No, I'm fine."

"Ron tells me that you have some important new information for me in the Julian Reardon case, is that correct?"

"Not really. You know how Ron exaggerates. He's a friend of yours, isn't he?"

"Not really. You know how he exaggerates." She smiled when she said the words but not in a friendly way. The woman was a poker player. "Do you have any information at all for me?"

"Well, I'm representing Julian for one and I believe that my client is innocent."

"That's a shocking revelation. Do you have any facts to support that belief?"

"Just that I know Julian and I know his mother. When I talked to him today, I believe he told me the truth."

"That's it?"

"That's it."

"And what would you like me to do now that you have shared your assessment—recommend to the state attorney that she not indict your client?"

She was a tough one, but Jack sensed that it was a front. He suspected they were still looking for information since the decision to indict had not yet been made.

"How about if Julian Reardon comes to the police station tomorrow and I allow you to interview him?"

"That would be nice." She took a moment to look at him. Jack could tell she was sizing up the situation. "I've done my homework on you, Mr. Tobin."

"Jack."

Danni ignored the offer to be on more familiar terms. "I don't know why you are handling this case, but I do know a lawyer of your caliber doesn't make an offer without wanting something in return. So why don't you tell me what you want in return for allowing your client to sit down for an interview."

"I want the name and the date of birth of the alleged victim."

"You know I can't do that. This is an ongoing investigation."

It was not an outright rejection. The language invited some negotiation.

"C'mon, Detective, you know I'm going to be entitled to that information eventually."

"Do I?"

"Look, the sooner we get to the bottom of this investigation, the better off we'll both be. I can help you."

"C'mon, Jack, I wasn't born yesterday. You don't want to get to the bottom of anything. You're a criminal lawyer. You want to get your client off. Who's kidding who here?"

"Your investigation of me was incomplete, Ms. Jansen. I spent my entire career as an insurance defense lawyer. I now represent people on death row out of choice and not for money. I want to find the truth. If Julian is guilty, he should be punished, although I will be a part of that process as well to make sure it's fair."

"You want the name and date of birth of the complainant so that you can do your own investigation?"

"Right."

"So you can vilify her in the press?"

"That won't happen. You have my word."

"And you are going to share information with me?"

"Immediately. You'll know minutes after I know."

Danni thought about his words again for a minute. It certainly would be nice to talk to Julian Reardon. And Tobin wasn't asking for the moon.

"All right, but I don't want any shenanigans. You double-cross me and I'll get the state attorney to throw the book at your client."

"Wouldn't think of it."

"Have your client here tomorrow at ten."

"Fine."

She stood up to let him know the meeting was over.

"How'd it go?" Ronnie asked when Jack showed up at The Swamp for lunch.

"She's a tough cookie."

"She is, but she's a good cop too. You're lucky she's on this case. Some of those other bimbos over there would have pushed for an indictment already. She won't do that."

"She's awfully young to be retiring."

"Not as young as you might think. I'd say forty-five or so. Still, it's young to retire from most jobs. We had a serial killer loose here about eight years ago. You remember because you called me in the middle of all that to find out how I was holding up."

"Yeah, I remember."

"Well, that situation affected Danni tremendously. Her daughter was ten at the time and Danni sent her out of town for a while—I don't know all the particulars because she didn't and still doesn't talk about it. I do know that ever since then she's been counting the days until her retirement."

"Why?" Jack asked.

"Like I said, I don't know."

"Well, I hope she doesn't retire before we get Julian's case resolved."

"I don't think she will, although you know how those public service jobs work. Even if you've got six months to go before you retire, if you've got enough sick time, you can just leave."

"Our tax dollars at work," Jack said.

"Tell me about it."

CHAPTER EIGHTEEN

Jack called Julian that night and made arrangements to meet him at eight o'clock the next morning at a coffee shop downtown. He wanted Julian to tell the truth in his own words, but he also wanted him to be prepared so that his answers were concise and to the point.

"Just answer her questions, Julian," he told the young man the next morning. "Don't anticipate what she wants to know."

"Do you think she might want to talk to Darryl?" Julian asked.

"Who's Darryl?"

"My roommate. He was with me that night. He didn't see anything but I told him what happened right after."

Jack wanted to smack himself in the head. *How did I not ask that question? I've been away too long. I'm slipping.*

"Is Darryl on the football team?"

"Yeah. He's the starting defensive end."

Several ideas hit Jack at the same time.

"Does the coach know that Darryl was there?"

"Yeah, but he hasn't disciplined Darryl or anything. Darryl has no problem telling you or anybody what he knows."

"Where is he now?

"He's back at the apartment. I told him you might want to talk to him."

"I don't need to talk to him. Maybe we'll just bring him along and give Detective Jansen an added bonus this morning."

"There was something else I didn't mention to you yesterday."

"What's that?"

"A lawyer from Miami called me right after this story was in the news. He said he could help me and it wouldn't cost me."

"That was generous of him. Why didn't you take him up on it?"

"I called my mom, and she said we should talk to you first."

"Did you get his name?"

"I know he told me but I forgot. I think I still have his number in my phone."

While Julian was scanning his phone, Jack tried to figure out how this new information fit into the puzzle. Every case started as a puzzle, but some proved to be more difficult than others. Maybe this was a lawyer trying to make a name for himself by taking a high-profile case. Maybe it was something else.

Julian found the number and Jack wrote it down. He decided not to give it to Detective Jansen until he had a little more information although if she asked about it, Julian would tell her.

Unlike the day before, Danni was very prompt. The desk sergeant had barely set the phone down when she came out to the waiting room to greet them. She wore black slacks and a white Oxford shirt with the sleeves rolled up halfway between the wrist and the elbow. A pair of small diamond earrings accompanied her silver watch.

"Good morning, Mr. Tobin," she said rather frostily as she extended her hand. "I recognize Julian, but who is this other individual?"

In contrast to Julian, who was slender and muscled, Darryl was enormous and muscled, kind of like the Incredible Hulk. He and Julian stood as Danni approached them; Darryl towered over her as Jack introduced him.

"This is Darryl Kennedy, Julian's roommate. He was at the bar on the night in question. I thought you might like to hear what he knows."

Danni shook his hand, which was enormous, and turned her attention right back to Jack.

"It was so thoughtful of you to bring along a witness to corroborate your client's testimony."

Jack wanted to fire back a zinger of his own, but this wasn't the time for repartee.

"I just thought it might be helpful. I have not personally talked to him."

"Considering your reputation, that is hard to believe, Mr. Tobin. However, I will accept your words at face value."

Jack didn't respond. He wanted this to go smoothly.

Danni was an experienced interrogator. It didn't take long for her to get both Julian's and Darryl's entire stories. She covered all the bases, except for the call from the Miami lawyer, and Jack noticed that she studied the faces of both young men as she listened to their answers.

"Well, what do you think?" he asked when she was done.

"I don't think anything. Your client's story completely contradicts that of the complainant. I've got to gather the facts and put the pieces together."

"Speaking of the pieces, you were going to give me some information today."

Danni reached into her shirt pocket and retrieved a piece of paper which she handed to him. "Remember, if you find anything, you're going to bring it to me."

"As fast as I can," Jack said, smiling.

He called Henry on the way to the parking lot and read him the name and the date of birth of the woman who had made the charge against Julian.

"The rumor is that she's from Miami."

"Good because I'm here. I drove home this morning to pick up some clothes. I'll call you back as soon as I know something."

Henry's knowledge of criminals, since he'd been one himself, gave him an innate ability that normal detectives or investigators did not have to find things out on the street. His time as an investigator for Exoneration had helped him hone those skills and learn the more conventional techniques as well. He had Sandra Davis's address and criminal record literally minutes after hanging up the phone with Jack.

"She's clean except for an arrest for prostitution ten years ago," he told Jack.

"She's thirty now so that means she was twenty when she got arrested. What do you make of that?" Jack asked.

"I don't know, Jack. She may have been in trouble back then and picked herself up. But it does give this whole rape claim of hers a fishy smell."

"It sure does. Why is a thirty-year-old woman hitting on a twenty-one-year-old kid?"

"I'm not sure but I'll find out. I'm heading over to her neighborhood now. She lives in Liberty City. I'm very familiar with the place. I'll just hang around and see what I can pick up."

"Keep me posted."

Jack knew it wouldn't take long, maybe a game of pool or a beer or two, but Henry would have the skinny on Sandra Davis in a matter of hours.

He dropped the boys off at their apartment and stopped at The Swamp to have another cup of coffee with Ron.

"How's the investigation going?" Ron asked.

"Terrific. Detective Jansen and I are going to work together to get to the bottom of everything."

"Really?"

"No, but at least we're sharing information."

"So she is at least cooperating with you on the investigation?"

"Somewhat. Her witness has problems and I think she knows it. She's letting me do the dirty work."

"You mean Henry is doing the dirty work?"

"Exactly. There's nobody better."

Henry called about three hours later.

"I met this druggie. He lives in the same apartment complex as our girl, Sandra. I guess they're friends. He says she told him the rape story was bogus."

"Will he talk to the police?"

"Probably, if somebody makes it worth his time."

"I'll let you handle that part. I've got to tell the detective about this. She'll probably want to interview this guy."

"Tell her she needs to come to Miami because this dude is not leaving the place where he gets his dope for any amount of money."

"I'll tell her. I've got a phone number I need you to look up. Some guy called Julian, said he was an attorney and offered to handle the case for nothing."

"Nice guy. It's understandable though. You represent a high-profile football player—it's advertising you can't buy."

"Maybe you're right. Check it out though."

"Sure thing. I'll be in touch."

Jack called Danni, but she had already left the office for the day. He had to track Ron down at The Swamp to get her cell phone number.

"I just need to relay some information to her," he told Ron.

"Sure, sure, I know. You can leave me in the dark if you want to even though I laid all the groundwork for you two."

"Thanks, Ron. I really appreciate it. I knew I couldn't hide this from you. Keep it under your hat though, will you?"

"Sure, sure. Your secret is safe with me."

Jack called Danni. "My investigator has uncovered a witness," he said.

"Where are you?" she asked.

"At The Swamp."

"I'll be there in five minutes."

She wasn't lying. Five minutes later she walked in the door, looking casual in a navy striped top and jeans. Jack raised his hand to let her know where he was sitting.

"So, Counselor, tell me about this new witness," she said after she sat down and ordered a glass of Cabernet from the waitress who had followed her to the table.

"My investigator has found someone who says he talked to your witness and that she made up the rape charge."

"That's a first-class investigator you've got. I gave you the woman's name this morning and you've already got a witness. Where did he or she find this person?"

"He found him in Miami. Apparently this person is a neighbor of Sandra Davis. My guy says he's a drug user."

"Not the most credible type of witness. For a few bucks he'd probably say anything. I'm not sure one witness is going to cause the state to drop the charges anyway."

"I figured that. Your case already has some problems though. You know about Ms. Davis's prostitution record."

"I do, but that was years ago."

"It has to make you pause at least. And the woman is thirty years old. What was she hanging around with this kid for anyway?"

"Wait a minute. You're assuming that his story is true—that she was hanging around with him. She told us he accosted her in the parking lot of the bar. We do have some questions though. That's why your client hasn't been indicted yet."

Ron stopped over in the middle of their conversation.

"How are you kids doing tonight?" he asked but didn't wait for an answer. "Why don't you guys let me buy you dinner. We've got some nice specials on the menu."

Danni was confused. She looked over at Jack, who just shrugged his shoulders. "Maybe another night," she said to Ron. "I'm not all that hungry tonight."

"Okay," Ron said walking away with a frustrated look on his face.

"What was that about?" Danni asked.

"Haven't the vaguest," Jack replied.

She looked at him for a moment, not knowing whether to believe him or not, then she was back on the case again. "I probably need to talk to your witness. Before I do that though, I want some assurances from you that this is on the up and up. I mean, you and I both know that you can find a drug user to say anything."

"I wouldn't do that nor would my investigator."

"No, I guess you wouldn't. I've been reading about the cases you've handled, and I know your reputation is pretty solid although I must tell you, I don't know how you represent the people you do. Don't get me wrong, I have some issues with the death penalty and how it's administered, but I think it's perfect for some people like that piece of shit who rampaged through this town eight years ago."

"I appreciate that you have a totally different perspective than me," Jack said. "But some people are innocent of the crime for which they were charged. The criminal justice system is flawed."

"But so is your sanctimonious position."

Jack smiled. She was testing him for some reason. Or maybe it was the mention of the serial killer case. Ron had said that case had affected her in a serious way although he didn't know the details. Jack could see that her demeanor had changed when she mentioned that case. She wasn't finished yet, though.

"You say people are innocent of the crime for which they are charged but that doesn't mean that they're innocent people. Take this Henry Wilson guy that you represented. He obviously wasn't guilty of the murder that he had been charged with, but he was a bad guy and you got him released back on the streets."

"After seventeen years for a crime he didn't commit."

"So, he's still a bad guy."

"Don't you have any belief in the power of redemption?"

"None. I guess I've been on the streets too long."

"Well, maybe you just continue to see the failures and not the successes and that frames your judgment. Henry Wilson is one of the finest people I know. He's my closest friend."

Danni looked genuinely surprised. "I didn't mean to offend you, Jack. I just thought he was somebody you represented. I didn't think you knew him personally."

"It's fine. I'm not angry. It's just that a lot of people think like you. They don't want to look at the person and ask how they got where they're at and what should or could be done to prevent it in the future. It's so much easier to look at them in that one-dimensional frame—as criminals—and snuff them out like cockroaches."

They were silent for a long minute. "I guess we can agree to disagree on that one, too," Danni said finally. Jack looked at her and saw a smile on her face. He smiled back.

"That's a good idea," he said.

Danni called the waitress over and handed her a ten-dollar bill for the glass of Cabernet. Then she stood up to leave.

"I'll be in touch," she said.

CHAPTER NINETEEN

The phone rang at eight the next morning. It was Henry.

"I got a line on the lawyer who called Julian. Are you ready?"

"Sure."

"Ted Collins."

"The sports agent?"

"Yup—the guy who wines and dines kids and tries to sign them before anybody else."

"It doesn't make sense. Why would a sports agent offer to defend a kid in a rape case? He's not qualified to do that."

"Maybe he gets somebody else to actually handle the case."

"But then he's coming out of pocket."

"Yeah, Jack, but remember, if he handles this for the kid, Julian would be indebted to him and would probably make him his agent. That could mean millions and millions of dollars. It would definitely be worth it."

"Maybe you're right, Henry, but I don't see any connection between Collins's offer and the rape charge itself, do you?"

"Not yet, but I'm not saying there isn't one."

"By the way, Detective Jansen wants to come down and interview our witness."

"Tell her to come soon. This guy is in bad shape. I don't know how long he's going to be around. Ask her if she can be here tomorrow. Tell her he's better earlier in the day than later."

"Will do."

Jack called Danni right away.

"I talked to my investigator and he says the witness can be available tomorrow morning."

"Good. I'll leave tonight. Tell him to set it up first thing in the morning and get me the details."

"Listen, since I'm driving down as well, do you want to drive together?"

"Let me make a suggestion to you, Jack. Stay here. If I'm going to go talk to this guy and he is truly an independent witness—and I'm not satisfied that he is—it's better if you're not there when I question him."

Jack rolled Danni's statement over in his mind for a few moments. What she said made sense, and the fact that she said it told him she was giving Julian a fair shake.

"Okay. My investigator will be there though."

"That's fine."

He called Henry right back. "Set it up. She's going to drive down tonight so she will be available first thing in the morning."

"Okay."

"Henry, I'm going to tell her about the sports agent when I call her back. I just want you to know she's going to have that information when she's there."

"She may want to talk to Sandra again."

"That's what I was thinking."

"I know she's an experienced cop and all, but Miami is a different ball game. Liberty City is a dangerous place."

"She's doing us a favor, Henry, by doing all this legwork before seeking an indictment."

"I hear you, Jack. I'll keep an eye on her."

CHAPTER TWENTY

Danni drove to Miami that night and on the way thought about the new information Jack had given her about the sports agent, Ted Collins. Being a detective in Oakville, she knew a little about sports agents who tried to prey on some of the more talented athletes at the university. Ted Collins was one of them. His nickname around sports programs was "The Eel" because he was a slippery, slimy son of a bitch. *So he was offering to represent Julian. He's located in Miami. Our victim, Sandra, is located in Miami. Is that just a coincidence or is there a connection? Maybe I need to talk to Sandra again while I'm there.*

In the morning, promptly at ten as instructed, she called the number Jack had given her.

"Good morning, Ms. Jansen."

"And who am I speaking to?"

"My name's Henry, ma'am. I'm Jack Tobin's investigator. I've got a small conference room at the Holiday Inn on West Flagler. We're here already but you'd better hurry. My man here is nodding in and out."

"I'll be there in ten minutes."

"Just give your name to the lady at the desk."

Fifteen minutes later a woman ushered Danni into the conference room where Henry was waiting with his witness. The room was fairly good sized for a small conference room although Henry made it look small. There was a table with four chairs in the middle and a credenza with a coffee urn and cups in the back. Henry put Danni at ease right away with a handshake and a smile. His witness was sitting in a chair, asleep.

"He nods out now and then," Henry told her. "You get yourself comfortable and I'll wake him up. Want some coffee?"

"No thanks." Danni settled in a chair across from the witness. "What's his name?" she asked.

"Pablo Ruiz."

"You can wake him up."

Henry gave Pablo a gentle shake and then another and another until the man couldn't help but wake up. "Pablo, this here is Detective Danni Jansen. She's the woman I told you about who is going to ask you some questions."

"Shoot," Pablo said in a daze.

Danni started off with a preliminary question to make sure Pablo could focus. "What's your name?"

"Pablo Ruiz."

"Do you know Sandra Davis?"

"Yeah. I know her real well."

"How's that?"

"We live in the same neighborhood—same apartment complex."

"What did she tell you about the rape charge in Oakville?"

"She said it was bullshit. She said she just did it for money. She does things for this guy once in a while, she says."

"What guy?"

"Hell if I know. Just some guy with money who pays her to do stuff."

"Like claim somebody raped her?"

"Yeah. Why not? Money's money."

"Why would she tell you?"

"I don't know. We were just shootin' the shit, you know. Kind of like what me and Big Henry was doin' the other day and now I'm here talkin' to you all formal and shit."

"And why are you talking to me now?"

"Why?"

"Yeah, why?"

"For the money, what else?"

"How much money?"

"Two hundred bucks for an hour."

"Okay, thanks."

Danni stood up and walked over to where Henry was standing in a corner.

"Tell your boss this isn't going to fly. Paying a drug addict to tell a story is not going to get your client off."

"I didn't pay him to tell me the story to begin with. I just paid him to come down here and talk to you."

"That's a distinction without a difference."

"Well, here's another one: You cops pay snitches all the time for information. At least I didn't pay Pablo beforehand." Henry turned his attention to Pablo, who was starting to nod off again. "Pablo, what would happen to you if Sandra found out you were talking to the police?"

Pablo didn't open his eyes. He just took his index finger and passed it across his throat. There was no need for words.

Danni did not have a counter to that so she changed the subject.

"How do I get to Liberty City? I want to stop and see Sandra Davis while I'm here."

"I'm going there to drop Pablo off. I'll take you and drop you back here."

"That's okay. I want to go alone."

"I can't let you do that, ma'am. I've got orders."

"Orders? From who?"

"Jack. I told him that neighborhood is dangerous day and night.

You wouldn't know what you were getting into. He asked me to stay with you."

"That doesn't sound like orders."

"No, ma'am."

"Listen, Henry. This isn't my first rodeo. I can handle this alone."

"I'm sure you can, ma'am, but if you walk in Sandra Davis's door, I'm gonna be with you."

Danni gave him her best defiant stare but Henry was not going to back down, she could tell.

"I could arrest you for impeding a police officer in the performance of her duties."

"You could but I'm not impeding you at all."

"If I agree to allow you to come, I don't want you interfering in any way."

"I won't as long as things don't get out of hand."

She thought about it for a moment. "All right, let's go."

Danni didn't like it, but there was a part of her that felt a little more secure with a man of Henry's size as backup. She didn't know if he had a gun, but she suspected he might since he was a private investigator. Besides, although she was an experienced homicide detective in Oakville, Miami was a whole different animal.

Sandra's apartment was on the fourth floor of a dilapidated apartment complex in a very poor section of town. Men and women, young and old were loitering in the parking lot. Danni was sure drug deals were being made at that very moment. The entire area was dirty and run-down as if everyone had lost the pride of at least keeping the place where they lived clean. The hallways held the stench of urine.

Everyone looked at Danni as she walked by. She obviously didn't fit for a lot of reasons. They could probably tell that she was a cop. Once again, she felt better that Henry was with her.

She knocked on Sandra's door and immediately heard scurrying in the apartment, like rats running for cover at the sound of a human approaching.

Nobody answered the door.

Danni knocked again. Finally a woman's voice answered from a distance.

"Who is it?"

"I'm Detective Danielle Jansen from the Oakville Police Department. I'd like to speak to Sandra Davis."

More scurrying. No answer. Then the door opened slightly. A beautiful woman with smooth coffee-colored skin appeared in the doorway.

"I'm Sandra Davis," the woman said.

Up to that moment, Danni had never met Sandra Davis. Someone else had taken the original complaint and Danni had followed up on it by telephone. This was the first time she had laid eyes on the supposed victim. The woman was drop-dead gorgeous.

"You and I spoke on the phone, Sandra, about the complaint you made against Julian Reardon."

"Yes, I remember."

"Well, I'm here in Miami on another matter and I thought it might be a good time for you and me to just meet and chat for a few minutes. I have some follow-up questions."

"I'm a little busy."

"It won't take long and it's really important."

Sandra stole a glance behind her. Danni figured there was someone else on the other side of the door.

"Okay, but only for a few minutes."

She opened the door, and Danni and Henry, who had positioned himself in the hallway so that Sandra could not see him, followed her into the apartment, which opened into the dining room. Danni looked around immediately. The living room was off to the left and the kitchen was to the right. There were no walls separating the rooms.

It was a dingy place but surprisingly clean. The walls looked like they hadn't been painted in years and the carpet was worn out. Danni saw two black men sitting in the living room, apparently watching television. They looked to be in their thirties and well-muscled. She couldn't tell if they were packing. Another man, much more rotund and maybe ten years older, was in the kitchen cooking. It must have been spaghetti sauce or something of that nature because the aroma from the various herbs was enticing. The two men in the living room ignored them totally. The heavy man looked at Henry as if he recognized him.

"You're Henry Wilson," he said.

"That's right."

"I heard about you."

Henry didn't reply. He just nodded. A lot of people in Liberty City had heard about him.

Danni looked at Henry as if for the first time. She hadn't put the pieces together. Jack's investigator, Henry, was Henry Wilson, the man Jack had freed from death row. *Is this a good thing or a bad thing?* she asked herself but could not come up with an answer at that moment.

Sandra sat at the dining room table and invited them to join her. Both Danni and Henry sat down.

"Like I told you, I only have a few minutes," Sandra said.

"Okay," Danni replied. She'd decided to get right to the point. "I know in the past you were arrested for prostitution."

"That was ten years ago," Sandra sneered.

"I know, but I recently received some information that you made this rape charge up because somebody paid you to do it. Is that true?"

"That's bullshit. I'm not working for anyone."

"Do you know who Ted Collins is—the sports agent?"

"Never heard of him."

"I don't believe you. Do you know what the penalty is for making a false charge like this? You can go to jail for a long time. I shake down Ted Collins, he's going to give you up in a heartbeat."

Danni was trying to play hardball to force an acknowledgment of some sort out of Sandra that the whole rape episode was a sham. At this point, even though Pablo was a piss-poor witness, she strongly suspected the rape charge had been trumped up.

Everything kind of happened all at once after that.

Danni had a written Miranda warning in her inside jacket pocket. She figured that putting the document in front of Sandra at that moment might bring home the seriousness of the situation to her.

The two men in the living room who had seemed to be ignoring everyone drew their weapons as soon as Danni's hand moved toward her inside pocket. The guns were pointed at Danni and Henry.

The fat man in the kitchen slammed the pan he was holding down hard on the stove and stormed into the dining room.

"Put your hand on the table slowly," the fat man said. Danni followed his directions. She was going to explain her intentions but thought better of it.

"You oughta mind your manners, lady," the fat man shouted. He had his own piece out now and was pointing it at her head, just inches away. "This isn't the sticks. You don't come around here bullying people in their homes and threatening to arrest them. My sister was nice enough to let you in. I'm not going to let you out."

Henry had been a passive presence up to that point. Now he stood up slowly, his hands in the air to let everyone know he either didn't have a gun or wasn't planning on using it if he did.

"Can we all just calm down for a minute?" he said in a low voice. He looked directly at the fat man who had recognized him initially. "I'd like you to know why I'm here. I'm here for Julian Reardon, the kid who's accused of this rape. His mother grew up just a few blocks from here. She's one of us and that makes Julian one of us. I'm not criticizing how anybody makes their money. I'm just saying you need to let this kid go."

"You can go," the fat man said, ignoring Henry's words. "We've got no quarrel with you."

Henry shook his head. "I can't do that. Listen to me, I know about these things. You do something to this detective, all hell is going to come down on you. Whatever else you've got going on here is going to be over and your life will be over. Trust me on that.

"On the other hand, Sandra just nods and lets us know that Julian is innocent and that she's going to withdraw the complaint, we're outta here. We were never here. You may lose a little money in the short run but in the long run you'll be a whole lot better off. It's smart thinking."

The fat man looked at Henry for what seemed like an eternity although his gun was still pointed at Danni's forehead. Henry knew he was weighing his options. He hoped he was smarter than most two-bit crooks.

"You speak for her, too?" the fat man asked.

Henry looked at Danni, who was still sitting. She nodded her head ever so slightly.

"Yes," he replied.

Again the fat man stared at Henry for what seemed like an eternity.

"Okay, the charge will be dropped," he said finally, lowering his gun. "Hector!" One of the two men came forward. "Walk them down to their car. Make sure they get in and drive away."

Danni stood up to leave. Henry turned toward the door.

"Henry Wilson," the fat man said, "this doesn't go down exactly the way you said, I will come looking for you and I won't be alone. Understood?"

"Understood," Henry replied.

CHAPTER TWENTY-ONE

W hew!" Danni said when they were in the car and Henry was driving away from the complex under Hector's watchful eye. "I'm sure glad I insisted that you come along, Henry."

Henry stole a quick glance at her to see if she had gone crazy. Danni was smiling. Henry got the joke and chuckled.

"Yeah, that was real good thinking on your part. Got any other great ideas?"

"How about a drink? I sure could use one."

"Lotta places to go around here."

"You pick one, Henry. I trust your judgment."

Henry picked a place over toward the beach. It had kind of a Caribbean feel to it with fake palm trees and stuffed parrots on the yellow walls along with a bunch of other junk. That was the thing with bars these days: Junk on the wall was supposed to be atmosphere. Bob Marley was playing on the jukebox, and a colorful mix of men and women of pretty much all ages were milling around, standing at the bar, or sitting at tables. It was a little after four in the afternoon. Henry and Danni settled in at the bar.

"What'll you have?" the bartender asked Danni. She looked to be about twenty-one herself, dressed in short-shorts and a bikini top.

"Gray Goose on the rocks. Make it a double. I'm celebrating life, or at least the continuation of my life thanks to my friend here. What are you drinking, Henry? It's on me."

Henry ordered a Red Stripe.

"I like beer," Danni told him. "But I don't drink it. Women my age with beer guts are not a pretty sight."

"I don't think you've got much to worry about in that regard," Henry told her.

"I'll take that as a compliment. Thank you."

"You're welcome. Now is the case against Julian Reardon officially over?"

"As soon as I get back it is. I've got to talk to my boss and the state attorney, but that's just a formality. We no longer have a witness. However, I haven't put this all together yet, Henry. I know it's Collins's modus operandi to hire women to get close to athletes, and I'm sure that's what he did with Sandra. I mean the woman is beautiful. But how do we go from there to the rape charge? I mean, I see the connection, but I haven't followed it through step by step."

"I've been thinking about it for a little longer," Henry said, "and I think I can connect the dots. Collins hires Sandra to get close to Julian. Maybe they will start dating. Maybe Julian will think he's in love. That's when Sandra will introduce Julian to Collins."

"I get that part," Danni said.

"Stay with me now. So Sandra meets Julian, tries to get close to him, but Julian rebuffs her. She tells Collins and they come up with plan B. She accuses Julian of rape. Collins comes in to represent Julian for free. Sandra drops the rape charge. Julian is indebted to Collins and makes him his agent."

"It sounds logical."

"The only thing I don't get," Henry said, "is why a sports agent would go through so much trouble to get one client."

"I think I can answer that," Danni told him. She'd already finished her first drink and had ordered another. "Collins is in trouble and he has been for a long time. The guy has a very lavish lifestyle and he's not his own man, if you know what I mean."

"I think I do. He has silent partners."

"Exactly! And this business is about millions and millions of dollars. Collins was probably on thin ice with his partners. He needed this score."

"It's amazing what people will do."

"It is." Danni was feeling her liquor now. "And by the way, you did great work on this, Henry. You saved my life. I've been a homicide detective for a lot of years and I walked into that situation like it was my first day on the job."

"What you did probably works where you live. You can usually put pressure on people and get them to talk. Down here they're all crazy. They'll shoot you as soon as they look at you."

"Well, I was lucky to have you there today, and Jack is lucky to have you."

"We take care of each other."

"When Jack told me you guys were close friends, that struck me as odd."

Henry noticed that she was almost done with the second double vodka. She was obviously shaken up by what had happened earlier and rightfully so. Henry wouldn't have taken odds against the fat man shooting her. Drug people were unpredictable and that crew was obviously running a small-scale drug operation out of that apartment.

"Why? Because he was my lawyer?"

"I guess."

"Jack is different from most people. He didn't just represent me. He got to know me. And after I was released from jail, he invited me to come live with him and his wife."

"His wife?"

"Yeah. Her name was Pat. She was a great lady."

Danni could see Henry start to tear up at the memory of this woman.

"What happened to her?"

"She died of cancer a few years ago."

"That must have been devastating for Jack."

"You have no idea. For a year he just drifted in and out. I thought I was going to lose him a couple of times, but he finally pulled out of his funk."

"I wish I could do that."

"Do what?"

"Get over things. They seem to linger with me."

"Everybody has their own coping mechanisms. I still wake up some mornings thinking I'm back on death row. It makes me shiver."

"I can't even imagine what you went through. I read about it. You were awfully close. They had you strapped in and had even started the process, hadn't they?"

"Yeah," Henry said as he downed his beer and picked up the fresh one the bartender had already set down for him. "Jack said he almost lost me."

"I thought you were going to lose *me* today, Henry."

"So did I, Danni. So did I."

CHAPTER TWENTY-TWO

The following Monday at 9 a.m. sharp, Jack and Julian were at the state attorney's office waiting to be ushered into a meeting that had been set up late Friday.

"Mr. Tobin and Mr. Reardon," the receptionist said, "would you please follow me?"

Jack and Julian, who was dressed in a blue suit just like his attorney, followed the woman to a large conference room. She opened the door for them and ushered them inside. Danni was there along with a tall woman and a husky man. Danni came around the table and shook hands with Jack and Julian. She was all smiles as she introduced the other two people.

"Jack and Julian, this is Apache County State Attorney Jane Pelicano and Oakville Chief of Police Sam Jeffries." Everybody shook hands and Jane Pelicano motioned them to be seated. She was now in charge of the proceedings.

After the arrest and subsequent conviction of the serial killer, Thomas Felton, Jane Pelicano, the prosecuting attorney, and Sam Jeffries, the head of the task force formed to apprehend the killer, were the two most popular people in the county. Jane used that new-found fame to successfully run for the position of Apache County state attorney. Sam became a double-dipper. He retired from the

Sheriff's Department and took the position as chief of police in Oakville. He was now Danni's boss.

Jane opened the meeting.

"We have asked you both here today because we have made some decisions regarding your case, Julian, and we wanted to talk about those decisions before we made a public announcement. Since this case involves the university's sports program as well as yourself, Julian, it has gotten a great deal of publicity. We want to make sure we tie up all the loose ends appropriately so that we are all on the same page, so to speak."

Jack was not sure where this was going. If they were just going to drop the charges, what was the need for a meeting? He decided to start asking questions.

"Are you going to drop the charges?"

"Yes," Jane Pelicano answered.

"What else is there to talk about?"

"We'd like your client to sign a release, releasing the police department, the City of Oakville, and the State of Florida from any and all claims arising out of this investigation. This is not normal procedure, but since there has been so much publicity already, some of it not favorable to your client, we thought it would be best."

Ah, Jack thought. *There's the rub. They're thinking about their own necks.* Now that he knew the game, he decided to work for some concessions.

"That's not a problem. However, we would like your announcement to say that you have completed your investigation and Julian Reardon has been completely exonerated. He is totally innocent."

"I'm not sure we can go that far, Mr. Tobin," Chief Jeffries said. "But we can work on some language with you."

"I'm sure you can but I like my language 'completely exonerated' and 'totally innocent.' It kind of goes along with releasing the police department, the City of Oakville, and the State of Florida from 'any and all claims arising out of the investigation,' doesn't it?"

"We're not charging your client. Isn't that enough, Mr. Tobin?" Chief Jeffries persisted.

"Let's put it this way. You want a release since you think you may have some exposure because of the adverse publicity my client has endured. We are willing to give that to you, but we want a statement that removes the stigma caused by that adverse publicity. That's only fair."

Jeffries looked at Jane Pelicano and shrugged. Jack could tell they wanted to get this over with. Danni just sat there and looked pretty. This was a political decision and she was not a part of it.

"Okay," Jane said. "We will agree with your language in exchange for the release if we can get it all done today. Time is important to all of us. We'd like to put this to bed."

Jack chuckled to himself. He'd gotten everything he wanted, but the state needed to feel that they had the final concession.

"Done. I'll draft the statement and you draft the release, and I'll review it. I only need an hour or so."

Pelicano stood up. "Fine. Detective Jansen will get in touch with you when the release is ready."

The meeting was over. Everybody shook hands and went their separate ways.

Julian had a few questions when they were standing outside the state attorney's office.

"I'm not sure exactly what happened in there, but I do know that you were just a little quicker than they were and they had a plan going in. How did you do that?"

"Well, Julian, when somebody wants to make a deal, you've got to make sure you seize the opportunity and squeeze everything you can out of it because it won't come again. It's just something that comes with experience. Now, they are going to make a wonderful statement clearing your name. I know because I'm going to write it. You will be reinstated on the football team and you can put this episode behind you.

"I hope that you learned something from this. As an athlete you are in a fishbowl. You can be innocent but still be perceived as guilty if you are in the wrong place at the wrong time. In your world, my friend, perception is oftentimes reality. Don't forget that."

"I won't, Mr. Tobin. My mother was right about you. You are the best. You know I almost went with that guy from Miami, but my mother wouldn't let me."

"It was the universe speaking to all of us, Julian."

Julian just nodded as he shook Jack's hand. He had no idea what that last statement meant.

Danni called two hours later.

"I've got the release."

"I've got the statement. Want to meet for lunch?"

"Where?" Danni asked.

"Where else?"

"I'll see you at The Swamp in fifteen minutes."

Jack was already at a back table talking to Ron when Danni arrived. She sat down and handed Jack the release. "I think it's pretty standard language."

"I guess I'll leave since I'm invisible anyway," Ron said.

"Don't go on my account," Danni said without much conviction.

"I know it will be hard for you two without me around, but I must go. You know, I've got to pay for the lights and all that. Lunch is on me, by the way. And, Danni, don't give me that city business crap."

It was Jack who protested. "Ronnie, I haven't paid for a meal since I've been here."

"And you won't, brother. Besides, I'm just softening you up for my big pitch down the road when I'm gonna need some real money." Ronnie walked away toward the front door to greet customers.

"He's something else," Jack said to Danni as he finally took a moment to look at the release she had handed him. "It looks fine." He pulled a piece of paper from his jacket pocket and gave it to her.

"Here's the statement."

Danni took a moment to read it. "It looks good to me, but as you know, I won't be making that decision."

"I understand. Tell the powers that be that the release seems okay with me, but I am withholding any final decision as to whether to have my client sign it until I hear back from them in writing about the statement."

Danni smiled. "You are a hardball player."

"Maybe so. I just know how the game is played and how people go back on their word."

"Unfortunately, I know about that myself."

Their meals arrived and as they ate, they watched the noontime crowd arrive. Ron was suddenly everywhere chatting with people.

"So Henry tells me you and he had an exciting time in Miami."

Danni almost choked on her veggie wrap. "You can say that again. And I'm with you about Henry, Jack. He's now one of my closest friends. He saved my life."

"Welcome to the club. So let's be optimistic and assume everything wraps up today. You and I will no longer be on opposite sides of a criminal investigation."

"That's true."

"So I think we should have dinner to celebrate."

Danni looked at him and smiled but didn't answer right away. For a moment Jack thought she was going to turn him down.

"I think so, too, and I've got the perfect place in mind."

"You're talking about here, right? Because I get my meals free at this establishment."

"No, Jack Tobin. Tonight you're going to pay. Assuming everything goes according to plan, you can pick me up at seven."

"I don't even know where you live."

"You'll find out. You're a resourceful man. I've got to go. I have an important deal to close."

Jack's eyes followed her to the door.

CHAPTER TWENTY-THREE

Danni called a little after three and said that the public state-ment had been approved. If they received the release in the morning, a joint press conference with the chief of police and the state attorney would be held tomorrow afternoon.

Almost as soon as he hung up, Jack received another call.

"Hello."

"You fucked up my mark."

"Who is this?"

"Shut the fuck up and listen. Nobody fucks me over and gets away with it. I heard about your orchestration of this whole deal. You may think you're a big shot but you're wrong. I don't work alone and my partners aren't nice guys like me."

"Don't even think about going near Julian."

"It's not about Julian anymore. It's about you, big shot. You're gonna get yours. It may be tomorrow, it may be the next day, but it's gonna happen. You can take that to the bank."

"You don't scare me, Collins. If people like you scared me, I'd have folded my tent up a long time ago. Have a nice day."

Jack called Henry right away and told him about the conversa-tion.

"I'm inclined to call the police. What do you think?"

"It was probably a throw-away phone so they won't be able to trace anything to Collins. They may question him, but that will only make him and whoever his so-called friends are a little bolder. Collins anticipates that you're going to call the police. He's prepared for that. Why don't you let me look into it."

"I don't want you doing anything that could get you in trouble."

"I'm going to look into this whether you call the police or not, Jack, so it doesn't really matter to me."

"Okay, I'll hold off for, say, forty-eight hours."

"That'll work."

Dinner was at an intimate little Italian restaurant in the town of Apache Hills. There were no more than ten tables in the place, each with a white linen tablecloth. They ate by candlelight with a nice bottle of Cabernet Sauvignon, the lighting so subtle that Jack could hardly read the menu.

"This is such a lovely area of the state. The more I stay here, the more I like it," he told Danni while taking a break from his delicious eggplant parmesan.

"When are you going home?"

"I don't know. I think I might stay a while. I'm in one of Ron's empty condos and, according to him, I can stay as long as I want."

"You don't have any pressing matters at home?" Danni asked.

Jack laughed. "Nope. I've got a gardener who takes care of the property, and Henry comes and goes whenever he likes. There's not a whole lot there for me these days."

"Henry told me about your wife Pat and how much you loved her."

Jack didn't respond right away. He was surprised by the remark, and any mention of Pat usually set him back for a second or two.

"What did he say? I don't know if I could put that feeling into words."

"It's not really what he said, it was the way he said it. He was quite fond of her himself."

"They became great friends in a short period of time. Henry used to read to her when she could no longer do it herself."

Danni could see the sorrow in his eyes. Maybe this subject wasn't such a good idea.

"I'm sorry. We don't have to talk about this."

"No, no, it's fine. I had some terrible marriages before Pat. I was a very successful lawyer, but I was dead inside. She taught me for the first time how to really love somebody, but she's been gone now for a few years. She'll always be with me, but I have to move on."

"Are you sure you're ready?"

"You're never sure of anything in this life, are you? But I can feel Pat kicking me out the door. She wants me to be happy and she's in a place where jealousy and all that other stuff don't matter."

"How do you know?"

"I don't really. I just feel it, and I trust my feelings. I believe in the universe and that Pat is part of the universe. I guess about now you're thinking 'This guy is nuts. I'd better get out of here.'"

"Not at all. You've got something that works for you. That's what we're all searching for."

"And what works for you, Danni Jansen?"

"I'm not sure. The universe sounds good. I need to move on from a lot of things. I just can't seem to get there."

"You will over time."

"I've heard that line—time heals all wounds. It hasn't worked for me, not in my personal or my professional life."

Jack decided it was time to change the subject. The past wasn't necessarily a good topic when talking to a beautiful woman over a bottle of wine.

"So you have a daughter in college, is that right?"

"Yes—Hannah. She's a great girl. She's at the University of Colorado. I sent her to Denver when she was a child under circumstances that were very stressful for both of us, and she fell in love with the place. I can't wait for her to come home for Thanksgiving."

"That's great. I'm sure you two are close."

"We are. She only has me. Her relationship with her father is superficial. We divorced a number of years ago and he spends most of his time chasing younger women."

"Really?"

"Really. It's a way of life in Oak Vegas. That's what I call this place. There are tons of pretty young women running around looking for rich men to help them along in life, and plenty of wealthy men who think with their little head."

Jack had to laugh at that line. "You haven't given up on men, have you?"

"I hope not. I haven't been looking really. I spent my time raising Hannah, and I always had my work."

"Hannah's gone now, and you're retiring soon."

"I know. And those changes will bring other changes. In the meantime I'm concentrating on adjusting and finding happiness in everyday life. I'm looking forward to Thanksgiving. I'm going to make a big turkey with all the trimmings. What are you doing for the holiday?"

"Nothing to speak of. Henry will probably come over if he doesn't have a better offer. We might cook a small bird or go out to eat, depending on how we feel."

"That doesn't sound like much fun. Why don't you and Henry come to my house for Thanksgiving dinner. Hannah would love to meet you. She's been talking about going to law school."

Jack didn't hesitate. "That sounds great to me. I'll ask Henry."

They left soon after, and Jack drove Danni home. She gave him a brief kiss on the cheek at the door before saying goodnight.

Maybe this is what I'm really here for, Jack thought as he walked back to the car.

CHAPTER TWENTY-FOUR

It was after nine when he swung his Mercedes SLS roadster into the driveway and clicked the garage door opener. He checked his watch to be sure. No calls to make tonight. He needed to get to bed early so he could run on the beach in the morning. *Got to work those extra pounds off right away. Maybe one cigar on the veranda before calling it a night. What's the use of living in a mansion on the beach if you can't enjoy it?*

It was a mansion—seven thousand square feet right on the water. Maybe it was too much for one person. Maybe the place needed a woman's touch. He wasn't ready for that, however. He'd just turned forty—way too young to settle down, especially when there were so many nubile young women out there eager to satisfy his needs. Marriage might happen down the road, but he didn't need a wife in his profession, so why have one?

The lights went on automatically when he pulled into the garage. He stepped out of the car and headed for the door leading into the house with his keys in his hand. He always kept the inside door locked. He'd read about burglars often coming through the garage door. He had an alarm system, but there was no downside to taking extra precautions in order to feel perfectly safe. He stuck the key in the door but before he could turn it the lights in the garage went out.

It was pitch black. He couldn't see anything. Before he could think, two powerful hands grabbed his arms and pulled them back. He could feel the handcuffs lock on his wrist. *What the hell is this, a bust by the cops?* He had some coke in the house but they'd never find it. He started to get angry to get his courage back. Then he lost it again.

Whoever it was that had handcuffed him grabbed his throat and lifted him up with his back to the wall *with one hand!* He could hardly breathe and he was too afraid to speak. He was sure he was going to die. All this work, all he had accumulated—for what? To lose his life to a two-bit robber? He needed to do something. Beg, plead, bargain. Whatever.

"What do you want? I'll give you anything you want."

No answer. The grip was tighter. He could feel himself losing consciousness.

"Please! Please! I'll do anything. Don't kill me."

"Shut up," the voice said. It was deep and threatening. He knew there was a big, powerful man behind that voice although he still couldn't see a thing. "I hear you like to use that word yourself when you're making threats. That right?"

"No, no. No threats. I'm a businessman."

The arm let him down but the hand stayed at his throat. He could at least breathe a little better.

"You threatened Jack Tobin."

"Who?"

"Don't fuck with me, boy. You wanna die?"

"No, no. I didn't threaten anybody though."

The hand squeezed his throat harder, cutting off the flow of air.

"Okay, okay!" he croaked. "Yeah, I threatened him."

The hand let up a little.

"It wasn't my decision. I have investors. They're pissed at Tobin."

"Here's the deal," the voice said. "Something happens to Jack Tobin, you die. Understand?"

"But I don't control that."

"You'd better."

"Somebody has already been hired."

"Then I might as well kill you now."

"No. No, wait. I'll call off the dogs. I promise. I don't know if I can stop what's already been done but I'll try."

"You better succeed," the voice said. "Your life depends on it."

Suddenly he felt weightless as the man kicked his feet out from under him. He landed on the hard concrete floor; his shoulder hit first and then his head.

Everything went black after that.

Henry called Jack the next morning.

"I think that your situation has been taken care of but I'm not one hundred percent sure."

"What does that mean?" Jack asked.

"Mr. Collins has other investors who he does not control. I convinced him, I believe, that it would be in his best interests to get them to follow his recommendation in this one situation."

"This is crazy, Henry. We're talking about a college football player and an agent."

"No, Jack. We're talking about millions of dollars and we're talking about people who want to send a message to others that messing with their business can cost you your life."

"So what do I do, wait and see what happens?"

"Do you still have that Sig Sauer you bought a few years back?"

"Yes, I've got it but not with me. Why?"

"I think you should start carrying it and maybe go to the range once in a while."

"I don't know if that's such a good idea, Henry."

"Maybe not, Jack. Maybe this is just smoke. But I would prefer that you at least have the gun in your house."

"I'll think about it. By the way, what are you doing for Thanksgiving?"

"I'm spending it with you. Why?"

"Wanda didn't invite you over for all the fixings?"

"As a matter of fact, she did. I'm just not ready to be the man of the house carving the turkey if you know what I mean."

"Gotcha. Danni invited us to come to Thanksgiving dinner. Whaddya think?"

"Speaking of calling the police."

"Yeah, right. I probably don't want to tell her about Collins's threat. So are you coming?"

"Sure. I'll bring your gun with me."

CHAPTER TWENTY-FIVE

Thanksgiving Day was cold and blustery, but Jack still got up early and went for a run in the woods. He'd found the running path just a few days after he arrived in town. It was literally two blocks from the condo and there was nobody around in the early morning but him, the birds, the trees, and a host of other small creatures. An armadillo had startled him just last week. They both jumped at the same time, the armadillo running about five paces or so in the opposite direction before stopping. So far as he could remember, it was the first time Jack had ever seen a live armadillo in motion.

He ran five miles at an easy pace, breathing in the fresh air and taking the time to enjoy the beautiful morning.

Part of his run took him down a giant sinkhole, a break in the limestone foundation that had formed over thousands of years. It was his favorite place. Looking up from the very bottom, he could see the tall trees clustered around the rim at the top, their branches rustling in the breeze causing the leaves to unhinge. A small stream snaked along from top to bottom, the sound so steady, so unchanging, yet altering forever the surrounding landscape. The sun filtering through the woods served as the spotlight for the leaves as they cascaded end over end.

Jack always stopped for a few minutes to take it all in. It was here in places like this that he could make sense out of the world.

Henry was at the condo when he arrived home. Jack had expected Henry to stay with him but Henry had declined the invitation, saying he was going to stay with a relative in town. He was dressed in sweats.

"Have you been working out?" Jack asked, noticing that his friend was sweating.

"A little bit," Henry replied evasively. "Now I'm hungry. Want to go for breakfast?"

"No. I'll eat too much if I go out. Dinner is at two and I want to be hungry. I'll scramble some eggs and make toast if you want."

"Sounds good," Henry replied.

It seemed strange to Jack that Henry did not stay with him then showed up sweaty in a jogging outfit. Something was going on.

A brown wreath made of bare branches hung on the front door of Danni's house, perhaps a symbol of autumn's end and Christmas to come. Jack rang the doorbell.

Danni answered wearing a snug brown sweater and jeans and the most beautiful smile Jack had yet seen. She gave Jack a big hug, then she opened her arms to Henry.

"Here's the man who saved my life. Welcome to my home, Henry."

She led them into the living room and sat them on the couch. A fire was just getting started in the fireplace, the wood crackling in the background. "Can I get you something to drink?"

"I'll have a beer," Jack said. Henry indicated that would be fine with him as well.

Danni left the room and returned a few seconds later with the beer and a beautiful young woman who bore a startling resemblance to her although her hair was dark brown.

"This is my daughter, Hannah. Hannah, these are my friends Jack Tobin and Henry Wilson."

Hannah greeted them both warmly. She had a mature confidence about her that was rare for a woman her age.

"Gentlemen, if you will accompany us to the dining room, dinner is ready to be served," she said after the introductions were complete.

The dining room was small, but it made the atmosphere even more intimate. Danni had decorated the table with a festive lace tablecloth, a gold leaf centerpiece, and deep orange candles. Danni and Hannah started bringing in the various dishes and setting them between the candles and the place settings: mashed potatoes, sweet potatoes, green beans, collard greens, corn, and cranberry sauce. Last but not least came the turkey, beautiful and golden brown.

"Gentlemen, please join us in a moment of thanks," Danni said after she and Hannah sat down. They all held hands as Hannah spoke.

"Dear God, please bless this food we are about to eat and these friends who have joined us today. Amen."

"Jack, will you carve the turkey?" Danni asked.

Jack stole a glance at Henry who just smiled and nodded.

"It will be my pleasure," Jack said.

The food was delicious and they talked and laughed as if they were old, old friends. Henry told stories about his and Jack's fishing excursions on Lake Okeechobee.

"The only thing that's always missing is fish. They seem to know it's our boat and that Jack's cooking. I don't want to eat what he's cooking and they don't want to *be* what he's cooking."

Henry was a good storyteller and everybody laughed. Hannah regaled them with stories of life in Boulder, hiking the Flatirons, and being a freshman in a college so far away from home.

"Mom sent me to Colorado when I was young and I hated it for a long time. Then I started to remember how beautiful it was. I couldn't wait to go back."

All in all it was a great meal. Both men helped with the cleanup. Jack cleared the table and Henry loaded the dishwasher.

"This is my job on the boat, too," Henry told Danni. "Only we don't have a dishwasher."

"Sounds like you need to speak up, Henry," Danni replied.

"It wouldn't do any good. There are only two jobs in the galley and Jack's a better cook but don't tell him I said that."

After dinner, Hannah sat on the couch with Henry and peppered him with questions about life in prison and what it was like on death row, issues Henry didn't usually talk about. She was so genuinely interested in his experiences, however, that he found himself telling her everything.

"There were times when I thought I would never see the outside world; never have a delicious meal like the one we just shared; never enjoy a good conversation like this. It certainly teaches you to cherish every day."

"And that made you and Jack friends forever, I guess?"

"We're joined at the hip. He's my brother as much as if we came from the same womb."

"Kind of like my mom and me. We had our differences along the way. For a long time, I resented her for sending me away to Colorado. Now that I'm older, I understand what the circumstances were back then. We're becoming friends. Like you and Jack, we only have each other."

"There'll be somebody else in your life eventually, Hannah. I'm sure of that."

Jack and Danni lingered in the kitchen, slowly putting the dishes and the pots and pans away.

"It was a great day," he told her. "Thanks for inviting us."

"Thanks for coming. You made it special for Hannah. It would have been boring with just her and me."

"You two seem very close."

"We are. It's been just the two of us for a long time. It's nice to have men in the house, though."

*   *   *

Jack didn't see Danni again until the next Wednesday. She wanted to spend all her time with Hannah before her daughter had to return to school. On Wednesday, they had dinner at The Swamp before going to the movies. Ron was there as usual.

"Jack, are you still in town?" he asked, faking incredulity. "I know your case is over. What is it that keeps you here—The Swamp? You want to help me with the rent on my condo? I can't figure it out."

Danni thought she'd have a little fun of her own at Jack's expense. "It's the free meals, Ron. Like tonight, for instance, Jack knows you're going to pick up the tab. That's why he insisted on coming here. I'm beginning to wonder about him."

"Beginning?" Ron replied. "He's got more money than God and he's living at my condo for half price and showing up here every night for dinner."

Jack laughed. "Okay, okay, I get the picture. Ronnie, tell Liz we're all going out Friday night on me—to the best restaurant in town. And then we're going dancing."

And they did. Ron and his wife, Liz, met them at a restaurant downtown called Preston's where they had a wonderful meal. Afterward, they went dancing at a nightclub called Stella's.

Jack wasn't much of a dancer, but he'd had a few glasses of wine at dinner and it didn't take long for Danni to get him out on the floor. She was smooth and, in no time, she had him dancing like he'd been a star pupil at Arthur Murray. Once they got into it, the two of them couldn't get enough of each other. No matter whether it was a fast dance or slow, they were in each other's arms, pressing close. Time had ceased to exist for them.

Ron and Liz left somewhere around midnight but Jack and Danni hardly noticed. They continued dancing until the lights came on and the bartenders were yelling for people to go home. Even after the band had stopped playing, they stood on the dance floor moving to music only they could hear.

"You guys gotta go," the bartender yelled at them. "Get a room, for Chrissakes!"

He finally got them to leave on the third try.

"I'm gonna call the cops."

That sobered Danni up quickly. "We've got to go," she told Jack. "I don't want any trouble at work. We can continue this at my house."

When they finally arrived at Danni's front door, there were no words between them. Jack simply followed her into the house. She closed the door behind them, took his hand, and led him to the bedroom.

They fell on the bed smothering each other with kisses. Jack lost all sense of everything but Danni. All he knew was the warmth of her skin, the sweetness of her smell, the moist touch of her lips. They made love slowly, softly, as if with a rhythm they had secretly known their entire lives.

In the morning, they awoke so enmeshed with each other it was hard to tell where one ended and the other began.

For the next two weeks, they saw each other constantly. The first weekend of their relationship, Jack had to speak at a conference in Siesta Key. Danni went with him. Friends of Jack's and their wives were there along with other folks neither of them knew. Danni fit in with everybody. They stayed out too late having fun on Friday and got up early the next morning and played in the surf. On Sunday morning, they just stayed in bed and talked about the people they'd met and the fun they'd had. Jack knew he was falling hard.

The next week was more of the same. They saw each other every day. On Wednesday night they went to dinner, drank a bottle of wine, and then went to the movies. Halfway through the movie he turned to look at Danni and she was sound asleep. *I love this woman*, he thought to himself. *She fits with me so easily.*

On Friday they went back to Stella's and, again, it was as if they were the only people on the dance floor although they left well before closing time. The dance at home was so much more fun.

They spent Saturday canoeing on the Santa Fe River. It was a glorious day, one that he would never forget. They were totally alone. The only sounds were the birds singing and the river flowing. The sky was cloudless and powder blue but they were shielded from the glare of the sun by the tall pines along the shore and the giant oaks a little further inland. Gators rested along the banks or glided effortlessly through the water. Turtles were everywhere, resting either on rocks in the water or on old tree limbs. Every once in a while, one would just slip off and disappear under the surface. The water itself was crystal clear and Jack could see mullet swimming along, seemingly oblivious to the boat above them. It was hard to believe civilization was only fifteen minutes away.

Civilization, Jack thought. *It's overrated.*

Danni was in the front of the boat in her bathing suit. She turned to look at him, a huge smile on her face. She was radiant.

"Isn't this gorgeous?" she said. "It's like we're the only two people alive in paradise."

"It's perfect," Jack replied.

CHAPTER TWENTY-SIX

Jack woke up on Sunday morning, gazed at the beautiful woman lying next to him, and felt blessed to once again have love in his life. He was happy beyond words.

He didn't know it was all about to come crashing down.

He drove to Bass Creek that day to get some clothes and go through his mail and, in general, to check things out. Henry arrived a short time later, which Jack thought was unusual. *What's going on with Henry? His behavior is strange. He stays with friends instead of me. He shows up at odd times.*

They went out on the boat for a little while that afternoon and again on Monday afternoon. Henry seemed to be his old self again although Jack could tell something was on his mind. He called Danni Sunday night and again on Monday evening and had a pleasant conversation with her both times although he sensed that she was acting strange as well. *What's going on? Is it me?* he asked himself.

On Wednesday he drove back to Oakville and showed up at Danni's house unannounced around six in the evening.

"Hi. I wasn't expecting you to be back so soon," she said when she opened her door and saw him standing there. She was dressed in jeans and appeared to be getting ready to go out.

"I never said when I was coming back. I just decided to come today. You look like you're going somewhere. Do you want me to come back later?"

"No, no. I was only going to get something to eat."

"Would you like company?"

"Sure." She hesitated halfway down the walkway and then stopped altogether. "Come on inside for a minute, Jack. I want to talk to you."

They both went inside and sat at the dining room table.

"I can't do this anymore, Jack."

"Do what?"

"Continue this relationship."

"What relationship? We just got started."

"You know what I mean. Time is no measure of a relationship. You and I have gotten so close so quick it scares me to death."

"What happened between Sunday morning and today?"

"Nothing happened. I've just had time to think. It's just been too much."

"We can tone it down. We don't have to end it."

"We can't tone it down, Jack. It is what it is. Hannah has gone off to college and I'm starting a new direction in my life."

"Does that mean you don't have time for a relationship?"

"It means I'm not ready for one right now. I need time and space to see where I'm going to land. I mean, I love the time we've had, but it's too intense."

"I'll lighten up."

"You can't. I can see it in your eyes. I can't either."

"We don't meet people that we have an instant connection with every day, Danni. Sometimes, we never meet them. You and I are lucky."

"I'm just not where you're at, Jack. It's the wrong time for me. I've got to end this now before we get any closer and I won't be able to do it."

They were both silent for a few moments after that last statement.

"Look, Danni." Jack finally broke the silence, speaking in a soft, low voice. "I know this has been quick, but I also know it's real. I know what I feel and I think I know what you feel. I can't just walk away from these feelings."

There were tears in Danni's eyes. "You're going to have to, Jack, because I'm not ready for this."

Silence again for what seemed like an eternity. Jack didn't know what to do or what to say. He could persuade a judge or a jury of his peers in the toughest of circumstances, but he had no words for this woman who had taken his heart. Deep down, though, he knew he didn't want to persuade her. This was a decision she would have to make on her own.

"I'm going to go," he said softly. "I'll be in town for at least another week. You've got my number. Call me whenever you have a mind to—about anything. I'll be there."

He stood up. Danni stood up, too, and hugged him tight. He felt from that embrace that this was just as hard for her as it was for him. Then he left.

CHAPTER TWENTY-SEVEN

Jack was sitting at the bar in The Swamp putting down his third beer when Ron showed up.

"Out on your own tonight, lover boy?"

"I am. Sit down. I'll buy you a beer."

"Can't. Don't drink in my own place. That's a rule."

"Well then, let's go somewhere you can drink."

They'd been friends for too long. Ron could tell there was something not quite right about old Jack. "All right, finish up. We'll go in my car."

They drove down College Avenue heading out of town.

"Henry was in The Swamp last night for dinner. I stopped and chatted with him a little bit," Ron said.

"That's funny," Jack said, more to himself than to Ron. "I thought he'd gone back to Miami. What the hell is he doing here?"

"I don't know."

Ronnie took him to a dark, quiet little spot east of town. There were a few people at the bar but other than that it was deserted. An attractive middle-aged brunette wearing a tight top and showing some great cleavage was tending bar.

"Well, if it isn't the grand pooh-bah come to visit the slums," she said to Ron who leaned over the bar and planted a kiss smack on her lips.

"Mabel, this is my friend Jack."

"Pleased to meet you, Jack. Any friend of Ron's is a friend of mine—only because Ron might buy this place someday and I need the job, know what I mean?"

Jack smiled. "I do."

"What are you having?"

"Give us a couple of martinis," Ron said. "Jack needs to talk and I've got to get him a little drunk first."

"Sure thing." She looked at Jack for a minute. "I'd say it's woman trouble. I've been doing this for a long time—usually get it right."

"Unfortunately you're right again, Mabel."

"Don't worry. A good-looking guy like you won't be lonely for long. Not in this town. As a matter of fact, I get off in five hours if you're still around."

That got another laugh out of Jack. "Thanks, Mabel, but I don't think I'll be making it that long. Not after this martini."

Mabel had just handed him and Ron their martinis. She worked as she talked, always in motion.

"I'm here six nights a week, honey. You decide to go slumming again, you come see Mabel."

Mabel moved on down her bar. The place was starting to fill up and she was greeting her regular customers.

"She's a great bartender for a place like this," Ron told Jack. "She's got the goods—not bad looking, big tits, and a great personality. She packs the joint."

"Why don't you hire her?"

"I've got a different type of place. We cater to the college kids, the professors, and the businessmen. This is a workingman's bar. You need a little fantasy and a little conversation. Mabel gives you all of it. She creates that little possibility in your mind that you might be the guy tonight. It keeps 'em coming back. Enough about Mabel; let's talk about Jack."

"Nothing to talk about really."

"Don't bullshit me, Jack. I see that puppy-dog look in your eyes. You're a great lawyer but you're a little sappy when it comes to the game of love."

"What the hell does that mean?"

"It means that you can tear somebody apart on the witness stand when they try to bullshit their way out of something, but a woman can wrap you around her finger in a heartbeat. Don't forget, I've been through all your relationships with you. Pat was a great lady, but you picked some doozies before her."

"Thanks for the compliment. If you're trying to make me feel better, you're doing a hell of a job. Remember you introduced me to Danni." Jack took a large sip of his martini, finishing it off.

"Take it easy," Ron told him. "You sip these drinks. It's not like a beer."

"Do you think I haven't had a martini before?"

"I've never seen you drink one. Let's get back to you and Danni. I thought you'd be great for each other. You've both been kind of out there for years. So what happened?"

Jack got Mabel's attention and ordered a beer. One martini was enough.

"She just said she couldn't do it anymore."

"Do what?"

"Be in a relationship."

Ron didn't say anything for a minute or two. He was thinking about the situation.

"Maybe she just needs a little time, Jack. You guys have been seeing a lot of each other. She may be overwhelmed."

"I'm an overwhelming guy."

"And then some."

Jack stayed in Oakville for another week although he never heard from Danni. He went jogging every day on his favorite path through the woods. On the morning he decided would be his last day, he came around a bend just after the sinkhole and found a man kneeling on the path maybe twenty feet ahead of him. The man had a ski cap on and a gun in his hand. The gun was pointed at Jack.

Jack had nowhere to go. The guy was obviously waiting for him. He desperately dove for the bushes. As he did so, he heard a *pop*. It wasn't a gunshot. Maybe the gun had a silencer. Jack hadn't noticed. He landed in the woods, hidden behind a decayed old oak amid a slew of dead leaves. He didn't appear to be hit. He wasn't in any pain.

What do I do now? Run, or just stay here?

He didn't hear any more movement so he decided to stay put. If the guy found him, he'd be helpless but if he got up and ran, he might be an easier target. At least here he was fortunate enough to be somewhat hidden. *A murderer doesn't have the luxury of spending too much time searching around for his victim.*

After about twenty minutes of lying completely still, when he heard no further sounds, Jack stood up and stepped back onto the path. What he saw shocked him.

The shooter was lying where Jack had first seen him with a pool of blood forming around his head. He was still in the kneeling position although he had fallen over. Jack carefully checked for a pulse. There was none. Then he saw the bullet wound in the temple on the right side.

So I come around this bend and this guy is kneeling ready to shoot me but instead somebody shoots him. Who? And why?

It took him a few minutes to think that one through but when he did, he decided it would be best to leave the premises. If he was there when the cops arrived, it wouldn't be hard to put two and two together. He stopped at a convenience store along the way, asked to use the phone, and called 911, giving the dispatcher the exact location of the body.

Oh yeah, Jack thought as he ran back to the condo. *It's definitely time to go home.*

PART THREE
Almost Two Years Later
January 2003

Route 27
Ten Miles South of
Perry, Florida

CHAPTER TWENTY-EIGHT

Jesus, can they make these damn trucks any smaller? If they're going to sell them in America, they should make them to fit Americans."

Jack was mildly amused watching Henry negotiate the passenger side of his Toyota pickup. The man was just too big. His knees were banging against the underside of the glove compartment and the rest of his body was squished against the passenger door. He'd been squirming for the last three hours. Now he was starting to voice his complaints.

"They do make them for normal Americans, Henry, but you don't fit into that category."

"You don't look so comfortable over there yourself," Henry grumbled.

It was true. Jack wasn't a small man either, although he wasn't Henry's size and he didn't have his bulk. Still, he'd have been a lot more comfortable in the Suburban.

"Why didn't we bring the Suburban?" Henry asked as if he'd read Jack's mind.

"They have a great tree farm up in Tallahassee. I want to buy some trees and stick them in the pickup and take them home."

"Haven't you ever heard of shipping? You order the trees, have them shipped, and we drive to Tallahassee in comfort."

"It's not that easy. I like to see the trees and get a feel for them before I buy them. And I like the idea of transporting them myself."

Henry just looked at him. "When did you become Chauncey Gardener?"

"What are you talking about? I've always liked to garden."

"Yeah, and I always liked to play the violin, only I never had one. Your gardener quit last year. That's when you started this stuff."

"Okay. And I found I liked it. It's soothing. It calms me. Do you have problems with that, Mister Macho Man?"

"No. Whatever floats your boat is fine with me, honey. The only thing I have problems with is this damn truck. What are we going to Tallahassee for anyway? I mean, what am I going for?"

"Ben wants to talk to us."

"Us? Ben has never talked to me in my life except to say hello a few times. Do you know what it's about?"

"I have no idea. I assume it's a case."

Ben Chapman was the executive director of Exoneration, the anti–death penalty advocacy group where both Jack and Henry donated their services, Jack as a lawyer and Henry as his investigator.

"Does he normally ask you to come talk to him personally about a case?" Henry asked.

"Never. It's usually done by telephone, mail, or e-mail."

"Then this must be something very unusual. What the hell does he want to talk to me about—how to investigate?"

"I have no idea, Henry. I have no idea."

They found out soon enough. Their appointment was the next morning, Monday, at nine sharp. Ben Chapman was waiting for them. He was a mid-sized portly man, mid- to late-fifties, with a shaved head, a short gray beard, and a deep voice. Chapman was an attorney like Jack, but that's where the similarity ended. He'd been a transactional lawyer with a tax background and had made his considerable fortune from acquisitions of all kinds, often taking a piece of a deal that he put together as his fee. After he'd been retired for a couple of years and bored stiff, he looked for a challenge to sink his teeth in. A Texas death penalty case he'd read about, in which a man had been executed for killing his wife and children and was later determined to be innocent, got him interested in the process. Then he started reading about other injustices, mostly across the South, and he was hooked. Unlike Jack, Chapman couldn't offer his legal services since he had no experience in the courtroom, so he offered his considerable organizational skills. Before long, he was running Exoneration.

"Good morning, gentlemen," he said in that booming voice of his. "Have you had any coffee?"

"We did. We just had breakfast," Jack replied.

"Well, come on in then." Chapman led them into his office, where they sat down in the two chairs in front of his desk.

"Are your accommodations okay?" He had set them up in a luxury hotel.

"Very nice, thank you," Jack said.

"Good, let's get to it then." He handed them both a one-page document. "This is a very brief summary of the case of Thomas Felton. Have either of you heard of him?"

"I have," Jack said. "He was the serial killer in Oakville about ten years ago."

"Correct, although he was never convicted of being a serial killer. He was convicted of a double homicide."

"But as I recall," Jack continued, "the murder weapon had been identified from a previous murder."

"That's almost correct," Chapman said. "Actually, there was an attempted murder, and the young lady who survived identified the weapon. She was subsequently killed, by the way."

"So I take it," Jack said, "that you want Henry and me to get involved in Mr. Felton's case."

"Precisely. The death warrant has been signed. His execution is scheduled for March fourteenth, and our office has been assigned to represent him in any post-conviction relief. The chief judge of Apache County has appointed Circuit Judge Andrew Holbrook to hear any post-conviction motions, and he's set a status conference for the thirty-first of this month. That's two weeks from now. We need to look at the case and decide if we want to file anything at that time. The judge, if he is going to set an evidentiary hearing, has to do it between the thirty-first of January and March fourteenth, leaving time for our client to appeal to the Supreme Court. We're under the gun, gentlemen."

"I don't—"

Before Jack could finish his sentence, Chapman cut him off. "Before you say no, Jack, I want you to hear me out. This is the case we've been looking for. Nothing is more high profile than a serial killer. This is a circumstantial evidence case and, frankly, the evidence isn't that strong. It's pretty much all hearsay, or hearsay exceptions. Since the girl who originally identified the weapon is dead, the police officer she identified the weapon to testified in her place. So the weapon from a previous attempted murder was found at the scene, outside of the apartment in the woods, and that was the sole basis for the conviction. This guy was convicted because they were desperate to catch somebody."

"You're forgetting a couple of things, Ben."

"What's that?"

"Felton's fingerprints were on the murder weapon and the murders stopped after Felton was arrested and convicted."

"All I want to do is stop the execution. If Felton stays in prison for the rest of his life, I'm okay with that."

"What if he gets off?"

"We don't necessarily want that."

"You don't always get what you want, Ben. We could find a technicality that nobody came up with before. If I took Felton's case, I would be ethically bound to give him the best representation I could muster. I can't pick and choose how I'm going to represent him. So I have to make a determination at the outset if I want to give my best efforts to represent an alleged serial killer knowing that I might possibly get him off."

Ben Chapman could see he was losing Jack. It was something he had anticipated. He had to approach the issue from another direction. This was where Henry came into the equation.

"Let's just take this out of the realm of Mr. Felton for a second and look at the bigger picture. What is our work here? What is our goal? We want to eliminate the death penalty. We know the criminal justice system is flawed. Henry is a concrete example of that. He wouldn't be here if you hadn't exposed the flaws in the system, Jack.

"You're the best lawyer we have. There's no doubt about that. You're a lawyer's lawyer. But frankly, Jack, you cherry-pick your cases. You look to represent only those people you believe are innocent. So, in your cases, you're not necessarily putting the death penalty on trial. The Felton case is high profile. It's a circumstantial evidence case. We have the best opportunity we have ever had to expose the death penalty and the flaws in the criminal justice system to the world."

"To what end though, Ben? I mean, is it better to expose the flaws in our system of justice and let a very dangerous man walk?"

"I'm not talking about letting this guy walk, Jack. I'm after the issue of capital punishment. I don't need an answer now. Think it over. We can meet tomorrow or possibly the next day, but I need an answer soon."

When they were outside the offices and headed for the parking lot, Henry finally piped up. "Boy, it's much colder up here in North Florida," he said, rubbing his hands up and down his upper arms.

"Yeah," Jack mumbled. He was still mulling over Chapman's words in his head. It was chilly, but the sun was shining and the wind wasn't too bad.

"Now I know why he wanted me here," Henry said when they were in the car and driving back to the hotel.

"Why is that?"

"He figures I'll convince you to take the case. I'm his ace in the hole. He brings the two of us up here, goes through that dog and pony show, and leaves me to work on you for the next day or so."

"And why is he so sure of you? You said he doesn't even know you."

"He doesn't. But he does know that I spent seventeen years on death row. He assumes that I am a staunch opponent of the death penalty because of my own experience."

"And?" Jack asked.

"You know I am. But I'm not necessarily opposed to some wacko serial killer being fried. I mean, nobody should ever mistake me for being a bleeding heart."

"I certainly wouldn't, Henry. Not after Oakville." Jack was referring to the killing of the man who had been about to shoot him while he was jogging. It was something they had never spoken about. Since he'd brought the subject up, Jack decided to get some closure at the same time. "That is over, isn't it?"

"Yeah," Henry said without acknowledging his part in anything. "The Eel called me a few days later and said it was finished. It's one less thing you have to worry about, Jack."

"Good. I won't bring it up again. Now back to this man on death row. You're forgetting something, aren't you, Henry?"

"What's that, Jack?"

"A lot of people said pretty much the same thing about you. Nobody gave a rat's ass about a career criminal like you going to meet his maker."

"One slight difference, Jack: You don't rehabilitate serial killers. They're like vampires. You have to cut out their heart to make them stop."

"Just because it's a serial killer case, everybody, including you, assumes this guy is guilty. He could be innocent."

"You're the one who pointed out that Felton's fingerprints were on the murder weapon and that the killings stopped after he was arrested."

"The prints are pretty substantial evidence, but I don't think the same way about the cessation of the murders. Serial killers for the most part are not stupid. And, contrary to popular opinion, most of them don't want to get caught. So somebody gets arrested for the murders. It's a perfect time to move on. The killings don't stop, they just move to a different location. That can be new and exciting for a killer."

"I guess you're right," Henry said. "You know, Jack, for a guy who has been clean as a whistle his whole life, you do a good job getting inside of the heads of criminals. So what are you going to do?"

"Don't know yet."

"And what's a lawyer's lawyer? I never heard that term before until Chapman said it."

"It's just a figure of speech."

"What does it mean?"

"It's a term to describe a really good lawyer—you know, the guy other lawyers want when they get in trouble."

They arrived at the hotel. Henry slid out of the passenger seat chuckling.

"What's so funny?" Jack asked.

"I was just thinking," Henry said. "What happens to the lawyer's lawyer when the lawyer's lawyer needs a lawyer?"

"Is that a tongue twister? And why would you think it was funny that I wouldn't have a lawyer?"

"I don't know—sick sense of humor, I guess. Besides, I'm the only one of us who gets in trouble and I've got you."

"Babe."

"What?"

Jack was laughing now. "I've got you—babe."

"I don't know about you, Jack. I think I just might get my own room."

Jack was still laughing. "More space for me. You were never meant for a double room anyway, Henry. And I won't have to wear earplugs anymore."

"Jesus, Jack, you're brutal. Gimme a break, will ya?"

"You don't mess with the lawyer's lawyer, Henry."

The next morning at eight, Jack called Chapman's office and set an appointment for eleven. He hadn't made up his mind yet but he wanted to set a deadline for himself. That left him three hours to bounce things off of Henry.

"I don't mind taking the case. I really don't. I think there's merit in arguing that this was a circumstantial evidence case and that it doesn't merit the death penalty. I mean, the murders were gruesome enough to warrant it, but the evidence was a little flimsy, at least according to Chapman. I haven't seen anything yet.

"The thing that bothers me, and I don't know why, maybe it's just a feeling—what if there's a loophole and this guy goes free? Do I want that on my conscience?"

They were at breakfast in the hotel dining room: silver coffee pot, cloth napkins, white table cloth.

"Don't you have to ask that question in every case, Jack? I mean, you weren't absolutely positive that I was innocent, were you? Yet, you got me set free."

"I was pretty sure of you, Henry. I'd have staked my life on you by the time it was all over."

"Why don't you give this Felton guy the same opportunity to convince you of his innocence? Tell Chapman you'll review the file and you'll visit Felton and then you'll make your decision."

"He won't like that. He wants me to represent Felton whether he's innocent or not."

"Who cares what he wants? You're not looking at him when you look in the mirror in the morning."

"I could still make a mistake."

"You could, but you convinced me of something last night, Jack. Something I had not thought about in a while. This man might be innocent and you, my friend, are probably the only person capable of saving him from his date with the grim reaper."

The two men's eyes met. They didn't often go back there because they didn't need to. Henry was reminding Jack, as Jack had reminded him just the night before, that one man through his faith and his tenacity can make a transforming difference in another man's life.

"Chapman made the right decision asking you to come along, Henry."

"Good, because it's going to cost him. Did I tell you I'm flying back to Miami, Jack? I want you and your trees to have an opportunity to bond."

The meeting at eleven didn't go that well. Chapman was furious that Jack put conditions on whether he would represent Felton.

"We've only got two months, Jack. What if you review the files and meet with Felton and decide not to take the case? It will be too late to get somebody else in and do an effective job."

"No, it won't. You've got the files right here." Jack pointed to four boxes leaning against the wall in Chapman's office. They hadn't been there the day before, and Jack correctly surmised that they were the files on Thomas Felton's case. Chapman had been pretty sure of himself.

"I can get through those files in a week and meet with Felton the following week. I probably want to meet with him at least twice before the case management conference with Judge Holbrook. Meanwhile, you can line up an alternate if I don't take the case. I will certainly work with whoever you get to bring them up to speed. I'll even attend the case management conference with that person."

Chapman wasn't satisfied although he had no choice but to acquiesce. Jack was not going to budge.

"Okay, Jack, you've got two weeks."

CHAPTER TWENTY-NINE

The trip to visit a death row inmate at Union Correctional Institute in Raiford, Florida, was something Jack would never get used to. The formalities of signing in, being searched, leaving the freedom of fresh air and wide open spaces for steel bars and narrow hallways always made him appreciate his life just a little bit more.

He had tried to get Henry to come with him, figuring Henry could pick out a cold-blooded killer, no matter how good a con man he was, by just being in the room with him. Henry was reluctant to do it but he couldn't say no to Jack. It was the warden who put the kibosh on the whole idea.

"The only way Henry Wilson is going to be allowed on death row is when he comes back permanently," the warden had told Jack. Apparently the man had not gotten over the fact that Henry had been set free. And he had seemed so concerned for Henry's well-being when Henry was about to be executed.

Jack could have fought the warden's decision, especially if Felton had agreed to the visit. However, it would have taken time, and time was the one precious commodity he did not have. So he went alone to meet Thomas Felton.

The circumstances of the meeting itself were different from the usual procedure afforded to Jack. In the past, he had been allowed to meet with his client in a room, face to face across a table. Today, he was allowed only to sit at a chair in one room and talk to Felton by phone in another room while looking at him through a set of bars and windows. Death row inmates had very strict monitoring regulations: they lived in a six-by-nine foot cell; they couldn't mingle with the prison population; they couldn't even take a shower every day. Apparently, serial killers had even stricter regulations. Jack saw two guards standing behind Felton as he sat on his stool on the opposite side of the bars.

For a brief moment before picking up the phone, Jack studied Felton. He was still a young man at thirty-three, tall, thin and surprisingly handsome although his head was shaved. Jack looked into Felton's clear green eyes. Felton returned the gaze. Jack picked up the phone.

"Hello, Mr. Felton. I'm Jack Tobin. I'm a lawyer with Exoneration and I've been asked to look into your case."

"I know who you are, Mr. Tobin, and I'm honored to speak to a lawyer of your standing."

That was unusual. The typical death row inmate, including Henry, practically spit on him when he introduced himself. They'd already been through a few lawyers and had been disappointed too many times to feel anything but enmity toward the litigators who came to visit bearing false hope.

Felton was different. Jack knew from reading his file that he had had only one appeal and that was right after his conviction, a perfunctory performance alleging the usual grounds—inadequacy of counsel and improper evidentiary rulings. It was as if the lawyer wrote on the brief, "I don't want to represent this guy but I have to, so here it is." After that, there was nothing. Nobody wanted to touch the serial killer's case. No wonder he was happy to see Jack.

"Mr. Felton, I've reviewed your entire file, and I've got a good feel for what happened on the night of the murder and what has happened with your case since then. Is there anything you want to tell me?"

"Just that I'm innocent. I didn't kill those two people. I think they convicted me because I didn't have an alibi."

"Well, they did find a knife with your fingerprints on it."

"I never saw that knife before they showed it to the judge and the jury in my trial. I don't know where they got the fingerprints from."

"You never gave a statement to the police after you were arrested, correct?"

"No, I didn't. I did tell them I was innocent."

"Why not give them details, I mean if you were innocent?"

"I was a law student, Mr. Tobin. I was always told that no matter whether you were innocent or not, don't talk to the police without a lawyer. When I did get a public defender, he not only didn't want me to talk to the police, he didn't want me talking to him. Would you have advised me to talk to the police?"

"Probably not. Listen, we've only got about seven weeks before your scheduled execution. I need something to take to the court. Can you give me anything?"

In fact, Jack had already found something substantial that would provide a basis for a motion for post-conviction relief and that indicated that Felton might be innocent. He was just testing Felton, trying to figure out in his own mind whether the man was innocent or not.

"I'm sorry, Mr. Tobin, I can't. The police came to my apartment two times before that last murder occurred. I was already a suspect in their minds because I had done my undergraduate work at the University of Utah and there had been a serial killer at that campus when I attended. I just think they wanted to solve this murder, and I was the best candidate they could come up with."

"That doesn't explain the knife with your fingerprints on it."

"No, it doesn't. I can't answer that question. All I can tell you is I never saw that knife and I certainly never held it in my hand."

*   *   *

Jack met up with Henry in Oakville, which was only a half an hour from the prison. The status conference and any evidentiary hearing that might occur before Judge Holbrook would take place in Oakville, so Jack wisely decided to make it his headquarters even though he had not yet decided to take the case. Ron had a two-bedroom furnished condo available at the time for him and Henry.

"I try to keep one open at all times for you, Jack, in case you want to come and visit," Ron told him.

The truth was that Jack had not been back to Oakville since he'd left two years ago. He'd tried to give Ron money for the place but Ron wouldn't take anything.

"I might be here for a month," Jack said.

"So what," Ron replied. "I shouldn't have let you pay me last time. What are you going to give me? Five hundred dollars? Seven fifty? I'm saving you up for when it really matters—you know, a hundred grand loan, maybe a hundred fifty. This is peanuts. I'm just making sure you stay committed to me for when I need you. By the way, since you're thinking of representing this serial killer, don't tell people you know me. It'll be bad for business and possibly my health."

"I'd better keep a low profile here. People are going to be upset," Jack said rather seriously.

The three men were sitting in the living room of the condo. Ron jumped on the remark.

"Upset? That's the understatement of the year, Jackie Boy. Some people are going to want your hide. Danni will be in the front of the line in that group, by the way. And don't come into The Swamp either. I'll have to close the place down if you do."

Jack just looked at Ron for a second, not knowing how to take that last remark.

"I'm just kidding," Ron told him when he saw the serious look on Jack's face. "I don't give a shit what people think. You know that."

Then he was back to being a jokester again.

"Henry, I'd drop him now. No percentages in being a friend of this guy. You can pick him up again when he moves back down to Pigeon Creek or wherever it is that he lives."

Henry laughed. Ron could make everybody laugh eventually.

"I'm just helping him decide not to take the case," Henry said. "Then I'm outta here."

"Everybody's a jokester," Jack said as Ron and Henry continued laughing. It was good for all of them because if Jack did take the case, they were all going to feel the pressure—Ron maybe worst of all.

When Ron left, Jack got down to business with Henry.

"I found something, something real substantial in Felton's case files."

"What is it?"

Jack went into his bedroom and came back with some papers.

"This is the coroner's report. Take a look at the description of the knife wounds on the woman's torso."

Henry's eyes scrolled down to where Jack was pointing. He read the description out loud. "The entry wound is approximately one-quarter inch wide *at each entry point* and extends into the body approximately three and a half inches *again at each entry point*."

"It's the same description for the man's torso," Jack said.

"So it was the same knife used on both."

"Exactly. And what kind of knife does that entry wound describe to you, Henry?"

"Probably a stiletto. Maybe a dagger although a dagger might be in excess of a quarter of an inch wide."

"And you know the murder weapon they used to convict Felton with?" Jack asked excitedly.

The light went on in Henry's head. "A bowie knife. It couldn't possibly have been a bowie knife. It's at least an inch and a half or two inches wide. They convicted him with the wrong murder weapon."

"That's right."

"Wait a minute, Jack. That just doesn't make sense. Somebody would have had to figure this out on the way to trial. Somebody would have had to see that this evidence doesn't add up. I mean *the coroner* would have had to blow the whistle."

"You'd think that would be the case unless they were all in on it."

"That's kind of hard to believe: Everybody agreed to set this guy up. It's crazy."

"Not if you think it through and I've been thinking about nothing else for days now. Let's say just one person believes Felton is the murderer and goes about setting him up."

"Okay."

"He's got Felton's fingerprints. The investigative file says that two officers on the task force surreptitiously obtained his prints from a cigarette case earlier in the investigation. By the way, one of those officers was Danni."

"Okay."

"And he knows the killer used a bowie knife with a gargoyle handle when he tried to kill that girl who got away, Stacey Kincaid."

"You're way ahead of me, Jack. I don't know all these facts."

"Trust me, Henry. They're true. And a bowie knife meets the MO of some of the other murders as well."

"Okay, I accept everything you're telling me. Keep going."

"So he searches and finds the exact knife and buys it. When he gets called to the next murder, he plants the knife in the bushes outside the apartment before he even goes in so he doesn't know he's planted the wrong murder weapon."

"This is too much, Jack. You've been reading too many mystery novels. Nothing ever happens like this or at least I've never heard of it. What about the fingerprints? How does he get the fingerprints on the knife?"

"You can transfer fingerprints, Henry. You can do it with Scotch tape as long as you have the fingerprints you're trying to plant. And the cops can do it another way: They can just say these are the prints we found on the knife. I don't think that happened in this case because too many people would have had to be involved."

"You already told me the whole damn criminal justice system was involved," Henry said.

"Not at first. In the beginning it was perhaps only one man. Then the scenario changed. They had Felton in custody and the killings stopped. A couple of months passed. Everything was back to normal. What would you have done if you were the prosecutor and you suddenly discovered the evidence didn't match up? Would you put somebody you were sure was a serial killer back on the streets to kill again? Would you put your community that had been living in terror for half a year in jeopardy again? Would you accuse a member of law enforcement of tampering with the evidence under these circumstances? Or would you just let it go—put Felton away and become a hero?

"You know the prosecutor just puts on a case. Of course, she's supposed to do it ethically, but it's up to the defense to challenge the evidence. The public defender was probably clueless—just going through the motions."

"I still can't believe this."

"Let's look at it the only other way you can look at it. There had been eight murders before these last two, and the police never found a trace of evidence. That excludes, of course, the evidence they obtained from Stacey, the girl who temporarily got away. Then all of a sudden this mastermind killer drops a bowie knife with his fingerprints on it outside the scene of a double homicide where he used another type of weapon to do his killing. Does that make any sense whatsoever to you?"

"No, it doesn't."

Jack, who was already standing and walking around the living room as if it were a courtroom and he was pleading his case, went to the kitchen and pulled two beers out of the refrigerator, opened them, handed one to Henry, and waited. He could tell Henry was going over all of it in his head again, challenging every premise, filtering it through the mind of a criminal, until he arrived at the place Jack expected him to get to.

"So I assume you have a person in mind who did all this?" Henry asked.

"I do."

"And who might that be?"

"Sam Jeffries."

"The chief of police?"

"That's the one."

"I can't wait to hear your rationale for this one, Jack."

"It's very simple. Sam Jeffries was the head of the task force back then. His wife had been murdered *by the serial killer* two weeks before this double murder. The man could not have been in his right mind. He knew about the bowie knife. He knew Felton was a suspect: Danni had tried to get a search warrant for Felton's apartment. And let me show you something."

Jack went in his bedroom and returned with a tape and popped it in the VCR. He and Henry watched a recording of Tom Felton's arrest. It started out fine with Sam reading Felton his rights. Then it got ugly: Felton nodded, telling Sam he understood his rights, and Sam told him he had to respond verbally. Then came the part Jack wanted Henry to see.

"I understand what you said to me but I'm innocent," Felton replied to Sam's prompting. "I didn't kill anybody. You've got the wrong man."

"We'll see about that, dickhead," Sam answered. "You're going down. And don't be fooled: that cocktail they give you up in Raiford—it may be quick but it's awful painful. They just paralyze you so nobody can tell."

"Wow!" Henry said when Jack turned off the VCR. "I see what you mean. That was one angry man there. So what are you gonna do with all of this, Jack? Most of it is supposition."

"I don't think I have to do anything but prove that the weapon found with Felton's fingerprints on it was not the murder weapon. At that point the court is going to have to set Felton free."

"So what was all that other stuff about?"

"I had to convince myself that this is how it went down."

"Why did you go over it with me?"

"Because if there were holes in my theory, you would see them."

"Let me say this: I don't know if your theory is totally accurate but you have convinced me that the bowie knife was a plant, and it certainly wasn't the murder weapon. So what are you going to do?"

"I don't know. After all this, I still don't know that Felton is innocent. I know that he was framed. I just don't know that he's innocent."

"What happened when you went to see him?"

"He proclaimed his innocence. He seemed honest and straightforward. He looked me right in the eye. I didn't detect any fidgeting, eye blinking, nothing. Of course, psychopaths don't display the symptoms that normal liars do."

"Well, if you don't represent him, nobody is going to. And all this stuff that you just brought to my attention is going to die with him."

"I know, Henry. I don't think I can let that happen."

"There's something else that you need to at least consider. Actually, it's someone else."

"You're talking about Danni."

"I know it shouldn't affect your decision, but—"

Jack cut him off. "It blew my mind when I read the file. She was a big part of this case. Besides obtaining the fingerprints, she's the one who interviewed the girl who identified the murder weapon in the previous attempted murder."

"The girl who was later killed?" Henry asked.

"Yes. Danni testified about that at trial. Do you remember Hannah and Danni telling us about Hannah going to Colorado when she was a young girl?"

"Yeah, I remember."

"She went there because the serial killer called Danni and intimated that he was going to kill Hannah."

"Jesus, Jack, she's going to be livid if you represent this guy."

"I know, but what can I do? I can't not represent him if I believe he's innocent just because Danni is going to be angry."

"No, you can't," Henry said. Then he started chuckling to himself.

"What's so funny?" Jack asked.

"I was just thinking that I'm glad I'm not you."

CHAPTER THIRTY

The case management conference on Thomas Felton's case was held in the courtroom in downtown Oakville at 9 a.m. on January thirty-first. Jack was present along with a lawyer from the attorney general's office named Mitch Jurgensen, and ten reporters.

Normally this would have been an informal affair but with the reporters in attendance, Judge Holbrook felt the need to go through the motions. He rescheduled the hearing from his chambers to the courtroom, and at the appointed hour he walked into the courtroom wearing his robe after the bailiff gave the order "All rise!"

"You can be seated," the judge said after sitting down. He was a good-looking man, probably in his early fifties, tall, with a full head of dark hair. Either he colored it or he was one of those rare people over fifty who did not have one gray hair on his head.

Judge Holbrook was a circuit judge in the northern part of the county. He had been chosen for this case on the theory that a judge from the northern part of the county would be fairer *or would at least appear to be more fair* than a judge who presided in Oakville where the murders had occurred. Jack, of course, didn't buy it for a second. He thought the Florida Supreme Court should have appointed a judge from a county far removed from Oakville. Unfortunately, time didn't permit filing a motion to get rid of the judge.

Jack had checked him out thoroughly, though. He wasn't a great

legal mind, but he wasn't thought to be an ideologue either. Ideo-
logues were the worst kind because they always *knew* what the truth
was and what should be done rather than listening to the evidence
and making a decision on the facts.

"Be simple and direct with him," one lawyer told Jack. "If you
start throwing case law at him and arguing complex legal issues,
he'll shut down."

Jack had that advice in mind when the judge called on him to
begin the proceedings. He also had a court reporter to transcribe
everything that was said. And if the judge allowed him, he was prepared to make some statements in open court that would send the
press corps into a frenzy. If Jack could have his say, what happened
in this case was definitely going to see the light of day.

Judge Holbrook unwittingly became a willing participant in
Jack's plan.

"This is a case management conference in the case of *State of
Florida v. Thomas Felton*. A death warrant has been signed in Mr.
Felton's case. He is scheduled to be executed on March fourteenth, approximately six weeks from today, and this proceeding is to determine
if there are any further motions or appeals that counsel for Mr. Felton
plans on filing. Mr. Tobin, are you here representing Mr. Felton?"

"Yes, Your Honor."

"And who is representing the State?"

"I am, Your Honor. Mitch Jurgensen from the attorney general's
office."

Jack had been back to see Felton one last time before making his decision to take the case and came away from that meeting as confused
as he was after the first meeting.

"He doesn't act guilty, but I just don't know," he told Henry.

"I don't know what to tell you, Jack. With these facts, though, it's
hard to let the man just be taken like a lamb to slaughter."

"I guess you're right, Henry. Now that I've seen what I've seen, I guess I can't stay silent."

"Okay, Mr. Tobin," Judge Holbrook said. "You know the drill. This hearing is for your client's benefit. Do you have any post-conviction motions that you intend to file?"

"Yes, Your Honor. As a matter of fact, I have a motion with me. It's a motion for an evidentiary hearing and a new trial."

Jack handed the motion to the judge and gave a copy to Mitch Jurgensen.

Judge Holbrook didn't even glance at the written motion. He saw the reporters out there behind the bar whispering among themselves. He knew they were just chomping at the bit to find out what was in the motion. On the spur of the moment, he decided to give them something.

"We've got some time, Mr. Tobin. Why don't you tell us about this motion."

"Yes, Your Honor. I have attached to the motion the coroner's reports on both murders. They were never admitted into evidence at the trial because the coroner testified in person, but he specifically stated that he was using his reports to refresh his recollection, and the record is clear that he had them in his hand when he was testifying.

"I also have attached to the motion pictures that I recently took of the knife that was admitted into evidence as the murder weapon. It's a bowie knife—a large bowie knife. As you can see from the pictures, I have a tape measure that measures the width of the knife at certain points and the length of the knife. I have also attached the transcript of the trial testimony in which the knife was referred to as the murder weapon. It is interesting, Your Honor, that the coroner never identified the knife as the murder weapon, and I have attached his testimony as well. One of the police officers who testified is the only person who identified the knife as the murder weapon.

The coroner testified first, and he was long gone when that police officer took the stand—"

"And your point is, Mr. Tobin?" The judge was getting frustrated, but that's where Jack wanted him to be—focused on the bottom line. Not just yet though.

"The public defender should have objected to the police officer's testifying about the bowie knife being the murder weapon. The officer was not qualified to give that testimony."

"Ineffectiveness of counsel was raised in the first appeal, Mr. Tobin. Are you really arguing that your client is entitled to an evidentiary hearing because the public defender failed to make a technical objection? Because if you are, I'm ready to rule on that issue right now."

Now was the time. The judge was ready and so were the members of his audience.

"No, sir, I'm arguing that the knife the police officer identified as the murder weapon was *not* the murder weapon and *could not possibly have been* the murder weapon."

That got the peanut gallery stirring. Judge Holbrook banged his gavel.

"If you people can't be quiet, I'll have you removed. Now, Mr. Tobin, how do you arrive at this seemingly outlandish conclusion? And for the record, I am not categorizing the evidence before I hear it. I only refer to the conclusion as outlandish because Mr. Felton has been through one appeal, has been on death row for ten years, and is scheduled to be executed in six weeks."

"I agree with you, Your Honor. It is outlandish and outrageous and whatever else you want to call it, but that doesn't make it any less true."

"And what is your basis for the statement you made?"

"Your Honor, if you would open the coroner's report on the deceased, Vanessa Brock, to page three—"

Mitch Jurgensen finally woke up.

"I object, Your Honor. This is not an evidentiary hearing, and the coroner's reports are not evidence. They are hearsay."

"I understand that, Mr. Jurgensen. I'm not taking testimony or admitting evidence. I'm just hearing argument, trying to get a feel for where Mr. Tobin is going in his motion. Proceed, Mr. Tobin."

"Yes, Your Honor. If you'll look at the second sentence of paragraph two. It reads, 'The entry wound is approximately one-quarter inch wide *at each entry point* and extends into the body approximately three and a half inches *again at each entry point*.'

"And if you look at my measurements of the so-called murder weapon, the bowie knife, even at its narrowest point, is more than a quarter inch in width. At three and a half inches in length, which was the stated penetration in the coroner's report, the bowie knife is two inches wide. Thus, if the bowie knife was the murder weapon, the entry wound would have been two inches in length."

Jack watched the judge's reaction. The man immediately started to fidget. His arms were moving, his shoulders were moving, his head and neck were moving—all in different directions. He looked like an old vaudeville comedian pretending to be drunk or afflicted with some rare disease. Those involuntary movements told Jack all he needed to know: Judge Holbrook was not a dispassionate, disinterested third party.

"There must be some mistake here, Mr. Tobin. Maybe it's a typographical error. That happens sometimes. The coroner will probably be able to explain all this as he would need to testify for you to get this document in."

"The coroner is dead, Your Honor. Perhaps there are contemporaneous notes he took at the time of the autopsy. Otherwise, this is the only record. And I ask Your Honor to take a look at the autopsy report of the deceased, Peter Diaz. On page two, paragraph four, you will see the same description of the entry wound. It is highly unlikely that a mistake would be made in both autopsy reports."

Several members of the press corps had already hightailed it for the exit, determined to get a leg up on everybody else. The majority stayed, however, eager to hear the State's response and to observe any further reactions from the judge.

"Mr. Jurgensen," the judge asked, "do you have any response to these allegations?"

Mitch Jurgensen wasn't born yesterday. Even though he had reviewed the file thoroughly before the hearing, he had not picked up on the discrepancies Jack had noted. This was not the time to respond, however.

"Your Honor, I have only glanced at this motion. I will need time to go through it in great detail before I comment. However, I assure the court that there must be a reasonable explanation."

Judge Holbrook didn't follow Mitch Jurgensen's cue to shut up. He prattled on for the benefit of the reporters.

"Mr. Tobin, if I'm hearing you correctly, you are basically saying that the state attorney, the coroner, and the police department conspired to convict your client. Now that is quite an accusation."

"I have never made that accusation, Your Honor. I'm merely stating the facts: The weapon identified by the police officer could not have been the murder weapon identified in the coroner's reports—period. I did point out that the coroner testified first and did not identify the murder weapon. The police officer did. It is difficult to believe that the coroner did not know that the physical evidence did not support the charge of murder against my client. It is also difficult to believe that the coroner did not tell the prosecutor. The way the evidence was presented, with the coroner going first and discussing his report but never identifying the bowie knife as the murder weapon, suggests very strongly that they did have that discussion. In any event, based on this evidence, my client should be granted a new trial although I don't know what a new trial would do at this point."

"Suppose I decide that the facts in your motion require me to set an evidentiary hearing. Do you intend to call anybody as a witness, Mr. Tobin?"

"I intend to call somebody from the coroner's office to verify the reports and to let the court know if there were any other contemporaneous notes made at the time of the autopsies. And I intend to call the police officer who identified the bowie knife as the murder weapon. I will have the knife here as well, Your Honor. I don't think my portion of the hearing will take more than two hours."

"What is that police officer's name, Mr. Tobin? Do you know?"

"Yes, Your Honor. His name is Sam Jeffries."

"Police Chief Jeffries?"

"Yes. He was the head of the task force at the time, and he found the weapon in the woods outside the apartment complex where Vanessa Brock and Peter Diaz were killed."

That was enough for the rest of the reporters. They all left in a hurry. It was like a stampede, causing the judge to pause the proceedings for a moment to watch them go.

"How about you, Mr. Jurgensen? How much time would you need?"

"I'd need at least two hours, Your Honor, since I have no idea what witnesses I'm going to call. However, I do object to an evidentiary hearing."

"I'm sure you do, Mr. Jurgensen, but I think Mr. Tobin has set out enough facts to warrant a hearing. I'll give you both the whole day. Now when are we going to schedule this? We've got approximately six weeks before the execution, but we need to leave time for an appeal to the Florida Supreme Court."

"I'll need at least two weeks," Mitch Jurgensen said.

"Is that okay with you, Mr. Tobin?"

"I'd like it sooner, Your Honor."

"Mr. Tobin, I'm sure Mr. Jurgensen has other matters to attend to as a public servant. I think two weeks is a reasonable time."

Mr. Jurgensen may have other matters to attend to, Jack wanted to say, *but my client only has six weeks to live.* However, he didn't say anything. There was no point in making the judge angry at this stage of the proceedings.

"That's fine, Your Honor."

"Okay, how about February fourteenth, Valentine's Day? If we start at nine, we should have plenty of time. I will rule at the end of the hearing and I assure you my written order will go to the Florida Supreme Court that day, which will give you and your client a month to appeal, Mr. Tobin."

"That's fine, Your Honor."

"Mr. Jurgensen?"

"That's good for me, too, Your Honor."

"See you then, gentlemen."

CHAPTER THIRTY-ONE

The story that the police and the state attorney might have conspired to convict Thomas Felton was not only the lead story on the local news at six, it was the *only* story. The state attorney had a spokesperson, the police department had a spokesperson, the sheriff's office had a spokesperson—and the message was the same: Thomas Felton was guilty as charged, and his lawyer was just blowing smoke because the execution was near.

"They're not saying very many flattering things about you, Jack," Henry said. They were in the living room of the condo. Henry had just arrived back from Miami. Jack had told him he might need him to run down some leads during the next two weeks. Jack was on the floor doing some stretching exercises. He'd just come in from his run.

"I'm crushed," Jack said. "I want so much to be liked by the media. After all, they are the truth seekers, aren't they?"

"It all depends on how you define truth. If it's synonymous with circus, then you're right. They are the circus seekers. They're looking to make a circus out of this thing."

"It's what they do," Jack replied.

"Well, you'd better be careful, my friend. They're going to work people into a lather and somebody just might come looking for you. Do you have that Sig Sauer with you this time?"

"I do."

"Good. Keep it loaded and keep it handy."

"You know, Henry, sometimes I think you're a little too para-noid."

"If I wasn't so paranoid, one of us wouldn't be here right now." It was the second acknowledgment between them concerning the sniper on Jack's running route.

Just then there was a hard knock on the front door, followed by several harder knocks.

"I'll get it," Henry said.

Jack knew that Henry was probably armed, but he never saw the weapon. Henry checked the peephole to make sure some whack job wasn't out there with a gun in his hand. Then he opened the door.

Danni walked right in, not even waiting to be invited.

"Where is he, Henry? And don't tell me he's not here. I saw his car in the parking lot." She was standing in the open area between the living room and the kitchen right by the dining room table but she didn't see Jack on the floor.

"And it's great to see you, too, Danni," Jack said, sitting up.

"That's not funny. Jack, how could you do this? How could you represent a cold-blooded killer like Felton and at the same time ac-cuse Sam Jeffries of being a crooked cop?"

"I didn't accuse Sam Jeffries of anything. I just told the judge he was the cop who testified about the murder weapon. That's it."

"That's it? Didn't you tell the judge that the knife wasn't the murder weapon?"

"I did."

"So you merely inferred Sam Jeffries was a liar."

"The judge made that inference, I didn't."

Jack was still sitting. He considered getting up but decided he was safer on the floor. *I don't think she'll kick me when I'm down.*

"You still haven't answered why you're representing that piece of garbage."

"Look, I know why you're upset and it's certainly understandable considering all that you went through."

"You have no idea," Danni said.

Henry was standing on the sidelines watching. He knew what was going on even if the two of them didn't.

"You're probably right but let me tell you why I'm here. You know I work for Exoneration. They were assigned this case. Ben Chapman, the director, called me and Henry to Tallahassee and asked me if I'd represent Felton. I was very reluctant to do so for a lot of reasons but I agreed to at least look at the file. Once I did and saw the injustice that had occurred, I couldn't let it go."

"For what it's worth, Danni, I agreed with him," Henry added, seeing that Jack might need a lifeline.

"It's not worth anything, Henry, and that's not a personal statement aimed at you. It's not worth anything because the man is guilty and he needs to stay guilty until he's dead."

"I won't say this in court because I don't have to and because I don't have the evidence to prove it, but from where I'm sitting, that man, Thomas Felton, was set up," Jack said.

"Jack, do you know what this community went through ten years ago? Do you have any idea what Sam Jeffries went through personally? What Hannah and I went through? You can't unleash this vicious killer on this community again. You just can't do it."

"Danni, it's not about me. I'm just a lawyer. The law gives Mr. Felton the right to counsel when he's about to be put to death. If it weren't me, it would be somebody else. And I hate to say this because I do understand what this community has been through, certainly not as much as those who lived here, but I didn't plant a knife in the bushes and claim it was the murder weapon."

"You're not just some lawyer, Jack, and you know it. And don't try and hide behind the law. You have a choice. I'm asking you— don't take this case."

"It's too late, Danni. It really doesn't matter who is representing Felton at this point. The cat is out of the bag. This judge or an appellate court is going to have to deal with the facts whether I'm presenting them or somebody else is.

"Part of me wants to do what you ask simply because you are the person making the request, but I can't."

"You mean you won't."

"If I had known how personal this situation was to you and Hannah, I probably would not have even looked into the matter. However, I took on this responsibility. I can't shrink from it at this late stage."

Danni stood there ramrod straight in silence, her arms locked across her chest for what seemed like an eternity. Jack wanted to bridge the gulf between them but he didn't know how.

"Damn you, Jack," she finally said as she headed for the door. "And Judge Holbrook is not going to give you a new trial. You can bank on that."

Then she was gone.

CHAPTER THIRTY-TWO

Danni was right about Judge Holbrook. Even though Jack was successful in getting all his evidence in at the evidentiary hearing, including the coroner's reports, the judge denied his motion for a new trial.

Mitch Jurgensen had someone from the coroner's office, a doctor named Jessel, testify that many of the reports ten years ago had typographical errors in them because the equipment was out of date and the staff was overworked.

Jessel's testimony gave the judge something to hang his hat on. He also threw in the fact that Jack's evidence was not *newly discovered evidence* since the public defender who had represented Felton at trial could have figured out exactly what Jack had figured out simply by reading the autopsy report.

Jack did have the opportunity to meet Sam Jeffries again since he subpoenaed him to the hearing. The two men had not spoken since the Julian Reardon incident.

"I testified that the bowie knife I found was the murder weapon because I believed it was the murder weapon," Sam told Jack under oath in Judge Holbrook's courtroom.

"Weren't you aware that the entry wounds on both victims were only one-quarter inch wide?"

"No. I was aware the victims were both killed because they had been stabbed. I found this bowie knife right outside the victims' apartment complex. We later tied the prints found on that knife to your client. This bowie knife or one identical to it was used in a prior attack by the serial killer. That was the basis for my testimony."

"Did you ever speak to the coroner?"

"No."

"Did you attend the autopsy?"

"No."

"Do you know anybody who did?"

"No."

Jack had half expected Judge Holbrook to deny his motion even though the evidence was overwhelmingly in his client's favor, so he had prepared in advance an appeal brief to file with the Florida Supreme Court. First, however, he needed his client's approval.

Thomas Felton was remarkably composed when Jack gave him the news. He now had less than four weeks to live.

"The evidence was all right there for the judge. I got all the evidence we needed on the record," Jack told him. "The only thing we can do is appeal."

"It's hard for me to believe that the police planted a bowie knife in the woods when the murder weapon was a stiletto and the judge let them get away with it when he had all this evidence in front of him," Felton said.

"I hear you, Tom, but it's never that simple. The judge lives in this community and he knows the murders stopped after you were arrested. He also knows that he wouldn't win an election for dog catcher if he set you free."

"So I'm to die so that Judge Holbrook can continue his career as a judge. Something's wrong with this system."

"Something is wrong with every system. People are fallible, so systems are fallible. Listen, we've got to make a decision on this appeal. Time is running short."

"File it, Jack. It's my only chance. I do want to live and be free again. And thank you for all you've done."

CHAPTER THIRTY-THREE

Two weeks later Jack was standing in the well of the Florida Supreme Court. The well was the area where the lawyers stood to face the court, seven judges who were on an elevated dais above them. Behind them was the gallery where the dark mahogany benches were gradually elevated like stadium bleachers though not as steep. The well was the lowest point in the courtroom—thus the name.

It was not a typical courtroom. It was the highest appellate court in the state of Florida. Such courtrooms were designed specifically for appellate arguments with an elevated dais for the judges, tables for the lawyers directly below the judges, a podium between the tables where the lawyers stood to face the court and present their arguments, and a huge gallery to accommodate hundreds of interested observers who almost never showed up. Appellate arguments were boring although today there were about forty people in the gallery, most of them reporters.

Jack had been to the court many times and in recent years it had all been on death row cases. He was not intimidated by the pomp and circumstance. The bailiff came out first. "All rise!" he said in a wonderful, deep voice. "Hear ye, hear ye, hear ye: The Supreme Court of the State of Florida is now in session. All those who have grievances before this court may now come forth and be heard."

Everyone in the courtroom stood up and the seven judges paraded out in their black robes and sat on their individual seats above the lawyers. Jack hardly noticed. He was there to save a man's life. In fact, he hoped the judges were aggressive and inundated him with a barrage of questions. "If they don't ask questions, they're not interested," he'd told Henry before he left for Tallahassee.

Nor was he affected by the bevy of reporters and cameras set up outside the courtroom. This case had gained national and international attention after the disclosure that the coroner and the prosecutor might have hidden evidence. It was a serious matter and worthy of the attention, but Jack knew that the reporters were leaning very heavily on the drama side—the serial killer, the powers of the state lined up against him, and the possibility of future mayhem. Now that was news!

Jack had walked right by the cameras.

"Mr. Tobin, do you have a moment—"

"No comment."

"Mr. Tobin—"

"No comment."

He'd never raised his voice. He'd never looked toward the camera. He'd simply kept moving.

Inside the courtroom, his demeanor was quite different. He was more than eager to respond to the justices' questions.

"Do you know what you're saying in here, Mr. Tobin? You're saying that the police and the prosecutor were all involved in one big conspiracy," Chief Justice Robert Walker said. It was the same question/statement Judge Holbrook had posed weeks before.

"No, Your Honor, I'm saying that the weapon found outside the premises where the victims resided and were murdered could not be the murder weapon based on the findings contained in the coroner's reports."

Jack knew they might need to connect those dots eventually. The standard on appeal of a death penalty case was *newly discovered evidence* and he could not meet that standard. The public defender had the coroner's reports and should have seen the discrepancy between the reports and the physical evidence. His only fallback then would be prosecutorial misconduct under *Brady v. Maryland*. Still, he didn't want to go there yet. He wanted the justices to lead him there. It was a dangerous tactic and Thomas Felton's life hung in the balance.

"It's inconceivable to me that the police, the coroner, and the prosecuting attorney did not see the disconnect between the murder weapon and the coroner's findings," Justice Juan Escarrez opined. He was a conservative and a key vote.

"I agree with you, Your Honor, at least as to the coroner and the prosecutor. The police officer, Sam Jeffries, who was actually the head of the task force, testified that he believed the bowie knife he found was the murder weapon. He was not at the autopsy and he never read the autopsy report. I have no evidence to quarrel with that testimony. The coroner, however, had to know about the discrepancy between the physical evidence and his findings. And I believe it is a reasonable inference that the prosecuting attorney knew since she never asked the coroner at trial if the bowie knife was the murder weapon, and she positioned his testimony in such a way that he was long gone when Captain Jeffries opined that it was."

"So you believe this is a *Brady v. Maryland* situation?" Justice Ray Blackwell, the newest member of the court, asked.

"Yes, sir. *Brady* held that if a prosecutor withholds material evidence, whether innocently or not, that is grounds for a new trial."

"But the evidence was not withheld. It was right there for the public defender to see. He had the coroner's reports and he had access to the murder weapon just as you did, Mr. Tobin."

"That's true, Your Honor, but he did not appreciate the discrepancy in the evidence. Should a man be put to death because the state attorney and the coroner succeeded in putting one over on the public defender? I don't think that's what *Brady* stands for."

For his part, Mitch Jurgensen kept hammering away on the fact that the report could have been mistaken.

"It was the coroner's *testimony* combined with Captain Jeffries's testimony along with the other evidence in the case that caused the jury to convict. This court should not go behind that decision."

"Even when we know this was not the murder weapon?" Justice Margaret Arquist, the only female member of the court, asked.

"You don't know that, Your Honor. The coroner isn't here and his reports were never evidence in the original case."

"The record is clear that the coroner testified from his reports, not from his memory, and it's inconceivable, at least to me, that the coroner would make such a blatant error in the reports of *both* victims. That evidence combined with the way the prosecutor presented her case, as Mr. Tobin pointed out, creates a pretty compelling case for his client, doesn't it?"

"I respectfully disagree, Your Honor." It was all Mitch Jurgensen could say.

Justice Arquist wasn't through, though. "Mr. Tobin, I still have some concerns because of the fingerprints on the bowie knife and the evidence that this knife or one almost exactly like it was involved in a previous attempted murder. We are dealing with a serial killer situation and we have to be very careful."

"Yes, Your Honor. I have the same concerns myself although my client was never charged with being a serial killer. Even if there is a basis here for a new trial, shouldn't we look at the bigger picture even if the law doesn't provide for that? The answer I come up with is yes and no. Yes, we should be particularly careful in evaluating the evidence but no, we should not apply a different standard. Should the presumption of innocence be any different when a man is being accused of a crime which *may* be a part of a series of crimes? Should he be entitled to less due process? On the other side of the dilemma are these questions: If the evidence at trial was contrived, what about the evidence found at the scene? If the bowie knife wasn't the murder weapon, is it reasonable to believe that the killer left it there? Or is it more reasonable to believe that the police, and it could be just one person, put the knife there with Felton's fingerprints on it since they already had surreptitiously obtained his prints on a previous visit to his apartment? Those are questions neither I nor this court can or must answer but in considering the bigger picture of the seriousness of this particular case, perhaps they should be part of the analysis."

It was a highly unusual oral argument. They were way outside the evidence in the case. However, Jack knew that the judges had to wrestle with that bigger picture just as he did.

"While we are exploring these so-called *other issues* that are not part of the record, Mr. Tobin," Judge Blackwell continued, "how do you deal with the fact that the murders stopped after your client was arrested?"

"There are two possibilities, Your Honor. Either my client was guilty or whoever committed the murders decided it was a good time to move on. I can't choose which of those two options is correct. I'm just a lawyer so I go back to what I know. The evidence in this case does not support a finding of guilt for the crime charged. The prosecutor knew that. The coroner knew that. The prosecutor chose to hide that fact from the jury and the unwitting public defender. I took the case for those reasons. I believe my client should receive a new trial for those reasons. The law is the law."

CHAPTER THIRTY-FOUR

On the day scheduled for his execution, Thomas Felton was moved from his cell on death row to the death cell near the execution chamber. Jack stayed with him all day. They had still not heard from the supreme court, and Jack tried to keep his client optimistic. The argument had gone very well, but Jack had had better clients and stronger arguments in the past and still lost, a fact he did not share with Felton, who was extremely nervous.

It was four o'clock. The execution was scheduled for six. Jack knew they would hear something before then. He just didn't know when or what the verdict would be. *Why do they always wait until the last minute?* he asked himself. On the other hand, maybe it was good to give people hope right up to the final hour.

Felton had been given the option of receiving a generic form of Valium, diazepam, which he had accepted, but it had not yet arrived. His last meal was due any moment as well. He was jumpy as all get-out, and angry.

"I'm gonna die because of the testimony of one stupid police officer. I can't believe it."

His analysis was off base but Jack wasn't going to correct him. His job was to keep Felton calm and hopeful.

"The judges have all the information. It's not over yet, Tom."

His meal finally arrived: a strip steak with mashed potatoes, green beans, and biscuits. Felton inhaled everything, his anxiety consuming him. Jack thought of an evening many, many years ago. He was a young boy waiting for dinner and he was famished. When his mother set his supper on the table, he wolfed it down.

"You ate that like it was your last meal," his father had said to him in a disapproving manner. Now, after all these years, he knew literally what his father had been talking about.

Thankfully, a guard came with the sedative as soon as Felton finished his supper. Then he was off for his last shower, leaving Jack alone in the cell. Jack knew what was coming next. A preacher would come in and talk to Tom. Then the warden would read the death warrant. Jack would have to leave after that as final preparations for the execution began.

Why do I put myself through this? he asked himself.

Felton came back from the shower dressed in a white shirt and prison pants. *All clean and dressed in white*, Jack thought. *Purified for the slaughter. Does that somehow relieve our collective conscience?*

The preacher came in to speak with the prisoner and Jack got up to leave.

"I'll be right outside the door, Tom," he said to Felton, whose demeanor had changed dramatically. He was totally subdued now and a look of resignation had settled on his face.

"Don't, Jack. Don't come back. Go now. I don't want to talk anymore." Felton hugged him. "I appreciate everything you've done for me. Nobody could have done more."

The warden offered his office for Jack to sit and wait and Jack accepted. *I'm not going out with the anti–death penalty protesters this time*, he told himself. At every execution, a group of protesters gathered outside the prison gates until the execution was postponed or the inmate was executed. They carried placards and sang hymns. In the past, Jack had joined them. He just wasn't up to it this time and he didn't know why.

He was sitting in the warden's office at ten minutes to six, imagining Tom being strapped onto the gurney and the medical team putting the heart monitors and the IVs in place, when the warden burst in.

"I just got the call. The supreme court granted your motion for a new trial."

Jack accompanied the warden back to the death cell where Tom Felton was waiting. The man was in shock. He was still a little subdued from the diazepam, but he was aware enough to know that he had been minutes away from death, strapped to a gurney with IVs in his arms and heart monitors on his chest when everything stopped. Nobody had told him anything yet.

The warden let Jack in and closed the cell door behind him.

"Let me know when you're ready and we'll move him back to his cell," the warden told Jack.

Jack sat in the death cell with his client for a minute or two before either of them spoke. Tom was sitting on the bed, his head down, his hands holding onto the cot for dear life.

"They should have finished it," he said finally. "I was ready. I won't be able to do this again. I'll have to find a way to kill myself."

"You won't have to do it again," Jack said.

Tom looked up, confused. "What's that supposed to mean?"

"The supreme court granted you a new trial."

"So that's what this was about. Why didn't anybody tell me?"

"I guess they figured you should hear it from me. You probably have a lot of questions, and it wouldn't be appropriate for the warden or the guards to try and answer them."

"I see. We never did talk about what would happen if I got a new trial."

Felton still seemed a little wary, as if he didn't or couldn't believe what was happening.

"No, we didn't. I don't think the State can retry you. They just don't have any evidence."

"You mean they're going to set me free."

"They could. I don't know. They could hold you on a different crime."

"They've never charged me with anything else, have they?"

"No. The guards are going to take you back to your cell. I'll check with the State, but I believe we'll know something within a few weeks."

"That long?"

"Maybe not. I can't say at this point. I hoped you'd be a little happier."

"I'm sorry, Jack. I'm still a little dopey from the drug, and I think I'm in shock as well. Thank you."

"No problem. I'll walk you back to your cell."

Jack went to the door and signaled for the guards.

CHAPTER THIRTY-FIVE

After leaving the prison, Jack went back to the condo in Oakville. He was emotionally exhausted and immediately went to bed but he couldn't sleep. Henry had bought a bottle of Jack Daniel's a few weeks back, and Jack decided to pour himself a shot and sit out on the patio and listen to the crickets sing. It was a beautiful night, clear skies with a slight breeze. He brought the bottle with him and poured another shot a few minutes later. After that second one, he could feel the tension rise from his body like steam from a natural spring.

When Henry was released, Jack was ecstatic. He didn't feel that way about Tom Felton because he still wasn't sure that Felton was innocent. There had always been a safety valve in the back of his mind to establish that innocence, something he hadn't discussed even with Henry.

For Felton to be guilty, some of the evidence had to be legitimate. Obviously, the bowie knife was not the murder weapon in the Brock/Diaz murders, but it could have been the actual weapon used by the killer when he attempted to kill Stacey Kincaid. If those fingerprints on the bowie knife were real and not planted, something that would be apparent to any fingerprint expert, the State could still charge Felton with the attempted murder of Stacey Kincaid. That was Jack's out. If they didn't charge Felton with attempted murder, the fingerprints were definitely bogus and Felton was innocent.

Jack took a long deep breath and poured himself one last shot. In a few minutes he wouldn't have any trouble sleeping.

After the new trial was granted, things happened a lot faster than Jack had expected. The supreme court's opinion in the case of *State of Florida v. Thomas Felton* was a scathing rebuke of the state attorney and the coroner's office. The police department escaped criticism because there was no real evidence to conclude that they were part of the plot to railroad Felton. The coroner was dead but Jane Pelicano, the prosecuting attorney and now *the* state attorney for Apache County, was still very much alive. The day after the supreme court's decision, the *Oakville Sun* ran a front-page headline summarizing that opinion and its castigation of the prosecutor and the coroner. Jane Pelicano immediately resigned.

The next day the governor appointed a man named Robert Merton as her successor. It was a logical decision. Merton was the chief assistant in the office, so continuity was assured, and he had not been around at the time of Felton's trial, so the taint was removed. Still, the quick appointment made Jack suspect that the governor had either known about Pelicano's resignation before it happened or had *caused* it to happen.

Merton wanted the whole Felton affair over with so he could start on a clean slate. Even though Sam Jeffries was adamant about initiating a new prosecution based on the attempted murder of Stacey Kincaid, Merton was having none of it.

"We've still got evidence to prosecute for the attempted murder, Bob. We can keep him in prison," Sam told the new state attorney when he visited him in his office almost immediately after the appointment.

"And how do we explain the knife at the Brock/Diaz crime scene? Felton, who was not guilty of the Brock/Diaz murder, just wandered by and dropped it off? Do you think the court's going to exclude evidence of what this office did in the Brock/Diaz murder prosecution when we try to introduce this knife into evidence in this new case? Of course not. This office will have yet another black spot on its reputation.

"That's not the way I'm going to start my tenure, Sam. There'll be no new trial and there'll be no new prosecution. Thomas Felton is going to be released."

Jack went to visit Felton two more times before his release. The first time was only a few days after the scheduled execution, and Felton asked some questions that Jack thought were slightly unusual.

"Everybody around here heard about my stay of execution. They all say I'm going to be released."

"Let's not get ahead of ourselves," Jack cautioned. "I believe you will be released as well but that hasn't happened yet."

"Somebody said I could file a claims bill and get paid for the time I've been in here."

That was the surprise. Jack had fully expected Felton to ask him to file a claims bill at some time in the future but not three days after the scheduled execution.

"You can. I've done it before and I've got the forms. It's fairly simple. I know a few state representatives who could introduce the bill."

"How much should I ask for?"

"How much do you want?"

"Twenty million dollars—two million for each year I was on death row. Do you think that's too much?"

"It's not too much to ask for as long as you understand you're not going to get it. You are more likely to get somewhere between three and five million if they decide to give you something. It's totally at their discretion. Asking for twenty actually gives them a little cover. No matter what they eventually give you, they can say you were asking for a lot more."

"No matter what it is, Jack, I want you to get a third."

"I didn't do this for money. You can give it to Exoneration if you want."

"Exoneration didn't save my life, Jack. You did. I'll give it to you. You can give it to them if you want."

Jack thought about it for a few seconds. It wasn't the way he wanted to do it but Exoneration needed the money. He had time, and he had the forms on his computer to get this taken care of in a day. He didn't want to give Felton's generosity any time to change its mind.

"Okay. How about if I do the paperwork tonight and bring it back tomorrow? That way, if you are released and as soon as you are released, we can file the claims bill."

"Sounds great," Felton said.

Jack returned the next day with a copy of a claims bill for Felton to keep and a contingency fee agreement for Felton to sign stating that Felton would give Jack one-third of whatever he received from the legislature as consideration for Jack's past representation and his representation during the claims process. Jack did explain that he would most likely have to go to Tallahassee a few times to convince the legislature to do the right thing. They made a copy of the signed contingency fee agreement at the jail and Jack left Felton with a copy of that as well.

"I can file the claims bill right away," Jack told his client, "but I have no idea when the legislature will act on it. It could take months or even years."

"I hope I can wait," Felton said.

Jack had no idea what he meant by that remark.

Jack was driving back from Bass Creek in a rainstorm when he heard the news of Felton's release. The warden called him to tell him it was imminent.

"I'd like to be there," Jack said.

"The paperwork is almost done. It will probably take no more than an hour to complete. After that I have no authority to hold him," the warden said. Since Jack was at least four hours away, there was nothing he could do.

Even though the only ostensible reason for Jack to leave his home in Bass Creek was to be in close proximity to the case, which had just ended abruptly, and his client, who would very shortly no longer be in prison, Jack continued driving to Oakville.

"I just felt I needed to be there," he told Henry later. "And I didn't know what for."

He would find out soon enough.

CHAPTER THIRTY-SIX

The rain was coming down in sheets as Kathy made her way home late Wednesday night. She could barely see the red brake lights of the cars ahead of her as she drove north on I-95. Her windshield wipers were on the fastest speed but the rain was coming down so fast that it was as if they weren't moving. Cars were pulling off on the shoulder to wait it out but not Kathy. She wasn't wired that way. She'd worked overtime, she was tired, and she wasn't going to stop until she was home.

She'd read somewhere that it was rain like this that spawned the phrase, "It's raining cats and dogs." The way she'd heard it, a hard rain in London around the turn of the century would cause cats and dogs to be swept into the sewers—thus the phrase. She didn't know if it was true or not but if it was, this was certainly a cats-and-dogs downpour. Kathy had never seen rain this hard anywhere but in Florida.

She'd almost missed her exit in North Miami, catching a glimpse of it through the sheets of rain at the last minute. Once off the highway, she could negotiate the side streets almost from memory. Still, she was careful.

"Shit!" she yelled out loud. She was on her street now and almost at her driveway when she remembered that she couldn't pull into the garage. Her ex-husband, Steve, had stored some of his stuff in there and had not yet picked it up although Kathy had been on him to do so. The divorce had been six months ago and his shit was still there. "If he doesn't pick it up this week, it's all going in the garbage!" she told the air as she reached into the backseat with her right arm and rummaged for her umbrella, which was on the floor back there somewhere.

She pulled into the driveway. The rain was coming down harder now, harder than she had ever seen it. She put the car in park, turned it off and half opened the umbrella. There was a trick to this. If she opened the door, stuck the half-opened umbrella out first and opened it fully, she might not get as wet as she sprinted from the car to the front door. The shoes were new. She wanted to save them if she could.

She opened the door, but the rain was coming down too hard, and she had not anticipated the wind, which suddenly shifted toward her. The umbrella was up quick enough but she was still soaked by the time she stood upright. Nothing to do now but make the mad dash. Between the rain, the darkness, and the wind, she had trouble finding her own front door. With the umbrella positioned in front of her, she never saw the dark figure to her left. If she had, she might have thought it was a tree anyway. There was a tree over there some-where.

Finally she was at the front door, key in hand. She opened it as quickly as she could, but as she pushed the door in, she felt a force from behind her propel her across the threshold. She knew it wasn't the wind; she could feel an actual contact with something. Then she was on the floor and heard the door slam shut. Someone, something was on top of her. She turned her head to look.

"This is going to be so much fun," a voice said as something struck her simultaneously on the left cheekbone. She felt a sharp pain, saw a flash of light, then nothing.

CHAPTER THIRTY-SEVEN

Two days after Felton's release, Jack received a phone call at the condo. It was about ten. He had just come from an early morning bike ride and had to retrieve his phone from the saddlebag under his seat.

"Hello?" he said, resting his empty hand on the bike.

"Jack?"

"Yes. Who's this?"

"It's me, Tom Felton."

Jack was a little embarrassed that he hadn't recognized his client's voice. "Hi Tom. How are you? Where are you?"

"Just driving around. I was wondering if you had filed that paperwork yet."

"Not yet, but I plan on doing it within the next week."

"Don't bother, Jack. I've changed my mind."

Jack couldn't believe what he was hearing. Why would a man turn down the opportunity to receive millions of dollars? It didn't make sense.

"Are you sure?"

"I am."

"You wouldn't want to tell me why, would you?"

"I just couldn't wait, Jack. I just couldn't wait."

"I'll hold on to them for you in case you change your mind," Jack said, not really understanding Felton's answer. Felton did not respond. He'd already hung up.

Jack had barely closed the cell phone when he received another call. It was Henry.

"Hey, what's up?" Jack asked.

"Are you sitting down?"

"Nope. I'm leaning on my bike as we speak. Had a great ride this morning. Why?"

Henry didn't answer right away, causing Jack to think he had lost the connection.

"Henry, are you still there?"

"Yeah, I'm here. Listen, Jack, I've got some bad news. I was listening to the morning news here in Miami and they were reporting the murder of a young woman. They wouldn't release the details. All they would say was that it was a brutal murder. Jack, the woman's name was Kathleen Jeffries."

"Oh my God. It's not Sam Jeffries's daughter, is it?"

"I'm not positive, but I remember reading somewhere—I think it was the newspaper accounts when his wife was murdered—that he had a daughter and her name was Kathleen or Eileen or something like that."

Jack let his bike fall over and almost fell to the ground himself. The realization of what might have happened was starting to sink in. He remembered as well that Sam Jeffries had a daughter although he couldn't remember her name.

Please. Please, let it be some other Jeffries, not Sam Jeffries's daughter.

It was Henry's turn to wonder about the connection.

"Jack, are you there?"

Silence.

"Jack?"

"I'm here, Henry. Are you checking into the details of the murder?"

"I don't have time, Jack."

"You don't have time?"

"No. The more I thought about this and the possibilities, the more I thought I need to get on a plane. I'm heading to the airport right now. My plane leaves in a little over an hour."

Jack understood, finally. Henry was putting the pieces together.

"Hannah?" he asked.

"That's my guess, Jack, although Danni's a possibility. I figure she's probably heading to the same place I am if she knows. Will you give her a call just to make sure?"

"I'll give you her cell phone number, Henry. I don't think she'll want to talk to me right about now. And frankly, I don't think I could handle that conversation."

"Jack, I know you don't want to hear this, but don't blame yourself if this turns out the way it looks. You were just doing your job. I'm as responsible as you. We just made a mistake, that's all."

"Is it just a mistake, Henry? Do you think Chief Jeffries will see it that way? Maybe I think I'm too smart sometimes. Maybe I think I know more than the people who put people away for a living. Danni kept telling me to leave this alone, but I just couldn't do it. I couldn't hear her."

"Stop it, Jack. We don't even know for sure that it's him. We're just speculating."

"Oh, it's him, Henry. I know it. I just talked to him. He told me not to file a claims bill. Said he couldn't wait. I didn't know what he was talking about until this moment. He couldn't wait to kill again."

"Jack, he's a psychopath. Nobody can read those guys. You can't blame yourself."

"If not me, Henry, who? Here's Danni's number. I can't talk anymore."

He gave Henry the number and abruptly hung up the phone.

CHAPTER THIRTY-EIGHT

Henry called Danni right after he hung up with Jack. He was ten minutes from the airport and his plane was leaving in an hour. He had to park and get through security in that time. He held the phone in his left hand as he sped down the highway doing close to ninety.

It had been two years since he'd spent any real time with Danni. She'd shown up at the condo that one day after Jack had taken Felton's case to express her displeasure, but that didn't count. He didn't care about the lapse of time, however. This wasn't a social call and now that he'd been put on notice, he wasn't going to let another person die if he could help it. If it was awkward, so what.

She answered on the second ring.

"Hello?"

"Danni, this is Henry Wilson."

There was silence on the other end of the line, which Henry expected.

"I don't know if you heard about the murder in Miami."

"I did. Somebody from the department called me about fifteen minutes ago."

Her voice was hard and cold. Henry could feel the antagonism on the other end of the line.

"Danni, I'm on my way to the airport."

"What for?"

"It's my understanding that your daughter is still in school at Boulder."

"Henry, I don't need your help. I'll take care of my daughter. Don't you think you and Jack have done enough?"

Henry ignored the remark. "My flight leaves in less than an hour. I figure now that you know, you're on your way as well. And I assume you've instructed Hannah not to go home."

"I have."

"And to go to a well-populated public place."

"Yes."

"When's your flight?"

"Four hours from now. I have to drive to Tampa."

"I'll be there three hours before you. Tell me where to meet her."

Again there was silence on the other end.

"Danni, this isn't about me or you, or Jack for that matter. It's about Hannah. I'll be damned if I'm going to let anything happen to her. Now where should I meet her?"

"The Boulder Book Store on the mall."

"Is there a coffee shop nearby?"

"There's one in the store."

"Okay, we'll go there and wait for you to arrive. Then you and I will come up with a plan. Will you call her and tell her to look for me?"

Silence.

"Danni?"

"Yes, I'll call her. I don't know why you're doing this."

"It's the least I can do."

CHAPTER THIRTY-NINE

J ack sat on the floor after hanging up with Henry. He didn't want to get up. Getting up meant dealing with what had happened. *Maybe if I just stay here it will all go away.* But he knew that was childish thinking. Besides, it wouldn't work. No matter where he was, he couldn't just turn off his mind. Couldn't force himself to go to sleep. There was at least one way to turn it off though. He stood up, walked to the kitchen, grabbed a glass with his right hand, the Jack Daniel's with his left, and headed for the patio.

He wanted to howl at the moon, although it was a little too early to do that. He wanted to scream about the unfairness of life. But life hadn't been unfair to him. He'd lost Pat, his wife, to cancer, but that was a far cry from losing both your wife *and* your daughter at the hands of a psychopathic murderer. Sam Jeffries, not Jack, had an absolute right to howl at the moon. Jack took a long pull from the bottle. He hadn't needed the glass after all.

Only when he was good and drunk could he return to the scene of what he considered his crime. When he was devoid of the ability to rationalize his actions—that's when he went back. His soul needed condemnation not vindication.

It was vanity! that little voice inside his head told him when he arrived at the state of mind he so craved. *It was all about your vanity! Nobody had ever gotten a serial killer off before—nobody but the great*

Jack Tobin. You should be proud of yourself, Jack. You did it! And don't let it bother you, don't let it ruin your night that the son of a bitch was actually guilty. Somebody else got killed, it's true, and there may be more, but there are always casualties on a man's road to success. Some have to fall for others to rise. It's the nature of the universe.

If Henry was there, Henry would have reminded him of the true facts: *You and I came to see Ben Chapman at Chapman's request, Jack. You didn't want to take this case. You didn't even want to look at the file. I talked you into it. Once you saw this man had been set up by the police, that's when you couldn't let it go. Vanity had nothing to do with it, Jack. Injustice was the culprit.*

But Henry wasn't there.

CHAPTER FORTY

Henry didn't find Hannah at the Boulder Book Store—she found him. She came running up to him as he walked in the door and gave him a big hug. He hadn't seen her since Thanksgiving two years before. She was a little taller and she looked more grown up and healthy. That zest for life that college kids possessed seemed to ooze from her pores. She was smiling from ear to ear at the sight of him.

Kids, Henry thought, even though he was referring to a twenty-year-old. *They're so open with their feelings. We could learn a lot from them.*

"Hi, Henry," Hannah said. "I hear you've come to rescue me."

"I don't know about that," Henry replied. "I'm just helping your mom out here."

"Do you really think this guy is after me?"

"I don't know, Hannah, but we can't take any chances."

"Where's Jack?"

"He's back in Gainesville. He's going to do what he can from there."

"Mom's pretty pissed at him."

"It's understandable, but Jack had his reasons for representing Felton."

"That's not what Mom said."

"I know. Don't they teach you at school to look dispassionately at all sides of a problem?"

"Yeah. What does that have to do with anything?"

"Well, this is one of those problems that has many sides, and since it's about life and death, it brings out the best and the worst in people. Are you hungry?"

"Kinda."

"We're going to meet your mother at the coffee shop here in three hours. Why don't we get something to eat."

"Okay. There's a great vegetarian restaurant right down the street."

"Are you a vegetarian?"

"No. I'm a vegan."

"And what exactly does that mean?"

"No meat, no dairy, no eggs, milk, or cheese, and no fish."

"So what do we eat, the bark off the side of a tree?"

"Very funny," Hannah said. "You just wait—you're going to love it."

Henry didn't know that he had consented to go to Hannah's restaurant but she was already on her way. *She's a lot like her mother*, he decided.

Danni had a lot of time to think on her drive to Tampa and her flight to Denver. Henry would probably have some suggestions about how best to protect Hannah. Danni felt that nobody could protect her daughter as well as she could. However, something else very powerful was building inside of her—the need to find Felton and kill him. While Hannah's security was still paramount, she trusted Henry to see to it. They weren't that close and Henry had participated in the decision to help Felton get out of jail, but there was that day in a small apartment in Miami when Henry could have walked away and saved his own life and didn't. He'd had her back, and he would have Hannah's back no matter what—Danni was certain about that. So if Henry's suggestions allowed her to go back to Oakville and find Felton or let him find her, Danni was going to listen. After all, finding Felton and killing him was the best security of all.

Henry watched Hannah bolt from the chair in the bookstore coffee shop, run to her mother, and throw her arms around her. He had seen Danni walk through the door a second before Hannah saw her. She'd looked stressed and troubled. Her daughter's hug had momentarily replaced that look with a smile of genuine joy. Hannah was slightly taller than her mother now but the two women looked so much alike. Other people glanced up from their computers, books, and lattes to watch and listen to the reunion.

"You look great!" Danni told her daughter.

"Not as good as you, Mom. You always look great."

The two women approached the table where Henry was waiting. He stood up and put out his hand. Danni didn't take it. She walked around the table and gave him a big hug.

"There's no animosity between us, Henry," she whispered in his ear. "You came all the way out here to save my daughter."

Henry's response came out before he had a chance to grab it. "I wish you felt the same way about Jack."

They separated. "Don't go there, Henry. Not now."

They all sat down. Danni ordered a coffee, and they chatted a little before getting down to the hard stuff.

"I almost missed my plane," Danni said. "I was on my way to the airport, stopped at a stop sign not too far from my home, when I saw this elderly gentleman on the corner struggling to maintain his balance. Suddenly, he went down. I jumped out of the car and ran to help him up. 'What happened?' I asked.

"'I dunno,' he says in an Italian kind of New York accent. 'I just kind of lost my balance.'

"'Where do you live?' I asked.

"'I dunno,' he says. Now I'm thinking he's either disoriented or he has other problems. I check him over, ask him how he's feeling. 'Fine,' he says but he's still holding onto me. So I get him in the car. I ask him his name and I try to look up his phone number on my phone. Nothing. I'm not exactly sure what to do—he remembered his name but he had no idea where he lived—so I asked him on a hunch what his telephone number was. He rattled it right off. Amazing.

"Anyway, I called the number and his wife answered. She told me he had Alzheimer's and the whole family had been looking for him for hours. He lived about two miles away so I drove him home. She was out there waiting for him when I arrived.

"'That's my wife, Rosemarie,' he beamed as we pulled up to the house. 'She's my heart. Everybody has to have a heart. Rosie is mine.'

"Rosemarie thanked me profusely and then she gently led him into the house. Why am I telling you this story? Oh yeah, I was telling you why I almost missed the plane."

"That's not the reason." Henry almost whispered the words.

"Maybe not," Danni said. "Maybe it affected me so much I wanted to share it. I mean, what a tragedy to see the love of your life walking around in a stupor. And yet, how beautiful it is to see two people who love each other so much."

"There's beauty in seeing a stranger help another human being too, Mom."

"There you go," Henry said. "A person to model yourself after."

Danni immediately changed the subject.

"So, Henry, you said we needed to make a plan. Do you have any ideas?"

"I do."

"Do you want to share them with us?"

"I thought maybe I'd listen to your thoughts first," Henry replied.

"I don't have any. I mean nothing concrete. So I'd rather hear from you."

"Okay," Henry began. He leaned in toward them, his arms resting on the table, his enormous hands surrounding his coffee cup so that it almost disappeared. "Hannah, you're not going to like this part. I know it's close to the end of the semester, but I think you're going to have to leave school. He knows you're here and there's too much open space here even if we moved your living quarters and tried to watch you all the time. It's too dangerous."

Henry paused to let his words sink in and to wait for a reaction.

"I already figured that," Hannah said, a slight look of disappointment on her face.

Danni didn't have a reaction to that part.

"Go on," she said.

"After that, there's a lot of options," Henry continued. "Danni, you could take Hannah to Europe or she could even go herself. The likelihood of Felton getting out of the country at this point in time is pretty low. It's not impossible but I think Hannah would be safe out of the country."

Danni wasn't buying it. Henry was holding back and she had an idea why.

"What would you do if Hannah was your daughter, Henry?"

"She's not my daughter," Henry persisted.

"What would you do if I entrusted her to your care?"

Henry didn't answer right away. He looked at Danni as if trying to read her thoughts. Danni nodded slightly to let him know that this was her wish if he wanted to do it.

"I'd take her to New York," Henry continued. "I have family there, my aunt in particular who lives in Harlem. It's a city of over eight million people. We'd drive up so there would be no flight record or anything. She'd be a needle in a haystack, assuming Felton even thought to look there. I can get her a new ID, if necessary, and

I have people to watch her at all times when I'm not available, which will be a rare occasion, I assure you.

"It's a short-term solution. I can't see keeping it up for more than a month, two at the max, but I think Felton will be caught by that time."

"I agree with you for the most part," Danni answered. "He may not be caught, but he'll be dealt with in that time period."

Henry stopped at that point. He'd been very reluctant to even offer the plan. Hannah was a twenty-year-old woman who he did not know very well, he was an ex-convict, and Danni was a retired cop. It didn't seem feasible that she would trust him to walk off with her daughter. But she'd asked. She'd even persisted. And he was convinced that he could protect Hannah.

"Do you really want to do this, Henry?"

"I do, Danni—for me and for Jack."

"Leave Jack out of this," she said. Then she looked at Hannah.

"What do you think, honey?"

"I don't want to leave school," Hannah said. "But if I have to, this sounds like another type of learning experience. I've never been to New York City. And Harlem—wow!"

"You'd be living with real black people, too," Henry added with a smile.

"That's the best part, Henry," she said, smiling. "A new cultural experience."

"You're sure?" Danni asked Henry again.

"I'm sure. Are you sure?"

"I can't explain it, Henry, but I don't think I'd trust Hannah with anyone else but you. Hannah, are you sure?"

"Yes, Mom. I feel the same way."

"Then it's settled. Henry, I'm going to write you a check for a thousand dollars. It should cover the first week or so."

"No, ma'am."

"'No' what?"

"No, I won't accept any money. We've all got some amends to make here, and I've got to do it my way. Besides, I've got a lot more money than you do."

Henry smiled when he said it, causing Danni and Hannah to smile as well.

"When are you planning on leaving?" she asked.

"Right away. We need to get out of here."

"But I need to pack and, Mom, you just got here," Hannah said.

"I know, honey, but we'll have plenty of time when this is over to enjoy each other's company."

"Would you take her to the apartment and help her pack?" Henry asked Danni. "If he's watching the place, I don't want him to see me. If he doesn't know that I exist, Hannah is a lot safer."

"Sure," Danni replied. "I want him to think she's coming home with me anyway."

Hannah walked ahead as they left the coffee shop, giving Henry an opportunity to say a few words to Danni alone.

"I know you're going after him and that's why you're leaving her with me. Don't make me feel like I made the wrong decision again. Be careful."

"I will, Henry. I'm going to make that son of a bitch come to me. And when he does, I'm going to be ready for him."

CHAPTER FORTY-ONE

Ron had been banging on the condo door for almost five minutes before he decided to use his key and just open it. He'd been calling Jack for hours before that to no avail so he decided to drive over. Jack's car was outside, but he wouldn't answer the door. Ron was worried. He'd heard the news about Sam Jeffries's daughter—it was everywhere now—and he knew that Jack would take it hard.

Once in the apartment he looked around but didn't see anybody. The place was a little bit of a mess but not too bad. Ron spied two bottles of Jack Daniel's side by side on the kitchen counter.

"Jack, are you here?"

No answer.

He checked out the two bedrooms and the bathroom. Nobody.

"C'mon Jack, where the hell are you?" Ron yelled, knowing that Jack could have gone out for a run or a bike ride or a plain old walk. It just didn't seem like he would after getting this news though. And the bottles of Jack Daniel's were a pretty good indicator that he was temporarily off his training regimen. Then Ron saw the curtain fluttering by the open sliding glass door leading out to the patio. He headed that way. Jack was sitting outside, a cigar in his right hand, an empty shot glass on the table in front of him, and a half-full bottle of Miller Lite in his left hand.

It was a tall table with tall chairs, and Ron's first thought was that Jack looked so unstable that he might fall off his chair.

"Jack, didn't you hear me calling you?"

Jack ignored the question. "Sit down, Ronnie." He slurred the words. "No, better yet, why don't you walk out to the kitchen and get the full bottle of Jack and a couple of beers from the refrigerator. I'd do it myself but I'm a little under the weather right now."

Ron figured it wasn't the right time for a lecture, and if he wanted to get Jack to open up and let the poison out, he was going to have to sit with him for a while and share a drink or two. Jack would eventually tell him, he knew that. He only hoped he had the right answers when the discussion started. His friend needed help but he wasn't in the right frame of mind to listen. Ron had to get through to him somehow.

In the meantime, he headed for the kitchen to get the beer and the whiskey.

A couple of beers and one shot later, the real discussion began.

"Did you ever make a monumental mistake, Ronnie? One you didn't think you'd recover from?"

"Tons of 'em."

"I'm not talking about failed businesses and shit like that. I'm talking about something that goes to your core, that affects who you are."

"I know what you're talking about, Jack. I left my first wife and my son. He grew up without me around. That was a fundamental, monumental fuckup that I still regret to this day."

"How do you deal with it?"

"I can't change it. I just have to go on and I have to make up for it in some way with the people I meet. I have to give more of myself because I didn't in the past."

"That's it?"

"I tried to make it up to my son but he resented me. We're a little better now but it'll never be great. At least I'm still here. At least I can help him if he needs it."

"I don't have that option. I caused a woman to lose her life and her father to lose his daughter after already losing his wife. How do you remedy that?"

"You didn't cause anybody to lose their life, Jack. You represented a man who you believed was innocent. Apache County set him free, for Christ's sake, not you. They could have prosecuted him for that attempted murder. A judge could have put him away for another twenty-five years but the county chose not to do so."

"I represented a serial killer, Ronnie." Jack leaned over the table until his face was almost in Ron's. He started to fall off his chair. Ron caught him and straightened him back up. He kept talking as if he hadn't noticed what had happened. "Danni told me not to do it. She told me I was getting into something I knew nothing about. I refused to listen."

"Think about all the people you've helped, Jack, because you didn't prejudge, you didn't listen to anybody—you relied only on the facts. You're not perfect, my friend. You were bound to make a mistake. If there weren't people like you, Jack, a lot of innocent folks would have been executed."

"You don't understand, Ronnie. This was a serial killer." He leaned in and almost toppled over again. Ron knew it wouldn't be long before he was sleeping it off.

"I'm sure I don't understand, Jack. It was an awesome responsibility. But it's over. You need to find a purpose again. Maybe you won't be able to do this death row stuff for a while, but you can do something for the greater good. Something worthwhile. That's who you are. Wasn't it you who told me you have to give back to the universe to even things out?"

"Don't hit me with that garbage now. And you're still not getting it. I'm not talking about responsibility, I'm talking about arrogance.

Why did I think I was smarter than the people who put this guy away?"

"I'm sure you had your reasons, and they were good reasons. I've met a lot of arrogant bastards in my time and you're not one of them. You're the opposite of that."

Just then the front doorbell rang. *The doorbell*, Ron thought to himself. *Why didn't I think of that?* He knew the answer. He'd knocked on doors his whole life. There weren't any tenement apartments in New York with doorbells.

"I'll get it," Ron said.

"No, no, I'll get it," Jack said as he once again almost fell off the chair.

"Then I'll go with you," Ron said as he caught Jack on his right side and steadied him. Together they went to the front door. Ron opened it to find two Oakville police officers standing there.

"Officers, can I help you?" Jack said.

"Are you Jack Tobin?"

"In the flesh."

It was apparent to the two cops that Jack was drunk since he was swaying back and forth, and Ron was still holding his right arm.

"We have been asked to give you a message by Assistant Chief Martin. He says to tell you that you might want to go back home," one of the officers said.

"What did he mean by that statement?" Ron asked.

"I don't know," the same cop answered.

The other cop spoke for the first time. "A lot of people in this town are angry about what happened and they blame him," he said, pointing at Jack.

That explanation didn't make a lot of sense to Ron. Cops coming to give a message to somebody to get out of town because the town folk were angry. It sounded like a scene from an old Western.

"Where's Sam Jeffries? Why didn't he tell you to deliver the message?" Ron asked.

"Nobody's seen him since he got the news. I was the one who told him. He didn't take it well," the officer who had spoken first told Ron.

"What do you mean nobody's seen him? Is he home?"

"No sir," the first cop continued. "His son is looking for him, too. Assistant Chief Martin is very concerned."

"Maybe he's in Miami making funeral arrangements."

"No, sir. The son took care of that. They're shipping the body here for the funeral and the burial."

So that was it. They weren't worried about Jack. They were worried that Sam Jeffries might kill Jack. At least that made sense.

"Would you give Chief Jeffries my apologies?" Jack muttered. "Tell him I'm going to kill that son-of-a-bitch client of mine myself."

"I wouldn't be making statements like that if I were you, Mr. Tobin," the second cop said.

To Ron's relief, Jack didn't answer. Jack didn't need to be making any more statements to the police in his current condition. Ron needed to end this conversation.

"Thank you, officers," he said. "And thank Assistant Chief Martin for his concern. I can assure you Jack will be relocating based on his advice."

Ron politely but firmly closed the door.

"What was that about? I'm not relocating," Jack said.

"I think you should. That was about Assistant Chief Martin telling you in a very subtle way that Sam Jeffries is temporarily out of his mind and that he may come looking for you."

"He should."

"Come on, Jack, stop that nonsense. Look, I've got another condo about two miles from here on the east side of town. It's fully furnished. You just need to take your clothes. Why don't we do that right now."

"Okay," Jack said to Ron's complete surprise. He'd expected an argument. "I need a change of scenery anyway," Jack continued, still slurring his words.

"I'll drive you over," Ron said. "And I'll pick you up in the morning and drive you to get your car."

It was an excuse to check on him the next morning.

CHAPTER FORTY-TWO

Two days after she returned from Boulder and a day before the funeral of Kathleen Jeffries, Danni received a surprise guest at her home. She opened the door and there stood Sam Jeffries, rumpled and disheveled with at least a three days' growth on his face, maybe more.

"Sam, come on in." She gave him a long hug after he entered the house. "I'm so sorry for your troubles, Sam."

"Thanks, Danni. You know the funeral is tomorrow."

"Yeah, they called me from the station and told me. That's pretty quick."

"I want it over with. I've got things to do."

"Why don't you come in and sit down, Sam. I'll get you some coffee."

"Thanks."

Danni had an intimate little table for two in her kitchen. They sat there to drink their coffee.

"How are you doing?" she asked, knowing at least part of the answer. Sam's hands were shaking, which told her he'd been doing what cops did in times of trouble—drowning his sorrows in alcohol.

"Well, you don't need to take my guns if that's what you're asking. I've had my moments but now I'm focused."

Danni was pretty sure she knew what he was focused on, but she felt obligated to ask the question.

"On what?"

"On finding Tom Felton and killing him. I'd like to cut his fuckin' balls off and stick them in his mouth and while he was choking slowly slit his throat, but I want to keep my job, so I'll have to settle for a bullet to the head or the heart, whichever is most convenient."

"Sounds good."

"I'd like to do the same for your boy Tobin."

"He's not my boy."

"He was at one time, Danni. You were head over heels for him. Don't deny it."

"What's your point, Sam?"

"My point is that he's a piece of shit and I'd like to spare the world his presence as well if I could get away with it."

"Is that what you came here to tell me?"

"No. I've been thinking about this constantly, even when I was so drunk I could hardly move. Felton's a smart boy. He had ten years in a small cell to figure out there was only a small group of people that had the ability to fuck him over. He likes to kill women so he went after my daughter first. I assume you figured this part out already."

"I have."

"And Hannah is safe?"

"She is."

"That leaves you, Danni. He's coming for you as sure as I'm sitting here. He's not going to back off. Killing the women of the people who fucked him, or, in your case, the woman who might have directly fucked him over, is probably the ultimate jolly for this sick bastard."

"Are you trying to scare the shit out of me, Sam?"

"Absolutely not. You were a homicide cop for fifteen of your twenty years. You know all this shit already. I'm here to ask you if I can stay here at night and wait for him. You can stay here, too, if you like. I won't be sleeping. Or you could go to my house. I want to catch this bastard, Danni. I need to catch him."

Danni understood the sentiment all too well. Her feelings mirrored those of Sam Jeffries although Sam's hunger was so much greater than her own. She would have let Sam do what he wanted but she just didn't agree with his reasoning.

"I want you to catch him, Sam, I really do, but you can't do it this way."

"Why not?"

"Felton is smart—you said so yourself. You won't be able to get in and out of this house every day without him seeing you. He wants me alone."

"Then I'll stay here all the time."

"It won't work, Sam. He'll know you're here."

Sam started rubbing his hair with his hands and then working them around to his neck. He was like a big agitated grizzly. If Danni hadn't known him so well, she would have been frightened. He was ready to snap. She needed to give him something.

"Where do you think he'll come at me from?" she asked.

"The woods would be my guess."

The street in front of Danni's house was well lit and her home was bordered on both sides by other single-family homes. She had a small backyard with nothing but thick woods behind it. There was a road on the other side of the woods. A person could enter from the road and walk for a half mile or so and exit in Danni's backyard. It was the logical place for Felton to come from.

"I think you're right, Sam. So if you weren't here waiting for Felton, where would be your next best spot?"

"The road on the other side of the woods."

"Exactly."

"But there's no place to set up a surveillance back there. The other side of the road is all meadow."

"I know. The best you could do is drive by—maybe do a circle of the front of the house and back by the road. You'd have to use unmarked cars and you'd have to change cars frequently. We don't want to scare him away. We want him to come."

"That's hit or miss."

"I know, but I'm going to be waiting for him every night, too, Sam. I'm going to sleep during the day. If a shot goes off or if you hear anything, it's nice to know you'll come running."

It was obvious Sam didn't like that option. He was rubbing his upper arms with his hands and then rubbing his hands together.

"I don't like it. You're too exposed."

Danni knew it wasn't about her being exposed. He'd already acknowledged that she could manage the risk. Sam wanted the kill, plain and simple.

"I could hide in the woods," he said.

"Sam, you are a big man and I hope you don't take this the wrong way, but you're not in great shape. You wouldn't be hiding in the woods, you'd be telling him you're coming—telegraphing your every move. It might be a good idea to put somebody from the SWAT team in there, though."

He didn't like that option.

"I don't want the department involved. Too many people know about this, it'll get all fucked up."

That wasn't true either. Sam was the chief of police, for Christ's sake. He could easily take a SWAT team member, give him the assignment, and swear him to silence. He didn't look or act like the chief of police though, sitting there at her little kitchen table.

He looked like a troubled, unstable man.

CHAPTER FORTY-THREE

Jack didn't know where he was when he woke up the next morning. The bedroom walls were the same dull off-white color as Ron's condo and they were bare of pictures like Ron's place, but the room was smaller, the sheets and the comforter were a different color, and the bed felt strange. Then he heard movement in another room.

Oh my God, he thought. *What the hell did I do last night?*

He didn't move, though. He stayed in bed and thought it through as he did with everything. It all came back slowly—the police; the decision to move to a new place; the drive over with Ron. *But who the hell was in the other room?*

He saw the knob on the door turn. He started to tense up. Then Ron walked into the room carrying a cup.

"I made you some coffee," he said. "Cream, no sugar, right?"

"That's it."

"How are you feeling?"

"How do I look?"

"Like shit."

"Well, I feel ten times worse."

"Maybe you ought to think about laying off of the hard stuff."

"Give me a chance to wake up and have my coffee before you start with the lecture, okay?"

"Sure. Anything you want, Jack. I'll be in the other room. I don't have much time, so if you want me to take you to your car, you need to get ready now."

Fifteen minutes later they were making the short drive to the old condo in Ron's white Lexus SUV in silence.

"Sorry I snapped at you, Ronnie," Jack finally said. "You've been a great friend to me."

"No need to apologize," Ron said, although it was exactly what he'd been waiting for.

"You're right, too. I need to stop wallowing in self-pity and do something."

"I think you should get out of Oakville, Jack. What that cop said last night is true—there are a lot of people in this town who are not thinking favorably of you right now."

"I probably should but I'm not leaving town. You said something last night that I've been thinking about. I need to get a sense of purpose again—focus on something else—and I know just what that something else is."

"What's that, Jack?"

"Finding Thomas Felton."

"Jesus, Jack, every cop in the state is looking for him. You're a great lawyer, but what makes you think you can add anything to this manhunt?"

"I know Felton better than any of them. I've spent some quality time with him in the last few weeks. I think I know what he's going to do."

"Do you want to share that information with your old buddy?"

"Only if you swear you won't tell a soul, except for Danni. I want you to tell Danni part of it."

"And what's 'it'?"

"He's going to try and kill Danni."

"How can you be sure?"

"Look, he told me that he couldn't wait. He meant he couldn't wait to kill again. The guy gave up millions of dollars. Yes, he's a serial killer, and he wants, probably needs, to kill again, but that doesn't explain it all. He was in prison for ten years. He has a good idea of the people who could have set him up, and Danni is right behind Sam Jeffries on that list. That's why he killed Sam's daughter.

"Danni's daughter, Hannah, could have been his next target, but Hannah presents logistical problems for him. And even if he drove out to Boulder, he'd know that by now Hannah's gone. That brings him right back to Danni."

"That would be suicide."

"He doesn't care at this point. He wants to kill. He wants revenge. He needs it like a junkie needs his fix."

"Do you think Danni's figured this out?"

"I don't know, but she needs to know and I want you to tell her."

"And what about Sam Jeffries?"

"He may have figured it out, too."

"That means the whole damn police department knows."

"Maybe."

"Maybe? He's the police chief, for Christ's sake."

"I wish you wouldn't say that," Jack said.

"Say what?"

"For Christ's sake."

"Okay. He's the friggin' police chief, dammit!"

Jack looked at Ron and burst out laughing. It was classic Ron.

Ron started laughing, too. "Where was I?" Ron finally said. "Oh yeah, and what about the FBI? They're probably already in on this, too."

"I don't think so. I'll bet they're still in Miami investigating that murder to establish some kind of a link. Then they'll be here."

"Still, there are a lot more people with a lot more expertise than you who can handle this problem. What are you going to add to this?"

"I don't know, Ron. I don't know. But I've got to try."

CHAPTER FORTY-FOUR

Danni had her plan in place. She was certain Felton was going to come at night so she planned on catnapping during the day and staying up all night. It wasn't much more elaborate than that. She was going to make a dummy body in the bed and stick a comfortable chair in the walk-in closet where she was going to sit and wait, a flashlight in her left hand, her gun in her right. Lights were out at ten o'clock. Before that she would parade about the house with the curtains open, letting the world know she was there. She knew Felton wouldn't shoot her through the window. He would want to be up close with a knife so he could watch *and feel* the life ooze out of her. That was going to be his downfall.

She'd finally convinced Sam to patrol the area rather than hang out in the woods. He wouldn't have made it in the woods for any period of time in his physical condition, and he most certainly would have telegraphed his whereabouts. Now, at least, he was watching somewhere from a car. Danni figured he'd be out there all day as well as during the night. It wasn't just conjecture. A friend at the department told her he had taken a leave of absence for an indefinite duration.

She was still worried about his emotional stability. And something else, *someone* else, added to that concern—Jack. Ron had called her and told her that Jack believed that Felton was going to come after her. It wasn't news to her but she appreciated the fact that Jack was concerned. Her animosity toward him had dissipated somewhat. Henry's actions had certainly contributed to her change of heart, but she also realized that when Jack had read Felton's criminal file, he had been presented with a set of facts that had led him to only one conclusion—that his client had been set up. He didn't listen to her when she told him to stay out of it, but it was his job to investigate the facts and test the validity of the police and the prosecution's case. He wasn't supposed to listen to her. She was never going to tell him, but she finally understood things from his perspective.

Now Jack was out there somewhere, according to Ron. If Jack ever crossed paths with Sam Jeffries, she didn't know what would happen. Sam might snap and shoot Jack on the spot. Considering Sam's state of mind, it was not a far-fetched possibility.

Jack had his own plans that he did not share with anybody, including Ron. He knew Danni's house and the surrounding neighborhood from the brief period of time when they had been together. After circling the neighborhood a few times to re-familiarize himself with everything, he too became convinced that Felton would attack from the woods. It was the only undetected avenue for entry and escape. So Jack decided he was going to stay in the woods.

He bought himself a pup tent and a sleeping bag. He didn't know what the police presence was going to be like, but he figured they would probably be checking any parked cars in that area and that they would also set up surveillance at the entry to the woods behind Danni's backyard, so, before daybreak, he rode his bike from the new condo and entered the woods a half a mile farther down from the area directly behind Danni's house. It was a longer walk and the woods were thick, but if he could do this, Felton could as well. He found a place to hide the bike not far from his entry point, under some fallen tree trunks that he covered with dead leaves. Then he walked to the area directly behind Danni's house, a walk of about twenty minutes, and started searching for a spot for his tent. It took him a while but eventually he found a hollow, maybe about three feet deep, that abutted a tree. He set the tent up and covered it with leaves and put a log in front of the entrance. Even in the daytime, he was sure it was undetectable.

Like Danni, Jack figured Felton would make his move at night, so he, too, planned on catnapping during the day and staying up all night. Unfortunately, at night he would have to stand up to look out over the log to be able to see all of Danni's backyard. Since he would be exposed then, he knew he had to be extremely careful. As an amateur, he also knew he would have to plan for any and every contingency. For example, on a moonless night it would be impossible to detect someone crossing the yard, so the next day Jack went to a gun store and purchased some night vision goggles. Every morning well before sunrise, he took his bike and bought his supplies for the day, mostly water and sandwiches, and sneaked back before the sun came up.

Contrary to his drunken statement to the police, Jack planned on catching Felton and turning him in. In the event that that plan didn't work, he hoped he could shoot the Sig Sauer straight.

Sam Jeffries didn't tell anybody at the police department that he thought Tom Felton was going to try and kill Danni Jansen. He didn't get a SWAT team member to hide out in the woods either as Danni had suggested. He wanted Felton all to himself.

In Sam's mind, he was going to park the car somewhere by the entrance to the woods behind Danni's house during the day and just sit and watch. In the evening he was going to drive around. He'd put the arm on a few friends who had second cars and had access to four different cars to drive.

Things didn't work out the way Sam envisioned, however. He'd always been a large man with huge arms and a powerful build, but in recent years he had been inactive and had gained too much weight. Consequently, his knees and his back ached with a minimum amount of stress. He could make the tour of Danni's neighborhood every half hour at night, but sitting in the car all day lasted less than a day. The pain was just too much. His backup plan consisted of driving up to the woods every hour or so and taking a very slow walk through the brush and the bramble up to Danni's backyard.

Jack heard Sam coming on his very first trip long before he saw him. Sam was huffing and puffing and making a racket trying to wade through the thicket. Felton would have been long gone at the first sound. Still, Sam was not going to give up.

With all of the activity going on around here, Jack thought, *Felton's going to have to be awfully committed.* Three people were absolutely counting on that commitment.

CHAPTER FORTY-FIVE

By the third day, Jack had settled into his routine somewhat. It was difficult to catnap during the day and even harder to stay awake all night, although the crickets chirping incessantly with the occasional accompaniment of a hoot owl did their part to keep him awake. The creatures of the night helped as well. He saw a slew of raccoons and possums, even a few armadillos. The animal that caused him the most concern, however, was a coyote. Jack saw him the first night, silently slinking by, his body close to the ground. Jack put his right hand on the Sig Sauer, hoping again that he would shoot it straight if the necessity should arise, but the coyote just kept going. He actually turned and looked right into Jack's eyes as he passed—a kind of "welcome to the neighborhood" look. By the third night, Jack's nerves had calmed. He was getting used to the place and, as a result, he constantly found himself waking up.

I've got to do better than this, he told himself each time.

There were other problems as well. The sandwiches were making him sick and constipated, and his body ached constantly. He was in excellent shape, but he wasn't a young man anymore. Lying on the cold hard ground combined with inactivity was taking its toll. On the fourth day, he took some time before he went shopping and went for a short run and stretched for about a half hour. It made him feel so much better. Then he bought a big bunch of fruit along with his sandwiches. He just hoped the fruit didn't give him the runs. Having the runs in the woods did not fall under the category of a good thing. In an abundance of caution, he put toilet paper on his list of things to buy the next morning.

The fourth night brought even a bigger problem. Jack was standing up just outside his pup tent looking at Danni's backyard over the tree trunk that covered the entrance, wearing his night vision goggles. He didn't remember falling asleep. All he knew was that at some point late in the evening he woke up to the feeling of cold hard steel pressed against his left temple.

"Bang!" a voice said.

Jack recognized it right away.

"Danni?"

"Jack, what the hell are you doing out here?" she asked, withdrawing the gun from his temple.

"I'm trying to catch my client."

It was true but it sounded funny. Danni *almost* laughed.

"You could get yourself killed. If I hadn't recognized you, I might have shot you."

"Yeah well, I'm still learning how to be an Indian."

Danni didn't say anything. She seemed to be debating something in her own mind.

"Why don't you come into the house and have some coffee," she said, not waiting for an answer as she headed for the house.

Jack didn't hesitate. It took him a few minutes to stumble out of the hollow, but he followed her inside.

Danni was already loading the coffeemaker when he arrived. It felt weird being back in this house under the circumstances. The last time he had been there, he and Danni were having a torrid love affair. Now a killer might be stalking her.

"Have a seat," she said, motioning to the little table where she and Sam Jeffries had had coffee just a few days before.

Jack sat down. He didn't know what to say to her so he didn't say anything. He just watched her as she made the coffee. She'd been at the condo to dress him down for taking Felton's case but under those circumstances, he hadn't taken the time to look at her as he did now. She looked great—hadn't changed a bit in two years. It was funny but he still felt connected to her. He'd known many women who were probably considered more beautiful than Danni but he hadn't been attracted to them. *What does that?* he asked himself. *How can I instantly feel connected to this woman all over again?* Maybe it was her personality. Maybe it was her strength of character. She was so straightforward and direct. Those things were certainly part of it but Jack was sure there was something else, something in the universe that was unrecognizable to humans, that attracted certain people to each other. Of course, Danni was no longer attracted to him, he was sure. She probably wanted to shoot him. Maybe that's why she invited him in.

"Do you want something to eat?" she asked. "I've got some apple pie."

"That would be great." Four days in the woods was enough to make him salivate over the thought of apple pie.

Danni set the pie and two mugs of coffee on the table and sat down across from him. Jack was still speechless so he filled his mouth with pie. Now he had an excuse not to talk and something to say when he was done.

"This pie is delicious."

"Thank you."

Another bite, a few chews, and he was cornered. Danni wasn't making it easy for him. She could have made some small talk but she didn't. He decided to wade right in.

"Why are you being so nice to me?"

"You mean besides the fact that you're putting your life in danger to protect me from a serial killer?"

"A serial killer I freed from death row."

"Don't give yourself too much credit, Jack. I think the supreme court and Apache County had something to do with your client going free."

"You know what I mean."

"Yeah, I do. You set the process in motion because you found some irregularities in the way he was arrested and prosecuted."

"You told me to let it go and I didn't listen to you."

"You weren't supposed to listen to me. I wasn't answering your questions; I was just telling you to leave it alone."

She was right but he couldn't believe her attitude.

"I put your daughter in danger."

"There you go again thinking you control the universe. You represented a client to the best of your ability. And my daughter is safe, by the way, because a man you freed from death row is protecting her."

Jack was dumbfounded. He stuffed another hunk of apple pie into his mouth. They sat there in silence for a few minutes, Danni sipping her coffee and Jack steadily making the apple pie disappear.

"Do you want some more?" she asked.

"Sure." The woods were looming in the background. He wasn't going to pass up a second piece of the best pie he'd ever eaten, or so it seemed at the moment.

"I see Sam Jeffries in the woods every day at least two or three times," he said.

Danni was cutting the pie. "Don't ever let him see you, Jack. He doesn't feel the same way about things as I do."

"Nor should he."

"Let's not go back there again. Just stay away from him. He's not himself these days. I shudder to think what would happen if he came upon you like I did. Speaking of which, I can't talk you out of going back out there again, can I?"

Jack finished chewing his newest piece of pie.

"Nope. This is something I've got to do."

Danni certainly understood that sentiment. She reached down into a cabinet below the sink off to the right and pulled out a thermos. She poured the rest of the coffee into it.

"Try and stay awake out there. Remember who you're dealing with."

"I can't forget," he said, taking the thermos from her and heading for the door.

"Thanks for the coffee. I'll bring this back in the morning."

"Just leave it by the back door. I'll refill it for you," she said.

Jack looked at her. "Really?"

"Don't read anything into it. If you're going to be out there, I want you to be alert."

CHAPTER FORTY-SIX

Felton finally showed up on a Sunday morning, debunking the predictions of all three of his antagonists who were sure it was going to be a nighttime assault.

Jack had already made his early morning run and had been back at the pup tent for about an hour. He'd lain down for a short nap and for some reason, he could never say why, he woke up and immediately stood up to look at Danni's backyard. He saw a figure dressed in black from head to toe enter the woods *from the backyard!*

Oh my God—Danni! he thought. *He's coming back from her house. What the hell has he done to her? I've got to go to her.*

He wasn't even sure it was Felton but he had a way to find out. Jack had Felton's number in his phone since Felton had called him at the condo to tell him that he no longer wanted to file the claims bill. *Two nights ago* Jack had called the number to see if Felton still had the phone. Somebody answered but didn't speak.

"Tom, are you there? This is Jack."

Felton never did say a word but Jack got the information he needed. He knew how to contact Felton.

Now, as he stood in his bunker paralyzed with fear, wondering what Felton had done to Danni, wondering whether the man in black was even Felton, wondering what he was going to do—go after Felton or go to Danni—he decided to call the number. He

pressed Felton's name in his cell phone directory and watched the
man who was now in the woods moving slowly toward the road. He
was maybe a hundred yards away from the bunker now. Jack didn't
hear a ring, but he saw the man first look toward his right pants
pocket then reach his hand in and pull out a phone and look at it.
He didn't answer it; he didn't need to.

Jack had his man and he made his decision in that instant. Whatever happened to Danni had already happened. This might be his
only chance to capture Felton. He sprang from his foxhole, taking
one last look toward the house. *I'll be there as soon as I can*, he
thought to himself and took off after Felton, the Sig Sauer in his
right hand. He closed the gap rather quickly since Felton wasn't
running. When he was within fifty feet or so and had an unob-
structed view of the man, Jack raised the gun and called out.

"Tom, this is Jack Tobin. I want you to stop."

Jack continued to move forward slowly, his gun aimed at the target. Felton looked back once, saw the gun and saw Jack coming and
started to slow down. For a moment, Jack thought he was going to
give himself up. Then Felton suddenly wheeled around, and Jack
saw something in his hand—it looked like a small gun.

"Don't do it, Tom."

Felton raised his arm. Jack had no idea if he was preparing to
fire or not. He had to make a split-second decision. He fired the
Sig Sauer. Everything after that seemed to happen in slow motion.
The bullet hit Felton in the chest. He knew it because Felton fell
straight back, his legs and feet flying in the air. He lay motionless on
the ground. Jack did not move toward him, though. Once the crisis
was over and Felton was down, his attention immediately turned to
Danni.

He ran in the opposite direction toward the backyard and Danni's
house. He saw her in his mind as she had stood in the kitchen just
two days before, smiling at him and telling him to be careful and

stay awake. He finally reached the back door. It seemed as if it took an eternity to get there. The door was locked.

"Danni, Danni!" he yelled as he banged.

When nobody answered, he took the heel of the gun and prepared to break the closest window. Just as he was about to swing his arm, the door opened and Danni stepped out.

"What's going on, Jack? I was sleeping and thought I heard a gunshot. Are you okay?"

Jack's face broke into the biggest smile.

"I couldn't be better now that I see you standing there."

"Was that a gunshot I heard?"

"Yeah. It was Felton. I shot him. I thought he was leaving your house. He's in the woods out there."

"Is he dead?"

"I don't know. I came to see about you."

"Don't tell me you left him there without making sure he was dead."

"I'm pretty sure he's not going anywhere," Jack said.

"Wait here. I'm going to go get my gun," she said as she retreated back into the house.

It was ten o'clock on Sunday morning when Sam Jeffries started into the woods to do his first walkabout of the day. Normally he was out earlier, but he'd had a few too many the night before and decided to sleep in. His walks into the woods were getting to be a routine and Sam was focused on negotiating through the trees and the brush rather than doing any observational investigative work. Then he heard voices and a shot directly ahead. Sam took off like the high-school running back he had once been. Branches were scratching his face and his body as he ran along but he hardly noticed. Felton was out there and Felton had killed his wife and daughter. He was so focused that he almost tripped over Felton's body, stopping at the last minute. Felton was lying on his back. Sam could see blood flowing from a bullet hole almost dead center in his chest. The face was untouched, but it was bearded and filthy and it took Sam a few minutes to realize who it was.

"Shit!" he said aloud to the trees and the wind. He was too late. Felton was dead. He'd been robbed of the opportunity to kill the man who had murdered his wife and daughter. *Danni had to be the one who did this. But where is she?* First things first. He called the station and made his report. He wanted a forensic team out there on the double along with a team of homicide detectives. Now that Felton was dead, he wanted to make sure his department handled everything efficiently.

After he made the call, he started looking at the scene and the surrounding terrain in greater detail. He removed a small pair of binoculars from his pants pocket and focused them on Danni's backyard. If Danni had done the killing, as he suspected, why had she left the scene? He caught a glimpse of someone banging on Danni's door. It was a man, a fairly tall man, with speckled gray hair.

Who is that? he asked himself, unable to pinpoint the man's identity through the small field glasses. *Maybe he's the shooter.* Then he saw the man take something out of his pants pocket—it looked like a gun, but he couldn't be sure—and reach his arm back as if he were going to break one of the back windows. Just then Danni came out of the house and started talking to the man. *She knows him!* Sam said to himself. *Who the fuck is it?*

He could have continued to watch them, or even better, he could have walked toward them and maybe gotten some answers, but he decided against it. His people would be there soon and he wanted to do his own investigation before they arrived. Danni and her friend weren't going to get far in the next few minutes. Besides, he couldn't have chased them if he'd wanted to. The old tank was empty.

He hesitated to move the body but he saw that Felton had a small backpack on. Putting his rubber gloves on first, he rolled Felton over rather easily and opened the backpack. Inside were some clothes, a toothbrush, toothpaste, and some papers. *Nice to know a serial killer brushes his teeth*, Sam thought. He perused the papers. One set was a document called a claims bill that had a lot of legal language in it and another set was a document called a contingency fee agreement. Sam scanned them quickly. The claims bill was basically a request by Felton for twenty million dollars from the Florida legislature for his wrongful incarceration. The contingency fee agreement was an agreement to give Jack Tobin one-third of whatever he got from the legislature on the claims bill.

So that's how Tobin does it, he thought to himself. *He puts himself out to the public as this great human being, and then he makes his money on the back end if he's successful. What a slimy son of a bitch.* Then he started laughing to himself thinking about all the money Tobin had lost when Felton killed again. It was a morbid laugh since Felton's victim had been his own daughter. *Serves the prick right. He makes his money getting maggots like this set free, it's only fair that he should get fucked good once in a while. He probably wanted to kill Felton himself. Too late, Tobin, Danni beat you to it.*

Wait a minute! Now he knew who the tall man was who had been banging on Danni's door. *Tobin!* He started putting the pieces together. *Tobin killed Felton. Danni never would have left the scene.*

Jeffries made his other big discovery while he was kneeling on the ground stuffing the papers back into the knapsack. There was a gun in the grass right next to Felton's right hand. He picked it up, careful not to smudge any fingerprints that might be on the handle, and looked it over. It was a small 22 caliber Ruger. *Almost missed it*, Sam thought to himself. *Must be slipping.*

He didn't realize how much he had slipped until he heard the moan. He looked down at the body and saw Felton make a jerking motion with his head and right arm. He'd never checked for a pulse!

He looked up at the blue sky leaking through the tall pines. "Thank you, God," he whispered.

Felton moaned again. He opened his eyes and looked at Sam, apparently not focusing too well. "Help me," he whispered to the man whose daughter and wife he had so brutally murdered.

Sam grabbed his head and jerked it toward him so that his face and Felton's were almost touching. "Look at me, fuckface! You killed my wife and daughter. You're asking the wrong person for help."

Felton did look at him. Sam could see the recognition in his eyes—the fear. He was so thankful for this moment.

"I had to," Felton whispered. "No control."

"Well then, you'll understand what I have to do—for my wife, my daughter, and all those other people you murdered—you piece of shit. I only wish I had more time."

There was a good-sized rock off to Sam's right. He reached for it and slid it in place under Felton's head.

"I hope this hurts real bad," he said just before he smashed the man's head on the rock over and over again. Blood oozed out and started leeching into the dirt and the grass, and the little life that had been there clearly left Felton's body. Still, Sam didn't stop until he heard the sirens in the distance—and something else: leaves rustling in the woods. Somebody was coming from the direction of Danni's house.

He stood up quickly then, taking off the rubber gloves and stuffing them into his pants pockets as he moved, fielded the binoculars, and looked through the trees. Danni *and Tobin* were running toward him.

Sam picked up the revolver off the ground where he had laid it while he attended to Felton, held it in the palm of his hand and looked at it for several seconds as he continued to listen to Danni and Jack rustling through the woods, getting closer and closer.

Then he smiled to himself as he placed the gun in his inside jacket pocket.

"Stop!" Sam yelled to Danni and Jack, putting his hand up when they were about twenty feet away. "I've got a dead body here. It's Felton."

Danni and Jack both stopped for a moment.

"We know," Danni said. "At least, we knew Felton was shot. We didn't know he was dead."

"How did you know?" Sam asked.

"I shot him," Jack said.

Just then the sirens stopped.

"I want you two to stay right there. This is a crime scene and my forensics team is going to be here in a moment."

The team arrived at the scene a few minutes later: three men and two women, accompanied by two male homicide detectives. The forensics people didn't need any direction. They saw the dead body and went to work.

Sam addressed the detectives.

"That's Jack Tobin over there. He says he was the shooter. I want you to read him his rights and then take a statement if he'll give you one. Take a statement from Danni, too. Same procedure. I know she's one of us but I want it done by the book."

"Jack says Felton had a gun," Danni said to Sam.

"I want someone to look for a gun," Sam said to the people on the ground. "You don't happen to know what kind of gun, do you?" he asked Jack.

"No," Jack said. "I was about fifty feet away."

"But you're sure it was a gun?"

"Pretty sure."

"Pretty sure?"

"Yeah, like I said."

Sam turned to the two detectives. "No need for you to be here. Why don't you take them down to the station and interview them there."

"What's going on, Sam?" Danni asked.

"Nothing, Danni. It's standard procedure—you know that. I'll have this team scour the area. We'll find the gun if it's here. Then you and Mr. Tobin will be able to go home."

CHAPTER FORTY-SEVEN

By the time they started for the police vehicles, Jack had made the decision to stop talking. He knew he shouldn't have said anything to begin with, but even experienced trial lawyers made mistakes, especially when they were innocent and wanted to help the investigation. When he heard his own words that he was "pretty sure" Felton had a gun and then heard Sam Jeffries repeat those words as a question, he instinctively knew he had said too much. So he sat in a small room for two hours across from a homicide detective named Cal. Cal asked questions, and Jack smiled and refused to answer.

"Do you want a lawyer?" Cal asked. "Because we'll get you one."

I'll bet you will, Jack thought to himself as he smiled at Cal and said, "No thanks."

Jack knew a slew of criminal lawyers, but he was not sure who to call or even if he wanted somebody at this point. At least Cal knew enough not to give him the usual line that things would go easier with him if he started talking.

Sam Jeffries had not yet decided what he was going to do with the gun. He wanted to let things play out for a bit. He was disappointed that he hadn't gotten the chance to shoot Felton, but that had been a long shot from the start. At least he had gotten in a few final blows. Now he had the opportunity to get Tobin, the prick who'd gotten Felton out of jail—*for money*—so he could kill Sam's daughter. It was a dangerous game. He'd have to beat Tobin in his own bailiwick—the courtroom. But he had nothing left to lose. He'd lost too much already. And it would be such sweet revenge to outwit the now infamous Jack Tobin.

His crew at the scene had already called and informed him that they had found a pup tent and some clothes, food, and a credit card with Jack's name on it.

So he was staying out there waiting for Felton. How do I spin this? Or can I? I'll just wait and see what else they come up with. In the meantime I'll work on Tobin.

He made his first move while Jack was sitting in the interrogation room.

He made sure nobody was in the observation room before walking in and tapping Cal on the shoulder.

"You can take a break, Cal." Cal didn't need any prompting. He left immediately.

"How are you doing, Jack?" Sam said when the two men were alone.

Jack didn't know what to make of the situation—Sam Jeffries being nice to him. Something was wrong.

"Fine."

"Listen, I'll have you out of here in no time. We just need to finish up some paperwork. Cal didn't bust your balls too badly, did he?"

"No. We had a nice conversation."

"A little one-sided, I'm sure. I want you to know that I've got people scouring those woods for Felton's gun. They'll be out there until dark and if they don't find it, they'll be back again tomorrow morning. If we find the gun, I'll call you right away."

"Thanks, I appreciate that. I'm surprised that you're even talking to me."

"You did a job and you did it to the best of your ability. I've got an obligation to do the same thing. I don't hold you personally responsible for my daughter's death if that's what you're thinking."

"It is. I don't know that I wouldn't hold you responsible if our roles were reversed."

"You wouldn't. You'd be angry in the beginning like I was but eventually you'd get to the same place."

"I hope I would," Jack replied.

"Let me check on that paperwork and I'll get you out of here."

Sam was back minutes later.

"Everything is in order, Jack. I've just got a statement for you to sign. It contains the things you said at the scene."

"I'm not going to sign anything, Sam. You know what I said and I know what I said and there are plenty of witnesses if you need them. I'm just not going to sign anything."

"I understand. You're free to go. You can pick up your stuff at the front desk They recovered some stuff of yours in the woods, too, including a credit card. You ought to be more careful with things."

"I'll keep that in mind," Jack said. "Is Danni still here?"

"No, she left an hour ago."

As soon as he left the station, Jack called Danni to make sure she was okay. He didn't get an answer so he left her a message letting her know that he was out.

"I'm just calling to let you know I'm okay and to make sure that you are as well. Talk to you soon."

Jack had an ominous feeling. Sam Jeffries had been too nice. Things had gone too smoothly. He knew that if they didn't find Felton's gun, however, he had some problems. If the cops were going to quit looking for the gun at dark, he was going to be out there with a flashlight. The gun had to be there somewhere—*unless somebody took it!* Jack wasn't ready to consider that possibility yet. He wanted to search for himself first.

CHAPTER FORTY-EIGHT

Danni hadn't sat out on her back porch in the evening for over a week. She loved to sit out there at the end of the day with a cup of decaf—no caffeine after six—and listen to the sounds of the evening. It was still pleasant this time of year when the sun went down. There was a cool breeze, fireflies were out, the crickets weren't too bad. It was peaceful and serene. She looked out at the woods and let the tension release itself from her body.

She'd gone about the task of waiting for Felton's assault with the precision of a professional. Now that the danger had passed, she could finally acknowledge how stressful it all had been and take the necessary time to let it go.

She'd called Henry as soon as she left the station and talked to both him and Hannah and given them a synopsis of what had happened. The decision was made that Hannah would head back to school immediately. The semester was not yet lost. Hannah could still bone up and take her exams. Worrying about exams was a whole lot easier than worrying about the threat of a serial killer.

"How's Jack holding up?" Henry asked, surprised to learn that Jack and Danni had been together when the police arrived. When they had actually started talking to each other again was still a mystery to him. It didn't matter though. He'd find out soon enough.

"I haven't talked to him since we went to the station. They split us up after that. You know, police procedure and all that stuff. He left a message though saying that he was fine."

"There aren't any problems, are there?"

"Well, Jack said Felton had a gun and so far they haven't found the gun. I don't think it's a big deal, but at this point, I don't know."

"I'll head straight for Oakville after I drop Hannah off, just in case."

"Good idea. I'll see you when you get here. And Henry—"

"Yeah?"

"Thanks for taking care of my baby."

"It was a pleasure. We had fun. And Hannah had her cultural experience."

Danni laughed. "Good. I'll see you soon."

As she sat on her porch that evening thinking about the events of the day, Danni heard a loud noise from the woods on her far left. It was a quarter moon so there was some light in the backyard and she thought she saw a figure emerge from the thicket.

Calm down, she told herself. *The danger has passed.* Still, she checked to make sure she had her Glock with her.

The figure moved closer. Danni fingered her weapon.

"Is somebody out there?" she yelled forcefully.

"It's me," came the reply. She recognized the voice immediately. It was Jack.

Thirty seconds later he was standing on the porch, dressed in jeans and a black tee shirt and carrying a flashlight.

"What were you doing out there?" she asked.

"Looking for Felton's gun."

"All the way over there? Felton's body was straight out from this porch."

"I circled around. There are SWAT team guys out there. Sam told me that he was pulling everybody off when it got dark so I was going to do my own search. Then I find he didn't do what he said he was going to."

"'Sam?' Is that what you said? You guys are on a first-name basis all of a sudden."

"Yeah, well, we had a fairly long conversation this afternoon. He was calling me Jack and I was calling him Sam. It was a little strange, really."

"Very strange. Don't go trusting him, Jack. The man isn't himself. I don't care how he acts."

"I hear you. He already didn't do what he told me he was going to do, and I'm not sure why."

"Would you like a cup of decaf?"

"Sure."

Danni went inside and returned a minute later with a cup for Jack. Jack watched her the whole way.

"Have I told you lately how beautiful you are?" he asked.

Danni smiled. "No, you haven't."

"Well, you are."

"Thank you, Jack."

Jack just sat there looking at her for the longest time.

"What happened to us, Danni? I know we started too fast and I know I was too intense, but I really thought we had something."

Danni took a sip of her coffee and looked away toward the quarter moon.

"We did, Jack. We definitely had something. I could tell you that we started too fast and that it was too intense and maybe I didn't feel as strongly as you did. I could tell you that we had different perceptions. You know, perception is reality, and we had two different realities going on. But what gets in the way of all that is truth. There is always an absolute truth even if neither of us sees it."

"I have no idea what you're talking about."

"I know. I'm going to tell you something—something I didn't

admit to myself until just recently, although I think you've always known. It wasn't about us starting too fast or you feeling more than me. It was my fear. I can't have a relationship with you because I can't trust, and without trust I can't open my heart. I thought it might be different with you, but it wasn't and it had nothing to do with you, so don't beat yourself up about it. I just run up against a brick wall and I can't get through it. That's the truth."

"Can't we work on it together? Can't I help you?"

"I'm sorry, Jack. The only way anything is ever going to happen is if I get through that wall myself. At least I now see the problem. I'm not lying to myself anymore."

"We can still be friends."

"Of course we'll always be friends but not close friends. I'm not going to do that to you and I won't allow you to do it to yourself."

Jack smiled at her. "I still think you're beautiful."

"That's just your perception."

"No. It's the truth."

Danni had another unexpected visitor at midmorning the next day. She was just getting ready to go out and run some errands when there was a knock at the front door. When she answered it, Sam Jeffries was standing there.

"Do you have a minute, Danni? I want to talk to you about something."

"If you can make it quick, Sam. I was just heading out to run some errands."

She turned and walked back toward the kitchen. Sam followed her.

"It will only take a few minutes. I just want to tell you a few things we found out about your boy Tobin."

"He's not my boy. And stop using that term. It's offensive."

"I'm sorry. I didn't mean it that way. I thought he was your friend at least."

"Just get to it, Sam."

"All right, we found some things in Felton's possession that are very interesting."

They were once again sitting at the little table in the kitchen. Danni wasn't offering any coffee this time. Sam pulled out some papers from his jacket pocket. He handed some of them to Danni.

"This is a claims bill that Tobin was planning on filing on behalf of Felton. They were going to ask the Florida legislature for twenty million dollars."

Danni scanned the document. "So? It's my understanding that every prisoner who has been wrongfully imprisoned for an extended period of time files a claims bill—especially people on death row. They might ask for twenty million but they're not going to get it. What's your point?"

"Take a look at this." Jeffries gave her the other papers in his hands. As she perused them, he kept talking. "That's a contingency fee agreement giving Tobin one-third of whatever Felton recovered from the legislature. This guy is a fraud. He's making money on these death penalty cases. Maybe Felton wouldn't have gotten twenty million but if he got five, Tobin's payout is over a million and a half. You hit one of these babies every couple of years and you're making a lot of money for very little work. He's motivated to get people off because there's a payoff at the end and not for the noble reasons that he pretends. He's a phony."

"You said that already."

"It's worth saying twice."

Danni wouldn't admit it to Sam, but the documents did trouble her. Jack wasn't doing anything illegal, but these documents showed that he was profiting from his work and not telling anybody about it, which made him exactly what Sam said he was—a fraud.

"Why are you showing me these things, Sam? Why do you want to involve me in this?"

"I care about you, number one. I really don't know your relationship with Tobin, and I want to make sure you're not taken in by this guy."

"And number two?"

"I figure Tobin had to be pretty pissed off when Felton killed his opportunity for a payday by killing my daughter. He might have had a little vendetta of his own."

Danni was starting to get where this was going. "Are you suggesting that the loss of a fee was a motivation for murder? That's outrageous. The guy was sitting out in the woods trying to protect me."

"That's what he told you. Felton had a cell phone on him. Tobin called him two nights before he was killed and again just before he was killed."

"So you're suggesting Jack lured him out there to kill him?"

"Why else would he be calling him?" Sam said.

"I don't know but why would he be out in the woods?"

"Why not? I don't know what he told Felton to get him into the woods but killing Felton behind your backyard is a perfect alibi for Tobin."

"It's just too crazy, Sam. How do you explain Jack coming directly to my house, concerned for my welfare? If he'd committed the murder, he would have gone directly to the body and put a gun in Felton's hand and said Felton had tried to shoot him—not run to my house. How do you explain that?"

"I think what you just said was Tobin's original plan. What he didn't plan on was me showing up. I think he heard me barreling through the woods as soon as that gun went off and decided he might not be able to get to Felton's body before I did. I was there pretty fast. So he went to your house, great guy that he is, to check on your welfare."

It was an incredible story but as a homicide detective Danni knew that the stories behind some murders were sometimes pretty incredible. So far, she wasn't buying any of it, not with Jack. She knew Jack, or at least she thought she did, and this was not the person she knew. And she didn't trust Sam. He'd been through too much.

"Let's follow this logically, Sam. If Tobin was going to plant the gun but didn't or couldn't, what happened to the gun? I mean, he was at my house right away. I was with him right up until the time we went to the station. You guys had him empty his pockets at the station. I'm sure somebody did a pat down."

"They did."

"So where did the gun go that he was supposedly going to plant?"

"The only thing he could have done was throw it away as he was running toward your house. He's right-handed so he probably threw it off to his right. I didn't piece all this information together until this morning so I didn't know enough to have somebody check that area before today. We had nothing to keep Tobin so we let him go late yesterday. I suspect that if he threw the gun away, he would have been back last night to retrieve it. You didn't happen to see him last night, did you?"

So that's why Sam is here. He's looking for this last little piece of information to incriminate Jack. Danni hadn't bought anything so far, but now she recalled seeing that dark figure coming out of the woods from the left as she sat on her porch. *That would have been Jack's right if he was running from the woods toward my house.* She remembered him saying he was looking for the gun and she remembered asking him why he was all the way over toward the left, nowhere near the body. *What was it he said? He was there because Sam told him the police were going to stop looking for the gun at dark. What else did he say? "I had to circle around because Sam sent a SWAT team out to the scene."*

"Sam, did you send a SWAT team out to the scene last night?"

"No."

"Did you tell Tobin you were quitting the search at dark?"

"Hell, no. He's a suspect. I wouldn't tell him anything. Now, did you see him last night or not?"

Danni had to answer the question. Thomas Felton's case had caused her to do things she never would have done before, and she regretted them. Now Sam Jeffries had asked her a question. She could lie and say she hadn't seen Jack last night or she could tell the truth. Lying meant making her own decision about Jack's guilt or innocence. Telling the truth meant letting the police, the state attorney, and possibly the judicial system make that decision.

She thought Jack was innocent, but she wasn't absolutely sure.

"Did you see him last night or not, Danni?" Sam asked for the third time.

"I did."

"Where was he?"

Danni got up from the table and walked to the back door that led out to the patio. Sam followed her. She pointed to her left.

"I saw him coming out of the woods over there. He told me he was looking for Felton's gun. He said there was a SWAT team up by the scene."

"One last question. I can check this out on my own but your answering the question will make my job easier. Did Tobin call you anytime in the last two days?"

"Yeah, why?"

"I'd like to see the number in your phone."

"Sure." Danni opened her cell phone and pointed to Jack's number.

"Did he leave a message?"

"Yes."

"Don't erase it. I'm going to need that phone eventually."

"Then you'd better get a warrant."

As she heard the words leave her mouth, Danni realized that giving Sam Jeffries any information had been the wrong decision.

CHAPTER FORTY-NINE

Sam Jeffries had one major obstacle left in his quest to try and make Jack Tobin pay for the murder of his daughter, Kathleen. He had to convince the new state attorney, Robert Merton, to prosecute Tobin for the murder of Thomas Felton.

Merton had made his reputation as an aggressive prosecutor but as the state attorney, he'd been rather conservative. He had made the decision not to prosecute Thomas Felton for the attempted murder of Stacey Kincaid, a decision that ultimately resulted in the murder of Kathleen Jeffries. Consequently, there was no love lost between him and Sam. Still, Sam needed Merton's help to prosecute Jack, and that was the most important thing right now. In his crazy mind, he needed the attorney who had made the decision to set Felton free, to prosecute the attorney who had started the process to set Felton free. It was nuts, and it made for strange bedfellows but Sam didn't care. He just wanted his revenge.

The two men met in Merton's corner office, the one he'd been occupying for just a short period of time. Sam quickly went over the evidence he had concocted against Jack. Merton had many of the same questions Danni did. Sam answered them all. His conversation with Danni had prepared him well.

"This is insanity, Sam," Merton said finally. "You want me to prosecute one of the most famous lawyers in Florida, maybe the whole United States."

"That's right."

"This guy probably doesn't have a speeding ticket on his record."

"So?"

"So I'm not going to commit political suicide here. If you recall, I'm the guy who wouldn't prosecute Felton on that attempted murder charge."

"Yeah. How did that work for you? You think you've got a shot at dogcatcher next election?"

"At least I can explain that decision and leave myself a chance. I prosecute Tobin and lose, I may as well leave the state."

"Let me give you a different perspective," Sam said. "Let's say the people in this county want Tobin prosecuted. Let's say they're angry at him for getting Felton off and for giving Felton the opportunity to kill my daughter. And let's say, as Kathleen's father, I'm grateful to you for at least taking the shot. Don't you think with my support, win or lose, you have a better chance at re-election by prosecuting this case? You took action. You didn't sit on your ass and let Tobin walk away when I presented you with these facts. People are going to appreciate that, Bob. It will make up for your past inaction."

Sam watched as Merton took in his words. He could see they'd had the desired effect by the look on Merton's face. He looked surprised. He hadn't thought of the situation in that light. But he still wasn't ready to take the big bite from the apple.

"Tobin will move for a change of venue. It won't even be tried here. People won't give a shit."

A change of venue was a request to move the trial somewhere else on the premise that the defendant would not get a fair trial in the jurisdiction where the criminal act had occurred. Evidence had to be presented for the court to grant a motion to change venue. Sam had anticipated this argument as well and he had an answer.

"What would be the basis for a motion for change of venue—that people here are angry at Tobin for getting Felton released, therefore he can't get a fair trial? You've got a great counter-argument. Think about it: The people here all know or at least believe that Felton was a serial killer. The fact that, in the eyes of the law, Felton was an innocent man at the time of his death is not going to make a difference here. Everybody here is going to know that Tobin is being prosecuted for ridding this county of a serial killer. That should even out any sentiment against Tobin and give you a pretty compelling response to any motion Tobin or his lawyer can file.

"They need evidence as well and they're not going to get it. I know Art Grumman, the editor of the *Oakville Sun*, real well. I've gotten his kids out of a few scrapes. He owes me. I'll make sure there are no editorials about Tobin's guilt, and I'll get the rabble-rousers under control, too. There will be no demonstrations or any of that crap. Tobin will be tried here in Apache County, I promise you. And if you try the case and seek the death penalty, win or lose, you will be re-elected to office. Hell, with the publicity from this case, you may become attorney general or governor."

It was a compelling argument by a man committed to his cause. All of Merton's fears about what would happen if he tried to prosecute Jack were replaced by new fears about what would certainly happen if he didn't.

"Okay," he said to Sam. "I'll take this case to the grand jury and let them decide. But I want your commitment that you will support me for re-election."

"You've got it but only on the condition that you try this case yourself."

"Done."

CHAPTER FIFTY

Jack returned to Ron's condo in town after Felton's death. Henry arrived the next evening. They didn't get to talk much until the following morning over coffee on the patio.

"You did a real good thing there, Henry, taking care of Danni's daughter."

"Can it, Jack."

"What?"

"I'll listen to that kind of stuff from other people but not you. This is what we do. I didn't tell you that you did a great job hanging out in the woods until you caught Felton, did I?"

"No, but you were about to."

"Hell I was. It was what I expected you to do just as you expected me to do what I did. Now let's get to the real stuff. What's going on with you and Danni?"

"Absolutely nothing."

"C'mon. Danni told me you guys were together the day Felton was shot."

"We were because I went to her house to check on her, that's all."

"So nothing's going on in the romance department?"

"Nope, and it looks like it won't ever be going on."

"Never say never."

"We had a good long talk. She was very honest with me. She told me she just couldn't sustain another relationship after her marriage. She said it's like hitting a brick wall."

"Well, you hadn't seen her in two years anyway. Now you can at least put it behind you completely."

"Yeah, I guess you're right."

"So what's going on with this investigation into Felton's death? Danni tells me they were looking for Felton's gun or something."

"Yeah. When I saw him in the woods, I yelled at him to stop, and he turned and I'm almost certain he had a gun but I'm not positive. That's why I shot him. Now they say they can't find the gun."

"Are they going to try and charge you with something?"

"I'm not sure. That's why I'm staying in town."

"What could they charge you with potentially?"

"I don't know—manslaughter maybe. I think Sam Jeffries still has it in for me. Part of me even thinks he took the gun out of Felton's hand."

"Really? It seems like a big risk for the police chief to set you up for something like this. I mean, Felton was a serial killer. You told him to stop. He didn't. You thought he had a gun. You shot him. What jury is going to convict you under those circumstances even if there wasn't a gun?"

"I don't know, Henry. But I wouldn't discount Sam Jeffries. He's lost his wife and now his daughter and I think he's dangerous. I also think he's got some things up his sleeve that we don't know about."

Jack's hunch turned out to be right. One week after his conversation with Henry, on a Monday afternoon, he was served with a subpoena to appear before the grand jury.

"I wouldn't go," Henry told him when Jack showed him the subpoena.

"I've gotta go."

"Well, I wouldn't say a word. That's a kangaroo court run by the prosecution. You need a lawyer, Jack."

"I am a lawyer."

"With a fool for a client. Who's the best criminal lawyer in Miami?"

"I don't know. Dez Calderon probably."

"Do you know him?"

"I know him to say hello to. I don't know any of those criminal guys that well. Remember, I did civil cases most of my career."

"Give him a call. Tell him the situation. Put yourself in his hands as you've had your clients do with you."

"All right, but I'm inclined to go to the grand jury and tell my side of the story."

"And they just might use it against you. You're not thinking objectively, Jack. You've seen enough of this stuff. You think just because it's you, you can do it differently. That's exactly why you can't represent yourself."

Jack called Dez Calderon that very afternoon but did not get to talk to him until the next morning when Calderon called him back. Jack filled him in on all the details.

"When are you scheduled to appear?" Calderon asked.

"Next Wednesday."

"I've got to reschedule some things, but I'll fly up Tuesday afternoon and we'll go over everything and make our decisions. Okay?"

"Sounds good," Jack said, but it really didn't sound good or bad. Calderon didn't give him any assessment of the case at all. He didn't even talk about a fee. Jack was totally in the dark about a potential strategy.

I'm beginning to understand how a client feels, Jack thought.

Dez Calderon arrived at Jack's condo in a limo the following Tuesday afternoon. Henry was there with Jack. Calderon was a smallish man, about five foot eight, with fine features. His short gray hair was groomed to perfection and his dark blue pinstriped silk suit was tailor made. He was all business as he set his briefcase on the dining room table and shook Jack's hand. Jack introduced him to Henry, and Dez immediately asked Henry to leave the premises.

"You understand. I need to talk to my client in private."

"No explanations necessary," Henry said. "I know the drill. Jack, I'll see you later."

Once Henry left, Calderon gave Jack his assessment of the case.

"I read my notes of our telephone conversation on the way up and I had my secretary prepare a little synopsis of the Felton case, which I read on the flight. You would think everybody in this town, especially the chief of police and the state attorney, would want Felton dead. I don't know why they're prosecuting you."

"I'm not sure either," Jack said. "But Sam Jeffries—"

"That's the chief?"

"Yeah. I think he might hold me responsible for Felton's getting out of prison and killing his daughter."

"The strongest motive in the world—revenge. Well, if they're out to get you, you're not going to help them. I'm going to call the state attorney right now and tell him you're not going to testify. We'll see if we can work something out so you don't have to show up at all. Sometimes, if you just tell them you're going to take the Fifth, they won't require you to come in. He'll probably want something in writing signed by you and me, but that's fine. I've already prepared the document."

"Wait a minute. I think I should testify. I mean, I already admitted I shot the man. I can explain to the grand jury exactly what I saw and why I was there."

Dez Calderon just looked at Jack for what seemed like the longest time.

"I know you're famous for your death penalty stuff," he said finally, "but I also know you're not a criminal lawyer, so let me be brief. Whatever case they have against you right now, it's because of what you've already said. They're going to get an indictment, you and I both know that. It's just the way this world works. If they are out to get you, talking some more will just lock you into your story and give them more information to twist into a coherent case against you. I know you're no boy scout, Jack, even though the newspapers make you out to be one. You know what I'm talking about. Bottom line—if I'm representing you, you're not testifying. Got it?"

"All right."

Calderon opened his briefcase, which was lying on the dining room table, and took out a piece of paper. "This is a written assertion of your Fifth Amendment right against self-incrimination. I want you to sign it and I'll sign it and then I'll call the state attorney."

Jack read the document quickly and signed it while Calderon called Robert Merton on his cell phone. By the time Jack had finished writing his name, Calderon was done.

"It's all settled. Merton said they'll probably be done today, which means you will be formally indicted probably tomorrow. Be prepared to be arrested in the next day or so. Are you with me?"

"Yeah."

All the time Calderon was talking, he was packing his briefcase. By the time Jack gave his brief answer, Calderon was headed for the door.

"I've gotta run. I'll be in touch with you in the next couple of days. Don't worry about a thing."

Jack *was* worried though. He followed Calderon and his silk suit out to the waiting limousine.

"Did he say what they were charging me with?"

"He did," Calderon said as the driver opened the limo door and he got in.

"What is it?"

Calderon lowered the backseat window.

"First-degree murder."

"What?"

"Don't worry. I'll handle it. I gotta go."

The limo driver took off for the airport and Dez Calderon's private jet, leaving Jack standing dumbfounded in the parking lot.

PART FOUR
April 21, 2003

St. Albans, Florida

CHAPTER FIFTY-ONE

Henry drove his own car, a Ford Explorer, to St. Albans, a city about an hour northwest of Tallahassee. It was a quiet, comfortable ride, a far cry from his last trip to Tallahassee in Jack's pickup.

He'd decided to go to St. Albans after his last conversation with Jack. When Dez Calderon left the condo, Henry was just pulling into the parking lot. He found Jack standing outside about as upset as he'd ever seen him, and that was saying something considering all the things that had occurred recently.

"What happened?" Henry asked after he'd parked his car and approached Jack, who hadn't moved.

"Nothing. I'm just pissed."

"At who?"

"Myself mostly."

"For what?"

"I've just abdicated making my own decisions since Felton's latest and last murder. I wanted to testify before the grand jury and then I listened to you and Calderon. That son of a bitch was in and out of here in about fifteen minutes and when he left, I was getting indicted for first-degree murder. I'll bet I get a bill for ten grand for that little visit."

"First-degree murder! I can't believe that."

"Well, believe it, Henry, because it's true."

"You can't blame Calderon for that, Jack. That's the prosecutor and Sam Jeffries. They've got it in for you. Calderon gave you good advice not to testify. You can't control what happens with the grand jury."

"Henry, you're my best friend and I love you, but I disagree with your assessment. Everybody says the grand jury is controlled by the state attorney but that's because there's no other lawyer in the room. It's just the state attorney presenting the state's case.

"If Calderon ever thought outside the box, he would have understood that if I testified, there would be two lawyers in the room and that the possibility existed that I could persuade those jurors by my testimony that there was no crime. I can be pretty convincing when I need to be."

"I know that, my friend. There's nobody better in a courtroom than you and there's nobody I'd ever want representing me but you. You can't represent yourself, though. You're too close to this. You need somebody dealing for you."

"Maybe so, Henry, but I've got to be part of the process even if I'm the client. That's not going to work with prima donnas like Calderon."

"We'll find somebody you can work with, Jack."

During those long years on death row, Henry, as part of his self-education, had read every book he could get his hands on. One of the first subjects he had read about was the civil rights movement, especially how that movement had played out in his home state of Florida. He figured that if he could understand the civil rights movement, its leaders, and what motivated them, it might help him understand himself and turn his life around. He'd read about a lawyer in St. Albans, Florida, a white man, who had put his life on the line on numerous occasions to protect innocent black people accused of crimes. The man's name was Tom Wylie. When he was released from prison, Henry eventually took a trip to St. Albans to see some of the historic sites from the civil rights movement. While he was there, he stopped to see Tom Wylie. He just walked into the office, gave the secretary his name, and two minutes later, he was shaking hands with the man himself.

"What brings you to these parts, Henry?" Tom asked after Henry had introduced himself and told Tom he was visiting from Miami.

"I know this city was a hotbed of action during the civil rights movement and I just wanted to visit the sites and meet you."

"Me? Why would you want to meet me?"

"Well, I read about Rufus Porter for one thing, and the civil rights committee of which you were a member. There's one particular story I recall, about you single-handedly taking on the local Klan on a dirt road one night. You were riding shotgun for a doctor on an emergency call to the black community and they stopped you. Is that true?"

Rufus Porter was a black man who had been accused of raping a white woman. There was no evidence to support the charge other than the fact that Rufus was in the vicinity of the crime, but, in those days, that was enough. Tom had taken Rufus's case even though he'd put his own life in danger, and he had gotten Rufus off. The other story was true as well.

"You can't believe everything you hear, son," Tom said. He was a tall man, not as tall as Henry but close. And he was thin like a reed, but strong. Henry could tell that from his handshake. His face and hands were tan and weathered, and he had a full head of thick brown hair, cropped short, with only a stray strand of gray here and there, even though he had to be in his midsixties. "I did represent a man named Rufus Porter but that story and the other one are way overblown."

"Sure they are," Henry said. "When I read Rufus Porter's own account of the hair on his forearms standing straight whenever he mentioned your name, that's exactly the word I thought of—overblown."

Tom changed the subject immediately. "Since you're here, Henry Wilson, I guess I should be neighborly and take you to lunch. After that, I'll give you a short tour. I'm sure you'd like to see the Monsoon Hotel where the manager poured the acid in the pool."

"I would," Henry replied.

At the height of the civil rights movement, when Congress was actually debating the Civil Rights Act and the southern senators were filibustering, the manager of the Monsoon Hotel had poured acid in the hotel pool while a group of black and white protesters were swimming. Somebody took a picture of the act and it made the newspapers all over the world. It was such a clear picture of the racism that existed in the South, and the backlash was so great that it caused the senators to end their filibuster and the Civil Rights Act to be passed.

Henry was so moved reading about the courage of the young demonstrators and people like Tom Wylie. *That's who I want to be if I ever get out of here*, he'd thought to himself at the time. Now he was out and he was sitting at a table having lunch with Tom Wylie.

"So what's your story, Henry?" Tom asked after they had ordered and had their drinks. Both men were drinking water.

"I was on death row for seventeen years. I just got released a couple of months ago."

"That's why your name sounded familiar to me," Tom said. "I read all about your case. Jack Tobin represented you. Fine lawyer. Good man, too. We've met a few times at different events over the years. Well, congratulations."

"Thanks."

The rest of the lunch went by quickly with Tom telling stories about St. Albans in the sixties and Henry telling stories about life on death row, which Tom found fascinating.

"Now that you've got a new lease on life, what are you going to do?" Tom asked.

"I'm not sure exactly but I'm going to try to make a difference like you and Jack have."

"Good for you, Henry."

Henry didn't know how to handle the compliment so he changed the subject as Tom Wylie had done a little while before.

"I want to ask you a question, Tom. I'm just curious."

"Shoot."

"Isn't it hard to be a criminal lawyer? I mean, you have to represent everybody that comes in the door, don't you?"

"I'm not a criminal lawyer, never was a criminal lawyer," Tom replied.

"But Rufus Porter, and those other people I read about…"

"I didn't say I didn't represent people who were charged with crimes. I just said I'm not a criminal lawyer. I never represented a person I didn't believe was innocent. I could never get my arms around the idea of representing people I knew were guilty, so I never did it."

Henry was thinking about that previous visit and his conversations with Tom Wylie as he drove to St. Albans to ask Tom to represent Jack. Both men were great lawyers and they shared the same values. It was only right that Jack should have somebody like Tom representing him. The words were ringing in his ears—*a lawyer's lawyer*. Henry knew he would have to be very convincing, though.

He'd called ahead and made an appointment but he didn't say what it was about.

St. Albans was one of the oldest cities in the United States. Originally it had been founded and settled by the Spanish, and the Old City reflected those roots. The city fathers had worked hard to keep the flavor of the Old City intact through zoning ordinances and other similar regulations. New buildings had to be built in the old Spanish Colonial style and no building could be over two stories in height. There was another part of St. Albans, the New City, that was modern and sleek and a commercial center. Tom Wylie, however, lived in the Old City, and that's where Henry was headed.

Tom was waiting for him.

"Henry, how are you? It's been a long time," he said as if they'd known each other all their lives. The two men had bonded in that one afternoon they'd spent together, and Tom had kept up somewhat with Henry's new life. He knew, for instance, that Henry now worked with Jack.

"I'm fine, Tom. How about yourself?"

Henry noticed that Tom had changed somewhat over the years. The handshake was still strong but he looked thinner and his thick brown hair had started to gray. For a moment he was concerned that Tom might be sick, but the handshake and the smile convinced him that the man was just getting older.

"Getting a little long in the tooth but I can't do anything about that. Come on into the office and sit down, and we'll have a chat. I know you've got something on your mind."

They went into Tom's office, and the two men sat in the client chairs next to each other. Tom didn't want his big desk to come between friends.

"So what is it, Henry? I assume it has something to do with our mutual friend Jack Tobin. I've been reading about the events down in Oakville."

Henry smiled. Tom was so perceptive. He probably knew what Henry was going to ask him already.

"It does," he replied. "As you know, Jack has been indicted on first-degree murder charges."

"They're going after him because he represented that Felton character. I know this game. I've been there."

"That's why I'm here, Tom. You and Jack are so much alike. You have a passion for the law and for people just like he does. Jack needs help, but he won't be represented by just anybody. He needs somebody who can see all sides of an issue and who will listen to his input. He needs you, Tom."

Tom sat back in his chair and put his index finger to his lip, thinking about Henry's words. After a few minutes he spoke.

"Have you talked to Jack about this?"

"Only to the extent that I told him I'd help find somebody for him. He knows he needs somebody."

"I'm sure Jack can handle the preliminary stuff, including the bail proceedings."

"He can," Henry replied.

"I can clear my calendar to do this," Tom said, thinking out loud. "I've been slowing down here for the last year or so. Henry, you need to go back and talk to Jack. Tell him I'm willing to represent him if he wants me to. I can probably get down there for a day sometime next week and we can go over everything in detail—start mapping a strategy."

Henry was elated. "I'll tell him. Thanks, Tom. And I know we haven't talked about money, but I'll pay whatever the fee is."

"I'm sure that won't be a problem. It will be a flat fee, and Jack and I will agree on a number together."

Henry smiled again. "You're the perfect lawyer for him."

"I wouldn't say that. I know this much though: When the state has it in for somebody—when it gets personal—they will move mountains to get a conviction. Jack has pissed off people in power for a long time. They are going to go after him with a bazooka."

CHAPTER FIFTY-TWO

The day Tom Wylie travelled to Oakville was a typical late-April day in Florida. Most of the drive had been relatively pleasant but during the early afternoon, when he was about thirty miles outside of town, thunderstorms rolled in, accompanied by fifty-mile-per-hour winds and lightning that persistently pierced the afternoon sky. A few of the thunder claps were so sharp they made Tom literally jump out of his seat. He wanted to pull over, but he considered it more dangerous to be parked on the side of the road than actually driving.

It was still bad when he arrived at the condo. He'd made arrangements with Henry so that he and Jack could meet alone for the first hour. Then, if the decision was going to be that Tom would come aboard, Henry and Ron would join them.

Henry waited for the call over at The Swamp. He sat at the bar and had a draft while Ron worked the room, stopping occasionally to chat.

"What does this guy want me there for anyway?" Ron asked Henry on his first stop. The storm had not yet hit, and people were still eating and drinking.

"I don't know. He just asked me if Jack or I had any trustworthy friends that lived in Oakville and could give him the lay of the land.

The only person I could think of was you. I thought of Danni, too, but I think she's a little compromised by all of this."

"She is. She was in here not too long ago and refused to talk about the case."

"I'm really surprised about that. I thought Danni would support Jack."

"You've got to remember, Henry, she's been in law enforcement all her life. Getting back to me again—what am I supposed to be able to tell this guy?"

"I don't know. Maybe he wants you to keep him posted about the mood of the people. You do know everybody in town."

"That's not true. There are about four or five people whose names I can't recall."

Then Ron was off again, hitting the tables, making sure that everybody was happy. The first rumblings of the bad weather that was coming could be heard off to the west. Henry saw the customers almost immediately start to quicken their pace. People at the bar drank up and headed for the door. Others at the tables were asking for their checks before they were done eating. *One sound and they know what's coming*, Henry thought to himself. *Nobody wants to be caught out in a bad thunderstorm.*

The thunder was closer now. The wind was picking up, and people were rushing to their cars. In a matter of minutes, The Swamp was nearly empty. Ron stood in the middle of his establishment and looked heavenward.

"You're killing me here," he said to the ceiling.

Henry was thoroughly enjoying his beer and the entertainment.

CHAPTER FIFTY-THREE

The rain was still coming down when Tom reached Jack's condo. He rang the bell and Jack answered right away. Both men were dressed casually in jeans and tee shirts although Tom's clothes were a little wet from the race from the parking lot to the condo.

"Hi, Tom. How are you? It's been a long time."

"Yes, it has, Jack. I was a young man last time we talked."

"That makes two of us."

"You're still a young man, Jack. You've got a lot of years ahead of you, and I'm here to make sure they're good years."

"Thanks, Tom. Let me get you a towel so you can dry off."

The two men had not spent a lot of time together in the past but enough to have developed a friendship of sorts. About ten years before, the Florida Bar had given Jack a professionalism award and Tom, the previous year's recipient, had made the presentation. They'd had a few that night and commiserated over the state of the profession.

"The professionals are losing, I think," Tom had said. "Now it's all about advertising and the money."

"You've got that right," Jack had replied. They were in a little beach bar in Daytona Beach across the street from the hotel where the awards ceremony had taken place. "The day the US Supreme

Court allowed lawyers to advertise is the day this profession started to turn south."

Tom had a son who was a lawyer in Miami, and Jack knew him as well, although the son, Kevin, never mentioned his father. Jack had learned through another lawyer that Kevin was Tom's son. He verified it that night in Daytona, but Tom wasn't very forthcoming about the relationship.

"I've met your son, Kevin, a few times. He seems like a nice young man."

"Except that he works for Bernie Stang. My son and I don't talk."

The way he'd said the words at the time assured Jack that he didn't want to discuss the whys and wherefores of why they didn't talk. Bernie Stang was a prominent criminal lawyer in Miami who represented drug dealers almost exclusively. His name didn't come up too often when people were discussing professionalism. Tom's remark told Jack that the man was disappointed that his son was working for Bernie.

They'd met a few times since then at bar functions and always set aside a little time to reconnect. There were phone calls as well over the years, usually to refer cases, or to ask about judges and the like. Even on those occasions, they took a few minutes to touch base with each other.

"So you already had the bond hearing, is that right?" Tom asked when he had dried off and they were seated at the dining room table.

"Yeah. The state wanted me held without bond but the judge did me a favor and let me out for a million."

"Some favor. Who is the judge and will he be doing the trial?"

"I believe so. His name is Holbrook. He's a retired judge from the northern part of the county and he handled the evidentiary hearing for a new trial in Felton's case. He's a special appointment, probably because he's familiar with all the underlying facts."

"Is that a positive or a negative for us?" Tom asked.

"I think he's probably a good trial judge, but he's susceptible to public opinion. He should have granted us a new trial in Felton's case but he didn't. I had to go to the supreme court, although, in retrospect, he made the right decision."

"Should we try and get him off the case?"

"We don't have any grounds. Last time I checked, having a judge rule against you wasn't sufficient grounds to have him kicked off your future cases."

"Wouldn't it be a beautiful world if that were so? Okay, we're stuck with Judge Holbrook. Why don't you tell me about the case."

"You probably know the basic stuff, Tom. I got a serial killer, Thomas Felton, released from death row, and he started killing again. The first person he killed was the daughter of the police chief, Sam Jeffries. He'd already killed the man's wife ten years earlier.

"I came upon Felton in the woods behind another cop's house, a female named Danni Jansen. I told him to stop. He turned toward me and I thought he had a gun in his hand and that he was going to shoot me, so I fired my gun and killed him.

"You don't know for sure whether he had a gun?" Tom asked.

"I can't say for sure and I didn't check the body after I fired my gun. Felton was coming from the vicinity of Danni's house. After I shot him and saw him go down, I immediately went to check on her. She was fine. When we got back to the scene, Sam Jeffries was already there. Danni and I told him the story, which, in retrospect, was probably not a wise decision, and everything happened from there."

"The amateur detective in me tells me there's more to the story between you and this Danni woman."

Jack smiled. "There is. We met two years before I took Felton's case, and we had a brief romantic relationship at that time. She wanted to shoot me when I took Felton's case, but right now we're back to being friends. At least, I think we are."

"You'll probably find out for sure sometime during this trial. What happened to Felton's gun?"

"They never found it. I told you I thought he had a gun. I wasn't a hundred percent positive but it was daylight and I'm pretty sure that's what I saw."

"If that's the case, somebody picked up the gun. It didn't just disappear into thin air."

"Nope."

"Whether there was a gun or not, it sounds like Sam Jeffries is the guy who's driving this train."

"He is, and that's something we need to discuss if you are going to be my lawyer, Tom. You and I both know that our best defense might be to go after Sam Jeffries. I mean, he's got motive to be angry at me and we can make a lot of hay with that, but I don't want to do it unless we have concrete evidence."

"Why?"

"The guy has been through hell. His daughter's murder is at least partially my responsibility. I've ruined his life enough. I just don't want to go after him and possibly ruin his reputation unless I'm absolutely sure."

"If he was the only one at the scene and he took the gun, you might not get concrete evidence, Jack. And he sounds like your best defense at this point."

"I know."

"It could mean your life. If it's tried here, these folks might execute you."

"I know."

"Any other conditions you want to tell me about?"

"I want to testify."

"That's not a problem. It sounds like this is now purely a self-defense case. You're going to have to testify."

"Good. There's nothing else."

"Okay. Now let's talk about the details for a minute. How are they ever going to prove premeditation for a first-degree-murder conviction?"

Jack reached for some papers behind him on the floor. He picked them up and set them on the table.

"It's all here in the grand jury indictment," he said.

"I'll read that eventually, Jack. Why don't you paraphrase it for me."

"They found two documents on Felton's body. One was a claims bill that I had intended to file with the legislature asking for twenty million dollars for his wrongful incarceration for ten years. The other one is a contingency fee agreement whereby Felton agreed to pay me one-third of whatever we recovered from the legislature.

"They also have Felton's phone showing two calls from me, one of them two days before he was killed and one minutes before he was killed. Lastly, they have the testimony of two police officers who said I threatened to kill Felton when I was drunk. You add it all up and the theory is that I was really representing Felton for money. Felton caused me to lose almost seven million dollars when he killed Kathleen Jeffries, so I killed him and set it up to look like I was protecting Danni Jansen."

Tom didn't react to Jack's very succinct summary right away. He was digesting Jack's words, rolling them around in his mind to see if all the parts fit. It took several minutes.

"It's a very persuasive argument, Jack, and it fits, except for the gun. If you were setting this up, you definitely would have planted the gun for the police to find. Jeffries didn't think that part through when he took Felton's gun."

"Probably not, and I've been thinking about that since I got this indictment. If that's their theory, they have to come up with a plausible explanation for no planted gun."

"And have you come up with anything?"

"I have. Sam Jeffries was in the woods when I shot Felton. That's why he was the first person who found the body. I think they're going to argue that I intended to plant the gun on Felton but I couldn't because I heard Jeffries coming. That's when I went to Plan B, running to Danni's house to see if she was okay."

Tom thought about that statement for a few more minutes.

"That'll work," he said finally. "There may be some flaws when we get into the minutiae, but it's a plausible theory and in this town that may be all they need. Have you formulated a defense to counteract their argument?"

"Somewhat. I haven't fleshed it out completely yet."

"Well, let's hear what you've got."

"I have never taken a death penalty case for money. Henry can testify to that. He got three million from the legislature. I didn't take a dime. Felton inquired about the claims bill and I told him we could do it. He wanted to do it right away, and he offered me the one-third fee. I told him to give it to Exoneration. He refused, so I let him sign a contingency fee agreement with me, and I planned to give the money to Exoneration."

"The only problem with this theme so far, Jack, is that it depends entirely on the jury's believing you. In this town that will be a difficult sell."

"Then we've got to change the venue."

"We can try but let's not get ahead of ourselves. Continue."

"I was in the woods behind Danni's house because I believed he would come after Danni next. The easiest access to her house was through the woods. By the way, Danni also believed he would come for her through the woods, as did Sam Jeffries. That's why he was there."

"That part is good but what about the phone calls between you and Felton?"

"He called me after he murdered Kathleen Jeffries. He said he wanted me to forget about the claims bill. I asked him why and he said he couldn't wait. I didn't understand what he meant at first, but when I found out about Jeffries's daughter, I got it. That's when I knew he was going to kill again, and it was going to be either Danni or her daughter, Hannah. Danni put Hannah in Henry's care so she could come back here and wait for Felton. That's how sure she was that Felton was coming after her."

"Let's stay focused on the phone calls."

"Okay. Two days before Felton's death, I remembered I had his phone number so I called it. Somebody answered but wouldn't speak. I figured it was him so when I saw a man in the woods and couldn't recognize him because he was so far away, I called the number. He didn't answer it, but I saw him check his phone. That's when I knew it was Felton. I went after him and told him to stop. When he turned to shoot me, I fired my gun. I hit him and he fell backward."

Tom was sitting at the table with his head down, listening intently. When Jack finished speaking, he didn't move for the longest time. Jack knew he was processing everything in his mind and evaluating it because it was exactly what he would have done.

"The phone calls have the same problem as the agreement, Jack. All the evidence is from you."

"I know."

"So we at least agree that we have to try and get a change of venue because the people in this town are not going to be sympathetic toward you."

"I'm with you totally on that, Tom. Does that mean you're considering taking the case?"

"Do you want me to?"

It was Jack's turn to hesitate before answering. "Are you okay with my conditions?"

"I wouldn't say I'm okay with them, especially the Sam Jeffries thing, but I understand why you feel the way you do. I'll honor your wishes on that issue, and you will testify, I assure you. Right now you are our entire case. I want you to know, though, that I will revisit the Sam Jeffries thing with you if we find more evidence, but I will follow your lead no matter what. It's your neck and you're entitled to stretch it out there for whatever reason you want."

"Thanks, Tom. Yes, I want you to represent me. You and I think alike and we'll be a formidable team. Besides, you're probably the only lawyer who would take my case on the conditions I just laid out."

"I disagree with you there, Jack. Money moves mountains."

"Maybe you're right, but I don't think Dez Calderon or guys like him would have gone along with my conditions. He would have wanted total control. Speaking of money, we need to talk about that issue now as well."

"Okay, how much do you want to pay me?" Tom asked.

Jack laughed. "I don't think it works that way. You're supposed to quote me a fee and I'm supposed to accept it or reject it or bargain with you."

"Okay. What's the going rate for a first-degree-murder case these days?"

"Somebody like Calderon would probably charge five hundred an hour and demand a retainer of two hundred grand or more."

"Well, I'm not Calderon, Jack. What are the middle-of-the-road guys charging on a flat-fee basis for a run-of-the-mill murder case?"

"In this town, probably around seventy-five grand."

"I'll do it for forty-five plus expenses."

"What are you doing, Tom? I've got the money."

"I know. I just don't want it to be about the money. I'd do it for nothing but I can't afford to. I see retirement looming in the near future, although I will hate to stop doing what I love."

At that moment, Jack knew that this man possessed what he had been striving for all his life, especially these past few years. Jack now took cases for nothing but only because he didn't need money anymore. Tom Wylie had taken cases for nothing all his life, even when he didn't have any money to speak of. Thus began one of the strangest negotiations ever between a lawyer and his client.

"I'll pay you seventy," Jack said.

"Fifty plus expenses, and that's my final offer—take it or leave it," Tom replied.

Jack laughed. "I guess I'm going to have to take it, Tom. You drive a hard bargain."

Tom laughed with him. "I do, indeed. Now let's call Henry and your friend the bar owner and start mapping out a strategy."

CHAPTER FIFTY-FOUR

It took Henry and Ron all of ten minutes to drive from The Swamp to the condo. The storm had passed, but The Swamp was still empty when they left.

"Once people go back to their caves to get out of the weather, they don't come out again," Ron told Henry on the drive over.

Ron was the only one who didn't know Tom Wylie, so Jack made the introduction when the two men arrived.

"I've heard of the legendary Swamp," Tom said as he shook Ron's hand.

Ron still couldn't let the bad day go. He was a businessman to his core.

"Yeah, well, today it should be called The Morgue because it's a dead zone."

Tom smiled. "I take it the storm killed your business."

"They fled like rats from a sinking ship."

"They'll be back tomorrow when it clears up. While you have some time, though, Jack and I would like to discuss his case with you and Henry."

"Are you on board?" Henry asked.

"I am," Tom replied. "Jack drove a hard bargain, but I wore him down eventually."

Tom stole a glance at Jack, who was smiling. The four men moved to the dining room table and sat down.

"I still don't know why I'm here," Ron said. "I can feed you guys and house you, but that's about it."

"Actually, you can be very helpful," Tom continued. "Jack says you know everything that's happening in this town. We want to get this case out of Oakville, and the only way we can do that is if we can produce some evidence to show that he can't get a fair trial here. We can look for editorials and letters to the editor and that kind of stuff, but we need to dig deeper."

"I'm not sure I know what you mean," Ron said.

"This case is going to heat up real fast. The national press and the foreign press are going to be falling all over each other trying to get stories. The people in this town are going to get caught up in that. They won't be able to stay out of the way. We believe the public sentiment is going to be overwhelmingly against Jack. Any time you hear about a group scheduling a protest or talking to a reporter, any reporter, we need to know about that so we can get the information and present it to the judge."

"I can definitely do that," Ron said. "I thought I'd be hearing things already, but I haven't. It's almost like people are being told not to say anything through some underground channel or something."

"How would that work?" Tom asked.

"This is a small town and it's run by a small group of people. Unfortunately, I'm not one of them. I can tell you who the people are, though, and it's not the mayor and the city council. It's the people who get them elected. Sam Jeffries is one of them. You can't discount Sam's influence in this community. Ever since his wife was killed ten years ago, he pretty much walks on water. Then you've got people like the state attorney, although this fellow Merton is fairly new, and it looks like he's following Sam's lead. There's Art Grumman, the editor of the paper, Jim Bentley who runs the chamber of commerce, the local ministers—people like that who control the money and the flow of information."

"I'll bet Jeffries has already met with these people and put the fix in," Jack said.

Tom agreed. "I think you're right. And if you are, we're going to be trying this case right here in Oakville where those same people control the message inside and outside of the courtroom. Still want to leave Sam Jeffries alone?"

"I do. We need to file the motion anyway if only to make a record for appellate purposes," Jack said.

"I agree but they probably have Judge Holbrook in their pocket as well. Didn't you say he was very much influenced by public opinion?"

"I did. And he's probably influenced more by the people we've been talking about—the people he sees at the golf course and the country club—than any other group. All of a sudden this case is looking a lot more difficult.

"Last chance, Tom. Do you want out?" Jack asked.

"Not on your life," Tom replied. "And one way or the other, it will be about your life, Jack."

CHAPTER FIFTY-FIVE

Tom and Jack were right about the fix being in. There were no editorials or demonstrations of any kind even though the national press and the foreign press were everywhere trying to foment outrage so that they could report on it objectively.

Still, after two weeks of watching and waiting in vain, Tom and Jack managed to prepare a pretty good motion for change of venue.

When Jack had first made an appearance representing Thomas Felton, the *Oakville Sun* had written some brutal editorials about Jack and his motivations for wanting to represent a serial killer. Numerous letters to the editor had followed, spewing the same vitriol. Not one letter had appeared supporting Jack for taking on the case. That wasn't the worst of it, though. The worst came after Kathleen Jeffries was killed. The editorials were harsh, but the letters to the editor almost uniformly linked Jack and Felton and called for both of their heads—literally.

It was powerful evidence and formed the basis for the motion.

Two days after they filed it, Judge Holbrook set it for hearing along with a status conference.

Tom was staying in a one-bedroom condo right next to Jack's that Ron also owned.

"We're paying for this one," Jack told Ron when he offered the place.

"Sure you are," Ron said. "I'm going to need you later on in life, Jack. Let me do this and you can pay me down the road."

Jack had just shaken his head at the time. There was no arguing with Ron.

"What do you make of this?" Tom asked Jack when he received Judge Holbrook's order.

Jack looked at the order. "I think the judge is sending us a message, Tom. He's setting the status conference at the time of the hearing to let us know before we get there that he is denying our motion."

"That's what I thought, too," Tom said. "This judge is really going to be a problem. He's also going to want to know our thoughts about a trial date when we get there."

"You're right. It's always been my inclination, if I didn't have a need to do any further investigation or preparation, to go as soon as possible. The State is always banking on the defendant's asking for more time and they are never prepared."

"I agree with you that we should go right away," Tom said. "But I've done some research on this Merton fellow. He's always prepared. And he'll want to go right away, too. I'll bet he has all his disclosures—names and addresses of witnesses and a list of the evidence—with him at the hearing. He'll hand them to us and tell the judge he's ready to go anytime."

"And when do you think anytime will be, Tom?"

"With a specially appointed judge it could be as quick as two weeks if we don't have any depositions."

"Do we?"

"I don't think so. I could take Jeffries's deposition but it won't get us anywhere and it will make him more relaxed than I want him to be."

"So we just tell the judge we're ready to go?" Jack asked.

"I think we should tell him he can set it three weeks out with the

understanding that we may need more time if there's anything in
the discovery Merton gives us that we haven't seen before."

"That's agreeable to me," Jack said.

The summer after Thomas Felton's brutal murder spree, Apache
County and the City of Oakville built a spacious new court complex
in downtown Oakville.

The previous courthouse dated back to the Civil War. The courtrooms were old and hot, the floorboards creaked, and the overhead
fans rattled so badly, you thought at any time one of them might
take off and power itself right out of the room like a wayward heli-
copter, or, even worse, land on some poor, unfortunate victim. There
were three courtrooms in the old courthouse. The main one was
enormous with its own balcony where the black folks often used to
stand and watch their kinfolk railroaded, but the other two were
very small.

Oakville had grown in population and in criminals, and the old
courthouse could no longer handle the volume of traffic coming and
going through its doors, so the county commission and the city council pooled their resources and built a new, modern complex with ten
courtrooms, all similar in size and shape, all with the same bland
gray walls and pine veneer tables, benches, and judges' dais, so that
you could not tell one courtroom from the other. They were small,
too, with five or six rows of benches in each to fit the observers who
wanted to come and watch a trial. That was usually enough and, in
most cases, more than enough. On a normal day, the benches in every courtroom would be empty except for criminals waiting to have
their cases called, or loved ones.

The old courthouse was not torn down, however, only because
it had become a historic landmark and could not be destroyed.
Although in plain sight, it simply became invisible like an old man
who had lived out his usefulness to society and stood on the corner

of the street every day, confident that his presence would go unnoticed.

Judge Holbrook, being from the north end of the county, didn't have an office in downtown Oakville, nor a courtroom for that matter. It wasn't a major problem. There was usually a courtroom empty for hearings, and an office had been located for the judge and his secretary while he was in town. However, the judge was eventually going to be trying Jack Tobin's murder charge and nobody knew how long the trial was going to last. It would be difficult to tie up one of the other judges' courtrooms for an indefinite period of time. Besides, none of the new courtrooms were equipped to handle the crowds that were anticipated for the trial of Jack Tobin.

The hearing on the motion was on a Monday morning in late May. The sweltering heat and humidity of the summer had not yet arrived but even though it was an overcast day, it was still in the eighties and humid. Tom had received a call late Friday afternoon advising him that the hearing was going to be in the main courtroom of the old courthouse.

"What do you think that's about?" he asked Jack. The two men had been through so many trials that they knew every little change could have some significance.

"I'm not sure," Jack said. "He's a visiting judge. Maybe they don't have a courtroom for him."

"Maybe. Maybe he's letting us know this is going to be one of those old-fashioned lynchings with a trial thrown in just to dress things up, like in the old days."

"Maybe so," Jack said. "But they can't get away with things today that they used to be able to get away with in the old days."

"You're right, but it won't stop them from trying. They've gotten this far."

They found a parking spot close to the courthouse, which was unusual since they arrived only minutes before the hearing was scheduled to begin.

They weren't surprised by the legion of reporters and television cameras. Both men knew this was going to be a media circus— a prominent lawyer on trial for murdering a serial killer. It didn't get any better than that. However, they were surprised by the small number of people in attendance and the lack of any signs supporting one position or another.

"No wonder we got a good parking spot," Jack said.

"Let's hope that's just the beginning of our good luck," Tom replied. "Get ready. We're going to plow through this slew of reporters ahead."

I've been in Tom's position so many times in my life, Jack thought to himself as they started side by side to push through the crowd of media people shouting questions and snapping pictures. *Now it's my turn to be the client, to rely on my lawyer and the system. God help me.*

CHAPTER FIFTY-SIX

Robert Merton was already in the courtroom when Tom and Jack arrived. He greeted them both amiably as if they were business rivals who had just arrived for a negotiation. Anyone looking at the tall, handsome defendant and his even taller elder statesman lawyer would have thought the State had no chance based on appearances alone. Merton was a short, thick, unattractive man with olive skin and black, greasy hair. Both Tom and Jack knew, however, that appearances didn't mean anything in a courtroom battle. Merton's reputation preceded him. He was an experienced, efficient, tough prosecutor who had aspirations for higher office. This was the beginning of a war and they knew it.

As the nine o'clock hour approached, the reporters and spectators filed in. By ten minutes to nine when the bailiffs closed the doors, the courtroom was more than half full. Jack knew that would change once the trial started.

Judge Holbrook walked in at nine and everybody stood.

"You may be seated," he said, almost shouting to be heard over the fans and the creaking benches. The courtroom was air conditioned but with window units. The windows were old and they leaked and the ceiling was thirty feet high, so there was a lot of space to cover and the antiquated ceiling fans that hung down from long poles to about fifteen feet from the floor had to stay on, swaying and creaking. Still, even with the courtroom only half full, it was warm. It didn't take long for people to start sweating.

"We have a motion for change of venue set for hearing today and then we have some housekeeping issues if we are going to proceed in this venue," the judge said. "Mr. Wylie, I have read your motion. Is there anything you would like to add?"

Tom stood up. "Yes, Your Honor. The newspaper articles we have attached to our motion show clearly and consistently that my client cannot receive a fair trial in Apache County. We have not attached any recent editorials or letters to the editor because, surprisingly, since Mr. Tobin was arrested for the murder of Thomas Felton, there haven't been any. Nothing has changed, however, and there is no reason to conclude that public sentiment has changed."

"Do you agree with that, Mr. Merton?"

"No, Your Honor."

"Do you have evidence to disprove it?"

"Yes, Your Honor. May I approach?"

"Come on."

Merton handed some documents to the judge and immediately gave a copy to Tom. "Judge, this is our response to the defendant's motion. I'd like to summarize it if I could."

"Proceed, Counselor." The judge seemed irritated with Merton's formality.

"Your Honor, the State doesn't take issue with the defendant's assertions in its motion. Those assertions simply do not tell the entire story and they don't accurately reflect public sentiment at present.

"Obviously, public sentiment was against Mr. Tobin's efforts to free a man who was convicted of terrorizing this town and killing its citizens ten years ago. I don't think the record reflects that those sentiments were against Mr. Tobin personally at that time. Now, after Kathleen Jeffries was killed, emotions were very high and they were personal in the immediate aftermath of that tragedy. There is no denying that. However, this public emotional sentiment is not static, it has been continuously changing.

"I would point out to the court—and this evidence is contained in the State's response—that there were letters to the editor attacking the State and the undersigned personally for setting Mr. Felton free, so the animosity was on both sides. Now, however, things have changed again. Jack Tobin killed a man who everybody in this town believes was a serial killer. People are happy about that. There are no recent editorials or letters to the editor against Tobin because the animosity is no longer there.

"Just two days ago, the *Oakville Sun* published an editorial questioning whether the State should even be spending the money to prosecute Jack Tobin. I submit to you, Your Honor, that the evidence shows that the worm has turned in Mr. Tobin's favor. Maybe the State should be asking for a change of venue."

"Well, do you want one?" the judge asked.

"No, sir. We'll take our chances with the good citizens of this county."

"The guy makes me want to barf," Jack whispered in Tom's ear.

"He's good, though," Tom said. "He tends toward the dramatic but he's making his point."

"Mr. Wylie," the judge asked. "Do you have a response?"

"I would just comment that it seems a little strange, Your Honor, that since Felton was killed, there have been no editorials about the killing and my client—none—until two days before this hearing when the *Oakville Sun* suddenly woke up and questioned the wisdom of my client being tried at all. This is a hometown setup all the way."

"Mr. Wylie," the judge said, "you can't base your reasons for a change of venue on the *Oakville Sun* and criticize the paper at the same time. You've got to take the good with the bad."

"I disagree, Your Honor. What's happening here is pretty clear."

"Maybe to you, Counselor," the judge replied, "but not to me. Your motion is denied. I will, however, agree to sequester the jury because once this trial starts there is going to be all sorts of stuff on the airwaves and in print. Now we need to discuss logistics."

It was the ruling both Tom and Jack had expected, but one never gets used to injustice. Tom needed a minute to collect himself, so he sat down and let Merton take the lead.

"Your Honor, I have my list of witnesses and evidence, which I am giving to the defendant's counsel this morning in open court. I believe these documents satisfy the state's obligation under Rule 3.220 of the Criminal Rules of Procedure. Having said that, Your Honor, we are ready to proceed to trial at your earliest convenience. This is a case that needs to be disposed of as soon as possible, respecting the rights of all parties, of course."

"Have there been any plea bargain discussions?" the judge asked.

"No, sir," Merton replied, "nor will there be."

That got the judge's attention. He looked at Merton as if to say, *Are you sure you want to do this? You can offer this guy a year, maybe two, save a lot of face and guarantee your reelection.*

Jack leaned over and whispered in Tom's ear, "Cocky bastard, isn't he?"

"He sure is but we wouldn't have it any other way, would we?"

"Nope. Makes our decision a lot easier."

"Changed your mind on Sam yet?" Tom asked.

"Not yet."

"Mr. Wylie, how do you feel about a trial date?" the judge asked.

"Your Honor, I obviously have not looked at the State's disclosures yet. My client is not opposed to setting an early trial date, say three weeks from today, with the caveat that if we decide we need to do further discovery after reading the State's disclosures, we can get a new trial date."

"What do you think, Mr. Merton?"

"That's fine with me, Your Honor, so long as we set a deadline as to when Mr. Wylie will make his decision."

"That sounds fair. How much time do you think you need to make your decision, Mr. Wylie?"

"Ten days, Your Honor."

"How about June sixth?"

"That's fine, Your Honor," Tom said.

"That's agreeable to the State, Your Honor," Merton said.

The reporters in the front rows were feverishly writing down the dates in their notebooks.

"Okay, if no request is made for a continuance on or before June sixth, we will have a pre-trial on June ninth and the trial will be set for Monday, June sixteenth. Mr. Tobin, if no continuance is granted, you will turn yourself over to the custody of the Oakville Police Department on the morning of June sixteenth at seven a.m. Is that understood?"

Jack stood to address the judge. "Yes, Your Honor."

"Okay, gentlemen, if there is nothing further, this hearing is adjourned." The judge stood up and walked out of the courtroom as the press moved in unison toward the lawyers and Jack.

"Let's get the hell out of here," Tom said.

CHAPTER FIFTY-SEVEN

For the next ten days Tom and Jack pored over the State's disclosures and its case, taking everything apart piece by piece, making sure they weren't missing anything before finally agreeing to the early trial date.

They met every morning in Jack's condo. Tom would bring the bagels and Jack would make the coffee. Henry was there for breakfast and he'd usually hang around for a while to see if they needed him to do anything. If not, he'd leave them alone.

"Let's go over the obvious first," Jack said after the seventh day when they had been through just about everything. "They're going to use the two cops to establish that I said I was going to kill Felton. We can deal with them. Then they put Jeffries on and he goes through how he found the body, that there was no gun, and that Danni and I both told him that I shot Felton. Jeffries then talks about motive—he brings in the claims bill and the contingency fee agreement and makes the argument that I killed Felton because he screwed up my payday. Merton has got to ask him then why I didn't plant the gun if I planned this all along, and that's when he comes up with his theory that I was going to plant the gun but he, Jeffries, thwarted that plan by arriving on the scene so quickly. We don't know they're going to do that for sure but there's no other way they can handle that problem that I can think of."

"That's the basic case. Now let's get into the nitty-gritty," Tom said.

The two men had developed a style between them of talking things out and taking them apart in brainstorming sessions. Jack found his older counsel to be sharp as a tack and totally flexible in going where the evidence took them. He was also brutally honest at times and Jack knew and appreciated that that was an absolute necessity.

"Let's talk about those documents for a minute," Tom said. "How are they going to authenticate them? They can't use you."

"They've listed a handwriting specialist. The contingency fee agreement is an original. If they can establish my signature on the agreement, I think it's in. Once they get the agreement in evidence, I think the judge will have to let the claims bill in even though it's a copy."

"Do they have enough original examples of your signature for the specialist to work with? They haven't yet asked for any samples," Tom asked.

"I sent a few letters to the police department a few years back," Jack said. "They can use those. And I filed some pleadings with Judge Holbrook, so they can look at the court file for those."

"Okay, so they have enough examples to establish your signature. They're going to get the documents in. Why don't we agree to their admissibility," Tom suggested.

"Why don't we wait," Jack countered.

"I'm not sure I understand."

"Wait until trial. When Merton calls his handwriting expert, you stand up in front of the jury and tell the judge in open court that you think Mr. Merton is calling this witness to establish the authenticity of certain documents. Then tell the judge there's no need for that—"

Tom cut him off excitedly. "We stipulate them into evidence right in front of the jury so the jurors know we're not hiding anything. It's brilliant."

"Thank you," Jack said. "I told you I was brilliant, you just weren't listening."

Tom smiled. "I'm an old man, I don't hear everything."

"You hear plenty. What were you going to tell me about the coroner's report?"

"She lists the cause of death as a gunshot wound but the back of his head was smashed in."

"I know. He fell backward, and it looks like he hit his head when he landed. Let's look at the pictures again."

Tom pulled out the pictures Merton had provided in the package he produced in open court. Tom turned to the pictures of Felton's head.

"Look at that. He'd have to hit the ground awfully hard to do that kind of damage," Tom said. "Maybe somebody smashed his head in because he wasn't dead when he arrived."

"Don't go there, Tom. Look at the rock under Felton's head. It's certainly big enough to cause that kind of damage, and there's blood all over it. Besides, the coroner didn't say anything about somebody smashing his head multiple times."

"The coroner probably didn't look that closely because of the gunshot wound. Maybe you're right, Jack. Maybe we should leave it alone, but this is your life we're talking about. Why don't we delay the trial and hire our own pathologist to look at this."

"Look, Tom, you've read enough of these reports in your day. The bullet nicked the aorta. Now it wasn't a big nick but that just means that it might have taken him twenty minutes to die rather than ten. There's no doubt that my bullet killed the man."

"You can get an expert to say anything."

"I've seen it a thousand times. You pay them, they'll say anything. We're not going that route."

"I didn't think so. I'm just raising possibilities."

"I know, Tom, and I appreciate that."

"You should at least let me explore the possibility that the head wound may have expedited Felton's demise."

"For what reason?" Jack asked. "To suggest to the jury the possibility that Jeffries bashed Felton's head in? I assure you that's not going to help our case. Besides, I'm not going to do it."

"Well, I think that's what happened," Tom said. "I think Jeffries took the gun and I think he bashed Felton's head in."

"You may be right, but those theories are not going to leave this room unless we have concrete evidence to support them."

"I understand. That was our deal. Let's move on. Do you think they're going to call that girlfriend of yours?"

"Danni? She's not my girlfriend."

"I know, she's just a friend. Do you think they'll call her?"

"Of course. She can buttress Jeffries's testimony that I said I shot Felton."

"Any other reason?"

"None that I can think of."

"Well, think hard because she's an unknown for me."

"I can't think of any other reason they'd call her."

"You're sure, Jack?"

"Sure as I can be."

"Okay, so far we have the cops, Jeffries, the coroner, your friend Danni—anybody else we can think of?"

"I was thinking about this—how are they going to establish it was me that called Felton?"

"I don't know. I expected them to call somebody from the telephone company but nobody is listed on their witness list."

"Dammit! I forgot," Jack said. "They can get that from Danni. I called her a few times."

"Let me ask you this one more time—is there anything else they can get from Danni?"

"No. I know I forgot about the telephone number but why do you keep pressing that issue, Tom?"

"Because she's your blind spot, Jack. You think only a certain way about her and you know as well as I do that in a trial for your life you can't have any blind spots."

"Well, I'm pretty sure that's everything."

"Keep thinking. We can't afford any surprises."

"I will, Tom, but as of now I've got nothing."

"So what do you think? Are we ready to go to trial?"

"I'm ready," Jack said. "If you agree, I don't want to wait."

"I agree," Tom said. "Let's get it done."

CHAPTER FIFTY-EIGHT

Monday, June sixteenth, was a cloudy gray morning. Magnificent storm clouds were looming in the distance. Flashes of lightning could be seen and vague rumbles of thunder could be heard—omens of trouble to come.

"I love days like this," Jack told Henry. They were standing outside the condo looking toward the horizon. "Cloudy skies are so complicated, as if secrets are hidden within them."

Henry slid into the driver's side of his vehicle. Jack settled next to him.

"Let's hope there's no secrets hidden in that courtroom today," Henry said as they pulled out of the driveway.

"It's just jury selection."

"Jurors don't have secret agendas?" Henry asked.

"You've got a point, Henry. Let's hope there are no hidden secrets today."

They picked up Ron in front of The Swamp. He had his hands full. He handed a bag to Jack, got in the back, and started handing out cups of coffee.

"Henry, you're black, no sugar. Right?"

"Are you insulting me? Of course I'm black," Henry said. "But I'm sweet."

It wasn't all that funny but it was good enough. This was a serious day and they all needed a little levity.

"Could have fooled me," Ron said as he handed Jack his coffee. "I thought you were Jamaican. Jack, there's bagels in your bag—one for each of us. I already toasted them and loaded them with cream cheese. Who knows if they're going to give you breakfast."

"Thanks, Ronnie. I appreciate that."

Ten minutes later, Henry pulled the car up in front of the jail.

"It's six thirty, Jack. You're early. Wanna just hang out in the parking lot for a while?"

"No, let's get it over with."

The three men exited the car. Thunder could still be heard in the distance.

"It's moving this way," Jack said.

"It's going to kill my business," Ron added, which made both Henry and Jack laugh out loud.

"What?" Ron asked. "That's funny?"

"You're funny," Jack said as he gave his friend a hug. "I'll see you in a few days."

"I'm counting on it," Ron said.

Then Jack turned to Henry.

"I was thinking we haven't been fishing much lately."

"Yeah," Henry said. "I miss our days out on the lake waiting for the fish to jump in the boat."

Jack smiled. The two men hugged.

"We'll do it soon," he said.

"Soon," Henry replied.

Jack turned and walked toward the jail.

Two hours later, Tom faced the crowds and the reporters on his own. The crowds were much larger today although there were still no signs or placards. And the media were there in full force—

newspaper and television reporters. Microphones were set up on the courthouse steps. As he walked toward the courthouse, Tom could see Merton standing in front of them pontificating as if he were a college professor and the reporters were his eager students.

I wish the storm hadn't passed by, Tom thought to himself.

Merton was walking away when he reached the steps so he decided to say a few words. *What the hell. I'm not going to let him try his case out here.* He could see the surprise on some of the reporters' faces as he stepped to the microphones.

He waited, as a good trial lawyer always does, until he had their undivided attention.

"I know it is often forgotten these days but one of the foundations of our democracy is that a man is presumed innocent until he is found guilty by a jury of his peers in a court of law—not the court of public opinion. Cases are tried in there, not out here." Tom pointed to the courthouse behind him. "That's the way it has always worked, folks. It's the one thing that hasn't changed much. This trial won't be long. The facts are pretty straightforward. I represent a good man who has dedicated his life to the law. When this trial is over, if he so chooses, he may stop and say a word or two to you on his way home."

Tom turned and walked into the courthouse with reporters shouting questions at his back.

The courtroom was empty. Reporters weren't allowed in for jury selection. Merton was already there with his files spread out on the table. Tom went to the opposing table and took a yellow pad out of his briefcase, laid it on the table, and sat down. The fans were churning, the air conditioners rattling. The old courthouse sounded like a factory. At exactly nine o'clock, Judge Holbrook walked in. The two lawyers started to stand but he motioned them to stay seated. There were no spectators and no reason for the pomp and circumstance. That would come soon enough.

"This is the case of the *State of Florida versus Jack Tobin*, Case Number 03-CI-759. Counsel, are we ready to proceed?" the judge asked in a loud voice.

Both lawyers stood up.

"The State is ready, Your Honor."

"The defendant is ready, Your Honor."

"Okay. Mr. Wylie has expressed a preference for examining one juror at a time so that is what we are going to do. What I would like to do is examine twelve jurors and then we'll have a conference and see where we are. Then we'll do another twelve and touch base again until we have a panel. Is that agreeable?"

Tom stood up. "The procedure is agreeable, Your Honor. I just want to make sure back striking is allowed."

Back striking was a procedure that allowed each lawyer to strike a potential juror at any time until the panel was finally selected and ready to be sworn in, even though that juror had already been passed over.

"Back striking is allowable, Mr. Wylie. However, I hope that you lawyers do not abuse the process. Is that understood?"

Both lawyers nodded.

"While we're on the subject of procedure, let me tell you how I want objections handled both during jury selection and throughout. You will stand and make your legal objection. If I want argument, I will have you approach sidebar. There will be no speaking objections. Is that understood?"

Speaking objections occurred when the lawyers stood and made arguments in front of the jury. Often it was a tactic to try to influence the jurors.

"Yes, Your Honor."

"Yes, Your Honor."

"Are there any other questions?"

"No, Your Honor."

"No, Your Honor."

The judge turned to the bailiff who was standing to his right by a closed door.

"Bring in the defendant."

The bailiff disappeared through the door and minutes later he came back in, followed by Jack and two uniformed police officers. Jack wore a blue suit, white shirt, and maroon tie. He walked over to where Tom was standing and stood next to him. The two officers stood by the wall directly across from him, maybe ten feet away. The bailiff went back to his position by the door.

The judge addressed Jack.

"Mr. Tobin, I'm pretty sure I don't need to tell you what is going to transpire during jury selection or how I expect you to conduct yourself. Am I correct in that assumption?"

"Yes, you are, Your Honor."

"Okay then, let's proceed."

Jury selection was one of the topics that Jack and Tom had spent a considerable amount of time on during their three weeks of preparation.

"We need to get into the nitty-gritty with each potential juror," Jack had said at the time. "So we need to question them individually outside of the presence of the other jurors."

But what was the nitty-gritty? They both believed that each juror had to be asked whether he or she believed that Tom Felton was a serial killer.

"When they say yes, then we've got to ask them if they know who you are," Tom said. "If they say yes to that question, which most of them probably will do, we have to ask them what they know about you. And when they tell us that you got Felton set free, we have to ask them how they feel about that. And then we have to ask them what they know about this case, or what they have heard."

Jack had agreed with Tom's assessment. They wanted jurors who thought Felton was a serial killer because they would be less inclined to convict Jack for killing him although that inclination might not trump their anger for getting him set free in the first place. That was the heart of it, and the two men would have to gauge each individual juror as they listened to the answers and watched the body language.

"It's a fine line we're walking here," Tom said.

"I'm not sure I understand."

"Well, we have to hammer home at every opportunity the notion that every man, especially you, is cloaked with a presumption of innocence and, at the same time, we have to hope and pray each juror does not extend that presumption to Thomas Felton. Remember, the Florida Supreme Court had freed him and the State of Florida chose not to prosecute him."

"I wonder if Mr. Merton will be bringing up the presumption of innocence that Felton enjoyed at the time I shot him," Jack said.

"Everything I've heard about Merton tells me he's not that stupid," Tom said. "Everybody knows Felton was guilty and everybody knows Merton chose not to prosecute him for the attempted murder of Stacey Kincaid. Merton's not going to try and play that card."

"He needs some emotional impact, though, to get the jury on his side. Without a victim, he's only got me and their anger at me for representing Felton."

"Maybe he figures that's enough."

"Well then, I guess jury selection is going to come down to finding the jurors who are least angry at me for helping to get Felton released."

"I think that sums it up, Jack."

Jury selection was surprisingly short. Both Jack and Tom had expected it to take a week, but it only took two days. Oakville was a small town. Every potential juror believed Felton was a serial killer and every juror knew Jack's role in getting him set free. Still, most asserted that they could decide this case on its facts alone and would not let their opinions about Jack's representation of Felton influence their decision.

"I'm never inviting Mr. Tobin over to my house for dinner," one woman said. "And I don't think we will ever be friends, but I can still hear the facts of this case and decide it on its merits. If that means setting Mr. Tobin free, then so be it."

Tom and Jack decided to keep her. Robert Merton disagreed.

CHAPTER FIFTY-NINE

The real show started on Wednesday. People were lined up at daybreak to get seats in the courtroom. Television kiosks were set up everywhere and reporters were reporting even when there was nothing to report. One was comparing Jack to the famous criminal defense lawyer, Clarence Darrow. Another was comparing the trial to the O. J. Simpson fiasco.

The reality was far different. Jack and his defender, Tom Wylie, were not interested in making the trial a spectacle. They were trying to reduce the issues to their simplest terms and get the spectacle over with as soon as possible. Merton liked the grand stage a little more, but even he planned to stick to the facts.

Judge Holbrook walked into the courtroom promptly at nine o'clock after being announced by the bailiff. The noise from the full courtroom standing up was almost deafening: The benches creaked, the floorboards creaked, the overhead fans squeaked, and the air conditioners, which weren't working all that well, rattled. Judge Holbrook had to shout for everyone to be seated.

Jack was dressed in a blue pinstripe suit and was seated next to Tom, who leaned over and whispered in his ear. "Now I know why people from the Old South talked so loud," he said, pointing up at the overhead fans. Jack smiled. His lawyer was trying to keep him loose.

Judge Holbrook began the proceedings by admonishing the spectators.

"A man is on trial for his life. You are here as spectators to witness the American justice system at work. However, you don't have an individual right to be here. You will sit and observe in silence and you will not react to anything that happens. If you react in any way, or if you do not remain silent, your privilege to observe will be revoked, and you will be removed from the courtroom."

He didn't ask them if they understood his words. He simply turned to the lawyers.

"Do you have anything you want to discuss before we bring in the jury?"

"No, Your Honor."

"No, Your Honor."

"Bring in the jury," the judge told the bailiff.

Moments later, the twelve jurors and one alternate entered the room—eight men and four women, the alternate being a woman as well.

"The lawyers are going to give their opening statements now," the judge told them. "Opening statements are designed to give you an overall view of each side's case. Listen carefully because the evidence does not often come in as timely and as precisely as we would like. Witnesses often testify out of order, depending on their schedules. And some evidence is never admitted. I caution you that what the lawyers say is not evidence. The only evidence is what is said from the witness stand and the documents that are admitted into evidence during the course of the trial.

"Mr. Merton, you may proceed."

Robert Merton strode to the lectern that was facing the jury, but he stood next to it, not behind it. Being small in stature, Merton had learned a long time ago that the lectern only diminished his stature.

"Good morning, ladies and gentlemen," he began. "This case is about this man, Jack Tobin." He took the time to point directly at Jack, a tactic that he would use over and over again during the trial. It had no effect on Jack, who had seen every tactic in a courtroom that there was to see. "This man, a very famous and successful trial lawyer, utilized his talents to free a serial killer on death row." Merton paused for effect. *"For money!* And when that serial killer double-crossed him by killing again before he could collect his money, Jack Tobin intentionally murdered his own client."

It was a very aggressive tactic—go for the jugular immediately, leave the details for later. Reduce Jack in the eyes of that jury as quickly as he could. Jack and Tom had expected nothing less. They didn't expect what came next, though.

"But this case doesn't start with the murder of Thomas Felton. It starts with the beginning of the deal. The defendant had to get Felton off to get Felton a payoff from the Florida legislature—and I will explain that process to you in a moment. And to get Felton off, the defendant had to attack the people who arrested him—impugn their character.

"You will hear from two of those officers: Danni Jansen, a retired homicide detective who was a member of the original task force, and Sam Jeffries, the head of the task force that tracked Felton down so many years ago and now the chief of police of our town. Sam had already lost his wife at Felton's hand. The defendant brutally and effectively attacked Sam's handling of the case, accusing the entire prosecution of planting evidence."

Tom was on his feet. Lawyers didn't usually interrupt other lawyers during opening statements, but Merton was way over the line.

"Objection, Your Honor. Mr. Merton is trying the wrong case here. Thomas Felton was released by the Florida Supreme Court. We can't try his appeal all over again in this case."

"That is a speaking objection, Mr. Wylie. I told you I won't have speaking objections in my courtroom. Overruled."

"But Your Honor—"

"Overruled, Mr. Wylie. Mr. Merton, you may proceed."

Tom sat down next to Jack, extremely frustrated. "This judge is going to be a big problem."

"We now know what Merton is going to use for his emotional impact. His victim isn't Felton, it's Sam Jeffries," Jack said.

"Exactly. And the judge is going to let him get away with it."

Meanwhile, Merton spent the rest of his opening putting meat on the bare-bones accusations he had made. He took the jurors through the facts he intended to prove in a meticulous fashion although he left a few things out. Tom didn't know if it was meant to keep the jury curious or to surprise him and Jack, or both.

"Mr. Wylie, are you ready to proceed?" the judge asked Tom when Merton had finished.

"Yes, Your Honor," Tom said and stood to face the jury.

Tom Wylie had a slow, easy manner about him that tended to put everyone around him at ease. It was a stark contrast to Merton's aggressive style. Because of his height, Tom could stand behind the podium and still comfortably address the jurors, although he preferred to walk about.

He started his remarks by reminding the jurors of the burden of proof, the same thing he'd done with each juror during jury selection. Tom believed firmly that, when it came to the burden of proof, you had to repeat it to the jury over and over again.

"When I talked to you during jury selection, I told you that the State has the burden to prove its case beyond a reasonable doubt. And I told you that the defendant has no burden and no obligation to put on even one witness in his defense, and, if the State does not meet its burden, you as jurors must acquit the defendant. And I asked each one of you if you understood and I asked if you could decide this case following that burden of proof, and you all assured me that you could. Now the trial has begun and I remind you of your promise and I ask you as you listen to the witnesses on both direct and cross-examination to always keep that burden of proof in your mind."

Tom paused to look each and every juror in the eye. By making eye contact, he was getting that individual commitment one more time. Merton didn't even notice. He was writing furiously in his yellow pad. Tom continued.

"Now you heard Mr. Merton say just a few minutes ago that this case really has its roots in the original appeal of Thomas Felton when the defendant—and I quote Mr. Merton—'brutally and effectively' attacked Sam Jeffries's handling of the investigation. Facts, ladies and gentlemen, you are guided by nothing but facts—not unfounded accusations, not character assassination."

Tom spoke the words softly. He wasn't pointing any fingers at Robert Merton. It wasn't his way.

"And the fact is, ladies and gentlemen, that the supreme court of this state, not Jack Tobin, set Mr. Felton free. And the supreme court of this state produced a written opinion about why Mr. Felton should be set free. That opinion is the law of that case, which every one of us, including Mr. Merton, is bound to follow. So please, do not be fooled by those deceptive words from the prosecution that would have you believe Mr. Tobin did something improper in his defense of Thomas Felton. They are false words designed to derive sympathy from you for Mr. Jeffries and anger from you toward Mr. Tobin. They have no place in this trial."

Tom paused for a moment, knowing what was coming. Merton rose from his chair, his face turning a darker shade of red at each movement so that when he was fully erect, his face was almost purple with rage.

"Objection, Your Honor." He shouted so loud that, despite the noise from the ceiling fans and the clanging of the air conditioners, every person in the courtroom could clearly hear his words. This was what they had come for—the showdown at the OK Corral. And it hadn't taken long for the fight to begin.

"Your Honor, Mr. Wylie is directly attacking my character and I won't have it."

Tom looked at Jack, who nodded. They both thought that Merton was high-strung despite his obvious talent in the courtroom. This was the initial experiment to see if they could get him unhinged, and it had worked to perfection. Merton was now headed toward the center of the courtroom and was out of control.

"May we approach, Your Honor?"

"Stay right there, Mr. Merton," Judge Holbrook said. "I want the jury to hear this.

"We are going to try this case in a professional manner. If you two want to go outside when this trial is over and have a fistfight, so be it. But in this courtroom you will conduct yourselves as professionals. There will be no personal attacks. Is that understood?"

Merton stuck his chest out triumphantly, looking at the jury as he walked back to his seat. "Yes, Your Honor," he said as if he were the conquering hero.

Tom was as calm as a man could be. He looked at Merton and then back at the judge. "Yes, Your Honor. And I apologize to counsel if he took my statements as a personal attack. They were not meant to be. I was merely commenting on the statements that he made to the jury."

Merton was not yet in his seat. "Your Honor?" he pleaded.

"Mr. Wylie," the judge said, "you heard my comments. Now, move on."

"Yes, Your Honor."

Tom was satisfied that he had significantly exposed Merton's character to the jurors. A lot of times close cases came down to what lawyer the jurors liked best. He spent the next ten minutes talking about the facts.

"You will hear from Jack Tobin. He does not have to testify but he is going to. And he will tell you that he was in those woods because he wanted to protect retired police officer Danni Jansen from harm. Was that a reasonable thing to do? You will have to make that determination. He saw Thomas Felton coming from the direction of Ms. Jansen's house. He called to him. Felton turned. Mr. Tobin thought Felton had a gun and that Felton was going to shoot him so he fired his gun. That's all there is to it—self-defense. And that, if nothing else, should create reasonable doubt in your minds."

They broke for lunch after the openings. Tom stayed in the courtroom with Jack. They shared a couple of Snickers bars and talked about the case.

"Good start," Jack told him. "Good opening. It will be interesting to see if Merton figures out we were pushing his buttons."

"I'm sure he will," Tom said. "But I don't know if that will help him. The guy is wound pretty tight. Who do you think he'll call this afternoon?"

Jack didn't hesitate. He had the State's case programmed in his mind—at least most of it. "I'd say the two cops and maybe the coroner if he has time. He'll save Sam for the morning when the jurors are fresh."

"I agree, but what about Danni?"

"She'll come after Sam just to buttress his testimony about what happened and about the phone calls. They'll put on the handwriting guy before Sam, but we'll make him go away."

"So they should be done tomorrow afternoon."

"That's it," Jack said. "Short and sweet."

The two police officers were the first two witnesses in the afternoon just as Jack predicted. Their testimony was pretty much identical. They were there to establish one thing—Jack Tobin said he was going to kill Thomas Felton. Tom's cross-examination was pretty much the same for both although he went into greater detail with officer Richard Brown. Tom never deviated from his soft-spoken, easygoing manner.

"Why were you at Mr. Tobin's condo in the first place?"

"We were told to go there by the assistant chief."

"Where was the chief?"

"We didn't know."

"So the chief disappeared after his daughter's death?"

"I wouldn't say disappeared. He could not be located for a few days."

"And the assistant chief was worried that Chief Jeffries might go after Mr. Tobin, isn't that correct?"

"I don't know that."

"Well, weren't you instructed to go there to tell Mr. Tobin to get out of town?"

"Yes."

"And didn't you tell Mr. Tobin that the chief of police, Sam Jeffries, was missing?"

"We may have."

"You may have? Wasn't the gist of the conversation—the chief of police is missing, we can't protect you, so get out of town?"

Merton couldn't sit still any longer. He hadn't gone into any of this stuff on direct examination.

"I object, Your Honor! This is beyond the scope of direct examination."

Tom saw his opportunity. He'd asked a question that didn't need an answer and he had a good idea what the judge was going to do.

"I'll withdraw the question, Your Honor, and move on. Officer Brown, what was Mr. Tobin's condition at the time you spoke to him?"

"He was intoxicated."

"Severely intoxicated?"

"Yes."

"So he was not of sound mind?"

"I don't think so."

"And this was at a period of time, right after the murder of Kathleen Jeffries, when tensions were high with everybody, correct?"

"Yes."

"And that includes Chief Jeffries, correct?"

"I don't know."

"Weren't you sent to Jack Tobin's condo because the assistant chief was concerned that Chief Jeffries might do him harm?"

Merton was on his feet again. "Objection, Your Honor."

"Sustained!" Judge Holbrook said. "Mr. Wylie, I've already ruled on this once."

"Yes, Your Honor," Tom said, even though the judge had not ruled on the first objection. "Thank you, Your Honor." Tom turned back toward the witness.

"Officer Brown, why did you go to Mr. Tobin's condo?"

Merton was up again—furious. Tom was pushing his buttons—again. "Objection, Your Honor."

"Sustained. Mr. Wylie, I have already ruled!" the judge shouted. Tom was pushing both their buttons now. Tom remained as cool and calm as ever.

"That was a different question, Your Honor. The State put this witness on to testify that he went to my client's residence. Surely I can ask him why he went there?"

Merton cut in at that point. "He asked that question already, Your Honor. Officer Brown said he didn't know. Asked and answered."

Tom had made his point again, or maybe not. You never knew with a jury. In any event, it was time to retreat.

"I'll withdraw the question, Your Honor, and move on."

"And don't revisit this subject again, Mr. Wylie."

"Yes, Your Honor." Tom turned his attention back to Officer Brown.

"How many officers do you have in the Oakville Police Department, Officer Brown?"

"I don't know for sure—fifty, fifty-five."

"So if an order went out, say, directing officers to look for Thomas Felton in a certain location—like the woods behind Danni Jansen's house—you would know about it, wouldn't you?"

"Yes."

"Did you or anyone in the department ever receive such an order?"

"No, sir."

"Thank you, Officer Brown. No further questions, Your Honor."

Merton called the coroner, Marie Vicente, next. Merton knew he needed to keep the jury focused since it was late in the day, so he introduced the coroner's report into evidence, and got to the important stuff right away, starting from when the coroner arrived on the scene and finishing with the autopsy itself, although he skipped most of the details of the autopsy.

"Your report is in evidence, Doctor, so we don't need to discuss all the details. Did you determine a cause of death?"

"Yes, I did."

"And what was that?"

"Mr. Felton died from a gunshot wound to the chest."

"And how did you determine that the gunshot wound was the cause of death?"

"Not to get too technical, the bullet, fragments of which we found in the body, nicked the aorta, causing severe internal bleeding."

Merton had her identify the bullet fragments, introduced them into evidence, and wrapped it up.

"Thank you, Doctor, I have no further questions."

"Your witness, Mr. Wylie," the judge said.

Tom stood and walked toward the witness stand. "Thank you, Your Honor." He didn't speak to Doctor Vicente until he was standing directly in front of her.

"Doctor Vicente, you said the bullet nicked the aorta, is that correct?"

"Yes."

"What does that mean in layman's terms?"

"It means there was a slight tear of the aorta caused by the bullet."

"And what is the difference between a slight tear and, say, a full-blown rupture of the aorta?"

"As far as cause of death, there is no difference."

"How about timing of death? Is it accurate that the smaller the rupture, the longer it takes to die?"

Marie Vicente hesitated for a second and looked at Robert Merton. Jack caught it right away. He didn't think the jury could see it, although he was sure Tom had.

"Not necessarily," she answered.

Tom didn't let it go. "What does that mean? Let me ask it another way: Is the blood flow greater when the aorta fully ruptures?"

"Yes."

"So a person dies faster when there is a complete rupture, correct?"

"Not necessarily. And let me explain. We can surmise that the bullet nicked the aorta from the trajectory of the bullet, which we traced from the entry wound and the path of destruction in the body cavity. Once the aorta is breached and blood begins to flow, a complete rupture can be instantaneous."

The doctor's answer had taken most of the wind out of Tom's sails but he had some left, so he kept on.

"You said 'can be' instantaneous, is that correct?"

"Yes, we're never sure."

"Okay, let's assume there is a complete rupture—how long does it take to die?"

"Approximately ten minutes maximum. It could happen in five or even less."

"And a partial rupture that does not become a complete rupture?"

"I'd say twenty minutes at the most."

"Can you tell whether Mr. Felton died ten or twenty minutes after the fatal bullet struck?"

"No."

Tom walked back to his table and retrieved the copy of the coroner's report that Robert Merton had just given him minutes before. He'd already reviewed his own copy in great detail over the past three weeks.

"Your autopsy report also references severe injury to the lower base of the skull, does it not?"

"Yes, it does."

"How did that happen?"

"I can only surmise based on the facts and the physical evidence."

"And what did you surmise?"

"That Mr. Felton, when he was shot, fell backward. His head hit a large rock very hard and that rock smashed the base of his skull."

"But that was not the cause of death?"

"It was not."

"Could it have hastened death?"

"Yes."

Tom looked at the judge. "Your Honor, I'm almost done. May I have a moment to talk to my client before releasing this witness?"

"You may."

Tom walked over and sat next to Jack.

"You know what I want to ask her, don't you?"

"I do. You want to ask her if it's possible that somebody could have come upon Felton still alive, put a rock under his head, and smashed it until he was dead—is that right?"

"That's right."

"Don't do it."

"Jack, listen to me for a second. We've already got the cops at your door telling you to leave town because they're worried Jeffries might be after you. Now if we can at least insinuate that Jeffries might have smashed Felton's head in for whatever reason, we are on the road toward establishing a hypothesis that Jeffries took Felton's gun to frame you. He was as angry at you at that point as he was at Felton."

"Two things," Jack said. "I don't want to do it because we don't have any direct evidence to support that theory and I don't want to ruin whatever life that man has left. Second, it's a bad strategy, Tom. It makes us look desperate."

"Mr. Wylie, are you ready to proceed?" Judge Holbrook asked.

Tom stood up. "Yes, Your Honor. I have no further questions."

When Tom finished cross-examining the coroner, it was close to five o'clock and the judge adjourned the proceedings for the day.

The stage was set for the testimony of Sam Jeffries.

CHAPTER SIXTY

Tom went directly from the courthouse to the jail to see Jack. He had to wait while Jack shed his courtroom attire for his prison attire: a yellow jumpsuit. Jack was lying on his bed with his back propped up against the wall and his hands behind his head when Tom walked into the cell.

"You look awfully relaxed," Tom said.

"I'm confident. I've got a good lawyer, and besides, worrying gets you nowhere. It was a decent day today."

"I think so," Tom said. "The cops didn't hurt us and neither did the coroner. You were right, by the way, about that last question. It would have made us look desperate."

"That's the benefit of having two lawyers on the case. The one that's watching can stop the other from going too far."

Tom sat on the bed opposite Jack.

"I'm with you so far, Jack, but Merton has made Sam Jeffries both the victim and the chief witness in this case. We need to take a bite out of Jeffries's hide if you want to walk out of here."

"I'm not opposed to that. I'm opposed to floating theories that we have no evidence to support. I'm opposed to ruining a good man's character."

"A good man? This guy wants to send you to the death chamber!"

"I know you believe that—and I believe it as well—but we can't prove it. Besides, Sam Jeffries *is* a good man. His mind is warped because he lost his wife and then his daughter to a man I helped set free."

"Jesus, Jack, I can fight the prosecutor, but I can't fight your conscience at the same time."

"I'm not asking you to. I just want you to play it straight—no intimation that Sam hid the gun or bashed Felton's head in, unless we get evidence to support it."

"All right. It's your funeral."

It was overcast and rainy on Thursday morning as Tom walked to the courthouse. The weather didn't deter the crowds though. People were everywhere and for the first time, there were signs. Merton had struck a chord when he made Sam Jeffries his victim. The signs made that clear.

"Let's Get a Little Justice for Sam," one read. "Kathleen, You Are Not Forgotten," read another.

I've got to be careful with Jeffries, Tom thought to himself. *The jurors have the same sentiments as these people.*

News stations had set up kiosks across from the courthouse, and the reporters practically stampeded toward Tom as he made his way to the courthouse steps. This was not a day to linger outside, however.

"No comment," Tom said as he pushed through the crowd.

"Your boy is going down," someone in the crowd shouted. Tom didn't even look up.

Inside the courtroom, the rain added to the cacophony of sounds. The doors had not yet opened for the crowds. The ceiling fans, the air conditioners, and the rain held court, so to speak. Merton was sitting at his table closest to the jury, writing on his yellow pad. A pretty brunette female attorney from his office sat next to him looking totally bored. Merton had brought her along but he hadn't given her anything to do.

One of the bailiffs saw Tom and immediately exited the room, returning a few minutes later with Jack and two more guards in tow. Jack wore a charcoal-gray suit. Tom was in navy blue. If looks could win, they were the winners hands down.

"All set?" Tom asked.

"I guess so."

The crowds started in a few minutes later, chatting away, adding to the symphony of sounds. The bailiffs squeezed them in, making sure every potential seat was occupied. The first two rows were saved for the press. When everybody was seated, the bailiff knocked on the door to the judge's chambers. Moments later Judge Holbrook walked into the room, his black robe flowing. Everybody stood up.

"Be seated," he said. They obeyed promptly, like cattle following the lead of their master. Judge Holbrook addressed the gallery again. "Those of you who are new, let me advise you that your presence here is a privilege. If you make any comments whatsoever or any gestures of any kind, you will be removed, and you may be held in contempt of court. Do you all understand?"

There was a collective "Yes, sir" as heads nodded in assent.

The judge next turned to the lawyers. "Do we have anything to discuss before I bring the jury in?"

"No, Your Honor," Merton replied.

"No, Your Honor," Tom said.

"Bring the jury in," Judge Holbrook told the bailiff.

After the jurors filed in and were seated, the judge looked at Robert Merton.

"Call your next witness, Counsel."

"The State calls Phillip Hughes."

One of the bailiffs left to retrieve the witness. Jack looked at Tom.

"The handwriting expert," Tom said.

Jack smiled.

Moments later Phillip Hughes entered the room and swore to tell the truth. He then took the stand and gave his name and occupation. That's when Tom stood up.

"Your Honor, if I may, it is the defendant's assumption that Mr. Hughes is here to identify the defendant's signature on the contingency fee agreement and the claims bill. In order to save time, we will not only stipulate that the defendant's signature is contained on those documents, we will stipulate them into evidence if the prosecution chooses to offer them as evidence."

The judge immediately looked at Merton, who knew he'd been had.

"Do we need this witness for anything else, Mr. Merton?"

"No, Your Honor."

"Mr. Hughes, you may step down. Call your next witness, Counselor."

Judges loved to move things along.

"The State calls Sam Jeffries."

It seemed as if everyone in the room shifted position at the sound of Sam Jeffries's name. There were some low murmurings as well, but they stopped immediately after Judge Holbrook stared into the crowd.

Sam entered the courtroom wearing a brown suit. Apparently Merton thought the uniform would be a little much. It wasn't needed anyway. Everybody knew Sam was the chief of police. The clerk swore Sam in, and he immediately took over the witness chair. He was so big that the chair just disappeared under him, giving the appearance that he was sitting on air.

Merton started slowly, having Sam tell the jury about his history in law enforcement, but he heated things up rather quickly, interrupting Sam at the part of his career where he was heading the task force.

"Was there anything wrong with the task force's investigation of the serial killings?"

Tom stood up. "Objection, Your Honor. Relevancy."

"Overruled."

"May we approach, Your Honor?" Tom asked.

"I have ruled, Counselor."

Tom did not sit down. "Your Honor, I have to make my record for an appellate court, if necessary. This is a very important point and I need to be heard."

The judge glared at him. "Your objection is noted."

"A general objection does not preserve the record, Your Honor."

The judge knew Tom was right. "Approach."

He laid into Tom when they reached sidebar. "Counselor, when I have ruled, I don't want any further discussion."

"With all due respect, Your Honor, I represent a man who is on trial for his life. I need to make my record, and the court has an obligation to allow me to do so."

"Don't tell me about my obligations, Counselor."

Tom didn't answer. He'd made his point and the judge knew it. There were a few moments of silence before Holbrook spoke again.

"Go ahead, make your record."

"Your Honor, we can't rehear the appeal of Thomas Felton. The Florida Supreme Court ruled on that case. The question Mr. Merton asked and the ensuing questions that I anticipate he will ask are an attempt to tell this jury that what the supreme court ruled concerning the evidence in that case wasn't true. This court cannot allow that to happen."

The judge looked at Robert Merton. "Mr. Merton?"

"We're not trying to overturn anything, Your Honor. You will not hear me mention the supreme court. I'm just asking this witness about what he did and what he observed. Mr. Wylie is free to cross-examine him as he sees fit. The testimony is relevant because it goes to Mr. Tobin's motive."

Tom interjected without being asked. "He's about to contradict the findings of the Florida Supreme Court. He can't do that."

"I'm going to allow it," Judge Holbrook said. "But only to a limited extent. Mr. Merton, I don't want you spending all day on this stuff and I don't want to hear anything about the supreme court's decision."

"You won't, Your Honor. I have only a few questions."

"And Mr. Wylie, I'm giving you a continuing objection as to this subject matter so you don't have to object to every question. You have made your record as to this issue, Counselor. Have I made myself clear?"

"Yes, Your Honor." Tom almost spit out the words.

Back at the table, Jack was more than curious. "What did he say?"

"He's going to let him go into it. This judge is killing us."

"Actually, he's only killing one of us," Jack replied.

Tom looked at him.

"It's a joke," Jack said. "A little maudlin, maybe, but I've got to keep you loose somehow, Tom."

Tom didn't look at Jack. He just smiled. *What client on trial for murder worries about keeping his lawyer loose?* he thought.

Merton continued his questioning of Sam Jeffries.

"I ask you again, Chief Jeffries, was there anything wrong in the task force's investigation of the serial killings?"

"No."

"What was the supposed problem that got Mr. Felton released?"

Tom couldn't help himself. Merton was doing exactly what he had said he wasn't going to do. He was asking Jeffries why the supreme court released Felton and in the next question, he would ask Jeffries, without specifically asking, why the supreme court was wrong. "Objection, Your Honor. This is a specific, blatant collateral attack on the ruling of the Florida Supreme Court."

"Sit down, Counselor," Judge Holbrook shouted. There was no problem hearing him above the din of the ceiling fans, the air conditioners, and the rain. "One more speaking objection and I will hold you in contempt of court! Your objection is overruled. Continue, Mr. Merton, but make it quick with this line of questioning. I'm giving you a short leash."

"Yes, Your Honor." To the witness: "Do you remember the question, Chief?"

"I do. The murder weapon in the Brock/Diaz murders was a bowie knife. I testified to that and the coroner testified. The coroner's report was never introduced into evidence. Ten years later, the coroner was dead and his report was used to show that there was somehow a discrepancy in the size of the entry wounds that were recorded on the document. It was nothing more than a typing error."

Tom was on his feet.

"Sit down, Mr. Wylie!" the judge shouted before Tom could say anything. "And don't say a word or, so help me, I will hold you in contempt of court!"

Tom sat down, livid. Merton and the judge were pushing his buttons now, a fact that did not go unnoticed by Jack.

"Stay calm. Stay focused," Jack whispered to his lawyer.

"So the basis of Mr. Tobin's legal appeal on behalf of Mr. Felton was what?"

"He argued that the evidence, the bowie knife, was not the real murder weapon. It was planted."

"And who found the bowie knife?"

"I did."

"So who was the finger pointed at?"

"Me."

"And at the time this man"—Merton took the opportunity to point his finger directly at Jack—"At the time this man was pointing the finger at you, you had already lost your wife at the hands of this serial killer, correct?"

"Yes."

"And when he was eventually released, what happened?"

Sam could not speak. It took minutes for him to compose himself so he could mouth the words. Everybody saw the struggle. Everybody *felt* the struggle. The eyes turned red and glassy. The massive chest heaved up and down. Sam tried to form the words but they just wouldn't come out. Everybody watched this giant of a man fall apart right in front of their eyes and they couldn't help but react.

When Sam finally weakly blurted out the words "I lost my daughter," there wasn't a dry eye in the courtroom, except for Tom, who was still livid, and the judge.

Jack Tobin was a pro. He'd represented men accused of murder. He'd represented men on death row, and he had tried hundreds of cases. He knew more than anybody that the demeanor of the people on trial was so important. Yet with all his knowledge and experience, Jack could not control his own emotions. He was almost as upset as Sam, knowing his part in this heartbreaking tragedy. His demeanor did not go unnoticed by the jurors, some of whom were looking directly at him.

Merton had now gotten to Tom Wylie *and* his client. And he wasn't through.

CHAPTER SIXTY-ONE

Sam Jeffries took the jurors with him on his imaginary tale about finding the body of the killer of his wife and daughter. He left out the fact that he had bashed the man's head in and taken his gun. Nobody needed to know those facts. Not when they were considering the fate of the lawyer who had set his wife's killer free, the lawyer who gave his daughter a death sentence. No, they didn't need those facts. Jack Tobin was finally going to get what he deserved.

"What specifically did you do when you came upon the body, Mr. Jeffries?" Merton asked.

"I didn't know whether he was alive or not, although there was blood everywhere. I checked his pulse."

"And?"

"And he was dead. I then looked around for the shooter. This was in the woods right behind Danni Jansen's house, so I thought it might have been Danni. She would never have left the body though. Nobody would have left the body unless there was foul play."

"Why do you say that?"

"You shoot somebody, whether in self-defense or because they are fleeing a crime, you go to them immediately to see what their condition is. You don't run in the opposite direction unless you want to hide something."

"What did Mr. Tobin want to hide?"

Tom was on his feet. "Objection, Your Honor. Speculation."

"Overruled."

"What did Mr. Tobin want to hide?" Merton repeated the question.

"He wanted to hide the fact that he had murdered Mr. Felton in cold blood."

Merton knew that he had gotten ahead of himself so he backtracked.

"What happened after you checked the pulse, determined that Felton was dead, and looked around for the shooter?"

"I called the station and ordered a forensics team and homicide detectives to come to the scene. I then pulled out my binoculars and looked toward Danni Jansen's house. I saw a man knocking on her door and then I saw Danni come out and greet him."

"Anything else that you did?"

"I saw a backpack on Felton so I put on some rubber gloves, turned the body over, and opened the backpack. There were some clothes, a toothbrush, and some papers."

"Did you look at the papers?"

"I did. One was a document called a claims bill and the other was a contingency fee agreement."

"Are you familiar with what a claims bill is?"

"Yes. As chief of police I have attended many seminars where claims bills have been discussed. A claims bill in Mr. Felton's circumstance is a request for the legislature to pay him for all the years he lost when he was wrongfully incarcerated."

"And the contingency fee agreement?"

"That was an agreement between Felton and the defendant whereby Felton was going to pay the defendant one-third of what he got."

"And how much were they requesting in the claims bill?"

"Twenty million dollars."

Somebody in the audience let out a loud gasp, which opened the door for the rest of the gallery to start whispering among themselves, causing Judge Holbrook to bang his gavel several times.

"Order in the court! Order in the court! I will have this courtroom cleared if there is not immediate silence."

The gallery stopped murmuring almost immediately.

"If that happens again," the judge said, "I will have you all removed." He then directed his attention to Robert Merton. "You may proceed, Counselor."

"So the claims bill requested twenty million dollars. What was Mr. Tobin's take?"

"Approximately six million six hundred and sixty-six thousand dollars."

The murmuring started again but stopped when Judge Holbrook picked up the gavel and looked out into the gallery.

"And what happened to Mr. Tobin's take when Thomas Felton killed your daughter?"

Tom could have objected. Nobody had ever determined that Thomas Felton had killed Kathleen Jeffries, but everybody assumed it, including Jack. An objection now would only make him look like an idiot when Jack later testified that he thought Felton was the killer.

"It was gone. The legislature was never going to give Thomas Felton any money. All he was going to get was a one-way ticket to hell."

"Now I want to go back to something you said earlier in your testimony: You said that Jack Tobin, the defendant, wanted to hide the fact that he killed Thomas Felton in cold blood. Why did you assume he had killed Thomas Felton in cold blood?"

"Because Felton had caused him to lose his payday by killing my daughter."

"And in your opinion, that was his motivation to kill Felton?"

"Objection, Your Honor. Opinion testimony."

"Overruled. Proceed."

"Jesus," Tom said to Jack. "You'd think the judge would at least want to make it look like a fair fight."

"You'd think," Jack said.

"Yes," Sam Jeffries answered. "That's my opinion."

"How do you know it was Jack Tobin who killed Felton?"

"He told me—right at the scene. He and Danni Jansen showed up minutes after I arrived on the scene. Tobin told me he had killed Felton."

"And what facts do you have that the defendant lured Felton into the woods?"

"One of the things we recovered was Felton's cell phone. Two nights before the shooting, Jack Tobin had called Felton and he called him again moments before Felton was shot."

The crowd started buzzing again. Judge Holbrook didn't say a word. He simply smacked down the gavel and everything was quiet again.

"How did those facts add to your investigation?"

"Well, once we saw the claims bill and the contingency fee agreement, we knew Tobin had the motive to kill Felton. The telephone told us how. The first call two days before was probably to set up the meeting in the woods. The call moments before the shooting was to make sure Felton was there and to pinpoint his location."

"But why the woods?" Merton was eliciting the testimony piece by piece as if he were solving a mystery right in front of his audience. It was working. The jurors *and* the gallery were on the edge of their seats.

"It set up a perfect alibi for Tobin. He was in the woods to protect Danni Jansen. Felton came by and he shot him—of course, after Felton supposedly pulled a gun."

"But there was no gun?"

"No. We searched every inch of those woods within a thousand feet of where the body lay and found nothing."

"I'm going to test you a little bit here, Chief Jeffries," Merton, the quizmaster said. "If the scenario you laid out for the jury is true, and the defendant set Felton up for murder, why didn't he plant a gun on Felton after he shot him? Wouldn't that have cemented his story?"

"Yes, it would have. I think Tobin was planning on doing exactly that. Unfortunately, I showed up before he could plant the gun. So he went to Danni's house instead, making up the story that he was concerned about her safety."

"Objection, Your Honor. Speculation."

"Overruled. You may proceed, Mr. Merton."

"Why didn't he just leave the scene?"

"He couldn't. He had set up a camp there in the woods. We found his credit card and clothes. There was too much evidence that he was there for him to flee the scene. Besides, we could trace the bullet to his gun. It was quick thinking on his part to do what he did."

"What about the gun you said he was going to plant—did you ever find that?"

"No."

"Did you take him into custody that day?"

"Yes, we took him to the station for questioning."

"Did you search him?"

"At the station, yes."

"So, where did the gun go?"

"We believe he threw it away, sometime after he shot Felton and before we took him into custody—before he met up with Danni. Danni Jansen is an experienced police officer. He wouldn't have been able to dispose of the gun in her presence."

"Did you look for that gun?"

"We did but I have to explain the timing. We initially were

searching for a gun that Felton supposedly had on his person, so we were searching in the neighborhood of the body. We only kept Tobin in custody a couple of hours. By the time we put all the pieces together and even considered the possibility of a planted gun, Tobin was free and had the opportunity to go back and retrieve the gun himself. So we never had any realistic expectation of finding it."

At this point in the questioning, Merton walked to the far wall next to the prosecution table and picked up a large rectangular object that looked like, and in fact was, a piece of foam board. There was an easel leaning against the wall as well, and his assistant, the pretty brunette female lawyer who had been doing nothing up to this point, grabbed the easel and walked with Merton. At his direction, she set up the easel and he placed the foam board on it. There was an elaborate diagram on the foam board and it was now facing the jury so they could see it clearly. There was a house and a yard and woods and they were all in color. Tom had been at the scene several times so he recognized the diagram right away.

"Do you recognize this diagram that I have set up in front of the jury?" Merton asked Sam Jeffries.

"Yes. It shows Danni Jansen's house, her backyard, and the woods surrounding her backyard."

"Your Honor, I have marked a smaller version of this diagram as State's Exhibit number ten. I'd like to introduce it into evidence at this point."

The judge looked at Tom. "Do you have any objection, Counselor?"

"No, Your Honor."

"State's Exhibit number ten is admitted. Proceed, Counselor."

"Now, Chief Jeffries, I have a pointer here and I would like you to come down and take this pointer and show the jury approximately where you found the body, where you first saw Mr. Tobin, and where you looked for this gun you believe Mr. Tobin threw away."

Sam Jeffries got up from the witness stand, lumbered down to the easel, took the pointer from Robert Merton, and proceeded to show the jury all of the important locations specified by Merton in his question. It was a very effective presentation.

"Once again, can you show the jury where you looked for the gun Mr. Tobin threw away?"

Again using the pointer, Jeffries showed the jury the specific area. "We looked here in the area of woods and backyard to the left of Danni Jansen's house."

"Why did you look there?"

"Jack Tobin is right-handed. If he is running toward Danni's house and he needs to get rid of the gun, that is the most logical place that he would have thrown it."

"I have no further questions, Your Honor."

"Cross-examination, Counselor?" the judge asked Tom.

"Yes, Your Honor." Tom stood and walked to the podium.

Tom had no intention of cross-examining Jeffries on most of the issues that he had raised. There was no need. Jack was going to testify and Jack would address just about everything. Tom had a few points he wanted to make and that was it. As an experienced trial lawyer, he knew less was sometimes more. Make it simple. Keep the jury focused.

"Chief Jeffries, why were you out there in the woods on a Sunday morning?"

"Why?"

"Yes, that's the question. Why?"

"I anticipated Felton might come after Danni. Danni was on the task force. Felton had threatened her in the past. He killed my daughter to get back at me. It was logical that he would come after Danni, and it was logical that he would come through the woods where he could not be seen."

"But why you?"

"Why me what?"

"Why were you out there on Sunday morning? You have a whole police force under you. You could have had two or four or six officers out in those woods or, even better, a SWAT team, couldn't you?"

"I could have but I chose to do it myself."

"Because it was personal."

"Yes."

"We've already had two of your police officers testify in this case, and I asked each of them if there were any general orders to watch the woods behind Danni Jansen's house and they said there weren't. Is it true that you did not put out any general orders to your officers to be especially vigilant of the woods behind Danni Jansen's house?"

"Yes."

"And again, that's because it was personal."

"Yes."

"If Felton was after Danni Jansen, why didn't you just wait for him in her house?"

"I wanted to. She wouldn't let me. She wanted to catch the son of a bitch as much as I did. Excuse my language, Your Honor."

The judge didn't respond.

"So you obviously wanted to get him because of what he did to your family. Why did Danni Jansen want to get him?"

"Objection, Your Honor. He's asking this witness to speculate about what was in Danni Jansen's mind."

"I'll rephrase the question, Your Honor."

"Proceed."

"Did Danni tell you why it was personal for her?"

"Yes."

"What did she tell you?"

"Objection, hearsay."

"Your Honor, I anticipate that Danni Jansen will be the State's next witness."

"Is that true, Mr. Merton?"

"Yes, Your Honor."

"I'll allow it."

"What did she tell you?" Tom asked again.

Sam was an experienced witness. He knew when Merton objected that he didn't want him to answer the question. But Sam couldn't help himself. He wanted the jurors, everybody, to know that Danni wanted Felton almost as bad as he did.

"She was on the task force when he was terrorizing this city. Danni has a daughter. Felton had threatened her daughter in the past. She wanted him apprehended."

"It was personal with her, too."

"Yes."

"So you were patrolling the woods—was that on a daily basis?"

"Yes, several times a day."

"And Danni Jansen was sitting in her house waiting for Felton to come?"

"Yes."

"And from the evidence you uncovered, Jack Tobin was living in the woods waiting for Felton?"

"No, he was luring Felton into the woods."

"I know that's your opinion and your opinion is based on the telephone calls to Felton's phone, correct?"

"Yes."

"But you didn't listen to those phone conversations?"

"No."

"In fact, you don't even know that there were phone conversations, correct?"

"No."

"And you don't really know for a fact why the calls were made, correct?"

"I've stated my opinion."

"I understand that, but you don't know why those calls were made, do you?"

"Not for an absolute fact."

"And you did find camping equipment, clothes—items that indicated that Mr. Tobin was living in the woods, correct?"

"Yes."

"Probably waiting for Felton just like you and Ms. Jansen?"

"I don't know that."

"Well, you've given a lot of opinions already on your direct examination. Isn't that a logical conclusion—you were waiting for Felton, Danni Jansen was waiting for Felton, and Jack Tobin was waiting for Felton?"

Merton was on his feet. "Objection, Your Honor. He's badgering the witness. The question was asked and answered."

"Overruled. Answer the question, Mr. Jeffries."

"I don't know."

"But the evidence—the clothing, the camping equipment—it doesn't coincide with your theory that Jack Tobin lured Felton into the woods, does it?"

"I don't understand the question."

"Let me ask it another way: The physical evidence shows that Tobin was camping in the woods waiting for Felton, not that Tobin was luring Felton into the woods."

"The camping equipment was all a ruse—all part of Tobin's plan."

"That's your opinion."

"Yes, it is."

"Were you armed when you were in the woods?"

"Of course."

"And did you anticipate that you might have trouble with Felton if you came across him?"

"Yes."

"And was Danni Jansen armed?"

"Yes."

"For the same reason?"

"Yes."

"And was Jack Tobin armed?"

"Yes."

"For the same reason?"

"No. He wanted to kill Felton. Danni and I are police officers. That's a big difference."

"Isn't Danni Jansen a retired police officer?"

"Yes."

"She has the status of a private citizen just like Jack Tobin?"

"Yes."

"So she and Tobin were armed as private citizens, correct?"

"If you say so."

"I'm not testifying, Chief Jeffries, you are. Please answer the question."

"Yes."

"Now, if you, walking in the woods, armed, came across Thomas Felton, maybe a hundred yards away, and you told him to stop, and he turned, and you thought he had a gun and was about to fire, would you shoot?"

"It all depends."

"On what?"

"If I thought I was in danger for my life, I might be justified— but I'd better be pretty damn sure he had a gun."

"What if he didn't?"

"Then I'd be facing discipline."

"From the police department?"

"From my superiors in the city and possibly the state. All police officers have standards they have to abide by. One of those standards is a use of force matrix. Essentially, you can only use force necessary to counter the force exerted against you."

"So you would be subject to disciplinary action but not criminal charges?"

"No. Not under the facts that you described."

"Okay. Let's take Danni Jansen walking in the woods, same circumstances."

Sam Jeffries had had enough. This lawyer was not going to squeeze him anymore.

"You're not getting this, Counselor. Danni Jansen was one of the finest homicide detectives this department ever had. This scum, Felton, threatened her daughter and he was out there. Still, she would have apprehended him if she had the chance. She was justified carrying a gun and I would put her in the same category as myself. She would not have shot unless she had to."

"Which means no criminal charges, correct?" Tom shot the question out quickly. He knew when he had a witness going his way, even though the witness didn't know it.

"That's correct."

Tom had what he needed. Going any further would have been a crap shoot. He'd set the scenario to argue to the jury that if they believed Jack's version of the facts, his good-faith belief that Felton had a gun, then according to Chief Sam Jeffries, there should be no criminal charges.

"I have no further questions, Your Honor."

"Great cross," Jack told him when he sat down.

"We'll see," Tom replied. "We'll see."

CHAPTER SIXTY-TWO

It was one thirty when the judge finally took a lunch break. The testimony of Sam Jeffries had been long and sometimes tedious and the judge rightfully didn't want to break before it was over. He gave the jurors an extra half hour for lunch, though.

"We'll reconvene at three," he told them.

Tom once again stayed in the courtroom with Jack, two old trial lawyers who couldn't get enough of it, although Jack didn't particularly like being the defendant. Tom produced two Snickers bars and handed one to Jack.

"You're such a thoughtful lawyer," Jack said. "You think of my sustenance along with everything else."

"Let's hope the everything else is as good as this Snickers bar."

"It is," Jack said. "Remember, I'm an expert at this."

Tom ignored the compliment. "So what do you think so far?"

"I think you set the case up exactly as it should be. Merton did an excellent job with Jeffries, but you got what you needed. It's going to come down to me or him."

"Yes and no. They are with him all the way. But he's out there on a limb all by himself and some of his stuff is very weak. The throwing the gun away into a certain portion of the woods is a little far-fetched. It could literally lose them the case if they don't have anything or anybody to corroborate the theory, and I don't see how they are going to come up with anything at this late date."

"Well, they've got nobody left except Danni," Jack said.

"We don't know that but it's our best guess. She's going to corroborate Jeffries's story about your knocking on her door and your saying you shot Felton. She's also going to testify about the telephone calls to Felton being from you because she knows your number, but that's not a big deal since we haven't denied that. She's not going to add much if that's all she's going to testify to."

Jack caught the note of sarcasm. "What's that supposed to mean?"

"I just have a feeling."

"And what's your feeling?"

"I think you trust this woman way too much. And I think we're in for a surprise."

"You're right, I do trust her. And I don't think there will be any surprises."

"We'll see," Tom said. "I hope you're right about that..."

They were both right about one thing—Danni was the next witness. She wore a black dress as if she were in mourning. Jack tried to catch her eye just to let her know he had no hard feelings about her testifying for the prosecution, but she wouldn't look at him. Even though he was on trial for his life, and even though she was about to testify against him, Jack still had intense feelings toward her that he could not suppress. Danni swore to tell the truth, took the stand, and answered Robert Merton's questions in a dull, expressionless voice.

As to the questions, Tom and Jack were right about most of them. Merton took her through Felton's death scene, and she corroborated everything Sam Jeffries had said. Then he asked her if she knew Jack's number and she said she did. He had called her on several occasions when they had been on opposite sides of a case. Merton then showed her the calls on Felton's phone—the one two days before the shooting and the one moments before the shooting. She identified both calls as Jack's number. Then came the surprise testimony—at least it was a surprise to Tom Wylie. He'd never heard it before.

"Now it's my understanding that after you and Mr. Tobin returned to the scene where Mr. Felton lay dead and Mr. Tobin told Chief Jeffries that he had shot him, you were both taken to the station for questioning, is that correct?"

"That's correct."

"How did you feel as a twenty-year veteran of the force, being taken in for questioning?"

"I felt fine. It was purely routine."

"Were you and Mr. Tobin separated at the station?"

"Yes."

"And you were eventually released?"

"Yes, about an hour later."

"Was Mr. Tobin released with you?"

"No."

"Did you wait for him?"

"No. I went home."

"When was the next time you saw him?"

"That evening."

Merton and his assistant set up the easel and the diagram again.

"Ms. Jansen, a smaller version of this diagram has already been entered into evidence as State's Exhibit number ten. Do you recognize what's depicted in this diagram?"

"Yes. It's my house, my back porch, my backyard, and the woods surrounding my house."

"Now if you would, I'd like you to come and take this pointer and point out a few things for the jury."

Danni stepped down from the witness chair and took the pointer as Sam Jeffries had done that morning.

"Now, would you point out approximately where in the woods Thomas Felton's body was situated."

Danni pointed to almost the exact same spot that Sam had pointed to.

"Thank you, Ms. Jansen. Now you said you saw Jack Tobin that evening—and you were referring to the evening of the shooting, correct?"

"Yes."

"Where did you see him?"

"I was sitting on my back porch, and he came out of the woods and approached my house."

"Were you surprised?"

"Yes, I was."

"And did you ask him what he was doing out there?"

"I did."

"And what did he tell you?"

"He said he was looking for the gun."

"What gun?"

"Felton's gun."

"The gun that Thomas Felton supposedly pointed at him?"

"Yes."

Danni was still standing in front of the diagram as she testified.

"Now would you show the jury on this diagram where you saw Jack Tobin come out of the woods that evening?"

"Sure." Danni pointed to the woods to the left of her back porch, the exact spot where Sam Jeffries had testified he believed Jack would have thrown the gun and where he believed Jack would have gone to retrieve the gun.

"Now, Ms. Jansen, were you surprised that Mr. Tobin was looking for Felton's gun in the woods to the left of your back porch?"

"Yes."

"And why were you surprised?"

"Because Felton was shot up here." Danni pointed to the area of the woods directly in front of the back porch—the area she had already pointed out. "If he had a gun on him when Jack shot him, it should be up there. I don't know why Jack was looking where he was looking."

"Did you ask him about that?"

"I did. He told me he could not look in the area surrounding the murder scene because there were SWAT team members up there. He said Sam Jeffries had told him nobody would be out there."

"Now did you see any SWAT team members out there in the area where the body was found at any time that evening?"

"No."

"And you were sitting on your back porch?"

"That's correct."

"Did you subsequently ask Sam Jeffries if he had deployed any SWAT team members at the crime scene that evening?"

"I did."

"And what was his response?"

"He said he hadn't."

"And did you ask Chief Jeffries if he had told Jack Tobin that nobody was going to be out there that evening?"

"Yes."

"And what was his response?"

"He said he hadn't. He said Tobin was a suspect. He wouldn't have given him any information."

"As a retired homicide detective did that answer make sense to you?"

"Yes."

"I have no further questions, Your Honor."

Tom could have objected to the questions about what Chief Jeffries had told Danni because Merton was seeking to elicit hearsay testimony, but Merton could have cured that problem simply by calling Jeffries back to the stand. The much bigger problem was that Danni Jansen had just corroborated Jeffries's testimony about the State's biggest hurdle—the fact that Jack had thrown away the gun he was going to plant on Thomas Felton's person and then had come back to retrieve it after he was released by the Oakville Police Department.

Tom knew he would have to go after her. He was searching his brain for anything he could use to attack her credibility. *She had once been involved with Jack; maybe she has some lingering animosity toward him from that relationship.* While he was thinking, Jack leaned over and whispered in his ear.

"Everything she said is true. Don't cross-examine her."

Don't cross-examine her! She just put a rope around your neck. Are you serious? We have to take a piece out of this woman's hide or this trial is over.

Up until now, Tom had abided by the deal he had struck with Jack. Now he felt he could no longer listen to his client. The man was not thinking rationally. He needed time. He needed an opportunity to talk some sense into Jack. He stood up.

"Your Honor, may we approach?"

It was ten minutes to five. The judge didn't know for sure what it was about but after twenty years on the bench, he had an idea. "Come on."

When they reached sidebar, Tom pleaded his case.

"Judge, it's ten minutes to five. The jury has already had a long day. If I start now, my cross could be very lengthy. If I wait until the morning and digest everything, it probably will be much shorter. At this time, I'm asking for a recess until tomorrow morning."

The judge looked at Robert Merton. "What says the State?"

Merton knew he had them on the ropes. He didn't want to let up on anything.

"I think we should finish this witness right now, Your Honor."

Judge Holbrook was inclined to go along with Merton on this one. He didn't like adjourning for the day when a witness was still on the stand, especially a major witness. He was about to rule in Merton's favor when he glanced at the jury box and saw two of the jurors yawning. His first obligation was to make sure they were able to listen to and absorb the evidence. And it had already been a very long day.

"I think the jury is tired," he said. "We're going to adjourn until tomorrow morning at nine a.m."

Tom was relieved. Merton was angry. Jack had no idea what had happened until the judge announced in open court that they were adjourning for the day.

CHAPTER SIXTY-THREE

Tom didn't talk to Jack before he was taken back to his jail cell. Instead, he went looking for Henry.

"I need you to come back with me to the jail. We've got to talk some sense into Jack."

Up to that point, Henry had not been involved much in the trial strategy and he had not been in on Jack and Tom's conversations during the trial, so he didn't know with any specificity what Tom was talking about.

"Sure, I'll go with you," he said.

Jack was in his usual position when they arrived, stretched out on the bed in his yellow jumpsuit with his back propped up against the wall and his hands behind his head. Tom sat across from him on an empty cot. Henry, not particularly fond of jail cells, leaned against the far wall after Jack gave him a big hug. They had not seen each other in a few days.

"So why did you ask to approach the judge there at the end?" Jack asked Tom.

"I wanted him to adjourn early so I could come back here and talk to you about the cross-examination of Danni Jansen."

"I thought I was clear. I don't want you to cross-examine her. Look, I know that last part was a surprise to you. I hadn't thought about the night I visited her and so I didn't tell you about it. I didn't expect her to testify about it either. I was almost as surprised as you. But she told you the truth today. All you had to do was look at her and you could see that she did not want to be there. She probably gave Sam the information in a conversation and then they subpoenaed her to court. I don't want you to cross-examine her. Period."

"Do you realize she just cemented the State's case against you with that testimony about you coming out of the woods? If we don't attack her credibility with every weapon we have, this case may be all over. I know you like this woman, Jack, but she's not your friend."

"It's not about me liking her, Tom. I trust her. I trust her to tell the truth."

"Henry, will you talk some sense into him?"

Henry looked at Jack, and the two men just smiled.

Tom thought they were crazy. Jack was on trial for his life, and they were smiling like two kids who had a big secret between them.

"What's going on here? Do you two know something I don't?"

"You're a fisherman, Tom," Jack said. "You've told me about your lake house and how you like to go out on your boat alone and fish."

"Yeah, so?"

"Well, Henry and I fish together, and we talk constantly. One of the things we talk about is how people always see others so clearly and never see themselves."

"I'm not following you at all."

"Jack trusted me," Henry said. "He believed in me when nobody else did. Both he and I trust Danni Jansen to tell the truth."

"I'm lost. How the hell does that have anything to do with your fishing conversations?"

"You," Henry continued. "You think you see us clearly but you don't because you don't see yourself."

"I can't believe I'm sitting in this jail cell and asking this question, but I guess I'll go along with you for shits and giggles—how do I not see myself?"

"You're just like us," Jack said. "You believe in your people when nobody else does. You believed in Rufus Porter—that black man you represented who was accused of rape—when nobody else believed in him."

"There's a big difference between my believing in Rufus Porter and the two of you believing in this Danni woman."

"And just what is that big difference, Tom?" Jack asked.

"Rufus and Henry were telling the truth. Danni Jansen isn't. Everything she said under oath today might be technically true, but deep down in her core, whether she comes to grips with it or not, she knows that Sam Jeffries has set you up. She may be lying to herself about it, but it's still a lie."

They were silent for a minute or two as Tom's words sank in. Then Henry spoke.

"Tom's right, Jack. She was with you that day. She has to at least suspect that Jeffries set you up. She also has to know something about what happened ten years ago when that bowie knife was planted. Jeffries is lying about that, too."

"Look," Jack said. "She worked with Sam Jeffries for twenty years. She went through the murder of his wife and then his daughter with him. She has to believe in him to a certain extent. She may have had some doubt but not enough to refuse to testify as to what she knows. I'm not going after her."

"It may cost you your life, Jack," Tom said.

"I'll take my chances."

"Don't be foolish, Jack."

"It may look that way to you, Tom, but this is who I am. I can't go after somebody I believe in."

Tom stood up to leave.

"I'm through trying to talk sense into you. That woman abandoned you when she took that stand today. She knew exactly what she was doing. She may not have liked it, but she did it."

CHAPTER SIXTY-FOUR

Tom Wylie felt terrible as he pulled into his parking space on Friday morning. An overcast sky with a light rain and thunderclouds in the distance would have been perfect weather to reflect his mood. Instead, he got bright sunshine, which made him even madder. *Why the hell does the sun have to shine every day around here? It should be dark and dreary at least two days a week. Disney World is a fantasy.*

He was mad at himself more than at Jack. He was frustrated with Jack but Jack was a good man, a man with principles. *Danni Jansen must be one hell of a woman*, he thought, *for both Jack and Henry to stand up for her like that.* He disagreed with them, but he didn't know the woman. He should have given their opinions more respect. *Hell, I can't afford to be nice and polite. I've got a guy on trial for his life.*

And that was the crux of the matter. He wasn't angry at Jack. He respected Jack's opinion. But he was so frustrated. This trial could be won if Jack would let him be just a little more aggressive. They could soothe people's feelings down the road—although he knew that wasn't true. You assail someone's character unjustly, you assail your own character. He wished some politicians could understand that.

No, Jack was doing the right thing and he was willing to accept the consequences of his actions. It was just so damn painful to watch this good man go down the tubes in the name of justice.

This was the last day of testimony by Tom's calculation. Closings would be on Monday and then the jury would get the case. There was a mob in front of the courthouse as he approached. They were jockeying for position in line. Everybody knew Jack was going to take the stand today. As he got closer, he could see the reporters start to run toward him like starving mice, desperate for that one unique morsel of information they could feed off of and disseminate to the rest of the world.

Tom put his hand up as he continued to move quickly toward his destination.

"I'm sorry. I'm late. I've got nothing to say."

One reporter, a young woman with short blond hair, got in his face. "A lot of people are saying Jack can't turn this around. It's already too late."

It was a teaser, a line designed to get Tom's blood pumping so he'd fire something back without thinking. She had probably worked on that line all night. This wasn't Tom's first dance though. He knew the game. Still, he felt the need to come to Jack's defense—to say something for him that he hadn't been able to say to him the night before. So he stopped, and when he did, the reporters fought to get their microphones in front of his face, and the crowd closed in around him.

"Jack Tobin believes in our justice system, more than you can ever imagine. And I am proud to be representing him. He will tell his truth today. It's never too late when you have truth on your side. I hope you will all remember that. There is no calculated hide-and-seek game by the defendant in this trial. Jack will tell his side. He will be subjected to cross-examination, and the chips will fall where they may. Now, if you'll excuse me, I need to get inside."

Tom put his head down and pushed his way through the crowd.

There were no surprises with the preliminary witnesses that morning. Tom started with Ben Chapman, the executive director of Exoneration. He took some time going over Chapman's very impressive credentials as well as the work of the organization. In Tom's mind, Chapman was actually there for two reasons.

"What is the purpose or the mission of Exoneration, Mr. Chapman?"

"Well, we have many purposes. First and foremost, we provide competent experienced counsel for individuals on death row. Some of them have never had that before. Second, but equally important, we try to shed light on the inadequacies of the criminal justice system with the ultimate goal of eliminating the death penalty as a punishment. We have cases that deal with inadequate defense counsel, improper identification, overzealous prosecutors—"

Robert Merton got the picture when he heard those words. "Objection, Your Honor. Mr. Wylie is trying to precondition the jury with this testimony."

The judge thought about it for a moment. "Sustained. Mr. Wylie, I believe the jury understands that Exoneration represents death row inmates. Let's move on."

"Yes, Your Honor."

He asked Chapman, "Did Jack Tobin work for your organization?"

"Not in a technical sense. Jack wasn't our employee and we didn't pay him a salary. He was an attorney who volunteered with us to represent death row inmates. He's been with us for about five years or so and he is an excellent attorney, the best we have."

"I move to strike that last statement, Your Honor," Merton said without standing up.

"Motion granted." The judge looked at the jurors. "Members of the jury, I'm directing you not to consider those statements by the witness about Mr. Tobin's abilities as an attorney." He then addressed Tom. "Mr. Wylie, I want you to control your witness a little better than that."

"Yes, Your Honor."

"And Mr. Chapman, I'm instructing you to answer the question and only the question asked. There will be no more editorializing, do you understand?"

"Yes, Your Honor."

"Let's proceed."

Tom only had a few more questions to ask Ben Chapman.

"Is it accurate that Jack Tobin has represented a number of people on death row?"

"Yes. I'd say at least ten."

"Have you ever known him to profit in any way from representing these people?"

"No. Never."

"He donated his time for free?"

"Yes."

"I have no further questions."

"Cross-examination, Counselor?"

Robert Merton stood up and walked to the podium with an air of confidence. Merton had made his reputation as a prosecutor primarily because of his ability to effectively cross-examine witnesses. Sometimes he tore them apart, making them look like liars—snakes who slithered off the stand when he was finally through with them. Sometimes he used them to support his own case. It all depended on the situation.

"I think the question you were just asked, Mr. Chapman, was *have you ever known* Jack Tobin to profit from representing death row inmates. Is that accurate?"

"Yes, that's correct."

"Which leaves open the possibility that Mr. Tobin could have profited from this representation and you might not have known about it. Is that correct?"

"I doubt that very much. I have known—"

Merton cut him off. "You doubt it very much. I'm going to hand you State's Exhibits numbers five and six. Have you seen these before?"

Chapman took a few moments to review the documents.

"No, I haven't."

"So you didn't know about them?"

"No."

"Exhibit number five is a document called a claims bill. Are you familiar with a claims bill?"

"I'm not familiar with this one but I am familiar with a claims bill."

"And what is a claims bill in the context of what you do?"

"If an individual on death row is exonerated, we almost always file a claims bill with the Florida legislature asking that body to compensate the individual for the time he or she was wrongfully incarcerated."

"And Exhibit number six. Do you recognize that document?"

"I have never seen this document but I recognize it as a contingency fee agreement."

"Can you see that this document is a contingency fee agreement between Jack Tobin and Thomas Felton?"

"Yes."

"Did you know that Jack Tobin prepared and signed a contingency fee agreement with Thomas Felton?"

"No, I did not."

"Did you know that Jack Tobin prepared a claims bill asking for twenty million dollars from the Florida legislature and then prepared a contingency fee agreement giving him, personally, a third of whatever Felton recovered?"

"No, I did not."

"Now, your organization has bylaws and rules and regulations that you and the attorneys who work with your organization must abide by. Is that correct?"

"Yes."

"Is this contingency fee agreement a violation of your bylaws and your rules and regulations?"

"Yes."

"Are the lawyers who work for you required to know about your rules and regulations?"

"Yes. They each sign a document saying they have read the bylaws of the corporation and the rules and regulations."

"And the term 'they'—would that include Mr. Tobin?"

"Yes."

"I have no further questions, Your Honor."

Jack leaned over and whispered in Tom's ear when Merton was finished. "What were we thinking?"

Tom didn't respond. The jury was watching and the judge was already addressing him.

"Redirect, Mr. Wylie?"

Tom didn't want to ask Ben Chapman another question but Robert Merton had so thoroughly used Chapman to his own advantage that he had to give it a shot.

"Mr. Chapman, what is your success rate in representing people on death row?"

"Oh, it's very low. Less than five percent."

"And is it accurate that it takes an awful lot of work to undertake a death row appeal?"

"The amount of work doing one of these appeals is incredible, not to mention the time constraints, the stress."

"It seems like counsel's theory in his questions to you was that Jack Tobin was running some kind of business where he would represent a number of these people, have the ones who win sign contingency fee agreements, and then make money off those success stories. Knowing what you know about the success rate and the work involved, does that theory have any rational basis in fact—I mean, does that make sense?"

Merton was standing before Tom had finished his question. "Objection, Your Honor. Speculation."

"Sustained."

"Your Honor, may I be heard?"

Judge Holbrook didn't like Tom's continuously questioning his authority, but he knew Tom had a right to make his record. His anger made him change his own rule about speaking objections.

"You may be heard, Counselor. Go ahead."

Tom was surprised that the judge was not calling him to sidebar. Perhaps the judge was trying to embarrass him. Whatever the judge's motive, Tom was happy to make his argument in front of the jury.

"Your Honor, Mr. Merton raised this issue with this witness on cross-examination. And I anticipate that he is going to try and tell this jury on closing, based on this witness testimony, that Jack Tobin was running some kind of business with these death row appeals. I think I am entitled to ask this witness if that argument has merit."

"Anything else?"

"No, Your Honor."

"Mr. Merton?"

"I don't intend to make that argument, Your Honor. I intend to use this witness's testimony to argue to this jury that Jack Tobin was clearly going to make money, possibly seven million dollars, on his successful representation of Thomas Felton and that he was doing it behind the back of the organization for which he was working. The loss of that profit was his motive for killing Felton."

"Thank you, Counselor. The objection is sustained. Any further questions, Mr. Wylie?"

Tom wanted to stick a knife in his eye, or his hand, or somewhere. Merton was killing him.

"No, Your Honor."

"Call your next witness."

The next witness was Henry Wilson. Tom kept it short and sweet. He didn't know what Merton was going to do with Henry.

"Mr. Wilson, you had been on death row for seventeen years when you met Jack Tobin, is that correct?"

"That's correct."

"And what did Mr. Tobin do for you?"

"He represented me. He went through my file with a fine-tooth comb and found that prosecutors had hidden evidence. I was exonerated—they set me free."

"And how long ago was that?"

"Five years ago."

"Now when you were set free, did Mr. Tobin file a claims bill with the legislature on your behalf?"

"Yes."

"And did you receive any money?"

"Yes. Three million dollars."

"Did you give any of that money to Mr. Tobin?"

"No."

"Did he ask you for any money?"

"No."

"Did he ever ask you to sign an agreement to give him money?"

"No."

"I have no further questions."

"Cross-examination, Mr. Merton?" the judge asked.

"Yes, Your Honor." Merton walked right up to where Henry was sitting but he didn't look at him. He looked at the jury so that each juror looking at Merton would see Henry in the background, putting the focus entirely on Merton.

"Now before you went to prison for this seventeen years and before Mr. Tobin got you out, Mr. Wilson, is it fair to say you were what one would commonly call a career criminal?"

Tom was on his feet. "Objection. Improper impeachment."

Merton knew the proper method. You ask a witness if he or she has ever been convicted of a felony and how many times and if they answered truthfully, the inquiry was over. Merton, however, didn't care about the answer. It was all about the question—the accusation.

"Sustained," Judge Holbrook bellowed. After a week, the jurors were as used to the judge's and the attorneys' loud voices as they were to the creaky floors and the fans and the air conditioners. They had adjusted.

Merton continued. "And after you got out of prison, is it true that you went to work with Mr. Tobin?"

"I volunteered to help out as an investigator for Exoneration on death penalty cases, if that's what you mean."

"Not on any death penalty cases, just the cases Jack Tobin was working on, isn't that right?"

"Yes."

"You became his right-hand man?"

"Yes."

"You were a team?"

"Yes."

"Mr. Tobin is your best friend, isn't he?"

"Yes."

"You would do anything for him, wouldn't you?"

Henry was about to say, "I wouldn't lie for him," but he knew that wasn't true. He'd kill for Jack. He already had.

"Yes."

"No further questions."

"Redirect?"

"No, Your Honor."

"Okay, folks, we're going to break for lunch. Remember the admonitions I have given you. Do not talk among yourselves about the case."

*   *   *

As usual, Tom and Jack stayed in the courtroom for lunch. Tom brought the Snickers bars.

"Jesus, Merton is good," Jack said. "I don't know what he's doing hiding in Apache County as a prosecutor. He could make millions as a criminal defense attorney on the big stage."

"He doesn't seem to be the type who is in it for the right reasons, either," Tom added.

"No. He wants to win no matter what the cost. Maybe he wants to be the governor or something like that and this is his path."

"Whatever the reason, he's doing a job on us."

"I'd have to agree with you so far, Tom, but it's not over yet."

"I was going to call Ron next to talk about the night you were drinking and said you were going to kill Felton, but I think I'm going to let him go. Merton will just do the friendship cross again and it will backfire in our faces."

"I agree. Just put me on. Let's get it over with."

There were definitely a few more press people in the room for the afternoon session, and it seemed like the gallery was even bigger as well. They all knew what was coming. You could taste the anticipation in the air.

"Call your next witness, Mr. Wylie."

"The defense calls Jack Tobin."

Jack stood up, walked over to the clerk, swore to tell the truth, and climbed up into the witness chair.

Tom first took Jack through his long and illustrious career as a civil trial lawyer. He wanted the jury to know not only how successful Jack was but how rich he was as well.

"So you started the firm and built it up, is that correct?"

"Yes."

"And how many lawyers did the firm have when you left?"

"Right around one hundred."

"Did the partners buy you out of your interest in the firm when you decided to leave?"

"Yes."

"What was the buyout figure?"

"Twenty million dollars."

"And was that in addition to your retirement package?"

"Yes."

"What were your plans at the time?"

"I was going to retire to the small town of Bass Creek and fish. I'd work part-time as a country lawyer but nothing too serious."

"So what happened?"

"An old friend of mine died in New York—my best friend when I was growing up. When I went up for the funeral, I found out that his son was on death row for a murder he had supposedly committed in Bass Creek. The fact that I was living in Bass Creek made me think that maybe I was supposed to get involved in my friend's son's case, so I took a look at it."

"And?"

"And I became convinced that his son—Rudy was his name—was innocent. So I undertook to represent Rudy."

"Was that representation successful?"

"No, it wasn't."

"What did you do after that?"

"I became a prosecutor for a while and I successfully prosecuted the detective who had arrested Rudy and whose testimony convicted Rudy.

"And then I started to represent people on death row. Representing Rudy gave me a different purpose in life as a lawyer. I found that I wasn't ready to just sit back in the rocking chair."

"Is that when you went to work for Exoneration?"

"Yes."

"Now, Mr. Tobin, I want to talk to you particularly about your representation of Thomas Felton. Why did you take that case?"

"Ben Chapman asked me to come to Tallahassee. He didn't tell me what it was about, he just asked me to come. When I got there, he told me about the Felton case and asked me to look at it. I didn't want to even look at it."

"Why?"

"Felton was a serial killer. A lawyer has an obligation when he or she takes a case to do the absolute best job he can. There is always a possibility that you could find a technical error in the prosecution's presentation of its case that could result in the defendant's being released. I did not want that on my conscience."

"But you eventually did represent Felton?"

"Yes."

"Why?"

"Henry Wilson, my friend and my investigator, convinced me to just look at the file. Henry said I shouldn't prejudge anybody, including an alleged serial killer. When I reviewed the file, I found a huge problem with the prosecution's case, and I became convinced that Felton had been set up as a fall guy."

"We've heard a little about this from Chief Jeffries. Why don't you tell the jury what you found."

"The coroner's reports indicated that the weapon that killed both Vanessa Brock and Pedro Diaz was one-quarter inch wide and three and one-half inches long. That description is for a stiletto or a similar type of knife. The police officer who testified, Sam Jeffries, testified that the murder weapon found at the scene was a bowie knife. If the murder weapon had been a bowie knife, the cut described by the coroner would have been two inches wide, not one-quarter inch. That's a huge discrepancy."

"You sat here and listened to Sam Jeffries tell this jury that you made a big case out of what was basically a typing error in the coroner's report and you were successful because the coroner was dead—how do you respond to that statement?"

"I certainly considered the possibility that the coroner's report contained a mere typing error, but I dismissed that possibility."

"Why?"

"There were two murders so there were two coroner's reports. The injuries to the deceased were to different areas of the body but the descriptions of the wound, in particular the width of the cuts, were the same. It was inconceivable to me that the coroner could make the exact same error on two separate reports. I then went back to the transcript of the trial and saw that the coroner had described the wounds and testified to the cause of death, but he had never testified that the bowie knife was the murder weapon, and his reports were never introduced into evidence. Only the police officer, Sam Jeffries, testified that the bowie knife was the murder weapon. In all fairness to Chief Jeffries, he had not seen the coroner's report nor had he attended the autopsy, so he could have believed that the bowie knife was, in fact, the murder weapon. The prosecutor and the coroner knew better. The Florida Supreme Court agreed with me on this, by the way."

Merton stood up at that statement as Jack and Tom had figured he would. "Your Honor, I object to the witness interpreting case law on the stand."

"He is not interpreting case law, Your Honor. He's just stating what he understands the case says."

"Is there a distinction?" the judge asked.

"Maybe, maybe not, Your Honor, but Chief Jeffries gave his interpretation. Mr. Tobin has now given his, and I have an actual copy of the Florida Supreme Court's decision that I'd like to introduce into evidence so the jury can look at it for themselves."

"The jury decides facts, not the law, Counselor. The decision of the supreme court is not going to be admitted into evidence. And I don't believe I ever heard Chief Jeffries interpret the supreme court's ruling. Therefore, I'm going to strike Mr. Tobin's interpretation of that case. Ladies and gentlemen of the jury, I instruct you to disregard that last statement of Mr. Tobin's where he told you the Florida Supreme Court agreed with him. Proceed, Counselor."

The entire discussion had been in front of the jury. Tom wasn't sure if that was good or bad. He then took Jack through his own personal ordeal of learning that Chief Jeffries's daughter, Kathleen, had been killed.

"How did you feel?"

"Responsible."

"Why did you feel responsible?"

"I had set the process in motion. I had uncovered the flaws in the prosecution's case. If I hadn't done that, Felton would still be in prison and Kathleen Jeffries would still be alive."

"You were sure it was Felton?"

"It had to be."

"What did you do when you heard this news?"

"First, I got drunk. Very drunk."

"Is that when the police officers visited you?"

"Yes. I vaguely recall them."

"Do you recall saying that you were going to kill Thomas Felton?"

"No, but I don't dispute it. In the state of mind I was in that night, I might have killed him."

Tom walked to the far side of the courtroom and retrieved the diagram of Danni's backyard and the easel and set them up in front of the jury.

"Now at some point in time, soon after learning of Kathleen Jeffries's death, did you set up a camp back here in these woods?"

"Yes."

"Why?"

"I thought Felton would be coming for Danni Jansen next and I wanted to stop him."

"Why did you think he would be coming for Danni Jansen?"

"She was one of the lead investigators in the original investigation, and he had threatened her and her daughter in the past. He had gone after Sam Jeffries's daughter, and it was logical that he'd go after Danni or her daughter."

"What did you intend to do with him if you caught him?"

"Turn him over to the authorities."

"You didn't intend to kill him?"

"Absolutely not."

"Did you have a gun?"

"Yes."

"Why did you have a gun?"

"Because I figured Felton would be armed and I didn't think he would come with me peacefully."

Tom then had Jack take the jury through the confrontation with Felton from the time he first saw him until he returned to the scene with Danni and was taken into custody by the police.

"Why did you shoot Thomas Felton, Mr. Tobin?"

"I thought he had a gun and I thought he was going to shoot me."

"Can you describe what you thought you saw?"

"I thought I saw a small pistol but I can't be sure."

Tom then handed him State's Exhibits #5 and #6. "I've handed you State's Exhibits numbers five and six. Did you prepare those documents?"

"Yes."

"Why?"

"Let's take them one at a time. Felton asked me to prepare the claims bill because he had heard about them while he was still in prison. This is something we normally do when a prisoner is re-leased, only this one was done a little earlier because of Felton's insistence."

"And the twenty-million-dollar figure—where did that come from?"

"It was Felton's number. I didn't have a problem with it because it doesn't really matter what you ask for. It only matters what the leg-islature decides to give you. He wasn't going to get anywhere near that amount."

"And the contingency fee agreement?"

"I prepared that as well at Felton's insistence. He wanted to compensate me for saving his life. I didn't want the money. I told him that he should give it to Exoneration. He said they didn't get him set free, I did. So I prepared the agreement the way he asked with the intention of giving any money that I got to Exon-eration."

"Had you ever prepared a contingency fee agreement for any other prisoner in the past?"

"No."

"Had you always done this work for free?"

"Yes."

"I have no further questions."

"Cross-examination, Mr. Merton?"

"Yes, Your Honor."

Tom was satisfied. Jack was Jack. He had answered every ques-tion directly and truthfully. He didn't avoid the hard ones, either. Now it was time to see how good Robert Merton really was.

Merton knew Jack was going to be a tremendous witness. The man was a great lawyer and communicator. He could not afford to play with him on cross. He had to make his points, make them quickly, and get out.

"Mr. Tobin, you would agree that there are many individuals, CEOs of major corporations for instance, who make more than twenty million dollars a year, wouldn't you?"

"Sure."

"And yet they still go to work. They still want to make more money, don't they?"

"Objection, Your Honor. Relevancy."

"Sustained. Move along, Mr. Merton."

"Let's talk about the contingency fee agreement for a minute. You testified that you planned to transfer any money you received to Exoneration, is that correct?"

"Yes."

"Did you tell Exoneration about that?"

"No."

"You could have just picked up the phone and called Ben Chapman, couldn't you?"

"Sure."

"But you didn't?"

"No, I didn't."

"And you heard Mr. Chapman testify that a contingency fee agreement like this was a violation of Exoneration's rules and regulations and the bylaws and that you knew it was a violation—is that accurate?"

"I don't dispute that the agreement might have violated the rules and the bylaws. I just didn't think about that at the time."

"So you are telling this jury under oath that a lawyer of your talent and experience never thought of talking to the organization you worked for about an agreement that you had never prepared before?"

"That's correct."

"You also testified on direct examination that the agreement was Felton's idea, is that correct?"

"Yes."

"What did he say—'Jack, I want you to prepare a contingency fee agreement'?"

"No, he said 'I want to give you a third of what I recover.'"

"Did he say, 'I want to put that in writing'?"

"No, that was my idea. I didn't want to leave him the opportunity to change his mind."

"So the contingency fee agreement was your idea?"

"The actual agreement—yes. The idea of giving money to me was Felton's."

"The idea of making it a legal obligation was yours, correct?"

"Yes."

"And do you agree that the killing of Kathleen Jeffries effectively ended any chance of getting a claims bill passed?"

"Yes."

"And effectively ended the possibility of your getting any money from this contingency fee agreement?"

"Yes."

"But you weren't angry about that?"

"No."

"You didn't want to get even?"

"No, I didn't."

"You're not a person who tries to get even?"

"No, I'm not."

"I want to revisit your testimony on direct examination about your representation of this young man named Rudy. You said that after Rudy was executed, you became a prosecutor and prosecuted the police officer who arrested Rudy and whose testimony convicted Rudy, is that correct?"

"That's correct."

"Is it also correct that you became a prosecutor for the sole purpose of prosecuting that police officer and after that prosecution was over, you resigned your position?"

"That's correct."

"You weren't trying to get even then, were you?"

"No, I was trying to prosecute a man who deserved to be prosecuted and who, in fact, was convicted."

"The police officer wasn't the only person you prosecuted over the death of this young man Rudy, was he?"

"No."

"You also prosecuted the former state attorney who successfully sought Rudy's execution, didn't you?"

"Yes."

"And at the time that you prosecuted that former state attorney, he was a sitting federal judge, wasn't he?"

"Yes."

"You weren't trying to get even with him?"

"No, I wasn't. I was seeking justice for Rudy."

"You were not successful against the judge, were you?"

"No."

"Is it correct that the judge you unsuccessfully prosecuted was assassinated by a sniper's bullet six months later?"

Tom was on his feet. "Objection, Your Honor." He didn't ask to approach sidebar. He just walked toward the bench.

The crowd started murmuring right after Merton finished asking the question. The jurors looked shocked as well. Judge Holbrook raised his gavel and lowered it again and again.

"Silence in the courtroom!" he shouted. "If you can't be silent, you will be removed."

Nobody stopped talking.

"Remove the gallery," the judge told the bailiffs who dealt with the gallery.

"Take the jury out," the judge told the bailiff who was assigned to the jurors.

In a matter of minutes, the courtroom was empty. The

press was gone as well. Only then did Holbrook speak to the lawyers.

"Mr. Merton, just what do you think you are doing?"

"Asking a question, Your Honor."

"A question that carries the implication that Mr. Tobin was involved with the murder of a federal judge."

"I never meant to imply that, Your Honor."

"Your Honor, I'd like to move for a mistrial," Tom said. "And I'm requesting that this court rule that my client cannot be retried since double jeopardy has attached."

"Relax, Mr. Wylie. There's not going to be a mistrial. The witness is not going to answer the question, and I am going to instruct the jury not only that it was an improper question and that they should disregard it but also that the only inference to be drawn from that question is that the prosecuting attorney committed an egregious error in asking it. Now are there any more questions?"

Nobody said a word.

"Bring in the jury."

The courtroom was still empty as the jurors filed in and sat in their respective seats.

"Ladies and gentlemen of the jury, sometimes things occur in trial that we don't expect. Sometimes lawyers ask questions without thinking. The last question Mr. Merton asked should never have been asked. It is not enough for me to tell Mr. Tobin he does not have to answer the question. I need to tell you that it should not be a part of this case and you should wipe it from your memory. And the only inference you should draw from that question being asked is that the prosecuting attorney, Mr. Merton, overstepped his bounds and committed an egregious or gross error when he asked it. Now, can you all do that?"

The judge asked each juror individually and had each juror say "yes" on the record.

"Okay, ladies and gentlemen, it has been a long day. We're going to recess for the weekend. Remember the admonitions that I have given you. This trial is almost over but it's not over yet."

After the jury left, Judge Holbrook addressed the lawyers.

"Mr. Wylie, do you have any other witnesses in your defense?"

"Not at the moment, Your Honor, but I'd like to have the weekend to assess everything before I rest."

"That's fine." The judge's attitude toward Tom and Jack had suddenly changed.

"And what about you, Mr. Merton?" the judge growled. "Are you going to have any rebuttal?"

"I don't plan on it at this time, Your Honor, but it will depend on what Mr. Wylie does on Monday."

"Fine. I'll see you both here Monday morning at nine. And Mr. Merton, I don't want to be seeing your face on television talking about the events that occurred here this afternoon. Do you understand?"

"Yes, Your Honor."

Tom stood up. "Your Honor, the press needs to at least be told that the question was determined to be improper by this court. It can't just hang there."

"I have placed no restriction on you, Mr. Wylie. I assume you will make the point in a professional manner."

"I will, Your Honor."

Jack and Tom stayed in the courtroom after everyone left. Jack's guards stood by the door leading out to the jail and waited for him while he spoke with his lawyer.

"So what do you think?" he asked Tom.

"I think your direct went as well as it could possibly go, but this Merton is damn good, and just a little crazy."

"A question like that last one can lose the jury for you, especially when the judge comes back and says what he said," Jack said.

"Under normal circumstances I would agree with you, Jack. But if these people are predisposed to have it in for you, Merton gave them all the rope they needed."

"He knew exactly what he was doing," Jack said.

"No doubt in my mind."

"Well, Tom, you're doing as good a job as can be done within the restrictions I placed on you. I wouldn't change or add anything. I appreciate what you've done for me."

"We've still got Monday, Jack. We're not done yet."

"No, we're not. Listen, do me a favor. Go grab Henry, and both of you have a beer tonight for me."

"I think we can do that."

"Good."

Tom watched Jack get up and walk over to the guards and say something that made them both laugh. Then all three walked through the door heading for the jail.

Such a good man, Tom thought. *We've got to find a way.*

CHAPTER SIXTY-FIVE

Tom and Henry went to The Swamp that night to have their beer and a little dinner. Tom did not want to go out at all. He wasn't in the mood to put himself out there where the citizens of Oakville could say anything they wanted to him. Henry reminded him, however, that if they were going to have a beer for Jack, Ron should be a part of that occasion. Tom agreed. Besides, when he thought about it, what rational human being would even attempt to say something nasty to him with Henry sitting at the table?

It was Friday night, but The Swamp was almost deserted.

"What's going on around here?" Tom asked before he actually thought about what was going on around there. They sat at a table by the window looking out over the street. Ron sat with them. He brought a pitcher of beer and three glasses.

"It's just a slow night," Ron said as he poured. "It happens sometimes."

Henry knew better. "Your fellow citizens are paying you back for sticking by your friend, aren't they, Ronnie?"

"I'm not sure, but it has never been this deserted on a Friday night since I opened the place. Even the college kids aren't here and they're not usually paying attention to what happens in the local courtroom."

There were a few college kids at the bar but it was a far cry from a normal weekend night, even in the summer.

"That really stinks," Tom said.

"It won't last long," Ron assured him. "People have short memories about where to eat and drink."

"Did you hear what happened in court today?" Henry asked Ron.

"Oh, I heard about it and a lot more. Tom, do Merton's actions today give you a basis for appeal?"

"Possibly, but not as strong as I would have liked. Judge Holbrook gave a curative instruction to the jurors and then polled them. He was making his own record. A denial of a motion for mistrial is within a judge's discretion. Why are you asking? Are you already onto the appeal stage?"

"Pretty much."

"Do you know something we don't?" Henry asked.

"Yeah, I know somebody who works for the paper. They've been doing exit interviews. I'm sure they're doing them for Merton since I haven't seen a word about them in the paper."

Tom became a little impatient hearing the news. "Did he tell you the results?"

"Yeah. They did it for two days—the day Sam and Danni testified and today."

"And?"

"There was no difference. Eighty-five percent think Jack's guilty, ten percent don't know, and only five percent think he's innocent."

"That's the gallery—it's not necessarily the jury," Henry said.

"If the gallery is that strong, the jury is the same way," Tom said.

"Where does that leave us, hoping for a lone juror or two to hold out?" Henry asked.

"That's not even a reasonable hope," Tom said. "This is a small town. A juror who even thinks about holding out in this town knows that he or she will have to move. People may have short memories about where they eat, but personal vendettas can last a lifetime."

"So we've got nothing?" Henry asked.

"Never say never," Tom said. "We'll go back in Monday and continue to slug it out. Who knows what may happen."

Ron raised his glass. "Let's have a toast," he said. "To miracles."

They all raised their glasses.

CHAPTER SIXTY-SIX

Henry rang the bell, barely touching it. He was reluctant to do it at first since it was not yet eight o'clock on Saturday morning. But Danni was an active woman. He figured she'd be up and about and he wanted to catch her before she left for the day. He had no idea what he was going to say.

He waited a few seconds. Nothing. He decided not to ring again. He'd try later. Just as he turned to walk away, the door opened. Danni appeared there wearing a pair of gym shorts and a pajama top. Her hair was everywhere and her eyes were squinting, telling Henry that he'd woken her up.

Danni spoke first, turning away from him and walking toward the living room.

"Come on in, Henry."

Henry followed her in, closing the door behind him. "I'm sorry, I thought you'd be up."

"Well, I've been sleeping a lot lately. Did you come here to thank me for doing my civic duty, or to crucify me? Let me see—*I saved your life. I saved your daughter's life. How could you do this to Jack?*"

"Stop it, Danni. I'd never say that to you."

"Why not? I say it to myself every hour or so." She slumped into a big chair in the living room, curling her legs under her.

Henry sat on the couch across from her.

She looked him in the eye for just a minute. "Sam came over one day. He asked if Jack had visited that night after he was released from custody. He told me about the claims bill and the contingency fee agreement. I didn't know who to believe so I told him what I knew. Then they subpoenaed me. End of story."

"Not yet."

"How's it going?"

"Bad. Very bad."

"That's what I heard."

"Ronnie found out that Merton did exit polls for two days—the day you testified and yesterday when Jack testified."

"Can they do that?"

"They disguised it as a news organization poll."

"Bastards. And?"

"And Jack's going down. It was eighty-five percent for conviction both days."

"Jesus, I'm sorry, Henry. I really am. For what it's worth, I think Sam's off his rocker and he's just out to get Jack. I wish I had never had that conversation with him. But there's nothing I can do. I told the truth."

Henry didn't say anything for a long time. He just sat there on the couch apparently looking at the stitching.

"You know, Jack didn't just get me out of prison," he said finally. "He taught me something. It was something I was starting to learn on my own from reading and working by myself, but Jack made it real by doing it. He taught me that if you put your life on the line for somebody, then you are truly living. That in itself is truth. He does it all the time. When he believes in people, he never backs off. He believed in me."

"Where are you going with this, Henry? I don't need you to make me feel any worse. I've already had a headache for two days."

"What was it that Thoreau said? 'Most men lead lives of quiet desperation.' Most men and women have acquaintances they call friends and lovers they say they would die for, but they don't mean it. It's all surface bullshit. Most times they walk away at the drop of a hat. Every once in a while, you might see an old woman in a hospital watching her husband die and you can tell by the look on her face she would gladly change places because she truly loves him like a mother loves her baby child—"

"Henry, if this is going where I think it is, stop right now. Jack and I were never in love. We had a fling, for Christ's sake."

She could tell that she had angered him with that remark but he didn't move.

"You're not getting it, Danni. I'm not talking about romance—maybe the couple was a bad example. I'm talking about real truth—not bullshit. When we were in that apartment in Miami, it was life and death—all the horseshit was gone. That's why you entrusted your daughter to me, because you knew I would protect her with my life. We'd already been there."

"What the hell do you want from me? I've already testified to everything I know."

"No, you haven't. I want you to put your life on the line.

"You know, I sat in Jack's cell the other night and listened to Tom Wylie tell him that if Jack didn't allow him to cross-examine you and attack your credibility, it could mean his life. Jack told him no. It wasn't about romance. It wasn't about feelings. It was about you. He believes in you. Life and death. Truth.

"Think about it."

Henry got up and let himself out.

CHAPTER SIXTY-SEVEN

Monday was a sunny day and Tom had a spring in his step when he bulldozed through the crowd and the press into the courthouse. He was late, and he did not have time to talk to Jack before the proceedings began.

Judge Holbrook entered the courtroom promptly at nine o'clock. He had a full courtroom again, and he was going to give them a piece of his mind before the jury was brought in.

"I reminded you all on the first day, although many of you were not here, that your presence in this courtroom is a privilege, not a right. I emptied the courtroom on Friday and I will not hesitate to empty it again. I sequestered this jury at the beginning of this trial to make sure they were not affected by public opinion. Your reaction in this courtroom affects this jury. If you react in any way to anything that happens in here, your privilege to be in this room will be revoked immediately."

Once again, he did not ask them if they understood his message.

Then he turned to the two lawyers.

"Gentlemen, I'd like to know what we're going to do today before I bring in the jury. Mr. Wylie, are you going to rest your case?"

Tom stood up. "No, Your Honor. I have one more witness."

"Who is it?"

"I'm recalling Danni Jansen."

The buzz in the gallery started and then stopped almost immediately as if people's emotions had reacted before their brains.

"And Mr. Merton, I assume that your decision will be based on what this witness says."

"That's correct, Your Honor."

"Okay, anything else before we bring in the jury?"

"No, Your Honor."

"No, Your Honor."

"Bring in the jury."

Tom sat down next to Jack. "When did this happen?" Jack asked.

"This morning. She called Henry at seven and said she wanted to testify for you. Henry called me."

"What is she going to say?"

"I don't know. Henry says she is going to talk about what happened ten years ago. She wouldn't tell him what she was going to say though."

"You don't know?" Jack asked.

"I hear you. Who calls a witness without knowing what they're going to say?"

"We have no choice, do we?"

"We always have a choice, Jack, but what are our options?"

"I guess we don't have any. I said I believe in Danni. When you believe in people, you have to trust them."

"You're making a believer out of me. I never thought this woman was going to testify on your behalf. Half of me is still a little worried."

When the jury was sitting, the bailiff brought Danni in from the witness room. She wore a blue suit with a skirt, not pants, and she looked terrific. This time she made eye contact with Jack. Her eyes were calm. She looked relaxed as she took the oath and sat in the witness chair.

"Ms. Jansen," Tom began, "when you testified in this case pre-
viously, you testified primarily about what happened on the day
Thomas Felton was killed. Is that accurate?"

"Yes."

"I want to go back a ways to the time when you were a homicide
detective and were in pursuit of Thomas Felton. In particular, I
want to talk to you about the murders of Vanessa Brock and Pedro
Diaz."

"Sure."

Tom didn't know exactly where he was going so he just asked
general questions.

"Were you involved in the investigation of those murders?"

"Yes."

"And what was your part?"

"Let me go back a bit and tell you very briefly where we were in
the investigation at the time of those murders."

Robert Merton stood up at this point. He, too, didn't know what
was coming, but he didn't think it was going to be good. "Your
Honor, I object to this line of questioning. It is totally irrelevant to
our reason for being here."

Tom was ready to make his argument but he didn't get the
chance.

"Overruled. You opened this door, Mr. Merton, with your direct
examination of Chief Jeffries. Continue, Mr. Wylie."

"Thank you, Your Honor." To the witness he said, "Ms. Jansen,
you were about to tell us where the investigation was prior to the
murders of Vanessa Brock and Pedro Diaz?"

"Yes. Those two people were the ninth and tenth individuals
murdered. The eighth was Alice Jeffries, Sam Jeffries's wife.

"One of the other people murdered was a young woman named
Stacey Kincaid. The killer had tried to kill Stacey earlier, but
she had managed to escape and she identified a bowie knife with

a gargoyle handle as the weapon the assailant tried to kill her with. Because of her identification, we were focused on that bowie knife."

The jury was listening intently. She was so much more compelling in her testimony this time.

"I was convinced that Thomas Felton was the murderer. I didn't have any real evidence other than the fact that there was a serial killer at the University of Utah when Felton was a student there and the fact that he had an unusual knife in his house, although it looked nothing like a bowie knife. However, with the number of people dead, I felt we needed to move on this flimsy evidence. I went to Sam Jeffries, the head of the task force, and asked him to get me a search warrant. He refused to support the request because he did not believe we had probable cause. I then went to Janet Pelicano, the state attorney at the time, and asked her for a search warrant. She refused me for the same reason.

"I must tell you also that the killer had threatened my daughter so I had a personal stake as well."

"Why are you telling us all this?" Tom asked. He really didn't know where she was going.

"Number one, I want the jury to know the pressure that was on us. People in our community were dying and it was our responsibility. And second, for Sam and me it was personal, although his loss was so much greater than mine."

"So what happened the night of the Brock/Diaz murders?"

"The night Vanessa Brock and Pedro Diaz were killed, I got a call from my partner to come to the scene. However, I didn't go to the scene right away. I went to Thomas Felton's apartment."

The gallery started to murmur at that revelation but Judge Holbrook merely had to raise his head and look out into the crowd for the murmuring to stop. Danni continued.

"Felton wasn't there, so I picked the lock and went in. I found the bowie knife that Stacey Kincaid had identified. It was located in a dresser drawer in a second or spare bedroom in the apartment. Felton had denied us access to that bedroom when we were there during the investigation. That was my main reason for requesting the search warrant.

"At that point, I knew in my own mind that Felton was the killer. I was so excited that I didn't put anything together as I should have. What I mean is that I should have realized that since Felton wasn't home, he must have used a different weapon in the Brock/Diaz murders. I just wasn't thinking straight.

"I also knew that I couldn't use the bowie knife as evidence because it was illegally obtained. I couldn't just close the door and walk away. I couldn't let another murder happen knowing what I knew. So I went to the Brock/Diaz murder scene and I planted the bowie knife in the woods where I knew it would be found."

There it was. What Jack had suspected and what he had argued to the Florida Supreme Court was, in fact, true. The bowie knife had been planted. Jack just didn't know that it was planted by Danni.

"Did you ever tell anybody what you had done before your testimony here today?"

"No."

"The state attorney, the coroner, Chief Jeffries—none of them knew?"

"I didn't say that. I said I didn't tell them. They all knew. These were experienced people but by the time the case came to trial, the murders had stopped. They were faced with essentially the same dilemma as I was—they had bad evidence, but the killing had stopped. They weren't going to release Felton. So they fudged it."

Merton's case was bleeding heavily at this point. He had to at least try to stop the flow. "Objection, Your Honor. Move to strike the last answer as unresponsive to the question and speculative."

"Overruled. You'll have your opportunity on cross-examination, Mr. Merton."

A change had come over Judge Holbrook ever since Merton had tried to suggest Jack had something to do with the killing of a federal judge.

"Nobody picked up on this major problem with the evidence?"

"Nobody discovered what had happened until Jack Tobin came along and read Felton's file."

"Thank you, Ms. Jansen. I have—"

"There's more," Danni interrupted him.

"I apologize. Were you not finished with your answer?"

"No. When Alice Jeffries was killed, I went to the scene. Sam was in his room and he was as upset as he could be. I was concerned about him. I didn't know what he would do so I asked him to give me his gun. He then gave me his Glock service revolver and I asked him if he had other guns. Reluctantly, he took a key from his top drawer and opened a hidden door in the back of his closet. He had a room back there with a number of guns in it—"

That was enough for Merton. Judge or no judge, he couldn't let this woman go on. He interrupted Danni in the middle of her sentence.

"Objection, Your Honor. Relevancy."

The judge thought about it for a moment. "Counsel, approach."

When the two lawyers reached sidebar, the judge asked Tom a question.

"Where is this leading?"

Tom had to come clean. "I don't know, Your Honor. I hadn't talked to her before she testified here today. However, I suspect she is about to tell us something very important."

"Well, it could also be objectionable and prejudicial. We've already had a little too much of that in this trial."

Tom knew the judge had a point, but he also knew this was an opportunity that could not be wasted.

"Your Honor, let me make a suggestion. Let's remove the jury and I'll proffer the testimony outside the presence of the jury. Counsel can make any objections and you can rule on them."

The judge thought about it for a minute. "I'd have to remove the gallery, too. I don't want this testimony floating out there if I deem it inadmissible."

Merton finally spoke up. "Your Honor, this is highly unusual and inappropriate. I have a client here, the State of Florida, and my client will be prejudiced by this last-minute surprise testimony."

Judge Holbrook glared at Merton. "You opened this door, Counselor. You brought in what happened ten years ago. Besides, this was your witness, you can't claim surprise. And one last thing: Your client is justice. Remember that. A man's life is at stake here.

"Okay, Mr. Wylie, I'm going to let you make your proffer."

He called the bailiffs over. "I want the jury removed and I want the gallery removed. Put the gallery in another courtroom and stay with them. I don't want anybody walking in here. In fact, lock the doors when you leave. But first, let me make a few remarks to the jury."

Everybody returned to their respective places while Judge Holbrook addressed the jurors.

"Ladies and gentlemen, we have some legal issues we need to address so I'm going to ask you to step out into the jury room. It should only be a few minutes."

As one bailiff marched the jurors out, two other bailiffs started removing the gallery. In a few minutes, the courtroom was again empty except for the judge, court personnel, the lawyers, Jack, and Danni.

When the jurors were gone but before the gallery was totally empty, Danni stole a glance at Jack, who met her eyes. She pursed her lips in a slight smile to let him know she felt good about what she was doing. Jack gave her an ever so subtle nod. Nobody in the courtroom noticed except Robert Merton, who leaned over to his pretty assistant. "Find Chief Jeffries," he said to her. "Ask him if there was ever anything between Jansen and Tobin. Get as much detail as you can. And make sure the guard at the door knows you're coming back so you can get in."

The woman gave him a look as if to say, *I can figure that out. I'm a lawyer, you know, not some ornament to make you look better in front of the jury.* She didn't verbalize her feelings, however. She quickly left the courtroom.

"What are we doing, making a proffer?" Jack asked Tom when Tom returned from sidebar.

"Yeah. I don't know what she's going to say though."

"I'm sure it's going to be good. I can't believe the judge is letting you do this."

"I can't either. He's done a complete one-eighty since Merton's big gaffe."

"Mr. Wylie, are you ready?" the judge asked.

"Yes, Your Honor."

"You may proceed."

Tom walked to the podium and addressed Danni on the witness stand.

"Ms. Jansen, you were telling us about a secret room in Sam Jeffries's house when Mr. Merton made his objection. Can you continue where you left off?"

"Yes. Sam had a secret room in the back of his closet and he had a number of guns in there. There were five semiautomatics, not including the Glock he had given me, a rifle with a scope, several shotguns, and an AK-47. I specifically noticed and mentioned to him that he didn't have any revolvers and he told me he didn't like them."

"Why is that so important?"

"Because I was never sure about things. Jack told me that he thought Felton had a gun, a small pistol, and Sam told me there was no gun, that Jack had set the whole thing up. I didn't know what the truth was so I just came in here and testified to what I knew. Then when I decided to tell the truth about what happened ten years ago and I specifically recalled what I had done, I thought there was a possibility that I could again find out for sure what happened in this case."

"I'm not sure I understand," Tom said.

"Ten years ago I assured myself that Felton was the killer by breaking into his house and finding the bowie knife. Early this morning I went over to Sam Jeffries's house, waited until he left, and broke in."

"What did you find?" Tom asked.

"I knew where the key to the secret room was so I got it and opened the door. There in the room, along with the other guns, was a small revolver, a 22 caliber Ruger. I knew Sam didn't like revolvers, so I was sure in my own mind that this was Felton's gun."

"Did you dust it for prints?"

"I did. It was clean. I figure Sam wiped it clean once he decided to frame Jack. That way, if anybody ever found the gun, although I don't know how they would, it would just be another gun in his collection."

"Where is the gun now?"

"I left it with the head of security at the courthouse entrance. I explained to him who I was and that this gun was potential evidence in this case."

"Is there anything else that you want to add?"

"No."

"I have no further questions, Your Honor."

As Tom finished, Merton's assistant came back into the room. She whispered something in Merton's ear that made him smile.

"There will be no need for you to cross-examine this witness, Mr.

Merton," Judge Holbrook said, "because I'm ruling this testimony inadmissible. This evidence has been obtained by the commission of a crime and Ms. Jansen is a former police officer. More important, however, I find this testimony has little probative value. Ms. Jansen's belief that this gun was Thomas Felton's is nothing more than her own speculation. There is no evidence whatsoever linking this gun to Thomas Felton."

Robert Merton was a good attorney, almost a great attorney, because he understood human nature, particularly the skeptical, jaded side of human nature. So far, Danni Jansen's testimony before the jury had been believable. She had made a dent in his case and he wasn't sure how to handle her on cross-examination—until this moment.

"Your Honor, I'm going to withdraw my objection to this testimony."

The judge looked shocked, as did Tom and Jack.

"Are you sure you want to do that, Counselor? Are you sure you want to allow that gun into evidence?"

"Your Honor, the Court has reminded me that my client is justice. If the defense wants to put this evidence on as truth, I think the jury should be allowed to evaluate it in that context."

The judge didn't say anything for a moment or two. He just gave Robert Merton a bewildered look as if to ask, *What the hell are you doing?*

"Very well," he said finally. "The objection being withdrawn, you are free to proceed, Mr. Wylie. Since this has taken a little more time than we anticipated, I think we should break for lunch. Who knows, perhaps we'll have different ideas after the lunch break."

Jack and Tom had to share a Snickers over lunch.

"I didn't get to the candy store last night," Tom said.

"I'll just take it out of your fee," Jack told him. "Interesting turn of events here."

"Very interesting."

"I can't believe Danni got on that stand and confessed to two crimes—to save me."

"I've got to say I was not a Danni fan no matter what you and Henry said about her, but today she stepped up to the plate in a big way. And I understand why she did what she did. She had to stop Felton any way she could, and she had a strong feeling that Jeffries was setting you up and that he was going to get away with it."

"Why did Merton drop his objection?" Jack asked.

"I think I know," Tom said. "Danni's testimony about what happened ten years ago was very believable. A jury could understand after that testimony why you decided to represent Felton. They could let you go without ever determining that Sam Jeffries did anything wrong. This gun testimony, even though it's true, requires the jurors to believe Danni over Sam Jeffries and makes Jeffries a criminal. Jeffries is well thought of in this community and he is the ultimate victim in this case. Making Jeffries look like a criminal is going to be a hard thing for them to do and that's what Merton is banking on."

"But it's the truth. Why would Danni lie? Why would she subject herself to criminal prosecution?"

"That's Merton's hurdle—finding a motive for Danni's having lied. I'm sure he'll come up with something. He's a very resourceful fellow. We could pull the plug on him though."

"What do you mean?"

"I don't have to ask another question. I don't have to put the proffered testimony before the jury. That way, Merton could only cross Danni on what she already testified to—and that's basically planting the knife ten years ago."

"What's our advantage in that?"

"If the jury believes her, they see you in a different light. They don't have to determine that Jeffries is a criminal. It's still a risk, but you and I both know that you win in this game hitting singles and doubles. Trying for a home run, like Merton did when he cross-examined you, can get you in a lot of trouble."

"What do you recommend, Tom?"

"Let's play it safe. Let's throw Merton a curve ball. We'll leave the gun stuff out."

"I can't do that. I hear everything you're saying, Tom, and I agree with you for the most part. But Danni put her life on the line by breaking into Sam's home and then by testifying about it. I can't just throw that away because it's good strategy."

"This isn't about Danni's feelings, Jack. We want to get you out of jail. You can spend the rest of your life with her if you like."

"What's that supposed to mean?"

"It's pretty obvious to me that you love this woman. I think Henry and Ron would tell you the same thing if they were here. I just don't want your feelings for her to cloud your judgment as a lawyer because this is your decision to make."

"You've been straight with me all the way through this trial, Tom, even though I don't agree with all of your assessments. And you stuck with me when I made decisions you didn't agree with. As a lawyer, I know how hard that is. But I'm going to ask you to do it one more time. I want Danni to testify to everything. That's what she came here to do, and it's the truth. I'll live with the consequences."

"Okay, Jack. I just hope Merton is not as good as I think he is."

CHAPTER SIXTY-EIGHT

Judge Holbrook re-convened the proceedings at one o'clock. Neither the gallery nor the jury was in the room.

"Do we have anything else to discuss before we bring everybody back here?"

"No, Your Honor," said Merton.

"No, Your Honor," said Tom.

"Just for the record, Mr. Wylie, you are going to ask questions about the proffered testimony, specifically about Ms. Jansen's breaking into Chief Jeffries's home and finding a gun and her belief that the gun belonged to Thomas Felton."

"Yes, Your Honor," Tom replied.

"And you have no objection to that testimony, Mr. Merton?"

"That's correct."

"Okay," said the judge, obviously a little exasperated. "Let's bring in the gallery first and the witness. Then when everybody is seated, we'll bring in the jury."

It took fifteen minutes to get the gallery seated and a couple more for the jury. Eventually, everybody was seated and ready.

"Mr. Wylie, you may proceed."

Tom went to the podium and proceeded to ask Danni the same questions he had asked that morning. She told the jury in a straightforward fashion how she broke into Sam's house, found the gun,

and why she believed it was Felton's gun. Robert Merton did not
raise an objection. When Tom was finished, the judge turned to
Merton.

"Cross-examination, Mr. Merton?"

"Yes, Your Honor."

Merton walked to his favorite spot close to the witness but
between the witness and the jury so that his questions could be
statements to the jury and they could see the witness behind him
answering the statements.

"So let me get this straight, Ms. Jansen. You broke into Felton's
home ten years ago, took the bowie knife, planted it at the last murder scene, and told nobody about that until this morning—is that
right?"

"That's correct."

"The burning question for me, as I'm sure it is for everyone here,
is why—why now?"

"I didn't want to see an innocent man go to jail."

"You didn't want to see an innocent man go to jail. You testified
last week for the prosecution; you knew they were prosecuting this
man for murder—did your feelings change between last week and
today?"

"Frankly, yes. I thought about it some more and I decided to tell
the whole truth."

"Did you talk to anybody about this between your testimony for
the prosecution last week and your new testimony this week?"

Danni hesitated—not a good thing when you were on cross-
examination. "Yes. I spoke to Henry Wilson."

"You spoke to Henry Wilson. Did he help persuade you?"

"He helped. The decision was mine."

"Now before you testified last week, you spoke to me on several
occasions and you never told me, the state attorney for this county,
that you had planted evidence in the Felton case, correct?"

"That's correct."

"So you talked to Henry Wilson, you made your decision, and then you woke up this morning and decided to break into Sam Jeffries's house, that's what you want this jury to believe?"

"It's the truth."

"The truth." Merton picked up the Ruger that Tom had introduced into evidence. "The truth is that you, me, anybody can buy this exact gun at Walmart, Kmart, or even better, at some obscure gun show that blows through town."

"That's correct."

"The truth is that this gun is clean, meaning there are no prints or any other evidence to connect this gun to Thomas Felton?"

"That's correct."

"The truth is that anyone could make the claim that they got this gun from Sam Jeffries's house and there would be no way to disprove it."

"Not everybody would know about Sam Jeffries's hidden gun room."

"A little gem to make your story more credible? And you want the jury to believe that the key to that room was in the same place that it was ten years ago, correct? And that just allowed you to walk right in?"

"I don't want them to believe anything. That's where it was. Otherwise I couldn't have gotten the gun."

"Unless you bought it at Walmart?"

Danni did not answer the question.

"That's a question, Ms. Jansen."

"I did not buy the gun at Walmart or Kmart or anywhere else."

"You were a homicide detective for twenty years, is that correct?"

"No, I was a homicide detective for approximately fifteen of my twenty years on the force."

"You interviewed witnesses, didn't you?"

"Yes."

"And you were constantly required to evaluate who was a credible witness and who wasn't, weren't you?"

"Yes."

"I've always heard it said that the worst witnesses are criminals who have their own self-serving reasons for offering their testimony: rats, prison snitches—those type of people. Do you agree?"

"Yes, I do."

"Now, what you did—breaking into Thomas Felton's apartment without probable cause—was criminal, wasn't it?"

"That's for the State to decide."

"Breaking and entering is a crime, isn't it?"

"Yes."

"You broke and entered into Chief Jeffries's house this morning, didn't you?"

"Yes."

"That's a crime, isn't it?"

"Yes."

"You are a criminal?"

"Yes."

"So now in evaluating your testimony as a criminal, our next step is to determine if you have any self-serving motive. Do you?"

"No."

"You're just here as a citizen, a criminal citizen, finally deciding to straighten up and do the right thing, is that what you're telling us?"

"I wouldn't put it quite that way. I don't have an agenda though."

"Aren't you having a love affair with Jack Tobin?"

The room erupted with that question. Judge Holbrook stood up as he banged his gavel. "I will have order in this courtroom."

The gallery settled down.

"Would you like me to repeat the question, Ms. Jansen?"

"No. I am not having a love affair with Jack Tobin."

"Have you ever had a love affair with him?"

Danni hesitated again. It was not going well. "Yes, we did have a brief affair two years ago."

"Two years ago? He shot Felton and ran to your house. You went to the crime scene with him. He went back to your house the same night. His best friend showed up at your house and you now come in here and tell this incredible story—two years ago?"

Tom was on his feet. Merton had asked the questions in machine-gun fashion. "Objection, Your Honor; he's badgering the witness. He's asking compound questions."

"Sustained. Mr. Merton, ask one question at a time."

"I'll withdraw that question, Your Honor.

"Didn't Henry Wilson tell you that Jack Tobin still loved you?"

"No."

"Ms. Jansen, can you look at this jury and tell them that you do not love that man?" He pointed at Jack, causing Danni to look at Jack.

"Object," Jack said to Tom.

"I can't," Tom replied. "I have no grounds."

"Object anyway."

"Can't do it, Jack. It's too late for that."

It had taken Danni so much to get to this place. So many walls had to come down. She had to admit that what she did ten years ago had led to everything that had followed, including the death of Kathleen Jeffries. It wasn't Jack who got Tom Felton released, it was her. She also had to finally see that Sam was on a warped quest to avenge the murder of his wife and daughter. And last but not least, when she had to decide to put her life on the line, she had to come to grips with her feelings about Jack Tobin. Now that the walls were down, she couldn't put them back up again.

The silence had been deafening. There was almost no need to answer the question anymore, but Merton felt it needed repeating.

"Can you look at this jury, Ms. Jansen, and tell them you are not in love with Jack Tobin?"

"No, I can't."

"I have no further questions, Your Honor."

"Redirect?" the judge asked Tom.

Tom started to stand. Jack grabbed his arm. "No," he said. "Let her go."

"No, Your Honor."

"The witness may leave the stand. Ms. Jansen, I am ordering you not to leave the jurisdiction, do you understand?"

"Yes, Your Honor."

Even though her answer to the last question had cemented his conviction, Jack wanted to go to her as she walked out of the courtroom. If he had one last moment of freedom, he wanted to hold her and thank her and tell her that he loved her too.

CHAPTER SIXTY-NINE

At eight o'clock on Tuesday morning, Danni heard somebody knocking on her door. She didn't want to talk to anybody. The evening before had been excruciating. She couldn't turn on the television without hearing her name. Hannah had called from Europe because she was worried about her. She had to assure her daughter that she was fine. Now somebody was at the door—at eight o'clock! She'd had just about enough.

She opened the door ready to give whoever it was a piece of her mind. There stood Ron and Henry. Ron had a big paper bag in his hand.

"We've got some bagels," he said.

"And cream cheese," Henry added, producing his own small paper bag. "Thought maybe you could supply the coffee."

Danni just looked at them and shook her head.

"It's hot out here," Ron said.

"All right, come on in." They followed her into the kitchen and sat at the table while she started the coffee.

"Don't just sit there," she said to Ron. "Here's the toaster. Start making the bagels. Henry, you can set the table."

"Yes, ma'am," Henry said.

When the coffee and bagels were done, they sat down to eat.

"So what's new?" Ron asked as he spread cream cheese on his bagel.

Danni looked at Henry. Henry looked at Ron.

"What?" Ron said. Henry just started laughing, which made Ron start laughing, which finally made Danni start laughing. It was totally unexpected, totally the opposite of how she was feeling, but it felt so good—for all of them. For the longest time they couldn't stop.

"What are we laughing at?" Ron asked, still unable to control himself.

"I don't know," Henry said, which made them start laughing all over again. Finally, they were laughed out.

"I needed that," Danni said. "I didn't know I needed it but I did."

"We just wanted you to know you're not alone," Ron said. "We're with you all the way."

"Thanks, guys. It's been a rough couple of days."

"You were awesome, Danni," Henry said.

"Yeah. Awesome. I think I got Jack convicted single-handedly."

"Don't say that. You did everything you could possibly do."

"It wasn't enough."

"It's not over. We have closing arguments today. Tom Wylie is a great lawyer."

"Nice try, guys, but I think Jack and I are both going to jail."

"Tom told me to tell you he's got your back no matter what happens," Henry said. "He would have come today but he's still got the closing to worry about before he can relax."

"They haven't arrested me yet although I'm in a prison of sorts. I can't go out in this town anymore."

"Sure you can," Ron said. "You can come to The Swamp and hang out with me and Henry. We'll be the oldest people in the place because none of my regular customers are showing up either."

"I don't blame them for feeling the way they do, Ron," Danni said. "They want to believe Sam so bad. His tragedies are everyone's tragedies. It's like we're all in collusion with Sam. Deep down, we all know he's lost it but we don't care."

"You cared. You came out of it," Ron said. "And you were closer to Sam than anybody."

"I was also very close to Jack, as you may have heard—the proverbial fallen woman. And Henry nudged me a little bit."

"All we need is one," Henry said. "One holdout on that jury."

CHAPTER SEVENTY

Tom finally got a day that matched his mood—dark, overcast, stormy. The wind blowing hard. He was deep in the clouds himself. Merton had outfoxed them completely. Jack had not made good strategic decisions, although Tom couldn't blame Jack too much. The man had a woman who not only broke the law to save him but came into court and testified about it under oath. Tom could understand why Jack wanted to stand behind her and her testimony. His Kate would have done the same thing, he was sure. Women like those two were rare indeed.

Those reflections didn't help him as he headed to court on this blustery morning. This trial had drilled home for him once and for all that in the criminal justice system, strategy trumps truth. It was the way of the world these days. He was about to make his closing argument and he had no strategy. All he had was truth.

Jack was waiting when he arrived in the courtroom. He looked relaxed and fresh.

"I'm ready," he said. "It's going to be a good day."

"Am I missing something?" Tom asked.

"I don't think so. Why do you ask?"

"You're awfully cheerful."

"All I can tell you, Tom, is that I believe in people and nobody has failed me yet."

Tom thought Jack had finally lost it. The man was delusional—speaking in riddles. There *were* no other people. Or were there?

Just then Merton arrived, resplendent in a blue suit and a flowery red tie. He, too, looked relaxed and confident.

The bailiffs were busy ushering the gallery in. When they were all set, promptly at nine o'clock Judge Holbrook entered the courtroom. Everybody rose.

"Be seated," he said. Then he addressed the lawyers. "Do we have anything to discuss before we bring the jurors in?"

Both of the lawyers said no. After Danni's testimony the day before, Tom had rested. Merton had no rebuttal. Tom had made a halfhearted oral motion for acquittal, and Judge Holbrook had denied it on the spot. Then they had briefly discussed the jury instructions.

The stage was set this morning for closing arguments.

"Ladies and gentlemen," the judge said to the jurors when they were seated, "the lawyers are going to make their closing arguments now. I want to remind you again that what they say is not evidence. You must use your own recollection of the testimony you heard from the witness stand in making your decision. When the lawyers are finished, I will give you the applicable law and you will apply the facts that you determine to the applicable law in making your decision.

"The prosecution will go first because the State has the burden of proof. Then the defense will have an opportunity to speak to you, followed by a brief rebuttal by the prosecution.

"Mr. Merton, are you ready to proceed?"

"Yes, Your Honor."

Robert Merton strode to his place next to the podium. He had no notes with him. He was confident that he could hit all the high points from memory.

"Good morning, ladies and gentlemen. First, I would like to

thank you for your attention during this trial. I know that you have
been separated from your families for the better part of a week, and
I assure you I will be as quick as I possibly can. This trial is almost
over but before it is over, you as jurors must do your job. It's not an
easy job deciding the guilt or innocence of a person, but it is an obligation you have agreed to undertake. I am confident that you will
make the tough decisions that are needed.

"I told you when this trial began that the State would prove that
Jack Tobin had intentionally planned and carried out the murder
of Thomas Felton. The evidence is undisputed that the defendant
shot Felton and that Felton died from that gunshot wound. It is also
undisputed that Felton signed a contingency fee agreement with the
defendant to pay him one-third of whatever he received from the
Florida legislature. The defendant was going to file a claims bill
with the state requesting twenty million dollars. The organization
the defendant worked for had no knowledge of the contingency fee
agreement and, in fact, the agreement was a violation of the organization's own rules and bylaws. The defendant himself testified that
when Felton killed Kathleen Jeffries, the claims bill and his contingency fee died with her. The defendant lost a potential fee of seven
million dollars—certainly enough motive for murder.

"What other facts support this murder by the defendant?" Merton took the opportunity to point his finger right at Jack. "Do you
remember the telephone calls? Both made by the defendant, one,
two days before the murder, setting up the meeting, the other, minutes before the murder, making sure Felton had shown up. You also
remember Chief Jeffries testifying that he believed that the defendant, after he shot Felton, planned on planting a gun on Felton but
was thwarted in this plan when he heard Chief Jeffries coming on
the scene. Chief Jeffries told you he believed that the defendant had
tossed the gun he was going to plant in the woods as he ran to Danni
Jansen's house. And you heard Danni Jansen, *before* she changed her

testimony, tell you that the very night of the murder, she saw the defendant, Jack Tobin, coming from the woods exactly where Chief Jeffries believed Tobin would have thrown the gun.

"Motive and opportunity, ladies and gentlemen. It's all there and it's undisputed. Mr. Tobin had an explanation for everything but his explanations didn't ring true. For instance, he said that the contingency fee agreement was Felton's idea, but then he admitted that Felton didn't know what a contingency fee agreement was. It was Tobin's idea to lock him in legally. Then you heard Tobin tell you that he was going to give any money he received to Exoneration. Unfortunately, he never told anyone at Exoneration about that. And, unfortunately for him, Ben Chapman, the CEO of Exoneration, testified that such agreements are not allowed by the organization *and Jack Tobin knew that.*

"You know, I expected a unique defense from these two talented lawyers. I just didn't know how diabolical it was going to be. The defense let me put on my case and then developed a story to refute it using one of the prosecution's own witnesses and a former police officer—Danni Jansen. They believed they could pull this off. They still believe it. But you must not let them. You must see Danni Jansen's testimony for what it is—a pack of lies.

"First, she told you that for the first time ever she was revealing that she had planted the bowie knife at the scene where Vanessa Brock and Pedro Diaz were murdered. When I asked why now, she said because she didn't want an innocent man to go to jail. I asked her if she had any interest other than that and she said no. We know that was a lie. Jack Tobin was her lover and is still her lover. She had an agenda and she lied about it. But that was just the beginning of her lies. In her first break-in, she stole a knife; in her second supposed break-in, she stole a gun—all in the interests of justice, not for her lover. You remember the revolver—no prints, nothing to connect it to Felton at all. You remember her admitting she could have bought it at Walmart or Kmart, or at a gun show. Well, I submit to you that she didn't buy it anywhere. I submit to you that this was the gun Tobin had planned to plant on Felton's body. *This vile woman was in on this deal all along.* Where did Tobin run when he shot Felton and heard Chief Jeffries coming onto the scene? To Danni Jansen's house. Who showed up with Tobin at the scene with the story of the self-defense shooting? His lover, Danni Jansen!

"Not only did she do everything to vindicate her lover, she also did everything she could to implicate Chief Jeffries in criminal activity—a man who had lost both his wife and his daughter at Felton's hand.

"You don't need to ask this woman if she has no shame. She doesn't."

Merton was like a preacher, his voice rising with every accusation. He was definitely on a roll when suddenly—

"Stop! No more! Do not say another word!"

Merton heard the shouts. He turned to look at the same time everybody else did, including Judge Holbrook, who was almost as indignant as Robert Merton that somebody had the gall to disrupt the proceedings in his courtroom.

Sam Jeffries walked down the middle aisle of the courtroom and inside the bar. He stopped right next to where Jack was sitting.

"Chief Jeffries, what is the meaning of this?" Judge Holbrook demanded.

"I have known Danni Jansen for over twenty years, Your Honor. She has dedicated her life to the city of Oakville. She was an outstanding homicide detective. I will not have you, sir," he pointed at Merton, "calling her a vile woman."

"Chief, I appreciate your feelings toward this woman but this is not the time or the place," Judge Holbrook said, seeing that the man was extremely distraught. The bailiffs were ready to move in at the slightest gesture from the judge.

"It's the perfect place, Your Honor, because Danni Jansen was telling the truth. She found that gun in my house. I took that gun from the crime scene. I took it because I wanted to frame Jack Tobin."

Bedlam broke out in the courtroom. People were in shock and they were talking about it. Judge Holbrook's prior admonitions were a distant memory now. He had lost control of his courtroom, but he wasn't giving up. He stood up, banging his gavel. "Order in the court! Order in the court!" When that didn't work, he changed his tune. "Clear the courtroom! Clear the courtroom!"

The bailiffs, the only people who were listening, began to clear the courtroom. Members of the press didn't need to be encouraged. They were running to get their story out. Everybody else needed a little urging. As the courtroom started to empty, order began to return.

Jack whispered in Tom's ear, "As soon as everybody is out, stand up and make a motion for dismissal."

"Okay," Tom said, still a little bewildered himself.

"Sam," Jack said. Sam Jeffries looked down to his right where Jack sat. "Don't say another word. You will only incriminate yourself more. Let Merton decide if he's going to dismiss the case. You've said enough."

When the gallery emptied out for the third time since the trial had begun, Tom stood up.

"Your Honor, I make a motion to dismiss this case against my client based on the admissions made by Chief Jeffries here in open court."

"Mr. Merton, do you have anything to say?" Judge Holbrook asked calmly.

Merton was still standing in front of the jury, but he was no longer the preacher breathing fire and brimstone. He was speechless and bewildered.

"Mr. Merton?"

"I don't know what to say, Your Honor."

"Well, Mr. Merton, your main witness, the chief of police, has just stated that he framed Mr. Tobin. Does that help you?"

Merton suddenly realized that the jury was still in the room. There was no coming back from this mess.

"The State has no objection to a dismissal of its case against Mr. Tobin based on the admissions of Chief Jeffries," Merton said finally.

"Case dismissed," Judge Holbrook said. "Mr. Tobin, you are free to go. I want those officers who have been guarding Mr. Tobin to take Chief Jeffries into custody."

Sam Jeffries had not said a word since Jack told him not to say anything, not because he listened to Jack but because he was struck dumb at the realization that the man he had set up for murder was giving him legal advice for his own good.

CHAPTER SEVENTY-ONE

Danni was kneeling in the dirt in her backyard garden picking weeds, the wind almost knocking her over. Gardening was her favorite pastime these days, regardless of the weather conditions. It soothed her. She wasn't sure why, maybe it was just being close to Mother Earth—or being part of the universe, as Jack might have put it. Jack—he was the reason she was out here this morning. She needed to do something to get him out of her mind. *What is happening? Is the jury deliberating yet?*

"Can I get some fresh tomatoes, ma'am?"

She recognized the voice but didn't turn around right away. It was her mind playing tricks on her. She stole a peek behind. He was standing right there in her backyard with a smile on his face and his arms outstretched. Was this real or just her mind playing tricks on her? Apparition or not, she went to him, her heart way ahead of her head. He was real. His arms encircled her as hers squeezed him. She melted into him, the tears coming in sheets. Tears of joy.

They held each other for a long time.

"I wanted to go to you right after you testified," Jack said. "But—"

Danni put her finger to his lips and shook her head "no"—no words. She took him by the hand, led him up the porch steps and into the house, shutting the door behind them.

*　　*　　*

They had a celebration dinner that night at The Swamp. Ron closed off the second floor for his friends—Henry, Tom, Jack, and Danni. Downstairs was almost full, which was a good thing for a Tuesday. Business was returning to normal quickly. News of the events in the courtroom that morning had spread like wildfire throughout the town. A lot of folks all of a sudden wanted to go to The Swamp. But Ron, the consummate businessman, was having none of it. He was staying upstairs with his true friends.

There were smiles all around and a little good-natured ribbing. It had been an ordeal for all of them. When everybody had a little twinkle in their eye from the joy and the alcohol, Jack stood up.

"I want to propose a toast." He almost had to shout to overcome the noise of the crowd below.

"To Danni, who told me she loved me for the first time from the witness stand in my murder trial. Well, it wasn't actually me she told, it was everybody—the whole world. Who can ever top that?"

"Way to go, Danni," Ron said.

"Danni, you put yourself in harm's way for me, and I'm going to spend the rest of my life thanking you for it. If Robert Merton even thinks about prosecuting you, he is going to face the most ferocious lawyer he has ever seen."

"Team of lawyers," Tom said.

Jack leaned down, kissed Danni, and whispered in her ear.

"I love you, too."

Then he was raising his glass again—the consummate toastmaster.

"And to Ron and Henry—every man should be so lucky to have friends like you. Ronnie, you supported all of us, fed us, stood with us when your neighbors wanted to shoot you. Put your business on the line for me. That is true friendship. I'm not sure I deserve it."

"I'm not sure I can afford it," Ron quipped.

"And Henry, the worst fisherman in the world."

Henry raised his glass. "Maybe the second worst," he said.

"You do the necessary, Henry. Whatever it is. I only know the part that Danni told me about, and that was enough. Thank you, my friend."

Henry couldn't help himself. He stood up and hugged his dear friend, the beer spilling everywhere.

Jack still wasn't done.

"And last but not least, to my lawyer, Tom, who was paid an ungodly amount to represent me."

"Keep that to yourself, Jack. I'd go broke with clients like you."

Jack waited for the laughter to subside.

"Tom, it was no picnic having me for a client. I overrode your suggestions at every turn. Yet you stuck with me. You pulled me through. I will never forget what you did."

"You know what this case makes him, don't you, Jack?" Henry asked.

"No, what?"

"The lawyer's lawyer's lawyer."

Nobody got the joke but Jack and Henry, who were laughing so hard they were in stitches.

EPILOGUE

Sam Jeffries was lying on the bed in his jail cell in his yellow jumpsuit when an Oakville police officer opened the door. Sam didn't know what was going on.

"You've got company," the officer said. Then Sam saw Danni.

"Danni, what are you doing here?"

Danni walked into the cell. "I came to see you, Sam. I heard what you said about me yesterday in court, and I wanted to thank you."

"Thank me? I got you involved in this whole mess."

"Sam, you weren't thinking straight. What man who went through what you went through would be thinking straight? You went a little crazy, that's all. But you didn't follow through on it. You came to your senses at the last minute."

"That's a nice way to put it, Danni, but I destroyed everything I stood for my whole life. I set up an innocent man for murder. I can't ever forgive myself for what I've done."

"Sure you can. The man you set up forgives you."

"What are you talking about?"

"He's here."

"Who's here?"

"Jack. He's right down the hall. He wants to talk to you."

"No. I can't. I wouldn't know what to say to him. I don't want to talk to him anyway."

"Sam, he wants to say something to you. Let me get him."

"No."

"Come on, Sam, do this for me. You know you owe me one."

Sam was sitting up on his cot now. His arms were resting on his thighs and his head was sunk so low it almost touched his knees. He didn't respond to Danni's question. He had nothing left.

Danni waited for a moment, then walked out into the hallway and waved to Jack to come along.

A minute later, Jack appeared in front of the jail cell. Danni opened the door. Sam was still in the same position.

"Hi, Sam," Jack almost whispered the words. Sam just stayed there, not moving. Finally, he raised his head.

"I can't believe this. I can't believe you. Did you really give me legal advice yesterday in that courtroom?"

"I did."

"Listen, Jack, I know words won't do it—"

"No, they won't, Sam, so don't even try. We all made mistakes to get us here—the three of us. Your loss, Sam, was unimaginable."

"I still can't get my arms around this. Why would you come here to see me, even if you don't have any hard feelings?"

"Danni loves you and I love Danni."

"Okay."

"Look, Sam." Danni cut into the conversation. "Jack and I have a proposition for you. Just sit back and listen for a minute."

Sam didn't know what to do or what was coming. "Okay. I've got all the time in the world. What's the proposition?"

"I'd like to be your lawyer," Jack said. "I think it would be a pretty hard case for Merton to prosecute when the man you supposedly set up for murder is representing you. I will make a speech every day on the courthouse steps as to why you are innocent and should not be prosecuted. Merton is still smarting from this defeat you handed him. He might be angry but he's not stupid."

Sam was silent for a long time. "I don't know what to say."

"Say yes," Danni said.

"I have no money."

"Money is overrated," Jack said. "I'm the lawyer who represents people for free. Remember?"

Sam was beside himself.

"I don't deserve this," he said. "I need to spend the rest of my life behind bars."

"Listen, Sam," Danni said. "I know you've been through a lot but so have your son and your daughter-in-law and your two grand-children. You can't bring Alice or Kathleen back but you can go forward and be a father to your son, and a grandfather to those kids."

"I haven't thought much about them, I know."

"It's time to move forward, Sam. Jack and I want to give you that chance."

"You two are unbelievable."

"I'm just passing it on, Sam," Jack said. "A few people just did the same thing for me, including this lady who connects the two of us."

Sam hesitated for a moment or two.

"Okay, Jack, if you're crazy enough to offer, I'm still crazy enough to accept."

The two men shook hands.

"I'd love to see Merton's face when he gets this news," Sam said.

ACKNOWLEDGMENTS

My greatest joy has always been my family and I have been blessed in that regard.

My three children—John, Justin, and Sarah—are my anchors. We have always been there for each other. John's wife, Bethany; Justin's wife, Becky; my children's mother, Liz Grant; my five grandchildren, Gabrielle, Hannah, Jack, Grace, and Owen; and my great-granddaughter, Lilly, make up the rest of my inner circle. The next band of the circle is my brothers and sisters: John, Mary, Mike, Kate, and Patricia and their significant others: Marge, Tony, Linda, Bill, and John. You form a unique bond when you grow up in a railroad flat in New York City with your mother and father and five brothers and sisters. My siblings have always kept my feet firmly planted on the ground. I also have an extended family of aunts, uncles, cousins, nieces and nephews, in-laws, close friends, three godchildren—Ariel, Madison, and Nathaniel—and a great-godchild, Annalyse, whom I love dearly.

I'm thrilled to have a new publishing home at Center Street, and I'm grateful to Publisher Rolf Zettersten and Associate Publisher Harry Helm for their enthusiasm for my work. Additionally, I would like to thank Marketing Director Andrea Glickson, VP of

Sales Karen Torres, Publicity Director Shanon Stowe, Web Publicist Sarah Reck, Publicist Sarah Beatty, and Jacob Arthur, who always responds to my e-mails.

Thank you to the staff at Center Street for the outstanding layout and cover design of this book, and especially to designer Tina Taylor.

Larry Kirshbaum, my agent on my first two books, has always given me tremendous support. Emily Hill, a friend and mentor, has taught me, and is still teaching me, how to promote my books on the Internet.

I owe a large debt of gratitude to my friends who have read my work and provided me with their honest analyses and opinions. I am tempted not to name names because I'm concerned that I might forget someone. But, having filed that disclaimer, I'm going to give it a shot:

Dottie Willits, Kay Tyler, Robert "Pops" Bella, Peter and Linda Keciorius, Diane Whitehead, Dave Walsh, Lindy Walsh, Lynn and Anthony Dennehy, Caitlin Herrity, Gary and Dawn Conboy, Gray and Bobbie Gibbs, Teresa Carlton, Linda Beth Carlton, Kerrie Beach, Cathy Curry, Dee Lawrence, Ron DeFilippo, Urban Patterson, Stephen Fogarty, Patty Hall, Brian Harrington, Paul Hitchens, Nick Marzuk, and Richard Wolfe.

I will always be indebted to Kate Hartson for giving me the opportunity to be a successful writer. Kate has been my mentor from the very beginning, my original publisher, and she also happens to be my sister.

ABOUT THE AUTHOR

JAMES SHEEHAN is the author of *The Mayor of Lexington Avenue* and *The Law of Second Chances*. He was a successful trial attorney for thirty years and now teaches law at Stetson University College of Law and is the Director of the Tampa Law Center, Stetson's satellite campus located in Tampa, Florida.